Available in
from Mills

QUESTIONING THE HEIRESS

"I'm attracted to you."

He was attracted to her? Better yet, he was admitting it? So maybe this thing wasn't one-sided after all.

"And I shouldn't be attracted to you," Egan continued. "It's unprofessional and dangerous. There's a reason for the regulation about a Ranger not getting personally involved with someone in protective custody. A personal involvement could cause me to lose focus. And that could get you killed."

And in that moment, Egan latched on to her wrists, then whirled her around and put her back against the doorframe. He moved closer until his mouth was almost touching hers.

"You don't want a piece of me," Egan warned. She reminded herself of what Egan said about losing focus. Oh, yes. This was the ultimate way to do it.

And she'd never wanted anything so badly in her life.

DAREDEVIL'S RUN

"God, you're just the same. Stubborn..."

Alex raked her hand over the top of her head.

"Hell, yeah, I'm stubborn." There was an edge to Matt's voice. "I didn't get to this point by quitting when things got tough."

And yet, you did. You quit on me*, dammit.*

But she didn't say that out loud.

Ah, hell. He took a deep breath and said softly, "Alex, be honest – do you really want to quit? Don't you want to keep going, too?"

She looked at the ground, then at him. "You did good out there. Really good. You saved him – you know that, don't you?"

"*We* did. We were good together, weren't we?" *Like old times.* He waited for her to say it: I've missed you. I need you here. I want you to come back.

All the characters in this book have no existence outside the imagination of the author, and have no relation whatsoever to anyone bearing the same name or names. They are not even distantly inspired by any individual known or unknown to the author, and all the incidents are pure invention.

First published in Great Britain 2009
Harlequin Mills & Boon Limited,
Eton House, 18-24 Paradise Road, Richmond, Surrey TW9 1SR

Questioning the Heiress © Delores Fossen 2008
Daredevil's Run © Kathleen Creighton-Fuchs 2008

ISBN: 978 0 263 87322 1

46-0909

Harlequin Mills & Boon policy is to use papers that are natural, renewable and recyclable products and made from wood grown in sustainable forests. The logging and manufacturing processes conform to the legal environmental regulations of the country of origin.

Printed and bound in Spain
by Litografia Rosés S.A., Barcelona

QUESTIONING THE HEIRESS

BY
DELORES FOSSEN

DAREDEVIL'S RUN

BY
KATHLEEN CREIGHTON

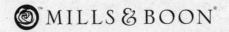MILLS & BOON

QUESTIONING THE HEIRESS

BY
DELORES FOSSEN

Imagine a family tree that includes Texas cowboys, Choctaw and Cherokee Indians, a Louisiana pirate and a Scottish rebel who battled side by side with William Wallace. With ancestors like that, it's easy to understand why Texas author and former Air Force captain **Delores Fossen** feels as if she was genetically predisposed to writing romances. Along the way to fulfilling her DNA destiny, Delores married an Air Force Top Gun who just happens to be of Viking descent. With all those romantic bases covered, she doesn't have to look too far for inspiration.

To Mallory Kane and Rita Herron.
Thanks so much for this wonderful experience.

Chapter One

San Antonio, Texas

Sgt. Egan Caldwell already had four dead bodies on his hands. He sure as hell didn't want a fifth.

"I need a guard in place by the entrance gate. Now!" he ordered into the thumb-size communicator clipped to his collar. And by God, the two rent-a-cops had better be listening and reacting. "Secure the area and await orders. *Do not fire*. Repeat. Do not fire. If this is our killer, he might have a hostage."

And in this case the hostage would be none other than Caroline Stallings, the Cantara Hills socialite who'd made a frantic call to Egan six minutes earlier. He'd been a Texas Ranger for over four years, and that was more than enough time on the job to have learned that six minutes could be five minutes and fifty-nine seconds too late to save someone from a killer.

With his Sig Sauer Blackwater pistol gripped in his right hand, Egan blinked away the sticky summer rain that was spitting at him, and he zigzagged through the manicured shrubs and trees that lined the eighth of a mile-long cobblestone driveway. He'd parked on the street so the sound of his car engine wouldn't alert anyone that he was there. He tried not to make too much noise, listening for anything to indicate the killer was inside the two-story Victorian house. Or worse.

Escaping.

Egan couldn't let this guy get away again.

Things had sure gone to hell in a handbasket tonight. Less than ten minutes ago, Egan had been eating a jalapeño burger, chili fries and going over forensic reports in his makeshift office at the country club. Less than ten minutes ago, the two-hundred-and-eighty-six residents of Cantara Hills had been safe with a Texas Ranger and two civilian guards they'd hired to stop anyone suspicious from getting into the exclusive community.

And then that phone call had come.

"This is Caroline Stallings," she'd said, her voice more breath than sound. Egan had felt her fear from the other end of the line. "There's an intruder in my home."

Then, nothing.

Everything had gone dead.

Well, everything except Egan's concerns. They were sky-high because two of the three previous murders in Cantara Hills and an attempted murder had been preceded by break-ins.

Just like this one.

And even though the person responsible, Vincent Montoya, had been murdered as well, there was obviously someone else. Montoya's boss, maybe. Or someone with a different agenda. Maybe that *someone* was now right there in Caroline Stallings's house.

Egan slapped aside some soggy weeping willow branches

and raced toward the back of the house. He didn't stop. Running, he checked the windows for any sign of the killer or Caroline Stallings. Enough lights were on to illuminate the place, but no one was in sight in the large solarium that he passed.

"I'm at the entry gate," one of the guards said through the communicator. "My partner's by the west fence. That covers both of the most likely exit routes, and San Antonio PD backup should be here soon to cover the others."

Soon wasn't soon enough. He needed backup now.

"I'm going in the house," he told the guard. Egan had to make sure Caroline Stallings was alive and that she stayed that way. "If the intruder comes running out of there *alone,* try to make an arrest. If he doesn't cooperate, if you have to shoot, then aim low for the knees. I want this SOB alive."

Because this particular SOB might be able to answer some hard questions about the four deaths that'd happened in or around Cantara Hills in the past nine months.

Egan glanced around to make sure the intruder hadn't escaped into the back or east yards. If he had, then it was a long drop down since the house was literally perched on the lip of a jagged limestone bluff. An escape over that particular wrought-iron fence could be suicide. But Egan did spot someone.

The brunette with a butcher knife.

She was standing just a few feet away on the porch near double stained-glass doors, and she had a white-knuckled grip on the gleaming ten-inch blade. Her blue-green eyes were wide, her chest pumping with jolts of breath that strained her sleeveless turquoise top.

It was Caroline Stallings.

Alive, thank God. And she seemed unharmed.

Egan had seen her around Cantara Hills a couple of times in the past week since the Texas Rangers had been called in to solve three cold-case murders and then a hot one that'd happened only forty-eight hours earlier. During those other sightings, Ms. Stallings had always appeared so cool, rich and collected. She wasn't so cool or collected now with her shaky composure and windswept dark brown hair.

But the rich part still applied.

Despite the fear and that god-awful big knife, she looked high priced, high rent and high maintenance.

She jumped when she saw him. And gasped. That caused her chest to pump even harder.

"Where's the intruder?" Egan mouthed.

She used the knife blade to point in the direction of the left side of the house. The opposite location from where he'd come. "My bedroom," she mouthed back. "I ran out here when I heard the noise."

Wise move. From her vantage point, she could see a lot through that beveled glass, including an intruder if he was about to come after her.

She reached over, eased open the door, and Egan slipped inside through the kitchen. The floor was gray slate. Potentially noisy. So he lightened his steps.

There were yards of slick black granite countertops, stainless appliances that reflected like mirrors, and in the open front cabinets, precise rows of crystal glasses, all shimmering and cool. He lifted an eyebrow at the half-empty bag of Oreo cookies on the kitchen island.

The A/C spilled over him, chilling the rain that snaked down his face and back. "Has the intruder come out of your bedroom or moved past you to get to another part of the house?" he asked.

"No one's come out of that room," she insisted.

So Egan turned his ear in that direction and listened.

Well, that's what he tried to do, anyway, but he couldn't hear much, other than Caroline Stallings's frantic breathing and her silk clothes rustling against her skin. She was obviously trembling from head to toe.

"When I came home from work, I noticed my security system wasn't working. Then I heard someone moving around in my bedroom," she muttered. "I dialed 9-1-1, they dispatched my call to you, and something or someone cut the line."

Yes. The line had indeed gone dead. Egan had hoped it was because of the rain, but his gut told him otherwise. It wasn't difficult to cut a phone line or disarm a security system, and perps usually did that when they wanted to sever their victim's means of communication. Murder or something equally nasty usually followed. Hopefully, he'd prevented the "equally nasty" part from happening.

"And I found this thing in my car," she added a moment later.

The vague *thing* got his attention. That wasn't good, either. Egan didn't want his attention on anything other than the intruder.

He glanced over his shoulder at Ms. Stallings and scowled at her so she'd hush. The scowl was still on his face when he heard the sound. Not breathing or rustlings on silk. It came from the direction of her bedroom, and it sounded as if someone had opened a door.

"What's the status of SAPD?" Egan whispered into the communicator.

"Not here yet," was the guard's response.

Egan silently cursed. It was decision time. He could stand there and continue to protect Ms. Stallings, or he could do something to catch a possible killer.

It didn't take him but a second to decide.

"Follow me," he instructed Caroline. "Stay low and don't make a sound."

She nodded and kept a firm grip on the butcher knife.

"And don't accidentally stab me with that thing," he snarled.

She tossed him a scowl of her own.

Egan took his first steps toward the bedroom, moving from the slate floor of the kitchen to some kind of exotic hardwood in the dining room and the foyer. He stopped. Listened. But he didn't hear any indication that the intruder was coming their way. So he took another step. Then, another. Caroline Stallings followed right behind him.

From the massive foyer, it was well over twenty feet to her bedroom. The door was open, and he paused in the entryway to get a look around. It, too, was massive. At least four hundred square feet. He wasn't surprised by all the space.

There were more dark hardwood floors and an equally dark four-poster bed frame, but nearly everything else was virginal white. The walls, the rugs, the high-end dresser and chest that were glossy white wood. It smelled like linen, starch and the rain.

No visible intruder.

However, there was movement.

Egan spun in that direction, re-aiming his weapon, but he realized the movement had come from the gauzy white curtains that were stirring in the breeze. He quickly spotted the breeze's source. Another set of French doors.

And these were wide open.

The doors shifted a little with each new brush of wind. That was obviously the sound he'd heard when he'd thought the intruder was escaping.

Mentally cursing again, Egan stepped just inside the room so he could get a better look at the floor. It didn't take any Ranger training or skill to see the wet footprints on the hardwood. The prints didn't just lead into the room. There were also some going out.

Hell. The intruder had likely left before Egan had even arrived.

"The cops are here," the guard informed Egan through the communicator.

Maybe it wasn't too late. "Have them check the grounds, but it looks as if our guy got away."

"He got away?" Caroline repeated with more than a bit of anger in her voice.

She went forward until she was right at his back and came up on her tiptoes so she could peer over his shoulder. She touched him in the process. Specifically, her silk-covered right breast swished against his back. That didn't stop her from looking and obviously seeing those tracks.

"He's gone," she mumbled, moving back slightly. She cursed, too, and it wasn't exactly mild. But it was justified. Judging from what the Rangers had learned about the murders, Caroline Stallings just might be on the killer's list.

The problem was—who was the killer?

And why exactly would he want Caroline dead?

So far, all the victims had been connected to a fatal hit-and-run that'd happened nine months earlier on the night of a high-society Christmas party at Cantara Hills. The now-dead Vincent Montoya was responsible for that incident, in which a young woman had died. In fact, everyone directly connected to the hit-and-run was dead.

Except for Caroline.

She'd been driving the vintage sports car that Vincent Montoya had slammed into.

Caroline had been injured, too, and supposedly lost her memory of not only the accident but that entire fateful night. The so-called amnesia bothered the hell out of Egan. Was she faking it to save one of her rich friends who might have caused the hit-and-run? Or was she covering for herself because she'd been negligent in some way? Egan didn't know which, but he was almost positive she was covering something.

Almost.

"The police will come inside any minute," Egan told her. He moved her back into the doorway so that she'd be away from the windows. "Then, I can question you and have them check for trace and prints. We might be able to get something off those shoe impressions and the doorknobs."

He didn't want to get too engrossed in processing the crime scene just in case the cops flushed out the intruder and the SOB came running back into the house. That's the reason Egan kept his service pistol aimed and ready.

"You're sure you had your security system turned on?" he asked her.

"Of course. Since the murders, I always make sure it's set. But as I said, it wasn't working when I came home." She looked around. "At least nothing appears to have been ransacked. And besides, there wasn't much to steal since I don't keep money or expensive jewelry in the house."

"This person might not have been after stuff," Egan grumbled.

She touched the highly polished dresser, which was dotted with perfectly aligned silver-framed photos of what appeared to be family members. "Do you think the intruder could have been the person who murdered Vincent Montoya?"

"It's possible." More than possible. Likely. Especially since the ritzy neighborhood of Cantara Hills had been virtually crime-free prior to the hit-and-run. But afterward... Well, that was a whole different story.

"Why isn't Lt. McQuade here?" she asked a moment later. "I figured he'd be the one to come."

Brody McQuade, the Ranger lieutenant in charge of the Cantara Hills murders. "He's in California trying to track down a person of interest."

"Oh. Then what about the other Ranger—Sgt. Keller?" She spoke in a regular voice. Not whispers. And Egan didn't have to listen hard to that shiny accent to know that she didn't seem to care for his presence. "He was at the country club earlier. Why didn't he come?"

"Hayes is in Austin at the crime lab. And before you ask, I'm in charge of this investigation right now, and you're stuck with me."

"Stuck with the surly one," she mumbled. Her chin came up when he glared back at her. "That's what people around here call you. Brody's the intense one. Hayes is the chip-on-the-shoulder one."

Egan's glare morphed into a frown. "And I got named 'the surly one'? That's the best you people could do?"

She nodded as if his *you-people* insult didn't bother her in the least. "It suits you."

Yeah. It did. But for some reason it riled him, coming from her. "You're the *richer* one."

"Excuse me?" She blinked.

Egan tried not to smile at her obvious indignation. "There are three young Cantara Hills socialites involved in this investigation. The 'rich' one is your lawyer friend, Victoria Kirkland. You're the 'richer' one. And Taylor Landis, the third socialite, who hosted that infamous Christmas party, is the 'richest of them all.'"

She gave him a flat look. "How original. That must have required lots of time and mental energy to come up with those."

"About as much time and energy as it took you and your pals to come up with *surly*."

They stared at each other.

There was a sharp rap at the front door, causing both Egan and her to jump a little. But even a little jump for Egan was an embarrassing annoyance and more proof that Caroline Stallings was a distraction he didn't need or want.

"SAPD," the man said from outside the door. "We can't find anyone on the grounds."

Egan didn't even bother with profanity—he was past that point. He went to the door and let the two uniformed officers in. Both were drenched from the rain, as were the two security guards behind them. That same drenching rain would likely wash away any tracks or evidence that the intruder had left in the yard.

"There are shoe prints in the bedroom," Egan informed them, and he hitched his thumb in that direction. "It looks as if that's the point of entry and escape. I want that entire area processed."

The taller Hispanic cop nodded. "I'll get our CSI guys

out here right away." He paused and looked at Caroline. "What about her? Does she need medical attention?"

"I'm fine," she insisted.

Egan slipped his pistol back into his leather shoulder holster. "Secure the crime scene," he instructed the officer. "Check for signs of forcible entry and a cut phone line. Someone probably tampered with the security system, too. And let me know the minute the CSI guys arrive. Ms. Stallings has to show me a *thing* she found in her car, and I'll question her about the intruder while I'm doing that."

"Oh, yes. *The thing*," Caroline said as if she'd forgotten all about it. "My car's in the garage. This way." She led him through the foyer and back into the kitchen—all thirty to forty feet of it. She slid the knife back into the empty slot of a granite butcher's block.

"You're sure you didn't see this person in your house?" Egan proceeded.

"No. Not even a shadow."

Egan kept at it. "But you heard a sound. Footsteps, maybe?"

"I'm not sure what I heard. Movement, yes. But not footsteps per se."

Too bad. The sound of footsteps could have given him possible information about the size of the intruder. Since they were nearing the solarium and the garage, Egan shifted his focus a little. "What exactly is this thing you found in your car?"

"A little black plastic box about the size of a man's wallet. It fell out from beneath my dash while I was driving home tonight."

That didn't immediately alarm him. "And you don't

think it's part of the car?" Though he couldn't imagine what part of the car that would be, exactly.

She lifted her shoulder. "I guess it could be. But it'd been secured with duct tape."

Now, the alarms came. She wasn't the sort of woman to buy anything that required the use of duct tape. "Did you open this box?"

"No. It fell as I was pulling into my garage so I let it stay put and went inside. I'd left my cell phone at the restaurant in the country club, and I was going to use my house phone to call someone about the box, but then I heard the intruder."

So, she'd had two surprises in one night. Were they connected? "What do you think this box could be?"

"Maybe some kind of eavesdropping equipment," she readily supplied. "My family and I are in the antiques business. Competition is a lot more aggressive than you'd think, and I'm within days of closing a multimillion-dollar deal."

That silenced some of those alarms in Egan's head. "So you think your competition could have planted a listening device to get insider information?"

"It's possible."

Egan followed her through the massive solarium. More lights flared on as they walked through, and those lights gave him a too-good view of his hostess's backside. In that short black skirt, it was hard not to notice that particular part of her anatomy. Ditto for her long legs, which looked even longer because of the three-inch heels she was wearing. She was no waif, that was for sure. Caroline Stallings had a woman's body with plenty of curves.

"The garage is through here," she explained, and she reached for a door.

Egan caught on to her arm and pulled her behind him.

There was renewed alarm in her eyes. "You think the intruder could still be around?"

"No. But I don't want you to take any unnecessary chances. I want you alive and well because if you ever get your memory back, we might finally be able to figure out who's behind these killings."

She made a noncommittal sound. "And that's why you set up the appointment for the day after tomorrow for me to see the psychiatrist. The one who specializes in recovering lost memories from traumatic incidents. She wants to try some new drug on me."

Egan didn't think it was his imagination that Caroline was upset about that. Probably because it threw off her daily massage schedule or something. But he didn't care one bit about inconveniencing her. He only wanted the truth about what'd really happened the night of that hit-and-run.

"The psychiatrist also wants me to keep a journal of my dreams," she added. "I was up at three in the morning writing down things that I'm sure won't make a bit of sense to her. I just don't think this'll do any good."

"You never know," he mumbled. "It might be the key to the truth." But even a long shot like this was a move in the right direction.

He preceded her into the garage. The lights were still on, and there were two cars parked inside. A vintage white Mercedes convertible, top up, beaded with rainwater, and a 1966 candy-apple-red Mustang with a coat of dust on it. What Egan didn't see were any signs of the person who'd left those tracks in her bedroom.

"The box thing is in the Mercedes," she volunteered, stepping ahead of Egan. She, too, made vigilant glances all around them. But the vigilance didn't seem necessary because no one jumped out at them, and no one was lurking between the vehicles.

She opened the passenger's door and pointed to the object on the floor. *Yep.* It was a small black box all right, and it had strips of black duct tape dangling off the sides.

"Like I said, I think it's an eavesdropping device," she commented.

And she reached for it.

Her fingers were less than an inch away when Egan practically tackled her so he could snag her wrist. In theory, it was a good idea because he didn't want her to smear any prints that might be on the box. But that snagged wrist and his forward momentum sent them sprawling onto the passenger's seat.

Caroline landed face-first. He landed with his face in her peach-scented, shoulder-length hair. And another part of him, a brainless part of him, hit against her firm butt. Egan grunted from the contact.

Her body nearly distracted him from hearing the tiny, soft sounds.

Clicks.

But Egan shook his head, mentally amending that. Not clicks.

Ticks.

The sounds were synchronized. One right behind the other. Marking off time.

Or rather counting it down.

Hell.

"Get out of here!" he shouted, dragging Caroline from the seat. "It's a bomb."

Chapter Two

Before Egan Caldwell's words even registered in Caroline's head, he already had hold of her and was running toward the door with her in tow.

Mercy, was that black box really a bomb?

She'd heard the ticking sound, of course. Not while she'd been in the car earlier when the engine was running. But now—when Egan and she had tumbled onto the seat. She seriously doubted that an eavesdropping device would have a timer on it.

The adrenaline jolted through her, and Caroline somehow managed to run in her unsensible business heels. Probably thanks to Egan. He had a death grip on her left wrist and practically plowed them through the door that led to a narrow mudroom and then the solarium on the back of her house.

"Evacuate now—there's a bomb in the garage!" he shouted. Which, in turn, caused more shouts from the cops and the security guards.

All of them began to run. Egan didn't stop, either. He hauled her through the kitchen, then the living room, and they exited through the front door, on the opposite side of the house from the garage. The cops were ahead of them. The two civilian guards, behind.

The rain was coming down harder now and lashed at them like razors. So did the blinding blue strobe lights from the police cruiser parked at the end of her cobblestone drive. It didn't hinder Egan. He barreled down the front porch steps with her and made a beeline to the driveway, getting her even farther away from the garage.

"Call the bomb squad," Egan shouted over his shoulder to one of the guards who was sprinting along behind them. He glanced around through the rain and the night until his attention landed on the other guard. "Keep everyone away from the house."

Because the place might blow up.

That "bottom line" realization sent Caroline's heart to her knees. Someone might get hurt. Also, her house might soon be destroyed, and there was apparently nothing she could do to stop it.

But who had done this?

A car bomb certainly seemed like overkill for an overly zealous competitor in the antiques business. *Sweet heaven.* Had the intruder also been the one to plant that bomb? And if so, why?

Of course, she couldn't discount the four previous murders. All people she'd known. All of them involved in some way with the City Board, of which she was a member.

Was she now the killer's next target?

Her legs and thighs began to cramp from the exertion. She wasn't much of a runner, and the heels didn't help. Caroline was wheezing for breath and her heart was hammering in her chest by the time they made it to the end of her drive.

Egan stopped, finally, and pulled her in front of him. Actually, he put her against the wet stone pylon that held the open wrought-iron gate in place. He got right behind her, pushing her face-first against the stones.

"Don't look back," he warned. "And shelter your eyes just in case that damn thing goes off."

That's when she realized he was *sheltering* her. It wasn't personal; Caroline was sure of that. She'd seen the disdain in his eyes. Sgt. Egan Caldwell was merely doing his job, and right now, she was the job.

"You really think the bomb's about to explode?" Caroline asked.

"It's a possibility, but I don't believe the device is large enough to create a blast that'll reach us here. At least, I hope not," he added in a mumble.

But the officers apparently didn't believe that because one of them began to sprint in the direction of her nearest neighbor. "I'll have them evacuate," the Hispanic cop relayed to Egan.

Mercy. Now her neighbor and best friend, Taylor Landis, was perhaps in danger.

Caroline wiped her hand over her face to sling off some of the rainwater. She wished she could do the same to the adrenaline and fear because it was starting to overwhelm her. "This doesn't make sense."

"If we have a vigilante killer on our hands, it doesn't have to make sense," he reminded her.

Yes. She'd heard that theory. Or rather the gossip. That Vincent Montoya might have been murdered by a vigilante who maybe wanted to tie up all loose ends of the hit-and-run.

"I can understand why a vigilante would go after Montoya," she mumbled. "But why try to kill me?"

"You got an answer for that?" Egan asked.

Since that sounded like some kind of challenge, she looked back at him. She didn't have to look far. He was there. Right over her soaking wet shoulder, and the overhead security light clearly showed his rain-streaked face.

Surly, beyond doubt.

Caroline tried not to let the next thought enter her mind, but she couldn't stop it. Egan Caldwell was a good-looking man. Okay, he wasn't just good-looking.

He was hot.

Dark blond hair, partially hidden beneath that creamy-white Stetson. Eyes that were a brilliant, burning blue. He had just enough ruggedness to stop him from being a pretty boy and just enough pretty boy to smooth out some of that ruggedness.

And Caroline hated she'd noticed that about him.

"What are you waiting for me to say?" she snapped. "That this guy wants me dead because I saw or heard something the night of the hit-and-run?" She didn't pause long enough for him to confirm it because Caroline could see the confirmation in those eyes. "Well, if that were true, why didn't he come after me nine months ago? If this is truly some vigilante killer, then I should have been one of the first on his list."

Egan stood there, staring at her, with the summer rain assaulting them and the sounds of chaos going on all around. The cruiser's lights pulsed blue flashes over him. Flashes that were the same color as his eyes. "Maybe the killer hasn't come after you before because you supposedly have no memories of the hit-and-run."

Again, that wasn't new information, either. "Nothing has changed about that. It's not *supposedly.*" Caroline froze and then eased around so that she was facing him. "But I have an appointment the day after tomorrow to see that psychiatrist to help me remember what happened."

He nodded and snorted slightly as if annoyed that it'd taken her so long to figure it out. "Did you tell anyone about that appointment?"

Oh, mercy. "Yes. I was talking about it today when I had lunch at the Cantara Hills Country Club." Actually, Caroline had verbally blasted the Rangers, Egan and Brody, for demanding the appointment. She'd already been through hours of therapy and had zero recollection of the time immediately before, during and following the accident. The dream log and the appointment seemed not only unnecessary but intrusive and a total waste of time—and hope.

"Who was there at this country club lunch?" Egan asked. He used his snarly Texas Rangers' tone that was only marginally softened by his easy drawl. Words slid right off that drawl.

"My parents. They were leaving on vacation this afternoon, a second honeymoon they've been planning for months, and I wanted to see them before they left." In the distance, she could hear the sirens. Probably the bomb squad. Maybe they'd get there in time to disarm it before it could hurt anyone. "And Kenneth Sutton and his wife, Tammy, joined us."

His mouth tightened. "Kenneth, who's chairman of the City Board. He's also a suspect."

"Only because the hit-and-run driver, Vincent Montoya, worked for him. But Kenneth told me he had no idea what Montoya had done."

"Yeah, yeah," Egan grumbled. "Because according to Kenneth, Vincent Montoya killed Kimberly McQuade in that crash because he was jealous she'd rebuffed him and had had an affair with another man. An affair she'd never mentioned to anyone. Funny that the guy's never surfaced, either, and there's not a lick of proof that Montoya had had any sexual interest in Kimberly. Or vice versa. According to people who knew her well, Vincent Montoya wasn't her type."

"Because he was a lowly driver?" Caroline instantly regretted her question. It sounded snobby, especially since Egan's own father was a chauffeur. And not just any old chauffeur but the one who worked for her father's close friend who lived in Cantara Hills.

"I'm sorry," she mumbled. "Talking about that night isn't easy for me." Caroline was still grieving. Always would. There wasn't a day that went by that she didn't regret what had happened. Yes, Montoya had caused the fatal crash, but Caroline couldn't help but wonder if there was something she could have done to stop it.

"Murder is rarely easy to talk about," he countered.

When Caroline continued, she softened her voice. "I'm just having a hard time believing that Kenneth Sutton, a man I work with on the City Board, a man I've known my entire life, is capable of ordering his driver to murder someone. Yet the Rangers seem to think that might have happened."

"You might think that, too, once I've had a chance to question Kenneth further and have more information." He shrugged. "But the point right now is Kenneth was there today at lunch with you. He heard you say that you had an appointment with the shrink. Who else heard?"

She started to shake her head but stopped. Oh, this was

not good. "My parents, Kenneth and his wife were the only people at the table with me, but some of my other neighbors were there. They could have heard."

"Give me names," he demanded, while he made a visual check of the area around them.

"Your father's boss, Link Hathaway, and his daughter, Margaret. Miles Landis was there, too. He's my best friend's brother. Half brother," she corrected. Miles had dropped by to hit her up for a loan, again. Caroline had turned him down, again. "Your father even came into the restaurant for a couple of minutes to talk to Link."

Egan mumbled some profanity under his breath. "So, what you're saying is that everyone in Cantara Hills knows about your appointment?"

She silently repeated the same profanity as Egan. "Yes. But I didn't think I had to keep it a secret. My parents and I were discussing it because my mom's upset about me being sedated with this drug and then interrogated. She wanted to cancel her trip, and I had to talk her out of it."

Egan jumped right on that. "Why is she upset?"

Caroline groaned. The adrenaline and bomb scare had obviously made her chatty. "Long story."

"I'm listening."

Of course he was. And he was scowling again. He apparently thought she was concerned about revealing something incriminating.

Which she was.

In a way.

But Caroline couldn't think about that now, and she didn't dare voice any of it to Egan. She'd already blabbed enough tonight.

She chose her words carefully. "My mother's afraid I'll

say something about a personal incident, and that the information will get around to everyone," she admitted. "The incident isn't pertinent to this case."

"I'll be the judge of that."

Caroline was sure her scowl matched his, and she had to speak through nearly clenched teeth. "All right. Three years ago I was involved with a jerk. Everybody knows about the broken engagement, but no one else knows that the jerk stole money from my parents. I want to keep it that way, understand?"

Egan responded with a noncommittal grunt. "I'll keep it that way if I decide it's not vital information that can help me catch a killer. You're not my priority, Ms. Stallings. And neither is your parents' need to keep their skeletons shut away in their walk-in closet."

"Oh, God," she mumbled, ignoring his last zinger. She checked her watch. "My parents. They'll be in Cancun by now, and one of the neighbors might have called them at their hotel. They'll be worried." She glanced in the direction of her parents' house. Just up the street. And even though she knew her parents weren't home, her concerns were verified.

The cruiser's lights had attracted the neighbors. All of them. One of the officers was guarding the street in front of her house and preventing anyone from getting too close. Including her parents' nearest neighbors, the Jenkins. She spotted them, a perky yellow umbrella perched over their heads. They were frantically waving at her, and Mrs. Jenkins had a cell phone pressed to her ear.

"They say they have your parents on the line. They want to know if you're all right," the officer relayed to

her. Because of the sirens and the rain, he had to practically shout.

"Tell them I'm fine," Caroline shouted back. "And that
I love them. I'll call them later."

If Egan had any response to her message, he didn't
show it. He looked at the approaching trio of bomb squad
vehicles before turning his attention back to her. "Other
than you, who had access to your car today?"

It was something that hadn't occurred to Caroline. Yet.
But it would have once she'd caught her breath. "I was
the only person in the car. My family's business office is
on San Pedro Avenue, and I parked there in my space in
the building garage. I came back here to Cantara Hills for
lunch around noon, and then I met with a client at his
office just off Highway 281 before returning to work."

He glanced around them again. "I noticed your car
doors were unlocked in the garage. Were they locked
when you were at any of these other places?"

Caroline really hated to admit this, but, hey, she hadn't
known that her every movement might have been watched
by a killer. "I had the top down most of the day so it
wouldn't have been hard for anyone to get inside. And
since it's a vintage car and I don't keep anything valuable
inside, it doesn't have a security alarm."

The bomb squad vehicles braked to a stop by the gate.

Egan stared at her. "So anyone could have overheard
your conversation at lunch, and those same anyones could
have gained access to your car and planted a bomb."

Because he made her sound like a careless idiot,
Caroline frowned. "That about sums it up."

But Egan was right. She hadn't been cautious, driving
with the car top down with a killer on the loose, and it

could have cost others their lives. She already blamed herself for Kimberly McQuade's death.

She didn't want this on her conscience as well.

The bomb squad personnel barreled out of their vehicles, and Egan stepped away from her to speak to a burly blond man wearing dark blue-gray body armor. Caroline listened as Egan briefed the man, describing the location of the device and the size.

The man tipped his head toward her. "Go ahead and get her out of here. I want those guards and uniforms out, too. I don't want anyone near the place until my guys have checked out this thing."

Egan turned back to her. There was more displeasure in his body language and expression, probably because he had to babysit her.

"Let's go," he grumbled.

But the grumble had barely left Egan's mouth when the sound of the blast rocketed behind them.

Chapter Three

Well, at least no one was dead.

That was the only good thing Egan could say about the events of the night.

First, an intruder. The intruder's escape. Then, an explosion. Egan was waiting for a call from the bomb squad so he'd know the extent of the damage, but he didn't have to hear a situation report to confirm that the killer had a new target.

Caroline Stallings.

She was in the corner of his temporary office. Soaked to the bone. She'd gotten even wetter when they had run from his car and into the country club. Her clothes were clinging to her body, and there were drops of rain still sliding down her bare legs and into those pricey, uncomfortable-looking heels. She was shivering. And using his phone to call her parents in Cancun, Mexico. Her calm, practically lively tone didn't go with her slumped shoulders and shell-shocked expression. The rain, and possibly even a tear or two, had streaked through what was left of her makeup.

"No. I'm fine, really," she assured her parents. "There's nothing you can do, and I have everything under control."

She caught her bottom lip between her teeth for a moment, probably to stop it from trembling. "I'm with one of the Rangers," she went on. "We're at his office at the Cantara Hills Country Club." She paused. "No. I'm with Sgt. Egan Caldwell." Another pause. "No." She glanced at him and turned away. "He's the surly one," she whispered.

Egan was just punchy enough that he couldn't stop himself from smiling. He didn't let Caroline see it, of course.

While she continued her call, Egan went to the closet behind his desk and took out one of the four freshly laundered shirts hanging inside. His jeans were soaked, too, but changing them would require leaving Caroline alone. Because they had a killer on the loose, that wasn't a good idea. So he settled for a fresh blue button-up. Either that or a white shirt and jeans were his standard "uniform" when he was on duty, which lately was 24/7. He changed and put back on his shoulder holster. Later, he'd have to give his gun a good cleaning to dry it out as well.

"Please don't come home," he heard Caroline say. She'd repeated a variation of that at least a half-dozen times since the call began. "Yes, I'll have the locks changed on all the doors and windows at the house. I'll make sure the security system is checked. And I won't stay there alone. I promise." She shivered again. "I love you, too."

She'd said that at least a half-dozen times as well. *I love you.* The words were heartfelt. It was hard to fake that level of emotion. Even though he was thirty years old and had been in his share of relationships, it still amazed Egan that some people could say those words so easily.

Not him.

But then, he'd never tried, figuring he was more likely to choke on them than say them aloud.

He finished transferring his badge to the dry shirt, turned, and Caroline was there holding out his phone for him to take. "Thank you," she said. No more fake cheerfulness. The shock was setting in, and she was shaking harder now.

Egan hung up the phone, extracted another of his shirts from the closet and handed it to her. "Put this on. As soon as the bomb squad clears the area, you can go to your friend's house and get some dry clothes." That might not happen soon, though, and her friends wouldn't be able to get to her since no one could use the road to drive to the country club. The bomb squad had sectioned it off.

She made a small throaty sound of agreement and slipped on his shirt. "Thank you again."

Caroline wearily sank down into the studded burgundy leather chair next to his desk and closed her fingers over the delicate gold heart necklace that had settled in her cleavage. Like the words to her parents, she'd done that a lot tonight as well.

Egan anticipated what she'd do next. She was wearing two dainty gemstone gold rings on her left hand. Opals on one. Aquamarines on the other. Another opal ring was on her right hand. She began to twist and adjust them. She was obviously trying to settle her nerves. But Egan was betting that settled nerves weren't in her immediate future no matter how many rings she twisted.

"I suppose the bomb squad will call when they know anything," she said. Not really a question. He'd already explained that.

Still, Egan nodded and started a fresh pot of coffee. Thank God for the little premeasured packets because that was the only chance he had of making it drinkable, and right now, he needed massive quantities of caffeine that he could consume in a hurry so he could stay alert and fight off the inevitable adrenaline crash.

"You didn't get to finish your dinner." Caroline pushed her damp hair from her face and tipped her head to the now-cold burger and fries on the center of his desk. He'd managed only a few bites.

"It's not the first time." And he hoped that wasn't concern for him in her voice.

Wait.

What was he thinking?

It couldn't be concern. He was the surly one, and she was the richer one. She was an heiress. He, the chauffeur's son. Concern on her part wasn't in this particular equation, and the only thing she cared about was getting through this. The only thing he cared about was keeping her alive and catching a killer.

The silence came like the soggy downpour that was occurring simultaneously outside. They weren't comfortable with each other, and they weren't comfortable being in the same confined space. Hopefully, that confinement would end when the bomb squad finished, and he could pawn this "richer" leggy brunette off on someone else.

Anyone else.

"I'm sorry I wasn't able to help more with the investigation of the hit-and-run," Caroline whispered.

That comment/apology came out of the blue, and Egan certainly hadn't expected it. More ring twisting, yes. Ditto for touching that gold heart pendant. But he hadn't anticipated a sincere-sounding apology. "And you're probably sorry that you were driving the car that night."

"That, too." She nodded. "But my memory loss is only of that night. I remember Kimberly."

So did Egan. Kimberly had grown up on the same street that he had. And her brother, Brody, was now Egan's boss.

"She was a kind, generous woman who worked hard as an intern for the City Board," Caroline continued. "I'm glad her killer is dead."

And yet her killer was also someone whom Caroline had known. Vincent Montoya, who'd rammed his vehicle into the passenger's side of Caroline's vintage sports car. The impact had thrown Kimberly from her seat, and she'd sustained a broken neck. Death had come instantly.

But not for the two other men Montoya had murdered.

Two men, Trent Briggs and Gary Zelke, who Montoya likely believed had seen him ram into Caroline's car, had been killed months later. Montoya had murdered them to eliminate witnesses and probably would have done the same to Victoria Kirkland, a third possible witness, if someone—the vigilante maybe—hadn't killed Montoya first. Since it was possible that Victoria was now in danger from this vigilante, she was out of state in Brody's protective custody.

Unlike Caroline.

She was here at Cantara Hills. Right in the line of fire.

"We still need to find out if Montoya was working alone, or if someone hired him to commit those murders," Egan reminded her. He stood and poured them both some coffee. "And if he was working alone, then who's this new intruder who came into your house tonight?"

She took the mug of coffee from him, gripping it in both of her shaky hands, and she sipped some even though it was steaming hot. "And you think that intruder might be Kenneth Sutton, the chairman of the City Board?" Despite all the other emotions, skepticism oozed from her voice.

Egan shrugged and sank down in his chair. "Stating the obvious here, but Montoya was Kenneth Sutton's driver, personal assistant and jack-of-all trades."

"That doesn't mean Kenneth ordered Montoya to kill anyone. Kenneth's a career politician and is running for the governor's office. He can be ambitious when it comes to politics, but I don't think he has murder on his mind."

Egan was about to remind her that rich politicians hid behind their facades just like everybody else, but his cell phone rang, and he snatched it up. "Sgt. Caldwell."

"This is Detective Mark Willows from the bomb squad. We've done a preliminary assessment. No injuries. Property damage is minimal. Definitely nothing structural. A few holes and dents in the garage wall. For the most part, the impact was confined to the Mercedes."

Well, that was better news than he'd expected. That blast had been damn loud. "There was enough damage to destroy the car?" Egan asked.

"It's banged up pretty bad, but we'll tow it to the crime lab and look for prints and other evidence. The explosion happened at 8:10 p.m. You'll probably want to question the owner to see if there's anything significant about that time. We'll question her, too, but it can wait until tomorrow. We'll be here most of the night collecting the bits and pieces so we can reassemble the device and try to figure out who made it."

"Thanks. Call me if you have anything else." Egan

clicked the end-call button and looked at Caroline. Who was looking at him, obviously waiting. "Good news," he let her know. "No one was hurt. Your car is totaled, but the house is okay."

The breath swooshed out of her, and her hand was suddenly shaking so hard that she sloshed some coffee on her fingers when she set the cup on his desk.

"Good. That's good." A moment later, she repeated it.

He debated if he should check her fingers, to make sure she hadn't scalded them. She certainly wasn't doing anything about it. Egan finally reached over and caught on to her wrist so he could have a look. Yep. Definitely red fingers. He rolled his chair across the floor to get to the small fridge, retrieved a cold can of soda and rolled back toward her. He pressed the can to her fingers.

She didn't resist. Caroline just sat there. Her head hung low. Probably numb. Maybe even in shock. "I didn't want anyone else's death or injuries on my hands," she said under her breath. "I couldn't live with that."

Since she seemed on the verge of tears, or even a total meltdown, Egan decided to get her mind back on business. His mind, too. He didn't like seeing her like this.

Vulnerable.

Fragile.

Tormented.

He preferred when she had that aristocratic chin lifted high and the ritzy sass was in her eyes. Because there was no way he could ever be interested in someone with a snobby, rich, stubborn chin. But the vulnerability and the genuine ache he heard in her whisper, that could draw him in.

Oh, yeah.

It could make him see her as an imperfect, desirable woman and not the next victim on a killer's list.

And that wouldn't be good for either Caroline or him. He needed to focus.

That was the best way to keep her alive and catch a killer.

He wrapped her fingers around the soda and leaned back to put some distance between them. No more touching. No more thinking about personal stuff. "The timer on the explosive was set for 8:10 p.m. Where would you normally have been at that time?"

Her head came up, and she met his gaze. "Since it's Monday, I should have been in the car, driving home from work."

He was afraid she was going to say that. "That's your usual routine?"

She nodded. "I always work late on Mondays. The security guard walks me out to my car at eight p.m., because that's when his shift is over. I leave at exactly that time so he won't have to stay any longer, and it takes me about fifteen minutes to drive home." She put the soft drink can aside so she could touch the necklace. "But the security guard wasn't feeling well tonight. He wouldn't go home until I did so I left about forty-five minutes earlier than I usually do."

That insistent sick guard had saved her life. Egan didn't need to spell that out for her.

"Who knows your work routine?" he asked.

The color drained from her cheeks. "Anyone who knows me."

Well, that didn't narrow it down much, and it certainly didn't exclude Kenneth Sutton. There was just something about Kenneth that reminded Egan of a snake oil salesman. Egan only hoped that his feelings weren't skewed that way because the guy was stinkin' rich.

"So did the same person plant that bomb and then break into my house?" Caroline asked.

"Possibly. Maybe he set the explosive to make sure you didn't come home when he was there."

She shook her head. "Why? If that explosive had killed me, why bother to break into my house?" She waited a moment, her gaze still connected with Egan's. "Unless he was there to make sure I hadn't survived."

It was Egan's turn to shake his head. Egan had already played around with that theory, and it had a major flaw. "Then the intruder would have been lying in wait and would have attacked the moment you walked in. You wouldn't have had time to make that 9-1-1 call or grab a knife."

She closed her eyes a moment, and her breath shuddered. "So, this intruder perhaps not only wanted me dead but also wanted something from my house?"

"Bingo." That was the conclusion he'd reached as well. "He probably thought you'd died in the car bomb, but when you came driving up, he'd perhaps already gotten what he came for or, rather, had tried to do that, and he fled because a person who sets a delayed explosive isn't someone who wants a face-to-face meeting with their victim. Now, the question is—what did he take? The usual is either money or jewelry. Something lightweight enough to carry away."

"I already told you I don't keep large sums of money in the house, or on me. I use plastic for almost everything I buy. And I don't own a lot of jewelry." Caroline held up her hands. "These pieces are all from family members. Aunts and my mother. My grandmother," she added, pointing to the gold heart necklace.

Family stuff. Something else he knew little about. "What about any small valuable antique that the intruder could have taken from your house?"

Another head shake. "I run an antiques business and love vintage cars, but I prefer modern decor." She paused. "Or rather, no decor. I'm not much for fuss or clutter."

He thought of her virginal white bedroom and glistening black kitchen and agreed. Modern, uncluttered and maybe even a little anal. Everything perfectly aligned and in its place, like the cool crystal.

Everything in place but those cookies.

Store-bought. Not the gourmet kind from some chichi bakery. Normal ones. Egan had a hard time imagining her standing in her kitchen. Surrounded by all that expensive glitter. Wearing silk designer clothes. And eating Oreos.

"Wait. There *is* something," she said a moment later. "I have a small clock that was a Christmas gift from my mother. It's portable and probably worth a lot. It's on the nightstand, next to the dream journal I've been keeping for the psychiatrist."

Egan didn't remember seeing a clock or a journal, but then his attention had been on those open French doors, not the nightstand. He grabbed his phone and punched in the number to the SAPD dispatch, who in turn connected him with Detective Mark Willows.

"This is Sgt. Caldwell," he said when Willows answered.

"Glad you called," Willows interrupted before Egan could explain. "I just got an update from the CSI guys. They took Ms. Stallings's lock from her bedroom door so they can test it to see if it was picked. They'll replace it with a temp so we can secure the house."

"Thanks. I'm sure she'll appreciate that."

"Well, we don't want another break-in. This is just preliminary, but those shoe prints left on her bedroom floor are about a size eleven. Some kind of athletic shoes. So, we're probably looking for a male."

Egan made a note to check Kenneth Sutton's shoe size. "I need you to check on the nightstand in the master bedroom and tell me what's there," Egan said to the detective.

"Give me a minute. I'm walking that way." Egan heard the sound of the man's movement. And waited. "There's a phone and a clock," Willows reported. "The phone is white, and the clock is about the size of baseball. It's gold, and it's got pearls and what looks like emeralds all around the dial. Heck, the friggin' hands look like they're made of diamonds. Caldwell, this is some clock."

Yes, and the intruder didn't take it. "Is there anything else on the nightstand?"

"Just a pen. Common, ordinary variety."

Oh, man. "There's no paper or notepad?"

"Nada."

"Thanks. Make sure CSI checks that nightstand for prints." Egan hung up, ready to relay that to Caroline, but he could tell from her expression that she already knew.

"My dream journal is missing," she mumbled.

"Yeah. The expensive clock is still there, though. So, let me guess—everyone at that lunch today heard that you'd been keeping a journal."

The color crept back into her face, and she looked as if she wanted to curse. She nodded.

Hell.

Egan leaned in and looked straight into her eyes. "Caroline, what exactly did you write in that journal?"

Chapter Four

"It's gibberish," Caroline concluded as she glanced over the notes that she'd spent most of the previous night and that morning making. Or, rather, the notes that Egan had *insisted* she make so she could try to re-create her stolen dream journal.

She'd told him the night before that it was futile, that the dreams hadn't revealed anything important. Caroline still believed that. But Egan had persisted anyway, right before the bomb squad had given her the all-clear to leave his office and go to the house of her best friend, Taylor Landis.

Taylor had welcomed Caroline with open arms. Literally. And her friend had hardly let her out of her sight since. They'd chatted, drunk some wine, and then Taylor had called her security expert to go over to Caroline's house to change all the locks on the windows and doors and to repair the security system. It wouldn't give Caroline peace of mind exactly, but it was a start.

"Okay, let me have a look at those notes," Taylor insisted. She had her long blond hair gathered into a ponytail, she gave it an adjustment and then waggled her fingers. "Maybe they won't be gibberish to me."

Caroline handed her the notes and proceeded with her so-called walk-through of her own house. Yet something else Egan had insisted that she do. With an armed security guard shadowing hers and Taylor's every move, Caroline checked her office to make sure everything was in place.

It was.

A PC, laptop and several thousand dollars worth of computer accessories. All still there.

She checked off another room from her list and went to the guest suite off the main corridor. She'd decorated this one all in blue. Pale, barely there blue, for the most part, with the exception of the glossy navy paint on the floor and a fiery abstract oil painting that hung over the natural white stone mantel. She no longer liked that particular bold shade of blue in the painting because it instantly reminded her of Egan's eyes.

Caroline made a mental note to replace it.

"You dreamed about clocks chasing you?" Taylor commented, reading from the reconstructed journal.

"Yes." Caroline frowned. "And don't you dare say anything about ticking biological clocks. I get enough of that from my parents."

"Wouldn't dream of it." However, Taylor's pun indicated she'd thought it. Caroline's frown deepened at her friend's grin.

Caroline checked the white marble guest bathroom. Nothing missing there. And she went into a storage room crammed with carefully stacked, unopened cardboard boxes. Things she'd bought to redecorate when she'd moved from her condo to the house five months earlier. The house had been a thirtieth birthday gift from her parents, and even though she had plenty of space—fourteen rooms—Caroline just hadn't gotten around to making the place *hers*.

She glanced inside the storage room, saw nothing undisturbed and then headed to the one area that she did indeed want to check out.

Her garage.

With her attention nailed to the notes, Taylor followed her. So did the guard, but he kept some distance from them.

"In the dream you had, a man saved you from the attacking clocks," Taylor concluded. "Looks like your rescuer was Egan Caldwell."

Caroline stopped so abruptly that Taylor nearly plowed right into her. "How did you come up with that?"

"Easily. In your notes, you said you were running through the woods with the clocks in pursuit. A man stepped out. He had blond hair, a blue shirt and a silver star embedded in his hand. He shot arrows at the clocks to stop them. Sounds like Egan to me. He has a star badge. He often wears a blue shirt, and he has blondish hair. And if you ask me, those arrows are phallic symbols."

Stunned, Caroline snatched the notes and read over them again. Oh, God. She was certain she hadn't dreamed about Egan and his phallic symbol, but if Taylor believed she had, then Egan might think that as well. She'd have to change the notes before he arrived. Except that she couldn't.

Could she?

No. If he found out, he'd view that as the equivalent of tampering with evidence.

A better solution was just to keep the journal from him and not let him read a single word. She'd wait and show the notes to the psychiatrist, especially since she was meeting with the doctor the following day. Maybe she could convince the psychiatrist to keep them private. After all, it was obvious to her that the dream wasn't connected to the murders or the hit-and-run.

Caroline tucked her journal beneath her arm and stepped into the garage. The doors were open, allowing in the humid breeze and plenty of light so she could see the damage. It was indeed minimal. A few small holes in the wall and some smoke stains—that was it.

Unfortunately, the minimal damage didn't extend to her.

Someone had violated her space, and Caroline wondered how long it would be before she could walk into her house and not think about being killed.

Maybe she never would.

The white Mercedes was gone, of course, towed away in the early hours of the morning by the CSI agents, who were probably now looking for clues about the person who had left that explosive for her. She prayed they'd have answers soon.

Caroline continued to look around the garage, and her gaze landed on the workshop door. It was wide open. And it shouldn't have been. Good grief. She hurried to close it. Except it wouldn't shut. The CSI had apparently busted the lock, probably to check for evidence, and she glanced inside the workshop at what they'd no doubt seen.

Her old secret.

Something she didn't exactly want to announce to the world, including Taylor, who likely knew about it but was too much of a friend to say anything. Caroline would have to do something about getting that door fixed.

Taylor ran her fingers over the remaining vehicle, the 1967 candy-apple-red Mustang. "You used to drive this car all the time," she reminded Caroline.

"Yes. But I gave up on hot, fast things." And for reasons she didn't want to explore, she immediately thought of Egan again.

Thankfully, she didn't have to think of him for long because she heard the voices in her backyard. Obviously, the guard heard them as well because he reached for his gun. Caroline waved him off, however, when she saw her visitors approach the garage.

Kenneth and Tammy Sutton.

She didn't want a gun drawn on her neighbors. Of course, Kenneth was also Egan's prime suspect, but Caroline didn't believe that. Except she hated the uncomfortable feeling that crept through her now. Egan was responsible for those doubts.

But the question was—were his doubts founded?

Twelve hours ago, Caroline would have replied with an emphatic no, but that was before someone had tried to blow her to smithereens.

"Are you all right?" Tammy asked, hurrying to her. She latched on to Caroline, hugging her, and engulfing her in a cloud of Chanel number-something. The woman's layers of thick gold chains dug into Caroline's breasts and her bloodred acrylic nails were like little daggers.

Caroline untangled herself from the hug and stepped back. "I'm fine," she said, realizing she'd been repeating that lie all night and all morning. To her parents. To Taylor. Even to the security guard lurking in the mudroom doorway. And now to Tammy Sutton.

Kenneth strolled closer. No hug. He had his hands in the pockets of his expertly tailored gray suit. With his dark hair combed to perfection, he looked ready for work. And probably was. Being chairman of the City Board often required a sixty-hour-plus week, and it was already past the normal start of his workday.

"You look tired," Kenneth observed.

"Caroline and I sat up chatting all night," Taylor volunteered. Covering for her. So that she wouldn't have to discuss the stress of the explosion and lack of sleep. "She's doing great, just like Caroline always does. Of course, she's anxious to catch the monster who did this."

Kenneth and Tammy nodded sympathetically. "So did the intruder take anything?" Kenneth asked.

Caroline inadvertently glanced down at the new dream journal squished between her arm and side. "Not really."

Tammy must have noticed that glance and the uncertainty in Caroline's voice. "Are you taking inventory?"

"Something like that."

Tammy opened her mouth, probably to ask more, but Caroline heard the movement just a split-second before Egan rounded the corner. Wearing a blue shirt again. And those butt-hugging jeans. No Stetson today. It was probably still drying out from the rain. But he did have his badge and that shoulder holster with the gun tucked inside.

He took one look at Kenneth, and Egan put on his best surly scowl. "Is there a problem?" Egan wanted to know.

"No," Kenneth answered just as quickly. "My wife and I were checking on Caroline. Last I heard, there was no law against that."

Egan's expression didn't change. He went closer to Kenneth and met the man's gaze head-on. "But there are laws against attempted murder, breaking and entering and interfering with an investigation. This is still a crime scene, and you shouldn't be here."

Tammy indignantly pressed her hand to her chest.

"And you don't think we know that this is a crime scene? We're not idiots, Ranger...whatever-your-name-is."

"Caldwell. Remember it, Mrs. Sutton, because you'll see me a lot in the next few days while I interrogate your husband and you." Egan looked down at Kenneth's feet. "What size shoes do you wear?"

"Why?" But it was Tammy who asked, not Kenneth.

"Because I want to know." His attention landed on her shoes as well. "And while you're at it, you can tell me your size, too."

"A perfect six," Tammy said, overly enunciating the words. "And my husband wears a size ten. Satisfied?"

"Not really. I'll have one of the CSI guys drop by to check your closet, just to make sure everything is as *perfect* as you say."

Taylor cleared her throat, obviously sensing that something even more impolite was about to be said, and she went to Kenneth and Tammy. She hooked her arms around both their waists. "Why don't you come on over to my house for some coffee? Egan and Caroline have to finish up this investigation, and we'd just be in the way."

Tammy looked back at Caroline. "Are you sure you don't need us here? Your mother will never forgive me if I don't try to help you at a time like this."

"I'm okay." Caroline hoped. "Please tell Mom that if you talk to her."

Egan looked at the security guard once Kenneth, Tammy and Taylor were out of sight. "Make sure Kenneth Sutton and his wife leave the premises. I don't want them back here, either."

The guard nodded and went after them.

"Tammy's a suspect now?" Caroline asked.

Egan shrugged. "Just about everyone around here is. Guilt by association."

Caroline had the eerie feeling that he wasn't exaggerating. "And her motive?"

"Well, if her husband did order Vincent Montoya to kill those people, then maybe Tammy wants to keep that their own little family secret. Of course, Kenneth has the same motive, so I'd prefer neither of them comes around here."

She huffed. "They're my neighbors. And Kenneth is my boss at the City Board. Any suggestions how to stop them from visiting?"

His gaze eased to hers. "I think my presence will deter them." She stared at him, but he didn't say more. Instead, he shifted his focus to the Mustang. "Nice car."

Yes. It was. "It's from my wild-child days. I guess I'll have to use it for transportation until I can replace the Mercedes." Of course, she was using the Mercedes because her other vehicle had been totaled in the hit-and-run.

His eyebrow lifted. "You were a wild child?" he said in the same tone as if he'd asked if she were a convicted felon.

"Afraid so. Six speeding tickets my senior year in college."

That earned her a hmmph. "Speeding tickets don't make you a wild child."

She didn't like that he dismissed it with that hmmph and raised eyebrow. Those tickets had really upset her parents and had caused her insurance to skyrocket. "Remember, I do have an ex-fiancé thief."

Egan shook his head. "That doesn't make you a wild child, either."

"My parents would disagree with you," she mumbled. And Caroline instantly regretted it. She didn't want to get into a discussion about how she felt she owed it to her parents to be a dutiful daughter.

"Your father had a pretty serious heart attack about the time your fiancé stole that money from him." Egan said it so nonchalantly that it took her a moment to realize the comment meant he'd had her investigated.

"Yes," Caroline admitted. "He nearly died. And please, spare me any psychoanalytical remarks about a guilty conscience."

"No comments." Egan tipped his head to the notebook still tucked beneath her arm. "That's your reconstructed dream journal?"

Oh, mercy. Another can of worms that she didn't want opened. "Yes. I'll give it to the psychiatrist tomorrow when I meet with her."

"*We'll* give it to her," Egan corrected, walking closer. He stopped just inches away.

"You're going to the appointment with me?" she asked.

"Actually, the appointment will be here at your house." He paused, studying her expression. "I shouldn't have to remind you that someone tried to kill you last night. I don't want you going out anywhere alone." He held out his hand. "Now, let me take a look at the journal."

Caroline had made up her mind to refuse, but she rethought that. Because Egan would want to know why. She'd stall him, of course. Then he'd demand to know why she was stalling and refusing.

He'd see right through her.

Because he could.

And in the end, Egan would be suspicious, very suspicious, which would only make him examine every word of gibberish she'd written.

Since she had already lost the hypothetical argument she'd had with him, Caroline handed him the journal as calmly as she could and then went to take a closer look at one of the holes in her garage wall. She waited. While he read the single page.

"Killer clocks, huh?" he commented.

"It was a dream," she snapped. "It doesn't have to make sense."

She heard his footsteps, turned around, and he was there. Practically looming over her. He smelled…manly, with his woodsy, musky aftershave. Looked manly, too, with just the hint of bad-boy stubble on his strong chin.

"You think time's running out?" he asked, handing her back the journal.

"For what?" She sounded cautious. And was.

"For catching a killer," he answered as if that were the only possible answer.

"Yes. That's it." Good. No mention of phallic symbols or blond, blue-shirt-wearing Rangers, which meant Taylor had obviously been wrong.

"Holy moly," Egan mumbled.

Caroline was startled and then realized he wasn't looking at her or the journal, but rather he was looking past her. She followed his gaze to the open door of the workshop. From his angle he could no doubt see her *old secret.*

And he made a beeline for it.

Mercy! She tried to step in front of him. For all the good it did. He merely stepped around her. Caroline maneuvered again. Not very well. She finally gave up the maneuvering and latched onto Egan with both hands.

It wasn't a good idea.

The journal dropped to the floor, and her hands were suddenly filled with his left arm and right shoulder. But her attempts were useless, anyway. He saw her old secret.

"That's a mint condition vintage 1952 Harley-Davidson Panhead Chopper," he announced, studying the motorcycle. His mouth opened slightly, and she thought she saw the pulse in his neck rev up a little.

"So?" she challenged. "I bought it, as an investment. And it's a 1951, not a '52."

He didn't react to the correction. "Not a dent, not one rust spot, not even a paint chip. So, you've obviously taken good care of it. You actually ride it?"

Caroline clutched her heart necklace. "Sometimes." But only at night. When her parents were out of town. They considered anything with two wheels to be dangerous.

"When's the last time you took it out?" he asked, still mesmerized by the motorcycle.

She cleared her throat. "A week ago."

Egan shifted those scorching blue eyes in her direction, and the corner of his mouth hitched into a smile. "Now, owning *that* beauty makes you a wild child."

For some reason, a stupid one, that sounded, well, hot coming from him. That smile helped. Heck, who was she kidding? That smile alone had no doubt seduced countless women because that smile created a too-familiar tug in her belly.

Something stirred between them.

It was followed by a long smoldering look. Oh, the things those eyes were conveying. The Chopper had obviously revved up more than just his pulse and his admiration for her wild-child label.

Thankfully, he must have remembered their too-close

situation because the smile faded until all that was left was the surliness.

He stepped back.

She let go of him and stepped back, too.

"*This* is not going to be a problem between us," Egan said like a general issuing an order to one of his lieutenants.

Caroline bypassed a clarification of *this* mainly because she didn't want it spelled out. "It won't be a problem. Because I'll stay with my friend, Taylor, until you have this killer behind bars. We won't have to be around each other, if at all."

Egan shook his head. "If you stay with Taylor, basically you'll be bringing the danger right to her doorstep, because I think the killer will definitely try to come after you again. And I don't think he'll care if he has to go through your friend to get to you."

Oh, God. Caroline hadn't even considered that. She *had* thought of hiring a security guard, though. But what if that wasn't enough? What if the intruder returned, and this time what if Taylor got hurt?

Caroline couldn't bear the thought of that happening.

"Well," she said, not knowing what else to say. She'd have to come up with a plan, of course. Caroline just wished the fatigue fog in her head would go away so she could think more clearly.

"San Antonio CSI confirmed that last night someone intentionally cut your phone line," Egan said, his voice calm and even. "The footprints on your bedroom floor also prove someone entered your house through your bedroom door. The person who did that had to have some familiarity with the layout of your place. He only took one thing, your dream journal, and he apparently knew exactly where to find it."

"I already know all of this," she said, frustrated. And scared.

"Yeah. But have you figured out that the shrink appointment tomorrow afternoon is no doubt going to make this guy come after you again?"

No, she hadn't. But it would have occurred to her soon enough. "So, what am I to do? Give up? Hide? Run? Because I'm a little short of solutions here, and I obviously have a massive problem."

"Brody called earlier with the solution." Egan let that hang there between them for several seconds, and she could tell from the tense muscles in his jaw that it was not a solution either of them would like.

"I'm listening," Caroline said, while trying to brace herself.

"Brody wants you in protective custody. *My* protective custody. You got a guest room, wild child? I sure hope so because I'm moving in with you."

Chapter Five

Egan tried to ignore the fancy feminine surroundings and instead forced himself to concentrate on the surveillance video he'd gotten from the manager of the Cantara Hills Country Club restaurant.

On the screen of his laptop, Egan watched the images of Caroline having lunch with her parents and the Suttons. There was no audio, so he studied the body language.

Nothing seemed out of order.

Neither Tammy nor Kenneth was exhibiting any suspicious or unusual behavior. They appeared to be enjoying a casual lunch with friends. But that was just the surface. Caroline had talked about her dream journal that day, and he watched, waiting for a reaction to that. If he got a reaction, any reaction, he'd have to send the surveillance disk to the crime lab so a lip reader could examine it. He might have to do that anyway unless he got a solid lead.

He heard Caroline's footsteps coming down the hall toward him, and a moment later, she appeared in the doorway. Barefooted. She had her shoulder-length hair scooped up off her neck and held precariously in place with a clip.

She still wore the pale yellow skirt and top she'd put on earlier when CSI had given her the all-clear to move back into her house. The top clung to her breasts. And the skirt skimmed her thighs and butt.

And how did he know this bit of fashion information?

Because he was brainless and couldn't seem to stop himself from gawking at her.

As usual, she looked uncomfortable being around him. She'd looked that way the entire day, even though Egan had tried to keep his distance. It was a big house, but it still felt like close quarters despite the fact that Caroline had spent most of the time working in her office. It was just up the hall from the guest suite that he'd be using as his office and bedroom until Brody could make other arrangements.

Egan intended to make sure those other arrangements happened *soon*.

"Find anything on that surveillance tape?" She had a cut crystal glass of garnet-red wine in her hand.

He shook his head and closed the box of pizza he'd had delivered earlier. "It'd be nice if I had audio."

"Well, maybe I can help." She strolled toward him, across the white rugs. Yes, white. The large bedroom and sitting area were blue for the most part, but the navy-colored glossy hardwood floor was dotted with a trio of white rugs that seemed to be made out of bleached raw cotton. "After all, I was there. Maybe I can fill you in on what was being said."

She stood behind the translucent ice-blue acrylic desk where he was seated. The desk was small and dainty, barely three feet across and had just enough room for his pizza box, laptop and a few papers. The chair, too, was dainty and definitely not a comfortable fit for his butt and back.

"Oh," she commented, looking at the screen.

When she didn't say more, Egan stared up at her. "Care to explain that *oh?*"

"That's Miles Landis, Taylor's half brother, standing at the bar. He's a freeloader so most people steer clear of him. That's why he's sitting alone. I didn't know he was there that early. I didn't think he came in until we were nearly finished with lunch."

He'd already noticed the guy. Lanky and with three shades of unnatural color—one of them purple—in his trendy chopped hair.

Egan also hadn't missed his own father, who'd dropped in for a short conversation with Link Hathaway, the sixty-something business tycoon and his father's long-time employer. Link's daughter, Margaret, was there as well. The two were at the table next to Caroline's during the entire lunch and could have easily heard everything she'd said about the appointment with the shrink and the dream journal.

"Do you have any reason to believe Link Hathaway could have something to do with the murders?" Egan asked.

"No." Then she shrugged. "Well, only because I don't want to suspect any of my neighbors. But you probably already know since your father works for him that Link can be ruthless, both in business and in his personal life. He's ruled Margaret with an iron fist."

And his father, Walt, had no doubt helped Link rule with that ruthless, iron fist. Egan didn't know if his father had ever done anything illegal for Link, but maybe it was time to dig deeper.

His attention shifted to the delicate-looking blonde across from Link. Link's daughter, Margaret. Egan had seen her a couple of times when he was a kid, on those rare occasions when his father had taken him out to the Hathaway estate.

"Margaret Hathaway is forty-five," Egan supplied. "She must not mind her daddy's iron fist or else she wouldn't be having lunch with him."

"It wasn't a pleasant lunch," Caroline explained. She shook her head. "They argued. In whispers, but it was still an argument."

It probably wasn't important, but Egan's training and instincts made him want to know more. "What was the argument about?"

She blew out her breath. "This isn't common knowledge, and I'd like to keep it quiet for Margaret's sake. But years ago, she had a baby out of wedlock, and from what I've heard Margaret say, Link forced her to give up the little boy for adoption."

That definitely hadn't come up in the background check, nor had he heard his father ever mention it, which meant it'd been hidden or perhaps even removed from public records. "How long ago was this?"

"About thirty years or so. Margaret was just fifteen or sixteen when it happened."

So, her son would be about Egan's own age, although it probably wasn't significant. He did wonder why they'd be arguing about it now, but he had no evidence to suggest that Margaret Hathaway or her illegitimate child had anything to do with this. In fact, in the background checks Margaret was one of the few residents of Cantara Hills who'd come up squeaky-clean. Besides, Egan had a personal angle on this—Margaret had always been nice to him. Unlike her father.

And unlike Egan's own dad.

Movement on the screen snared his attention, and Egan spotted someone else he recognized.

"Carlson Woodward. He's the tennis pro at the country club," Caroline provided, pointing to the dark-haired man who'd just walked into the restaurant. He wore his athletic clothes and carried a leather bag over his shoulder. "Rumor has it that you have a history with him."

"Oh, yeah." And he wasn't surprised that info had gotten around. "Carlson, Brody, Hayes and I all grew up in the same neighborhood."

She made a sound of agreement, indicating she knew that. "Carlson *really* dislikes you."

"Well, I *really* dislike him. He's a twit." And Carlson had made Egan's life hell when they were growing up. Always tattling. Always scheming to get Egan into trouble. Always picking fights.

"Carlson seems jealous of you," Caroline added.

It was such a simple statement, but it gave Egan a new angle to look at this. Carlson was close enough to the table to have heard Caroline's conversation about the dream journal and the therapy appointment, and that meant Carlson could have repeated it to any and everyone.

Including the killer.

"What happened between Carlson and you to cause all this friction?" she asked.

He frowned at her question. "Too much happened."

"There must have been something to start it all."

His frown deepened. But since it wasn't anything secret and since Caroline apparently wanted to dig up old dirt, Egan cooperated while he watched the surveillance disk. "He stole something from me. A golden Lab puppy that Margaret Hathaway had given to me for my eighth birthday."

"He stole a puppy?" She sounded as outraged as Egan still felt about it.

"Stole him and hid him. Carlson locked him in a shed without any food or water and then demanded a ransom. If I didn't pay him twenty bucks, he was going to let the puppy die. I didn't have *one* dollar, much less twenty."

"You're right. He's a twit." Her forehead bunched up. "Please tell me you got the puppy back?"

"Oh, yeah." After he'd beaten the crud out of Carlson, forcing him to confess where he'd hidden the dog. Egan had gotten in bad trouble with his dad when Carlson had gone tattling to his parents, but it'd been worth it.

Because he wasn't enjoying this trip down memory lane, Egan focused on the screen. But that was it as far as surveillance. The end of the lunch. Caroline and her parents stood from the table. So did the Suttons. Hugs were exchanged all the way around, Caroline's father signed the bill and the five dispersed, walking out of camera range.

"I'm sorry Carlson did that to you," she said, her voice practically a whisper.

"So am I." And he was even sorrier that he'd told her the story. It wasn't a good connection for them to have.

Frustrated with himself and frustrated that he hadn't gotten more from the surveillance tape, Egan clicked it off. He was missing something. He was sure of it.

But what?

"What about the shoe search?" she asked, propping her right butt cheek on the corner of the desk.

Although it wasn't necessary, Egan looked at his notes.

It was better than looking at Caroline, who was now so close that he could touch her. And smell her. The woman knew how to make subtle scents work for her. "Kenneth does indeed wear a size ten shoe. Tammy, a perfect size six. Just as she said. The intruder wore a size eleven."

"So, it's a dead end." She set aside her wine, lifted the pizza box and looked inside.

"Help yourself," Egan said.

However, she'd already declined once when he'd offered to share it with her when it was first delivered. Instead, she insisted she would eat a deli-packaged fruit salad she'd taken from her fridge.

"I'm supposed to be eating healthier," she commented. "Family history of high cholesterol and such." But she didn't refuse now. Caroline took out a slice of the sausage and pepperoni and bit into it. She made a sound of pure pleasure.

A sound that hit him hard below the belt.

Get your mind back on business.

"What about your dream journal?" he asked. "Were you able to remember anything else to write in it?"

She nodded and then held up her index finger in a wait-a-second gesture. Caroline ate a hefty bite of the pizza and washed it down with her wine. "Not much. I remembered a dream about driving fast with the wind in my hair. Nothing about Kimberly, though, and that night."

He thought about it a moment. "Well, you were in car that night. A convertible. So, there would have been wind in your hair."

As if she'd suddenly lost her appetite, she put the remainder of the pizza slice back in the box and closed it. "Yes. It was a blue convertible." She paused. "The last thing I remember about that night was getting dressed for the party. That's it. And afterward…" She paused again. "I woke up in the hospital, and the only memories I have of those lost eight hours are what people have told me."

Caroline stared at him. "You don't believe me."

Egan hadn't expected the blatant accusation. "No." But he immediately shook his head. "Wait, I didn't mean that exactly. I don't think you're lying." And he hoped to hell his change of opinion had nothing to do with her great-fitting skirt and hot legs. "But I do think you're scared of learning the truth."

Caroline didn't say anything for several long seconds. "I *am* scared. Those six speeding tickets keep coming back to haunt me. And I hope I didn't do anything to contribute to what happened."

So did Egan, but he kept that to himself. He also resisted the urge to reach up and wipe the dab of pizza sauce from the corner of her mouth.

"From all accounts, Montoya was waiting for your car, waiting to kill. Maybe both of you. Maybe just Kimberly McQuade," he reminded her. "I don't think speeding would have helped or prevented him from doing what he'd set out to do. And my guess is the only reason you're alive is because you had on a seat belt. Kimberly didn't. And because you were unconscious, that saved your life. I think Montoya might have killed you, too, if you'd seen what he did."

"Maybe I did see," she whispered.

He looked up, caught her gaze, just as a tear streaked down her cheek. She quickly swiped it away and got up. She was halfway to the door before he made it out of that dainty chair and caught up with her.

Egan caught on to her arm and whirled her around to

face him. There it was again. That punch. That feeling of lust so deep that he had to release the grip on her. Touching her was just plain dangerous.

"Sorry about that," she mumbled.

Surprised, he shook his head. "About crying?"

"Yes. You don't need that. And I wasn't looking for pity."

"Good. Because I wouldn't have given you any. I'm not very good at providing pity."

She gave a choppy nod and turn to leave again.

"Caroline, there's a, uh, strict rule about Rangers getting personally involved with someone in their protective custody."

He didn't touch her.

But she stopped.

"Yes. I figured there would be. It's just as well. I couldn't get involved with you anyway." She frowned. "Don't look at me like that. It doesn't have anything to do with your being a chauffeur's son. It's just I can't do anything else to upset my father. I love him more than life itself, but he can be a snob. He thinks my only path to happiness is for me to be with what he calls 'my own kind.'"

None of this surprised Egan, but for some reason, it riled him. How was this any different from Link Hathaway's ruling his daughter's life? A powerful, rich daddy trying to manipulate his family's gene pool. "So, what does that mean—you marry some guy of your father's choosing?"

Caroline smugly lifted her shoulder and her chin. "Who says I have to marry at all?"

He saw it then. That defiance that went bone-deep. It wasn't just in her silky voice but in her body language.

Yeah. She'd been a wild child, and that rich, polished demeanor barely disguised it.

"You're smiling," she commented.

Hell. He quickly changed his expression.

Egan went closer, and because it was driving him crazy, he reached out and skimmed his thumb over the corner of her mouth to get that pizza sauce.

Except it turned into something else.

Caroline, obviously not realizing what he was trying to do, moved. It caused his thumb to slide over her bottom lip. Her breath shivered a bit and brushed against his thumb. It was a heated moment that Egan felt in every inch of his body.

Before he pulled back his hand.

And cursed.

She cursed, too.

What they didn't do was move away from each other. Bad idea. Really bad. Because his primed body came up with a suggestion as to what to do about that closeness, and about that shiver in her breath.

The doorbell rang.

Thank God.

But then Egan remembered it was well past 10 p.m. Hardly the hour for visitors. And with the killer on the loose, he instantly went on alert.

"Expecting anyone?" he asked Caroline.

When she shook her head, he withdrew his service pistol from his shoulder holster and made his way to the front door. Caroline was right behind him, but he motioned for her to stand back.

The bell rang again. Not just once. But a series of frantic jabs, followed by a heavy-handed knock.

"Caroline!" the visitor shouted. "It's me, Miles. I need to talk to you. It's important."

Miles Landis. The half brother of Caroline's best friend, Taylor. "Any idea what he wants?" Egan asked Caroline.

"No. Maybe," she amended. She crossed the room and reached for the doorknob, but Egan stopped her. Catching on to her arm, he positioned her on the other side of a large plant, and after he'd made sure that she was out of the line of fire, Egan disengaged the security system and opened the door.

Miles Landis had his fist poised for another knock but quickly withdrew his hand. The man looked disheveled, but Egan didn't know if it was because Miles was making some kind of a fashion statement or if this was an emergency visit.

"I need to speak with Caroline," Miles insisted.

"About what?"

Miles dodged eye contact with Egan. "It's personal."

"He's here to ask me for a loan," Caroline provided.

Apparently following the sound of her voice, Miles tried to stick his head inside, but Egan blocked him from doing that. However, he heard Caroline walk closer, and she didn't stop until she was right at Egan's shoulder.

"The answer is no," she told Miles. "I won't give you another loan. And neither will Taylor."

Miles swallowed hard, and if a person could smell as though he was desperate, this guy had accomplished it. "I wouldn't have come if it weren't important. I need money, Caroline, and you know you wouldn't miss it with your bank account."

She folded her arms over her chest. "That won't work with me. Taylor and I have talked about this, and we agreed no more bailing you out of sticky situations. Go home, Miles. Stop gambling and you won't need to hit up your friends and family for loans."

Egan knew from the background check that Miles had major financial problems. What he didn't know about were these loan requests.

Something flashed in Miles's eyes. A strong mixture of emotions. Disappointment. Fear. And even anger. *Nope*—make that rage. Miles was one pissed-off guy.

And that made Egan look down at the guy's feet.

"What size shoes do you wear?" Egan asked.

Some of the rage faded, replaced by what Egan thought might be amusement. "Size eleven. Why, is that the size Caroline's intruder wore? I heard rumors that the crime scene guys found some tracks."

Egan didn't verify that. Instead, he took out his cell phone and called his fellow Ranger, Hayes, who was at the office at the country club.

"Hayes, we need a search warrant, fast," Egan instructed. "And have SAPD go over to Miles Landis's condo. Mr. Landis won't be allowed in until the place has been searched. Specifically, we're looking for his size eleven athletic shoes."

"I take it this Landis is a possible match to those tracks left on Caroline's floor?" Hayes asked.

"Oh, yes." Well, in the shoe department, anyway. Since only the dream journal had been stolen, this hard-up-for-money guy obviously hadn't broken in to get stuff to sell for his much-needed loan.

But then, maybe Miles intended to sell that dream journal to someone.

"There's some good news and bad news on those shoe

prints," Hayes let him know. "The tread indicates that the shoes are Razors. That's a fairly new brand name and an expensive one, so only a few people should have them. They're mainly tennis shoes."

"Interesting." And Egan knew they were both wondering if this was connected to their old nemesis, Carlson Woodward. After all, Carlson was a tennis pro at the country club and had easy access to of any part Cantara Hills. Plus, he knew all the victims. "What's the bad news?"

"It's possible that the person wearing those Razors isn't a size eleven. The CSI guys say there's something off with the pressure points of the tracks. Either the intruder could have been wearing shoes that were too big or the person was just walking funny."

"What does that mean?" But Egan already suspected what it meant, and if so, it wasn't good.

"Apparently, the guy could have purposely used the balls of his feet to throw off the way the soles landed on the floor. In other words, our intruder might or might not actually wear size eleven shoes."

And since the intruder had picked such an unusual brand of footwear, those shoe prints could have been made to encourage them to go after the wrong person. Was that break-in really just a setup to cast suspicion on someone else other than the real killer?

Miles smiled when Egan finished the call and slipped his phone back into his pocket. "Get your warrant, Sgt. Caldwell, but I don't have anything to hide. I don't have the kind of shoes you're trying to match."

Egan shrugged. "How do you know what I'm trying to match?"

"I don't, but since I wasn't the one to break into Caroline's house, I couldn't have possibly left those tracks. Therefore, I don't have the shoes you're looking for." He couldn't have sounded more arrogant if he'd tried.

Egan returned the arrogant attitude. "But you won't be offended if I don't take your word for it." He shut the door in the man's face, locked it and used the keypad on the wall to reengage the entire security system. Earlier, Egan had already checked all the doors and windows to make sure they were locked. He'd check them again before heading off to bed.

Still, even with all the precautions, it was going to be a long, restless night.

For a lot of reasons.

"What bad news did Hayes tell you?" Caroline wanted to know.

He stopped there in the foyer and looked at her. "The intruder might have worn bigger shoes to throw off the track marks."

"Oh. So this doesn't let Kenneth off the hook."

"It doesn't let anyone off the hook." Egan tipped his head to the door where their visitor had just been. "Do you think Miles could have stolen the dream journal with maybe the idea to blackmail you with it?"

She shrugged. "I guess that's possible. But that leaves the bomb. I don't know of any reason why Miles would want me dead."

Neither did Egan, but that didn't mean there wasn't one. Miles was a desperate man, and desperate men often did dangerous things.

And speaking of dangerous things…

There was a problem that Caroline and he hadn't discussed yet. Best to get it over with. Like ripping off a bandage.

"I need to modify the sleeping arrangements," he told her. "Your bedroom is on the other side of the house from the guest suite. Plus, there are those two French doors in your room that would give an intruder easy access."

She pointed to the keypad, where he'd just punched in the code. "But the security system is on."

"True. But this person's already cut a phone line and tampered with your old security system. I can't take the chance of not being able to hear you if something goes wrong."

He watched that register in the depths of those blue-green eyes. It didn't register well, especially after that pizza sauce–wiping incident. All that mouth touching had created a weird sort of intimacy that neither needed.

"What exactly did you have in mind?" Caroline asked cautiously.

Egan tried not to think of what he really had on his mind. Sex on the foyer floor wasn't going to happen despite his body's insistence that it should.

"The guest suite where I'm staying has fewer windows and no outside access. It's the room that'd be the easiest to monitor and secure." He hoped the next part didn't sound as troubling as he thought it would. "You take the bed. And I'll take the floor."

Caroline blinked. "You want *us* to sleep in the same room?"

He nodded, hoping that it looked authoritative and confident, and then Egan put his hand on the small of her back to get her moving in the direction of the guest suite.

"You *really* think this is a good idea?" she asked. Apparently, he'd failed at looking confident.

"No," he admitted. But sleeping in the same room was better than the alternative of not being able to protect her if something went wrong. Egan planned to do whatever it took to keep Caroline alive.

That included spending the night just a few feet away from her with all those hot images of raunchy floor sex scorching his body.

Man, he wanted her bad.

Chapter Six

Caroline dreamed.

The images were spliced together like fragments from a half-dozen different situations. She was in the car, wind in her hair. And it was dark. She had the feeling that someone was seated next to her.

A woman.

Caroline tried to turn her head to see who the woman was, but she couldn't. She could hear only two words. *Seat belt*. The words pounded in her head, repeating themselves over and over until they became painful.

Then the scene changed. Different images. The clocks were after her again. Not some cute timepieces. These clocks had fangs and had removed their hands to use as spears, which they hurled at her.

She ran. So fast. So hard. Until she thought her heart might explode. And the man came and began shooting arrows. The arrows worked because the clocks retreated.

Then the man kissed her.

That kiss relaxed her. Just like that. Fear faded from her mind, and in its place was the slow, hungry sensation of being seduced. He took off her clothes. Not in some hurried frenzy but gently, as if time didn't matter.

But it didn't last. Things changed again. Someone was calling out her name, and someone had hold of her. Not in a seducing kind of way, either. This person's grip was frantic. The danger had returned. She wasn't safe.

Caroline fought to release herself from the grip. She punched at the person. Not once—several times, but she couldn't break the hold he had on her.

"Caroline!" he said. "Wake up!"

And his command was clear. *Very* clear.

She forced open her eyes and realized why it was so clear. Because Egan had indeed said her name. He was still saying it, and he had hold of her hands. And she wasn't exactly cooperating. She was thrashing and trying to kick him. Obviously, she'd gotten caught up in the dream.

But why was Egan there…in bed with her? And there was no doubt about that. In the moonlit room, Caroline had no trouble seeing him. He had her practically pinned to the mattress.

"Wake up!" Egan insisted, sounding frustrated and in pain.

Caroline was in pain, too. Her right fist was stinging, and it took her a moment to figure out why. She replayed the last moments of that "dream" and figured out what she might have done.

She quit thrashing and fighting and went limp. "God, did I hit you?"

"Yeah, you did." Huffing, Egan rolled off her and landed on his back next to her. His breath was coming out in rough, short bursts. "You hit like a girl," he grumbled. "Well, except for that last punch." He rubbed the right side of his jaw and winced.

She fought through the haze left by the dream and got hit with a full dose of reality. "I hurt you."

And that wasn't all she'd done.

She'd put on pj's for bed. Her most matronly pair—cotton, at that—but the top was now shoved up high, and her bare breasts were exposed. Caroline quickly tried to right it, but she had, no doubt, given Egan an eyeful.

Speaking of eyefuls, she looked at him. And got one, too. He was naked. Well, from the waist up, anyway. Shirtless, he lay there, obviously trying to gather his breath, while the moonlight bathed over him. What a vision. All those toned and tanned pecs. Washboard abs. Of course. But that wasn't the best part. The best part was that he'd removed his belt, and his jeans had dipped down low on his hips.

Very low.

There was a thin strip of hair that led from his navel right down into his jeans, where there was an eye-catching bulge that made her go hot all over.

Mercy.

She couldn't want him this much. Or even half this much. But Caroline couldn't deny that her body was suddenly warm and wet in a place it shouldn't have been. Her breasts began to tingle, and she felt her nipples tighten. That tug in her belly became a hard pull.

This was *so* not going to happen.

"I'm never going to admit you hurt me with that last punch," Egan said, his voice not much more than a growl. That turned her on, too. "So let's get past it so I can tell you why I tried to wake you up. It's because you were talking in your sleep."

That didn't turn her on. Just the opposite. "Was I?"

Good grief. "What did I say?" *And please no melting kisses or clothing removal. No sex stuff at all.*

"You kept saying 'seat belt' and that you'd hit your head."

Okay. She nodded. Caroline remembered the seat belt but not the head part. "I think I was dreaming about that night of the hit-and-run."

"I thought so, too. I figured if I woke you up, the dream would still be fresh, and you might recall something."

Did she? Caroline sat up and turned on the lamp next to the bed. Just on the other side of that on the floor was Egan's crumpled sleeping bag, which he'd obviously vacated in a hurry.

"Seat belt," she repeated. There was something, but it was just out of reach. She closed her eyes, concentrated hard, and it just wouldn't come. "I'm sorry."

He continued to stare at the ceiling. "What about your head? Do you remember why it was hurting?"

"No. I only remember that it was hurting because I kept hearing the words *seat belt.* I'm sorry."

"Don't be. It was a long shot." He got up off the bed and walked toward his sleeping bag. He rubbed his back. Perhaps because he was sore from sleeping on the floor. Or maybe she'd injured him there in the struggle.

He stopped by her side of the bed, looked down and reached for her neck. For a moment, one body-warming moment, she thought he was going to touch her. But he didn't. Instead, he touched the collar of her pj's and pulled something from it. She heard a soft pop.

"The price tag," he said, dropping it onto the night-stand. "I guess you don't wear those very often."

"No. I usually—" Thank heaven she didn't finish that.

"Sleep commando?" he finished for her.

Caroline's mouth dropped open. How the heck had he figured that out?

"You have very smooth sheets," he said as if anticipating her question. "They feel damn good on bare skin." He shrugged. "Plus, it's how any wild child, former or otherwise, sleeps."

So, that meant he slept naked, too. Caroline didn't ask him to confirm it.

But she could envision it.

"Get some rest," he insisted, returning to the sleeping bag. She watched him climb in and got a great view of his butt. The man was delicious eye candy.

She turned off the light, lay back on her pillow and closed her eyes. She had to get her mind off Egan. Better to think about the dream instead. So that's what she did as she tried to drift back to sleep.

Caroline saw it then. The fringes of the dream that she hadn't been able to focus in on before.

"Seat belt," she mumbled.

She heard Egan sit back up, but she didn't look at him for fear that the murky image would go away.

"Kimberly is upset about something," she said, repeating what she saw in her head. "And she's not wearing her seat belt. I tell her to put it on. She's reaching for it…and that's it." Caroline slowly opened her eyes and glanced at Egan. "I'm sorry, but that's all I can see."

"Kimberly didn't have on the seat belt when Montoya hit your car," Egan reminded her. "So that must have happened just seconds before impact."

That made sense. "Maybe this means I'm regaining my memory."

"Maybe. And maybe the new drug the shrink's giving you tomorrow will make you remember everything."

Yes.

Everything.

Caroline only hoped that whatever she'd done, or hadn't done, she would be able to live with it. But she was terrified that she was the one responsible for killing Kimberly McQuade.

"THIS IS A NEW BARBITURATE drug," Dr. Elsa Whitaker explained to Caroline and Egan. "Fast acting. Ultra, we call it. Caroline, you should go under quickly, within minutes, and you'll only be out for a half hour tops. I'm aiming for fifteen minutes. That seems to be the optimum range for the effectiveness of this drug."

So, since it was 3:00 p.m., that meant by three-fifteen, Egan might finally have some answers about that night when all these murders had started.

Caroline was already lying on the white leather sofa in her living room. She was barefoot, dressed in jeans and a loose green top, and she had several pillows tucked beneath her head. The phones had been silenced, and there was a Do Not Disturb sign on the door. In short, everything was ready to get this show on the road.

"And you're positive the drug is safe?" Egan asked.

Dr. Whitaker flexed her dark eyebrows. "As safe as any drug like this can be."

Yes. Dr. Whitaker had already explained that to Brody and him when they'd first brought up the idea. Safety hadn't seemed as much of a concern then as it did now. "Could you go over those safety issues again?" Egan requested.

"Of course. The drug has been tested on nearly a

hundred people, with the only side effect being a temporary headache, followed by fatigue. Also temporary." The doctor volleyed glances at both of them. "This is the best drug for this session. I've gone through Caroline's records, and she's already had hypnosis, therapy, and her therapist even administered the more traditional drug, thiopental. If you want these memories recalled, then this is our best bet."

"Let's do it," Caroline insisted.

But the doctor didn't move until Egan gave the nod.

Egan hoped he wouldn't regret this.

He watched as the doctor gave Caroline the injection. She winced a little and looked over at him. He could see the worry in her eyes. He was worried, too. Worried that this was all for nothing and worried they might learn something that would be too hard to hear.

He didn't even want to vocalize what "too hard to hear" might entail.

Dr. Whitaker was a tall woman, over six feet, and she had the wide shoulders and hips to go with that height. However, her face was gentle, and she spoke in soft whispers. Egan hoped that kind voice would make Caroline feel at ease.

Because he sure didn't.

He had the tape recorder in his hand, and he knew once Caroline was under and talking, he'd have to start recording. A recording that would be dissected by not only himself but Hayes, Brody and God only knew how many other Rangers and law enforcement officials.

Which brought him to something he needed to clarify.

"There's no need to ask her any questions about her previous personal relationships," Egan told the doctor. "It isn't pertinent to the case."

That earned him a questioning raised eyebrow from Dr. Whitaker and a puzzled look from Caroline. "Thank you," she mouthed.

He wasn't doing this for Caroline, Egan told himself. But the problem was, he couldn't figure out why he was doing it. Still, there was no reason for the world to know about Caroline's thieving ex-fiancé.

Dr. Whitaker sat in the chair next to Caroline's head, and after the fifteen minutes had passed, Egan turned on the recorder.

"I read your dream journal, Caroline." The doctor picked up the notebook from the granite-and-steel coffee table and glanced through it again. "You have a lot of things going on. I'd say there's some anxiety about your future. Maybe biological clock issues. And then there are the phallic symbols. All of these are perfectly natural for a young woman like you."

Phallic symbols?

Egan glanced at Caroline to see if she could clarify, but her eyelids were already fluttering down.

"Caroline, let's talk about the seat belt dream, the one you had last night," the doctor continued. "Go back into that dream for me. Can you do that?"

Caroline gave a wobbly nod.

"Good. Think about the dream and what happened with the hit-and-run. Talk to me about Kimberly McQuade. You're driving from your friend Taylor's house. You're in your car. It's night, and even though it's December, it's unseasonably warm. Do you remember all of that?"

Egan held his breath until Caroline nodded again.

"That's good, Caroline. Keep thinking about that night,"

Dr. Whitaker instructed. "Think about what you were doing. You said Kimberly is upset. Why is she upset?"

Caroline didn't answer right away, and she mumbled something indistinguishable before she finally spoke. "She's had an argument with Kenneth at the party. She wants to leave, but her car isn't there so she asks me to take her back to her apartment. We get in my car, and we leave."

"What did Kenneth and Kimberly argue about?" Egan immediately asked.

But the doctor frowned and put her finger to her mouth to indicate he needed to stay quiet.

"Did Kimberly tell you about the argument with Kenneth?" the doctor said to Caroline.

"In a way. We're in the car, and she says she's, uh, disappointed and angry. But she won't tell me why. She says she's going to look into the matter further."

Egan motioned for Dr. Whitaker to jump on that, and she did. "Did Kimberly tell Kenneth, too, that she was going to look into the matter?"

"Yes." The answer came fast, with no shred of doubt. "She says that's when he got angry with her. He threatened her. She wanted to leave the party after that."

Hell. That was motive. But Egan still didn't know what had caused the argument. He needed more pieces of this puzzle.

He hurried to the sofa and used a blank page in the dream journal to scribble down the next question. "How did Kenneth threaten Kimberly?" the doctor read aloud.

"I don't know." Caroline shook her head. "Kimberly's not saying."

The doctor and Egan shared a look of frustration. "Did Kimberly say anything else about Kenneth?"

Caroline's forehead bunched up. "No. She doesn't want to talk about him because she's so upset." She hesitated. "Kimberly wipes some tears from her cheek. And I notice that she's not wearing her seat belt. 'You need to put on the seat belt,' I tell her."

Egan could almost see it. Brody's little sister's last moments of life.

"Kimberly tries to put on the seat belt," Caroline continued. "But it's stuck. So I reach over to help her, but the belt's caught in the door. I need to pull over, so I slow down and look for a place to stop. I can't stop in the road. It's too dangerous. Someone coming over that hill wouldn't see us."

Caroline's expression changed. Her face was no longer relaxed, and he could see her eyes moving frantically beneath her lids.

"What's happening, Caroline?" the doctor asked.

She swallowed hard. "There's a car. Just a blink of an eye. And it's there. From a side street. It comes at us so fast." She began to shake. "It's there. It's there. God, it's there!"

Egan walked toward her, but the doctor waved him off. Instead, she laid her hand on Caroline's arm and rubbed gently. "It's all right. You're safe." She waited a moment until Caroline quit repeating those two words, *it's there.*

Egan would remember those words and that pain on her face for a long, long time.

"Did you see the driver of the other car?" the doctor continued.

Caroline shook her head. "No. Too fast. The car was there, and then everything went black."

"Because your head hit the steering wheel. Did you feel it when you hit your head?"

Caroline didn't answer right away. "A second of pain. Then, nothing."

Egan had been afraid of that. If Caroline was unconscious, and she likely was at this point of the hit-and-run, then even the drug wouldn't be able to uncover what had happened during those critical moments.

"What about sounds?" the doctor pressed. "Footsteps? Someone's voice?"

"I don't hear Kimberly. And not footsteps—" She stopped. "But I hear a sound. There's another car coming."

Yes. Another car had indeed come, and the driver had been Gary Zelke, who'd sideswiped Caroline's car, possibly even contributing to her injuries. Of course, Gary wasn't around any longer to question about that since he'd been murdered.

Caroline's eyelids fluttered, and the doctor looked back at Egan. "She's not going to be under much longer. Is there anything else you want me to ask her?"

"I want to know more about what Kimberly said to her." Egan was going on gut instinct here, but his first thought about what could have caused that argument was something he hadn't considered before. "Ask her if Kimberly was having an affair with Kenneth."

Dr. Whitaker looked even less comfortable with the question than Egan did. "Caroline, leave the accident and go back to the party. Kimberly and Kenneth have argued, and Kimberly's upset. Did she tell you anything about having an affair—"

"Yes," Caroline interrupted. "We talked about that. I was a little distraught. I'd heard gossip at the party. Gossip about my ex-fiancé. I went to the bathroom, and Kimberly was there outside the door. She asked what was wrong with me, and I told her I was having guy troubles. She laughed. Said she was having guy troubles, too—an affair. But it was complicated. She didn't want anyone to know until she'd sorted it all out."

Egan couldn't stop himself from asking the next question. "Was the affair with Kenneth?"

"No." She frowned. "I mean, I don't know. Kimberly didn't say, and I didn't ask."

So…Kimberly had been having a secret affair. And it was a secret. Well, from her brother at least. If Brody had known about it, he would have already told Egan. But now the real question was, was this some clue to discovering the identity of a killer?

It was if her lover had been Kenneth.

Kenneth might have ordered his goon, Montoya, to murder Kimberly if she'd been about to expose the affair. Kenneth's wife, Tammy, didn't look the sort to forgive and forget such an indiscretion, and as a career politician, Kenneth would need his high society, rich wife by his side when he made his bid to be governor.

Caroline's eyes opened, and even though she obviously had trouble focusing, her gaze landed on Egan.

"Are you okay?" he asked.

She nodded. "I'm dizzy. And I have a mild headache. But I remember everything I said."

"Anything else you remember?" Dr. Whitaker pressed.

"No. I can see bits and pieces of the hit-and-run, and I can recall that conversation about the affair, but that's it." She tried to sit up, and that's when Egan saw her blink back the tears. "I didn't cause Kimberly's death. I slowed down. I tried to get her to put on her seat belt."

"Yes," Egan managed to say, but it was hard to speak

even that one word with the sudden lump in his throat. He could feel the emotional burden that Caroline had been carrying all these months.

Dr. Whitaker patted Caroline's hand. "You did great." And then she stood, facing Egan, and picked up her medical bag. "That's it for today. I can give her another dose but not for at least forty-eight hours."

Egan would have to talk to Caroline about another dose. He walked the doctor to the door. "She'll be okay?"

"From the drug—yes. But she might have trouble dealing with these memories. If she does, give me a call, and I can have someone bring over a mild sedative."

Alarmed, Egan turned off the recorder and set it on the foyer table. "You think that'll be necessary?"

"Never can tell how people will react when being confronted with trauma. Just don't leave her alone." She reached for the door and then stopped. "Oh, and it's possible she'll remember even more. You might want to brace yourself in case her dreams aren't dreams tonight but rather nightmares."

Hell. What had he gotten Caroline into?

"You know I don't want you to repeat anything Caroline said here today," Egan reminded her.

Dr. Whitaker nodded, said her goodbye and left. Egan locked the door behind her and engaged the security system.

"So, I might have nightmares," he heard Caroline say. "It's okay," she added before he could apologize. "It was worth it. It's a huge relief to remember that I didn't do anything to hurt Kimberly. And now we know about the argument with Kenneth."

Egan walked closer and looked at her. She was pale. And he suspected that her mild headache wasn't so mild.

He reached down and scooped her up into his arms.

Obviously shocked, she stared at him. "Where are you taking me?"

"To bed. No, not for that," he clarified when she gave him a puzzled look. "I want you to take a nap, and if your headache doesn't go away, I'll call the doctor and ask her what you should take for pain."

"Okay." She settled her head against his shoulder as if she completely trusted him.

Egan walked to the guest suite, placed her on the bed and draped the side of the comforter over her.

"Caroline, I don't want you to say anything to anyone about what you remembered."

"I didn't remember much," she insisted.

Egan silently disagreed. Caroline might have remembered just enough to get her killed.

Chapter Seven

Using the controls on the wall of the marble shower, Caroline adjusted the trio of showerheads to "deep massage" and let the steamy hot water go to work. The pressure felt good on her muscles, and mercy did she need it. That four-hour nap following the session had given her a foggy head and a stiff neck.

Still, those minor discomforts were worth it. She'd learned the truth.

Or at least part of the truth.

She hadn't caused the accident that'd killed Kimberly. It was a hollow victory, though, because obviously nothing would bring back the young woman, but Caroline thought she might finally be able to get a decent night's sleep.

Well, she might if she could quit thinking about the killer.

And about Egan.

This whole sexual thing she was feeling for him had to stop. He wasn't a scumbag criminal like her ex-fiancé, Julian, but Egan was equally dangerous in the sense that a relationship with him, even a purely sexual one, would cause her parents to worry. And the last time they'd *worried,* her father had nearly died of a heart attack.

So, no more sexual fantasies and dreams about Egan.

Besides, this was just a crazy crush or something. Temporary. Mostly one-sided. Certainly not based on anything with emotional substance. She wanted to sleep with him, that was it, and since that couldn't happen, she would just have to put him out of her mind.

Bolstered by her little lecture, Caroline finished the shower, dried off and dressed in her black jeans and her favorite comfortable top, a tomato-red sleeveless tee that stopped loose at her waist. She debated putting on some makeup. Opted against it. There wasn't any reason for her to look her best.

She opened the bathroom door.

And heard the voices.

Not friendly voices, either. Egan was obviously arguing with someone.

Alarmed, Caroline rushed through her bedroom, following the sound of those voices. It wasn't difficult. Because someone was shouting.

When she got to the foyer, she realized that someone was Link Hathaway. He wasn't alone, either. He was in the doorway with Kenneth, and Egan's father, Walt, and the men appeared to be trying to barge their way into her house.

Link wore his usual starched jeans and black leather jacket. Practically a uniform for him. And he also had on his usual semi-scowling expression. Caroline had never seen the man smile, and she'd known him her entire life.

Kenneth wasn't exactly smiling, either. He was aiming a venomous glare at Egan.

Wearing a real uniform for his job as a chauffeur, Walt stood behind the other two men, and even though Caroline had known of him for years, it was really the first time she'd ever looked at him. There were no traces of Egan in his face. His coloring was different with his gingerish hair and cold, steely eyes. Plus, he lacked Egan's air of authority. The only air that Walt seemed to have was one of indifference. Not for his boss. But for his own son.

"What's going on?" she demanded.

"I was about to shoot all three of them," Egan said drily. "Because I've asked them to leave, and they won't."

"We had to make sure you were okay," Kenneth volunteered, aiming a final glare at Egan. His expression softened a bit when it rested on her. "Your phone's turned off, and that Do Not Disturb sign has been on the door all afternoon. Tammy and I got worried."

"Sorry. But I was…resting." Best to leave it at that. "I'm fine. Nothing's wrong."

Kenneth studied her face and wet hair and gave her a look that hinted as if he might challenge her nothing's-wrong comment. "Tammy saw the strange car drive up to your house earlier and then she noticed the woman visitor who came to your door. We figured you'd had the appointment with the psychiatrist."

She had no idea how to answer that, but she didn't have to. Egan spoke up. "Caroline decided not to go through with the session."

Link and Kenneth exchanged a puzzling glance.

"We learned the drug's still experimental," Egan continued. "It was too risky. I'll just have to find the killer another way. Maybe through his shoes."

"I'm a size twelve," Link snarled when Egan looked in that direction. "And you aren't going to catch me wearing any half-assed tennis shoes. Besides, if I wanted somebody dead, I wouldn't go sneaking around in a woman's bedroom to do it. That's something only a coward would do."

Caroline believed him. But she was puzzled as to why Link and his chauffeur were there at her house. Link wasn't the sort to cower, or to personally check up on people. Well, other than his daughter, Margaret.

"Mr. Hathaway, Mr. Caldwell, why are you here?" Caroline just came out and asked.

Walt didn't utter a word, and Link's scowl intensified. "Your father called," Link explained. "He asked me to check on you. When I got here, Kenneth had just pulled up with plans to do the same. You got a lot of people worried about you, girl, but obviously you're all in one piece."

"Obviously. If my parents call again, please tell them there's no need to send anyone over to check on me. I'll tell them myself when I phone them tonight."

"Do that," Link snarled. "It'll save me from playing messenger." And he strolled away. Walt didn't even look at his son when he followed his boss.

Kenneth, however, didn't leave with them. "Caroline, why don't you come and stay with Tammy and me? Your parents would like that."

Again, Egan answered before she could. "She's in my protective custody," Egan reminded Kenneth. "And I doubt that invitation to stay at your house extends to me."

"No. It doesn't." Kenneth spared Egan another glance before returning his attention to Caroline. "Tammy and I are here for you. Call if you need anything."

"I will." She'd hardly gotten the words out of her mouth before Egan shut the door and locked it. He also rearmed the security system. "I'm sorry about that," she told him. "I obviously have protective neighbors."

"Or nosy ones." He kept watch out the sidelight window. "I made you a sandwich. It's in the kitchen. And I called Dr. Whitaker, and she said it was all right if you had a glass of wine. Or Oreos, whichever you prefer."

"Thanks. Oreos for dessert. But I'll start with the wine." Since she was starving, she headed for the kitchen. "Can I pour you a glass?"

"No. I'm on duty."

Of course he was. Sometimes, it was easy for her to forget that. Like when he was half-naked on her bed. But now, with his hand on the barrel of his gun and with his intense stare out the window at her departing guests, there was no doubt that this was *duty* for him.

"Did anybody else come by when I was napping?" she asked from the kitchen. The sandwich, ham and cheese on wheat, was waiting for her on the counter, but first she opened a bottle of pinot noir and poured herself a glass.

"Hayes came by. He picked up the recording of your session with the shrink, but I don't think he'll hear anything we didn't hear."

Caroline made a sound of agreement and sampled the sandwich. It was good, but then she was starving. She realized it was the first thing she'd eaten all day. She'd wanted to lose a few pounds, but this wasn't a diet she could recommend to anyone.

"I also got a call about the shoes that we took from Miles Landis's closet." Egan stopped in the doorway and bracketed his hands on both sides of the frame. The muscles in his arms and chest responded to the simple movement.

So did Caroline.

"Miles is definitely size eleven," Egan explained. "But

there was no match. Of course, he could have gotten rid of the shoes."

That was true of any of their suspects. "So, we still don't know who's trying to kill me."

"Well, we're pretty sure it's connected to Kimberly's death. Because the attempt to murder you didn't start until everyone heard that you were trying to regain your memory."

"Yes." Caroline groaned softly. "Something I regret broadcasting."

Egan shrugged. "You couldn't have known the consequences."

Nor could she know where it would end. That bomb had been designed to kill her. No doubt about that. But would Egan's lie that she'd changed her mind about taking the memory drug be enough to get the killer to back off? She ate more of the sandwich and contemplated that.

And then she noticed he was staring at her.

"What?" she asked.

Egan shook his head. And that didn't exactly seem to be a lustful look he was giving her. "What is it?" Caroline repeated.

"Nothing. It's just the pinot noir brings back some old memories."

She smiled. She liked this conversation better than the other. "What, memories of wild college parties?"

"No." He took his right hand from the frame and rubbed his forehead as if he'd regretted bringing this up. "When I was growing up, we used to live on the same street with an elderly woman who used to drink a lot of that particular kind of wine. I mean two or three bottles a day, and she'd pay my dad to get it for her since she couldn't drive. Because there were lots of times when my dad had other things to do, he made an arrangement with the seedy liquor store owner for me to be able to pick it up for her on my walk home from school."

Caroline's smile faded completely. "Good grief. How old were you?"

"It started when I was seven. Once, the bag broke, and I dropped one of the bottles on the way back to the house. Got in a whole boatload of trouble for that."

Caroline could only imagine, and it outraged her. "It's your father, the stupid store owner and your neighbor who should have gotten in trouble. They shouldn't have had a seven-year-old picking up alcohol."

He dismissed it with a shake of his head. "It was a long time ago."

She had a sudden desire to pour the rest of her wine down the drain, but that would be too obvious. Plus, she instinctively knew that would be even harder on Egan. It'd probably been a while since he'd discussed this with anyone, and he wouldn't want her to make a big deal of it.

"Why didn't your mother stop what was going on?" she asked.

"She left when I was just a baby. I figured that's why my dad hated me." He rubbed his forehead again, indicating a change of subject was on the way. "Brody and Victoria haven't had any luck finding the person they were looking for, so they're coming back from California tomorrow. I figure the three of us—Hayes, Brody and me—will take turns staying here."

The bite of the sandwich she took nearly lodged in her throat. "That makes sense, I guess."

He stared at her. "You think I'm doing that because I don't want to be around you."

She obviously hadn't hidden her emotions, or else he could read her well. "Isn't that why?"

"Yes." He didn't even hesitate, and he looked her straight in the eye when he said it.

That stung, more than she had imagined it would. Great. So much for her shower lecture about not getting involved with him. Caroline finished off her glass of wine, poured herself another one and walked closer to him so she could, well, start an argument or something. Anything was better than feeling the sting of his rejection. It, too, brought back old painful memories of her breakup with her ex-fiancé.

"Don't take it personally," Egan said, his voice low and husky. "This is my fault. I'm attracted to you."

Caroline stopped. Just a few inches away from him. And there was no argument to start because she couldn't think of what to say in response to that.

He was attracted to her?

Better yet, he was admitting it?

So, maybe it wasn't one-sided after all, and maybe it wasn't just her Harley that had him in a lather.

"And I shouldn't be attracted to you," Egan continued. "It's unprofessional and dangerous. There's a reason for the regulation about a Ranger not getting personally involved with someone in his protective custody. A personal involvement could cause me to lose focus. That could get you killed."

Caroline took a deep breath. Hearing it all spelled out that way, she couldn't disagree with him. He was right. If they were lusting after each other, then their focus wouldn't be on catching a killer.

Their gazes connected, and the corner of his mouth hitched. "I never figured I'd have this problem with you. You're not my type."

Oh, he was so her type, though. Caroline obviously didn't voice that. Besides, she'd had nothing but rotten luck with her type. It was time to try something...

She couldn't immediately fill in the blank. *Boring* finally came to mind. But maybe boring was exactly what she needed.

Too bad it wasn't what she wanted.

What she wanted was Egan.

The wine was going straight to her head, and the need was going straight through her body.

"What *is* your type?" she asked. She was playing with fire, and she was so close that she took in his scent. No aftershave today. Because he hadn't shaved. He smelled like clean cotton from his shirt, leather from his boots and the rest was all just the scent of a man.

He opened his mouth. Closed it. Shook his head. "You don't really want to know."

"But I do. What's your type?" she repeated, touching the rim of her wine glass to his chest.

Something dark and dangerous went through his eyes. "My type is someone temporary."

"Temporary," she repeated. She felt another sting and set her glass on the counter. "As in love 'em and leave 'em?"

"I don't love them. I've never said that to anyone I was involved with, and I've never implied it."

Her mouth dropped open. "You've never said I love you?"

"Never. I have fun with them, period. And they know that's all it's going to be right from the start." Egan mumbled a four-letter word. "That's my type, Caroline, and that's why you should back away."

So, she was dealing with a man who'd never said I love you. A man, from the sound of it, who'd never had a serious relationship. Why didn't that make her listen to him and back away?

Because she was obviously as warped as he was.

Caroline couldn't help herself. She wanted to put a dent in that rugged facade, although she wasn't entirely sure it was a facade. That was part of the lure. The uncertainty of what he would do.

The lack of boredom.

The attraction so strong that it could consume her.

She leaned in—to do what, Caroline didn't know. She just wanted to get closer to see how he'd react.

He reacted all right.

Egan latched on to her wrists, and in the same motion, he whirled around and put her back against the door frame. He wasn't exactly gentle. And his eyes burned with a fire that Caroline understood all too well.

He moved closer all right, until his mouth was almost touching hers. Until his body was closer, too. Until his shirt brushed against her breasts. Now *that* sent a nice shiver through her.

She wanted him to touch her. And she wanted it more than her next breath. But he didn't touch. Instead, that fiery blue gaze went from her hair. To her eyes. To her cheeks. To her mouth.

Caressing her.

And he was doing it in a way she'd never thought of as intimate. Leave it to Egan to make air kisses as potent as the real thing.

"You don't want a piece of me," Egan warned.

But it sounded like an invitation to her aroused body. An invitation she couldn't accept. She reminded herself of what Egan had said about losing focus. Oh, yes. This was the ultimate losing-focus activity. Air kissing and with her body so ready that she was imagining sex on the kitchen island.

Caroline couldn't make the desire go away.

Egan apparently didn't have that problem.

He let go of her as if she'd scalded him, and using his forearm, he eased her aside. He no longer had those baby blues on her lips. He was looking at the underside of the cabinet next to them.

"Did you know that was there?" he mouthed.

Expecting to see a brown scorpion or some other unsavory critter, Caroline followed his pointing index finger. It took her a moment to spot what had grabbed his attention, but she finally saw the "thing" stuck to the bottom of the cabinet. It was black, round and about the size of a quarter.

"What is it?" she asked. God, please don't let it be another bomb, but it looked too small for that.

Egan motioned for her to stay quiet. He moved her away from it and into the living room. By the time they made those few steps, she was more than a little concerned. Her heart was racing. So were her thoughts. And these weren't good thoughts, either.

"Did you know it was there?" he asked, putting his mouth directly against her ear.

"No. What is it?"

"An eavesdropping device. Caroline, someone's listening to us."

Chapter Eight

Hell.

And Egan silently repeated that profanity multiple times when the full realization about the eavesdropping device hit him.

Someone had likely overheard Caroline's entire drug-induced session with the psychiatrist. That someone could have also heard Caroline's and his conversations. Both the personal ones and the ones involving the case. And that meant this someone would know she was recovering bits and pieces of her lost memories.

Critical memories that could identify a killer.

"What do we do?" Caroline whispered. Because he was so close to her, he could feel her arm trembling.

"Play along," he whispered back. "I think I'll get started on some of that paperwork," Egan then said louder. "Go ahead and finish your sandwich and save me some Oreos."

It was, hopefully, a casual-sounding comment that Egan wanted the listener to overhear so the person would think all was normal. He didn't want to set off alarms just yet in case it was possible to trace where the device was transmitting.

A killer could be on the receiving end.

Egan motioned for Caroline to follow him, and he led her through the kitchen. He used a dish towel from one of the drawers to muffle the little beeps that sounded as he disengaged the security system. And he eased open the door that led to the back porch.

It was dark already, and there wasn't much of a moon because of the cloudy sky. He didn't turn on the lights, but there was more than enough illumination from the lagoon-colored pool. Egan maneuvered her away from that area and to the corner of the porch. There was still too much light to make him feel secure with having her outside, so he took her to the side of the house and pulled her behind a row of mountain laurels where they were in the shadows.

The ground was wet and soggy, not just from the recent rain but from Caroline's automatic sprinkler system that had obviously come on. He could hear the spraying water on the other side of the house. Maybe the sprinkler and the pool filtering system would drown out what they said. While he was hoping, he added that maybe the range of the eavesdropping device wouldn't extend to the yard.

"There could be other devices inside," he explained. "It's not safe to talk in there."

Caroline gave a choppy nod and looked exactly as he expected her to look. As if she'd been delivered another blow. Which she had.

Egan took out his cell phone and called Hayes at the Cantara Hill Country Club. "We have another problem," Egan started. He kept his voice low just in case. "There's a listening device in Caroline's kitchen."

"You're kidding?" Hayes grumbled.

"I wish."

"Well, this just keeps getting more and more complicated."

Yes. And Egan didn't like this particular complication. "How fast can you get equipment up here to check it out? I want to find the source of reception."

"Yeah. I'd like to know that, too," Hayes agreed. "I don't have any equipment like that here with me, but the San Antonio office will. I'll call them and have someone bring it over right away. It might take a half hour or so, but just hang tight, I'll get there."

"Thanks." Egan clicked End Call and put his phone back in his pocket.

"Who's doing this to me?" Caroline whispered.

"I don't know." But they knew it was probably the killer. Or someone working for the killer. "I don't know how long that device has been there, but I couldn't see any dust on it. Did anyone recently have access to your house when you weren't here?"

She took a moment, obviously thinking. "I have a housekeeper who comes in twice a week. She doesn't even have a key because my mother lets her in. The woman cleans both our houses, and I don't suspect her."

Neither did Egan, but he'd still check her out. It was a long shot, though, because it wouldn't have taken much time to plant that bug. Mere seconds. Which led him to his next question. "Has Kenneth been inside the house since we started the investigation?"

Caroline shook her head. "No. Wait, yes. Tammy and he were here with my parents the night Vincent Montoya's body was discovered."

"Of course they were." Now, that didn't surprise

Egan, and it was the reason Kenneth was still his number one suspect.

"What if the intruder is the one who put the device there?" Caroline asked.

Unfortunately, Egan couldn't rule that out. "If we go with the possibility that the intruder didn't set the bomb, that he didn't try to kill you two nights ago, then he could have planted the listening device. Maybe in addition to the dream journal, he wanted to hear what you were saying. Maybe he was listening for any clues as to what you knew. Clues that could ultimately incriminate him."

She hesitated, then nodded. "That means we're back to my memory issues."

"But the question is—what would a killer think you could remember that would point the finger at him?"

Caroline lifted her shoulder as if the answer were obvious. "Something to do with the hit-and-run."

"Maybe." Egan played around with that in his mind. "And maybe it's connected to that conversation you had with Kimberly the night she died. The secret affair she mentioned and the argument Kimberly had with Kenneth."

"You think her secret lover could be behind this?"

Egan opened his mouth to say yes, it was entirely possible, but he didn't have time to respond. That's because he heard the snap. That was it. Just a snippet of a sound that made him reach for his gun.

But it was already too late.

Someone fired a shot.

CAROLINE'S HEART JUMPED to her throat.

She heard the sound. Not loud. More like a swish. In

itself, it wasn't enough to be alarming, but it was Egan's reaction that made her realize what was happening.

That swishing sound was a bullet being fired.

Egan drew his firearm and pushed her to the muddy ground, behind the flowering lantana and sage that grew beneath the mountain laurels. He didn't stop there. He got in front of her. Protecting her.

He jerked out his phone again and pressed a button on it. Probably to redial Hayes. Thankfully, he wasn't far away, and if he responded immediately, he should be there in just a couple of minutes.

She prayed that would be soon enough.

"Someone's shooting at us," Egan said softly. "We're on the west side of Caroline's house."

Another shot.

This one whistled through the darkness and landed mere inches from her feet. She drew up her legs, trying to leave as little of herself exposed as possible. But that wouldn't do anything to help Egan. He was there. Right in front of her. Where he could easily be killed.

Oh, God.

Why was this happening?

The bomb had been one thing. Sinister, yes. But she hadn't even known it was there. If it'd gone off with her in the car, she literally wouldn't have known what had hit her. But this…she knew these bullets were being aimed at her.

Egan lifted his gun. Aimed at a thick live oak that was just on the other side of the wrought-iron fence in Taylor's yard. He fired. That sound wasn't a swish or soft whistle. It was a blast that nearly deafened her.

Caroline covered her ears with her hands, but it was too little too late. Egan fired again.

So did the shooter.

Not just one bullet, either. But the gunman fired three shots in rapid succession. Egan had no choice but to drop down, taking himself out of position to return fire. But hopefully, this new position would save his life.

The next shot went to the right of their heads. It was too close. And it shattered the limestone flanking at the base of the house and sent shards flying through the air. Caroline felt one of those sharp pieces slice across her cheek, but she didn't react. She stayed quiet. Because any noise might give away their exact position. Right now, that was all they could do to keep from being killed because they were literally pinned down with no place to run.

"Stay low and don't move," Egan whispered.

Caroline wished that he would do the same thing, and she nearly latched on to him and dragged him back when he levered himself up and returned fire. She couldn't tell where his shots had landed, but they seemed to go in the direction of that live oak.

Was the shooter perched in that tree?

If so, the person must have cut through Taylor's yard. So did that mean it truly was someone she knew? Someone familiar with the landscape and points of access to her property? Of course, it wouldn't be that difficult for an intruder to sneak through the darkness, climb the tree and deliver those shots.

But how had the gunman known that Egan and she would be outside?

Damn.

Maybe the intruder had used the eavesdropping device. Or were there possibly other devices planted outside? Or worse—did the intruder have them under actual surveillance?

Caroline wanted to curse and scream. When would this dangerous invasion of her life end? And when was that danger going to stop extending to people around her? The danger was especially high for Egan, who was literally in the line of fire. With each of those bullets, he'd endangered his own life while saving hers.

Another bullet smacked into the mountain laurel overhead, and the shattered branches rained down on them. Egan immediately returned fire, sending two bullets in the direction of the shooter.

Caroline heard sirens in the distance. Probably Hayes. Thank God. Egan needed the backup, and if they got lucky, the sirens might stop the shooter.

Or not.

The thought had barely formed in her head when there was another shot. Then another. And another. Until Caroline lost count.

Egan dropped back down to cover, and they waited there. Long, agonizing moments. For what seemed an eternity. Until the frantic rounds of gunfire stopped.

Just like that.

The sirens got louder and closer, and so did the sound of the approaching vehicle. From what she could tell, the driver braked to a screeching halt at the end of her driveway.

"Egan?" Hayes yelled.

"Over here. Use the nightscope to check the big tree in Taylor's yard."

Silence followed. It was both a good and bad sound. There were no more shots fired, but the silence meant the shooter was likely getting away.

"We can't move yet," Egan explained to her. "This could be a trick to draw us out."

She hadn't thought of that. And here she was just beginning to think that this latest attempt to kill her would soon be over.

It might have just begun.

"I don't see anything," Hayes shouted. "But I'll have a closer look. Stay put."

Caroline wasn't sure she could move anyway. So she lay there on the wet ground next to Egan. With the adrenaline pulsing through her and her heart beating so hard that she thought it might crack her ribs, it was hard to imagine that her life would ever get back to normal.

"I'm sorry this happened," Egan said to her.

"Yes. I'm sorry, too."

Even with all the precautions they'd taken, they hadn't been able to prevent the attack.

She heard another vehicle come to a stop in her driveway and then heard Hayes call out to them. It was the private security guards, obviously coming as additional backup.

"Nothing," Hayes relayed.

That single word caused Egan to curse. And Caroline knew why. It meant the gunman had gotten away again. They weren't safe, and they wouldn't be until this guy was caught.

Egan stood and pulled her to her feet. Thank goodness he kept his arm around her waist because her legs were wobbly, and she wasn't sure she could stand on her own.

Hayes walked toward them. "I'll take a look around the area."

Egan nodded. "I think the shooter used a rifle rigged with a silencer. He wasn't close enough to use a handgun."

"Obviously this wasn't a pro, or we wouldn't be standing here talking," Hayes concluded.

If there was a silver lining in this, there it was. The irony of this crazy situation. The gunman hadn't been a professional assassin but more likely a friend or a neighbor.

Hayes tipped his head to Caroline. "You might want to go ahead and get her out of here."

Egan looked at her first, and he must have seen the shock and the fear that was still no doubt on her face. "I'll take her to the office at the country club." He turned to the guards. "I want all gates to Cantara Hills closed and locked. No one gets in or out."

Probably because he'd barked that order and had fire in his eyes, the guard issued a "yes, sir" and got moving.

Egan turned back to Hayes. "As soon as you've checked out that tree, start rounding up everyone in the entire neighborhood. Everyone is going to be tested for gunshot residue."

Hayes's eyebrow lifted. "Everyone?"

"*Everyone,*" Egan confirmed through clenched teeth.

Chapter Nine

Egan wasn't mad. He was a dozen steps past that particular emotion.

And along with being past mad, he was plenty tired of hearing rich people complain about having to be tested for gunshot residue. He didn't care a lick about the inconvenience to them or about their feelings.

He had one goal.

Find the shooter.

He wanted to deal personally with the SOB who'd nearly killed Caroline.

Egan glanced at her to see how she was holding up. She was seated in the corner of his office, sipping a cup of reheated coffee. She'd changed into his shirt because hers had been coated with mud, and she'd washed up. But water and a clean shirt couldn't erase the worry he saw on her face.

He wished he could get her away from all of this, but he couldn't. Brody's flight still hadn't landed, and he needed to assist with the GSR testing. Besides, Egan wanted to be there if and when they identified the culprit.

Kenneth Sutton and his wife, Tammy, were the next to

be tested. When they walked through the door of the office, both glared furiously at Egan, and expressed their extreme displeasure at being called into the temporary office and treated like criminals.

Hayes used the surface of the desk to hold the supplies for the procedure, which involved four nitric acid swabs per person—swabs for the fronts of their hands and the backs. That way, if there was any GSR present, they would detect it.

The security guards were in the adjacent office, testing some of the residents. Along with them was a CSI that SAPD had sent over. With luck, they wouldn't have to swab everyone before they got a match.

"She's clean," Hayes announced when he swabbed Tammy's hands.

"I told you," she grumbled. She folded her arms over her ample chest and waited while Hayes repeated the procedure on her husband.

Egan stepped closer. He didn't want to miss this. Because if he had to put money on who had fired those shots, his money would be on Kenneth.

Hayes did the first swab and drew it back. Clean. Egan's stomach sank a little. He really wanted to nail this guy. But Hayes produced another clean swab.

"I'm innocent," Kenneth declared. "I appreciate that you want to find this person. I want to find him, too. But it's not me. Nor my wife."

The third swab was negative, too.

Kenneth locked his gaze with Egan's just as Hayes declared the fourth swab to be clean.

Kenneth stood and looked at Caroline. "Is there anything I can do for you? Anything you need?"

Caroline shook her head and seemed totally unconvinced about the man's concern. That's probably because Egan had already alerted her that Kenneth, Tammy or any of the other residents could have showered and changed their clothes after the shooting. That could be the reason there was no gunshot residue on their hands. In other words, Kenneth and/or his wife could still be guilty as sin.

Kenneth and Tammy stormed out, and Hayes motioned for the next person to enter the room. It was his father, Walt.

Walt didn't acknowledge him. Looking completely at ease, he strolled into the room. Of course, his father was likely familiar and even comfortable with every inch of the country club as well as the rest of Cantara Hills since he'd worked for Link Hathaway for nearly thirty-five years, five years before Egan had even been born.

Hayes started the swabs on Walt while Egan tested the next resident, a young woman who lived in the Cantara Hills condos.

"You do know you're riling a lot of people," Walt said, his voice practically a whisper.

Much to Egan's disgust, he couldn't ignore his father's warning. Not because his father had given him many warnings when he was growing up. But because Walt almost never interacted with him unless he was extremely upset—like the time Egan had beaten up Carlson Woodward.

"Yeah, I get accused of riling people a lot," Egan commented.

That's when Walt looked at Egan. A surprise, since he wasn't big on eye contact, either. "Be careful not to rile the wrong people," his father mumbled.

Egan stared back at him. "That sounds like a threat."

No confirmation of that. When the four swabs showed negative results, Walt stood and calmly walked out.

However, there was nothing calm about the way Egan felt. He cursed his reaction and wondered how many lifetimes it would take him to become immune to the cold disinterest of the man who'd fathered him.

Egan dismissed the woman he tested after her swabs were all negative, and he motioned for the next person to enter. It was Miles Landis, and he had that smirky grin on his face. A smirk he aimed at Caroline. That's when Egan knew that Caroline couldn't be subjected to this all night. He went to her and helped her stand.

"Come with me," Egan instructed.

He led her to the back of the room where there was a door to his adjoining suite, the place he'd been staying since the investigation. Egan opened the door and ushered her inside. "Why don't you take a shower and get some rest."

"Right," she said, both of them knowing that rest wouldn't come. "I want to know who's responsible."

"I want to know that, too, but having you out there won't make it happen any sooner." He heard the anger in his voice and knew it shouldn't be aimed at her. "You'll be safe here. The other entrance is blocked off. I'll make sure no one gets in."

She nodded. And stood there. Staring at him. "Thank you for saving my life, again."

"You shouldn't be thanking me. When I took you outside, I nearly let you get killed."

"You nearly got yourself killed." She pulled in a long breath.

Man—Egan wanted to hold her, to assure her that he would make things right. But he couldn't. Because he wasn't certain he could fix things. And one hug wouldn't be enough. Not with the adrenaline churning through both of them.

He settled for skimming his finger over her cheek. "I'll help Hayes with the testing. The sooner we swab everyone, the sooner we'll know who fired those shots."

She nodded. "Tell me the second you find something."

"I will," he promised.

Egan went back into the office and could deduce from Miles's continuing smirk that he hadn't tested positive. Still, there was something that Egan wanted to ask the man.

He motioned for Miles to go to the corner of the room. "I didn't fire those shots," Miles volunteered. "I don't have a reason to hurt Caroline."

Egan didn't even address that. "How well did you know Kimberly McQuade, the woman killed in the hit-and-run?"

Miles looked more than a little surprised. "I knew her. Why?"

"Any idea if there was a man in her life?"

"You mean a lover." Miles didn't wait for confirmation, and he appeared to give that some thought. "I never saw her with anyone, but I know that Trent Briggs wanted to get in her pants."

Briggs, Kenneth's aide, one of the murder victims. During the investigation, Egan had heard rumors that Trent had unsuccessfully pursued Kimberly, but if he'd succeeded, there would have been no reason for Kimberly to keep an affair secret.

"How about Kenneth?" Egan asked. "Any idea if he wanted to get in her pants, too?"

The smirk returned. "Kenneth? Not a chance." Miles

glanced back at the line of people waiting to be tested. "But you'll want to ask our tennis pro about that."

"Carlson Woodward?" The bucket of slime who'd made his childhood a living hell? "Why do I want to ask him?"

Miles leaned in and lowered his voice. "Figure it out." And with that ominous comment, he sauntered away.

"Next," Hayes called out.

Egan heard the guards in the other office call out the same. At the speed they were going and with five of them doing the processing, it might not take all night. Of course, he'd have to do a follow-up to make sure everyone had been tested because it was entirely likely that the shooter might try to evade this whole process.

But the one person who had his attention now was Carlson. It boiled Egan's blood to think this man might have had something to do with anyone Egan knew.

Link Hathaway entered, and he wasn't alone. His daughter, Margaret, was with him, and Egan could see his father still in the makeshift waiting area. Walt had probably driven the two of them there and would drive them back home.

As expected, Link complained, cursed and threatened to sue them while Egan swabbed his hands, but that wasn't what caught Egan's attention.

It was Margaret.

She trembled as Hayes processed her. Her behavior was enough to alarm Egan, but he relaxed when she tested negative.

Her father didn't test positive, either.

Finally, it was Carlson Woodward's turn. Tall, dark and slimy. He still wore his tennis clothes, and his hair was damp. Perhaps he'd been giving a lesson. He didn't have

Miles's smirk. No, he was in a public place. Egan knew firsthand that Carlson saved his smirks and taunts for times when he didn't feel the need to impress anyone.

Egan caught his arm and pulled him to the other side of the room. "Talk to me about Kimberly McQuade."

Carlson stared at Egan's grip and waited until he let go of him before he answered. "She's dead," Carlson said under his breath. He glanced behind him, probably to see who might overhear this conversation.

"Did you try to start something with her?" Egan asked.

He studied Egan a moment. "Define *something*."

Egan debated how much he should say and finally decided to put it all out there. "An affair."

Carlson's eyes lit up as if he'd just been handed a delicious morsel to savor. Egan didn't like being the one who gave him that morsel, but he had to question people about this affair because it could provide him with information about the identity of the killer.

Egan thought of Caroline. Of the shock and fear he'd seen on her face. And he knew he had to do whatever it took to get answers. He couldn't continue to risk her life.

"You think I slept with your Ranger buddy's sister?" Carlson clarified. He grinned.

It took every bit of Egan's willpower not to punch that grin right off his face. "Just answer the question."

Still grinning, Carlson leaned in and put his mouth close to Egan's ear. "She came on to me, but I turned her down. I don't sleep with the trash. That's the exact reason I turned down Caroline. She might be rich, but that doesn't change the kind of woman she is. Trash is trash, no matter how big the trust fund."

Egan didn't bother with willpower. He shoved Carlson

against the wall, and that had Hayes barreling across the room. "What's going on here?"

"I'm just telling the truth," Carlson gleefully explained. Oh, he was enjoying this, and Egan instantly regretted the burst of temper. Carlson fed on that kind of crap.

Hayes gave each of them a long, hard look before he latched on to Carlson and pulled him back to the desk. "Hold out your hands," Hayes ordered.

Egan didn't assist him, mainly because he'd end up breaking every one of Carlson's fingers.

Hayes stiffened, and Egan went closer to see what had caused his fellow Ranger's reaction.

And there it was.

The swabs had turned blue.

An indication that gunshot residue was present. This was no small amount, either. The entire swabs had lit up.

Egan stared at Carlson, almost hoping the man would go for a gun or try to escape. "Well?"

No gun and no escape. Carlson grinned again. "Oh, did I forget to tell you that I was at the firing range this afternoon? With all the crime in Cantara Hills, I thought I should learn how to defend myself." He shook his head. "You just can't get good law enforcement help these days."

Egan stepped closer, but Hayes stood, blocking him. Which was probably a good thing. Best not to beat the hell out of a suspect.

And Carlson was now, indeed, a suspect.

"What's the name of the firing range?" Hayes asked.

"Millford Crest. It's about fifteen minutes from here. My instructor is Jerry Bradshaw. He gives lessons to lots of people from Cantara Hills."

Hayes jotted down the information. "This Bradshaw will verify you were there today?"

"Of course."

Hayes grabbed the phone and used 4-1-1 to get the number of the firing range. While he was busy with that, Egan continued the questioning. "Where were you at eight-fifteen tonight?"

He shrugged. "Well, I wasn't shooting at you, Sgt. Caldwell."

Egan leaned in, violating his personal space. "Where. Were. You. Tonight?" He overly enunciated each word.

"Here, at my office at the country club. Besides, what possible motive would I have for wanting you dead?"

"Bad blood," Egan readily answered. People had killed for less. "If what you say is true, if you were really in your office tonight, then that'll be on the surveillance cameras." He hoped.

"Oh, that might be a problem," Carlson volunteered. He made a show of looking disappointed. "The one outside my office has been broken for days. I reported it, I think."

"Yeah, I'll bet you did."

Egan was more than ready to arrest this sorry excuse for a human being, but he heard Hayes say something that he didn't want to hear.

"The firing range instructor confirmed that Carlson was there," Hayes relayed. "Don't worry. After Brody arrives, I'll go out and have a chat with this guy and see if there are any holes in his story."

If that concerned Carlson in the least, he didn't show it. In fact, he seemed to enjoy it. Was he playing some kind of deadly game of cat and mouse? Because he could have intentionally gone to the firing range just to cover up the premeditated attack on Caroline and him.

Egan quickly worked through how that info fit the rest of the murders. Maybe Carlson was the one who'd hired Montoya to cause that hit-and-run so he could get back at Brody. There was bad blood from childhood between Carlson and Brody. And all the other killings and attempts could have resulted from that.

Carlson had just moved to the top of his list of suspects.

"Am I free to go?" Carlson asked.

It truly pained Egan to say this. "For now. But don't go far."

"Wouldn't dream of it. Cantara Hills is my home away from home." He looked around the office, and his gaze landed on the door to the suite. Where Caroline was. "In fact, I know every room in this entire club."

It sounded like a threat. A bad one. And Egan had to force himself not to bolt to go check on Caroline. He waited until Carlson had issued a smug "See you later" before he took Hayes aside.

"I don't think it's a good idea for Caroline to be in that room alone," Egan explained.

Hayes nodded. "I can make sure the rest of the swabs get done. Don't worry about it."

But Egan was worrying. And he was thinking. About what Caroline was no doubt feeling. She needed someone, a shoulder to cry on, and he was tired of pushing her away.

"Officially, I want Caroline in your protective custody," Egan insisted. "I want that in the paperwork, and I'll add it when I do my report about the shooting."

Hayes flexed his eyebrows. "Does that mean you want me to stay with her tonight?"

"No." And Egan was fully aware of how that sounded. "But I'd like you to stay put out here, to make sure no one tries to get inside."

"Right." Hayes paused. Then, paused some more. "I've seen the way you look at Caroline. You think being with her is wise?"

"No." It was probably the biggest mistake he'd ever make. But knowing that wouldn't stop him.

Chapter Ten

Caroline nearly jumped out of her skin when she heard the doorknob turn. Every inch of her was on edge, and she couldn't stop reliving the terrifying images of lying in that mud while someone had tried to murder Egan and her.

She waited, with her hand flattened against her chest, and she watched as the door opened.

Egan walked in.

Relief flooded through her. Well, as much relief as she could feel after everything that had happened. Egan obviously felt the same. She could see the tension in his face and shoulders.

"What's wrong?" she asked.

"Maybe nothing." But it didn't sound that way. It sounded like something big. "Carlson Woodward tested positive for gunshot residue."

Of all the people she'd thought who might test positive, he wasn't one of them. "He's the shooter?"

Egan shrugged. "He was at a firing range earlier in the day. That could account for it."

He didn't add the obvious—that the other explanation was that not only had Carlson been at the firing range but he had also tried to kill them.

But had Carlson really done that?

It seemed extreme. Unless he was linked to Vincent Montoya and those other murders. Or maybe the childhood grudge between Egan and him was a lot more than just a grudge.

Egan locked the door, using the deadbolt and the chain, and he walked closer, studying her clothes. She was wearing one of his blue work shirts and a pair of his boxers.

"This is all I could find," she explained. Maybe if she concentrated on conversation or anything else other than the shooting, those images would go away. "You really don't own any pajamas, do you?"

He stopped just inches away from her. The corner of his mouth lifted. A half smile. But the smile didn't make it all the way to his eyes. "I'll see if Taylor can bring you something to wear."

"She's not home tonight. I already called her. She's on a business trip for her charity foundation and won't be back until tomorrow morning." Caroline wanted to keep talking. She wanted to keep thinking about clothes, about Taylor, about anything that would keep her mind occupied.

She refused to cry, but she felt the tears building. And the fear. *Mercy,* when was that going to pass?

"You're no longer in my protective custody," Egan said. It sounded like an announcement.

And it apparently was.

Because he immediately pulled her into his arms.

That embrace was more than warm strength and comfort. It was necessary. And she needed it. Just like that, Caroline shattered. She couldn't fight it any longer. The tears came, and she fell apart.

Egan was right there to make sure she didn't fall too hard.

"I don't usually cry," she heard herself say.

"It wasn't a usual night."

She didn't accept that as an excuse. "But you're not a basket case."

Egan leaned back a little and looked down at her. "Yes, I am."

Their eyes met, and she saw it then. Not just the tension. But the uneasiness that ran bone-deep inside him. This shooting had been a nightmare and had brought them together like nothing else could have.

They'd cheated death, together.

He understood everything she was going through, and she instinctively knew that no one but Egan would be able to comfort her. Or maybe it was simply that she didn't want anyone else to.

Caroline stood there, blinking back the tears. Egan wiped the ones that fell from her cheeks, and in the same motion, his mouth came to hers.

She was stunned. But for only a second. Her mind barely had time to process the surprise before she felt the other sensation. Pleasure. It wasn't just his embrace that she needed. She needed this, too, and Egan gave it to her.

His mouth moved over hers. He wasn't rough, but he wasn't gentle. He took her, sliding his hand behind her neck so that he controlled the movement of her head.

Caroline didn't care about the loss of control. She allowed the searing heat from that kiss to fire through her, and she took everything Egan was offering.

She wrapped her arms around him. No gentle motion from her, either. That kiss had sparked a torrent of feelings that immediately became an avalanche. Caroline pulled him closer, until their bodies were pressed against each other, breath against skin, and she returned the kiss.

Egan did indeed taste as good as he looked.

She'd felt passion before. Had even been on the receiving end of some good kisses. But this went up several levels. And in the back of her mind, Caroline realized this kiss, this moment, would become the benchmark she would to use to measure all others.

That wasn't exactly a comforting thought.

Still, it didn't stop her. Nothing would at this point. She wanted to feel. She wanted the heat.

She wanted Egan.

His grip tightened around the back of her neck. The kiss deepened, and his tongue touched hers. More fire. More need. She fought to get closer.

Egan kept control. Well, at least until she slid her hand between their bodies and touched the front of his jeans. He made one rough sound. A hitch in breath that was muffled by the kiss, and then he backed her up against the wall. Using just one of his hands, he cupped her wrists and pinned them in place over her head.

They were going to have sex.

That was the only conclusion Caroline could see happening from this. The emotions were too high. The heat too intense.

And he was such a good kisser.

He didn't stop with just kissing her mouth. He went to her neck and started some major fires there as well. Caroline was aware of that heated sensation in that particular part of her body, but it was competing with all the other sensations. Especially those caused by his hand, as it slid down to cup her right breast.

Egan swiped his thumb over her nipple.

Then, he unbuttoned her shirt and replaced his thumb with his mouth.

Oh, mercy.

That nipple kiss made her want to beg for more, but it was mild compared to what happened when his mouth returned to hers. He adjusted their positions, until his hard sex touched hers. His boxers that she was wearing weren't much of a barrier. Hardly anything at all.

And she felt every inch of him.

She wanted him inside her right then. Just anticipating it nearly made her climax.

Caroline fought to free her hands so she could go after his zipper. But Egan just held on and slid them both to the floor. With her back still against the wall, she landed with her knees cradling his hips. It wasn't quite enough contact, so she maneuvered her hips closer so she could rub against his erection.

It was an overwhelming sensation.

But soon, it wasn't enough.

Egan seemed to know the exact moment when she had to have more.

Now, Caroline said to herself. Finally, it was going to happen. They were going to have wild, hot, crazy, rough sex.

But he still didn't let her go after his zipper.

Caroline groaned in protest, but the groan died on her lips when he gave their bodies another adjustment. He turned, laying her on the floor, and he finally released her hands. *Yes!* However, the zipper thing didn't happen.

Because he turned the tables on her.

Before Caroline even knew his intent, the boxer shorts

came off her. She felt the chill of the A/C on the inside of her thighs. For only a second. Then, she felt Egan's warmth.

And Egan's mouth.

Now, this was a French kiss to remember.

He literally made love to her with his mouth. Caroline considered, briefly, a protest. She considered telling him that she wanted him inside her. She wanted them to find release together, but after a flick of tongue and the not-so-gentle coaxing of his mouth, she gave up and slid her fingers into his hair.

She lifted her hips, moving with his kiss. He was so good at this. Not a surprise. And it didn't surprise her that within seconds, he had her close to that edge. Caroline wanted to savor it, to savor him, longer. But Egan would have no part of that. He continued to do what he was doing until she felt her body do the only thing it could.

Surrender.

The climax racked through her. It was as hard and as intense as the man responsible for what she was feeling.

She couldn't move right away. The aftershocks continued to ripple through her. Her heart reacted by racing like crazy. And her breathing was labored. But all those bodily reactions didn't make her forget the aroused man between her legs.

Caroline reached for him, but like before, he caught on to her hands and shook his head.

She couldn't believe that head shake. "No fair," she insisted.

"It's fair." He made his way back up her body and kissed her.

She tried not to let that kiss distract her, either. "How do you figure that? I got all the pleasure. You did all the work."

"That wasn't work." Egan freed her hands, rolled away from her and sat up, propping himself against the wall. "Feel better?"

"Oh." It took her a moment to process that. She didn't process it well. "That was to make me feel better?"

"No. It was to make *me* feel better. But I was hoping it'd do the same to you."

Caroline didn't know whether he was lying or not. Or whether to be insulted. She wasn't into sympathy orgasms, though secretly she had to admit that a sympathy orgasm from Egan was better than a regular one. Still…

"Caroline," he said, looking down at her.

Uh-oh. She knew that look and that tone. She was about to get a talk about how this couldn't mean anything. He'd probably remind her of the case, and the danger.

She pulled up her boxers, sat up and met him eye-to-eye. Best to nip this in the bud.

"I feel better," she announced. Caroline held out her hand to prove that she was no longer trembling—thank goodness, she wasn't—and just in case Egan hadn't gotten the point, she hiked up her chin. "You're better than a prescription sedative. So, consider your job done for the night, Sgt. Caldwell."

His "look" changed, and something primal and dangerous went through his scorching blue eyes. She'd pushed him too far.

Good!

Caroline wanted to push him farther.

She wanted to see if she could put a crack in that cool, imperturbable composure. Part of her, the obviously aroused, insane part of her, wanted to know what it would feel like to cause Egan to take her completely.

But he didn't take her, completely or otherwise.

He calmly got up, without saying a word, and disappeared into the bathroom, leaving her there with a lot of questions about what the heck had just happened.

They had an insane so-called relationship going on here. Oral sex and anger. Anger because Egan Caldwell thought it was perfectly all right to give her the orgasm of her life without allowing her the opportunity to do the same to him. This was his way of keeping his distance. That love 'em and leave 'em garbage. Or rather that have sex and leave 'em philosophy that he'd lived by.

Caroline was still in the middle of her mental tirade when there was a knock at the door. She froze. Egan didn't. He must have heard the sound because he came rocketing out of the bathroom, and before he reached the door, he already had his gun drawn.

"Sgt. Caldwell?" someone said from the other side. Caroline recognized it as the voice of one of the civilian security guards. "You have a visitor."

"Who is it?" Egan didn't put his gun away, and he certainly didn't sound welcoming.

"Carlson Woodward. He's the tennis pro here, and he says he needs to speak to you, that it's important."

"Go into the bathroom," Egan instructed Caroline.

She considered refusing because if Carlson was indeed guilty, she wanted to face him down. But Egan would never allow that. To save them both an argument, she stepped into the adjoining bathroom, but Caroline left the door ajar so she could see and hear everything.

Egan waited until she was in place before he opened the main door. The guard was there, and behind him was Carlson.

"We finished the swabs," the guard explained. "Mr. Woodward here is the only one who tested positive. He left and then came back because he said he had to talk to you. I searched him. He's not carrying a weapon."

Egan peered out into the office. "Where's Hayes?"

"With the club manager, Michael DeCalley. They're checking the surveillance camera outside Mr. Woodward's office. They're just around the corner and said they'd be back in a couple of minutes. The other Ranger should be here shortly, too. Lt. McQuade called, and he's on his way from the airport now."

Good. Caroline wanted Hayes and Brody there for backup, just in case.

Carlson stepped forward, moving to the guard's side. "I didn't come armed. I'm merely here with information."

"About what?" Egan snapped. The guard dropped back, walking in the direction of the desk, where they'd done the GSR testing.

But Carlson didn't answer. He looked past Egan, and his gaze landed right on her. His eyes immediately lit up, and Caroline didn't have to guess why. She no doubt looked as if she'd just gotten off the floor with Egan.

"Well, well, Caroline Stallings," Carlson said. He grinned from ear to ear. "How do you think your parents are going to take the news when they hear you're bedding down deep with the likes of a lowly Texas Ranger? A chauffeur's son, at that."

She did not need this.

Egan latched on to a handful of Carlson's shirt and dragged him closer until he was right in his face. "There's nothing for Caroline's parents to hear."

"Perhaps not, but you know how gossip is around

Cantara Hills. Hard to keep a secret. Now, if you'll quit manhandling me, Sergeant Caldwell, I'll tell you what you want to know about Kimberly McQuade."

"What about her?" And Egan didn't ask nicely, either.

But Carlson didn't speak until Egan released the grip he had on him. "Miles Landis said you were asking about Kimberly's lover."

"So?" Even from across the room, Caroline could see Egan's jaw tighten.

"Soooo, I know who he is."

Carlson didn't say more. Probably because someone came into the office and spoke Egan's name. Caroline recognized that voice, too. It was Lt. Brody McQuade, apparently back from his trip to California.

"What's going on here?" Brody asked.

Egan didn't take his eyes off Carlson. "Carlson was about to tell me the name of Kimberly's secret lover."

Brody came to the doorway. He glanced around. First at Egan. Then he spotted her. Brody no doubt noticed what Carlson already had, and she felt uncomfortable under his brief scrutinizing gaze.

"Welcome back, Lt. McQuade," Carlson greeted. It was syrupy sweet and sickening. He obviously detested Brody as much as he did Egan. "And how's your lovely fiancée, Victoria?"

"She's fine and with a bodyguard. Since I'm anxious to get back to her, I'd rather cut the BS. If you know something about Kimberly's affair, then spill it now or I'll just arrest you for obstruction of justice."

"Oh, I have no desire to keep this to myself. Miles won't mind if I share with you what he told me. Call it a guilty pleasure, but I'd love to see you Rangers at each others' throats, and news like this will do it. Maybe if you're fighting among yourselves, you'll leave the good citizens of Cantana Hills, me included, alone."

Egan got in Carlson's face. "Miles said he didn't know anything about her lover."

"Miles was a little, well, wasted, when he was in here. You just have to keep pushing, and it's amazing what he can remember. For instance, he recalled hearing a phone conversation."

"And?" Egan snarled when Carlson didn't immediately add anything.

"Miles overheard Kimberly talking to her lover. She was confused about her feelings."

Egan grabbed him by the shirt again. "I want a name, and I want it now. Tell me who her lover was."

Carlson's smile took on a sick, dangerous edge. "Well, it's none other than your fellow Texas Ranger, Sgt. Hayes Keller."

Chapter Eleven

Egan let go of Carlson and shook his head. He was about to tell Carlson that accusing Hayes of being Kimberly's secret lover was a sick joke.

But from Carlson's expression, he wasn't joking.

Carlson stepped back and straightened his clothes. "I'll give you all some privacy so you can discuss this Ranger-to-Ranger." He tossed one last glance at Caroline. "When I talk to your parents, I'll tell them you said hello."

"Please do," Caroline jabbed right back. She was glaring at Carlson when she walked closer. "And when I talk to them, I'll remind them that you're an ass. Oh, and if you call them to gossip, I'll have my own little chat with your boss. I know for a fact all employees here at the country club sign a confidentiality statement. Gossip won't be tolerated, even if that gossip might be true."

"You wouldn't have me fired," Carlson snarled.

"If she doesn't, I will," Egan volunteered.

Carlson gave Caroline a look meant to kill.

Egan wanted to pound Carlson to dust for that look and for saying those things about her. And for that other accusation against Hayes. But he didn't have time. Hayes came into the office, and he had a surveillance disk in his hand.

"Good news," Hayes announced, smiling. "The camera outside tennis boy's office wasn't working, but the one just up the hall is. We've got surveillance footage of the time before, during and after the shooting."

Egan saw just a split-second of what appeared to be concern in Carlson's eyes. But Egan didn't have time to deal with that now. He had a more pressing problem on his hands.

Hayes's smile faded. "What's going on?"

Brody and Egan exchanged glances. A dozen things passed between them, and none of those things were good. For starters, they had to ask Hayes what would have been unthinkable just minutes earlier.

"I'll excuse myself," Carlson said. "Obviously you have some business to discuss."

Egan grabbed his arm again. "This isn't over. And if you call Caroline's parents, you're going to regret it."

"Ohhhh." Carlson made a show of being afraid. "And what will you do?"

"I'll come after you." And Egan meant it. He had no doubts that his tone and expression conveyed that.

Carlson dropped the gleeful expression, and Egan got a glimpse of the raw anger lurking just beneath the surface. "Egan Caldwell, I'll see you dead before I let you put your low-rent hands on me again."

But it was Carlson who was shaking when he stormed out.

Egan didn't say anything else until Carlson and the guard were out of the room. Then he shut the door. Best to just put it all out there and get it resolved. "Carlson's stirring up trouble," Egan explained to Hayes. "He said you were the one having an affair with Brody's sister."

Egan expected Hayes to deny it. That they'd all share a laugh and curse Carlson for the petty lie he'd just told.

But Hayes didn't deny anything.

Egan's heart went to his knees. Judging from Brody's silence he was having the same reaction. Or worse.

"It just happened," Hayes said. He laid the surveillance disk on the desk. "Kimberly and I didn't plan it. She came to my place one night. She was upset. We had a few drinks…"

"Any reason you didn't tell us this sooner?" Brody's voice was low, intense and dangerous.

"I know, I should have." A moment later, Hayes repeated it. He groaned, sat down and put his face in his hands. "But I didn't know how, and Kimberly wanted to keep it a secret until we'd worked out our feelings for each other."

Hell. This was not what Egan wanted to hear. "Why not tell us after she was killed?"

"Because it wasn't pertinent to the investigation."

The look that went through Brody's eyes was dangerous. "You should have let me decide that."

Brody had said exactly what Egan was thinking. However, after what had just happened in the bedroom with Caroline, Egan was at least a little sympathetic to giving in to forbidden temptations.

But this?

Hayes had crossed a line by essentially withholding information. "Please tell me you haven't kept anything else a secret." Egan couldn't help but make it seem like an accusation.

Hayes pulled his hands from his face and stood. There

was some fire in his eyes, too. "You'd better not be suggesting I had anything to do with her death."

"Just asking." Egan had a tough time hanging on to his temper. Hayes was a fellow peace officer. Someone he'd grown up with. Gone to school with. A friend.

It seemed to take Hayes a moment to get his teeth unclenched. "You shouldn't have to ask. You know I wouldn't do anything to hurt Kimberly or any other woman."

"How would I know that?" It was Brody's turn to go on the attack. "You kept your affair secret."

Hayes lifted his hands, palms up, in the air and got back on his feet. "Because I knew this was how you'd act if you found out."

"I have a right to act this way." Brody's index finger landed on Hayes's chest. "Did you seduce her?"

"No." Though Hayes said it quietly, his voice was filled with emotion. And a warning—for Egan and Brody to back off. "She came on to me."

That wasn't the right answer because Brody charged at Hayes. He grabbed Hayes's shirt and shoved him against the wall.

Egan didn't know who was more surprised, Hayes or him. Brody had always been intense but never much of a physical fighter. No, the fights had usually erupted between Hayes and Egan. Childhood squabbles they'd settled with their fists and then gotten over it.

But Egan wasn't sure even a good fight would resolve this.

"Stop it!" Caroline yelled. Despite the fact that fists were about to be thrown, Caroline got between Brody and Hayes. "Go to your separate corners, guys, and cool off. I'm not going to let you beat each other senseless."

Surprisingly, Hayes and Brody stopped, even though their panting and angry stares meant this wasn't over.

"Carlson wants all of you at odds," Caroline announced.

She was right, of course. Carlson did want them at each other's throats. Why? Maybe to cover up that little detail about his testing positive for gunshot residue. And he didn't have an alibi for the shooting.

"Carlson might be the killer," Egan reminded Brody and Hayes. While he was at it, he reminded himself.

His gaze landed on the surveillance tape that Hayes had found, and he remembered Carlson's brief but intense reaction to it. "And there might be something on that tape to prove it."

CAROLINE SIPPED her morning coffee during her phone conversation with the antique broker from upstate New York. With everything else going on in her life, it wasn't exactly a conversation she wanted to have right now, but she was on the verge of a huge deal with this broker, and even with the murder attempts, she had to take care of her family's business. In this case, that meant rescheduling a meeting to sign the final paperwork that would seal the deal.

The broker wasn't happy with the delay; she could tell from his tone when he uttered a terse goodbye and hung up.

Heck, she wasn't happy, either. But leaving Egan's suite at Cantara Hills to go to her lawyer's office in downtown San Antonio just wasn't a smart idea. Nor did she want her lawyer to come to her because of the potential risk to him if he happened to get in the way of another attempt to kill her. She was feeling a lot like Typhoid Mary.

Besides, until the gunman/killer was caught, Egan

probably wouldn't let her leave, nor have visitors. He certainly seemed to be guarding the door to the suite. In fact, that's where he'd spent the night—in a chair bracketed right in front of the door while she took his bed.

Of course, neither of them had gotten much sleep.

At least she wasn't still having to wear his boxers and shirt. Along with the breakfast delivered to the suite, clothes for her had also arrived. Egan had sent one of the security guards to her house to get an outfit and her toiletries.

The guard had chosen a white knee-length bohemian skirt and a garnet-red tank top. Not exactly work attire, especially since they'd brought her funky jeweled flip-flops as well, but it beat the alternative. Everyone who'd seen her in Egan's boxers and shirt had assumed she'd had sex with the undergarment's owner. Which she hadn't. Well, unless that old analogy was correct—that a little bit of sex was like being a little bit pregnant. Degrees didn't matter.

The intimacy had been there.

And speaking of her partner in intimacy—like her, Egan was now involved with work. He was at the desk in the corner talking on the phone to someone at the Ranger Crime Lab in Austin while he continued to review the surveillance disk that Hayes had located. There were images taken on the day of her break-in and on the day of the shooting. And there were a lot of frames that included Carlson Woodward.

"Carlson," she mumbled under her breath. He'd likely phoned her parents by then. He was her parents' tennis instructor, and even though they were far from being best friends, they did talk and had occasionally gone out to lunch together. Carlson would use that connection to phone them and see what kind of trouble he could stir up. Because he probably thought the more trouble he caused, the harder it would be for Egan and the investigation.

If Carlson had indeed phoned them, her parents had likely tried to call her. There'd be messages on her still-missing cell phone. More messages at her house. And she was betting they had called friends and neighbors. She couldn't put off talking to her parents much longer, but she wanted to wait until she at least had some good news.

Judging from Egan's body language, that wasn't going to happen any time soon.

So, she bit the bullet and called to access her messages from her home phone.

First message, from her parents: "Caroline, Kenneth told us about the shooting. Call us now."

Second message: it was also from her parents. Her mother this time, and the gist, the same—call them.

Message three through eight were repeats of the same. But nine was the message she'd been expecting. And dreading.

"Caroline, this is your father, and I need to talk to you. Carlson called with some disturbing news about you and one of those Texas Rangers. Carlson said he was doing me a favor, that he was sure I wanted to know. Well, I do, but the news should have come from my daughter and not my tennis pro. I've already phoned the club manager, and he knows I'm not pleased about having Carlson Woodward, his employee, contact me about a private matter."

Sweet heaven. Carlson had done it. But she wasn't

going to take this lying down. She immediately called the concierge, who in turn put her through to the club manager, Michael DeCalley, an old friend of her father's. Michael informed her that based on the conversation he'd had with her father, he intended to talk to Carlson and that it was entirely possible that he would terminate Carlson's employment.

Caroline didn't feel any guilt at all about Carlson's losing his job. After the turmoil the man had gleefully created the night before, he deserved what he got. Plus, this would mean he wouldn't have access to Cantara Hills.

One less suspect who'd have the run of the place.

"Thanks," she heard Egan say to the caller on his phone. Egan hung up and glanced back at her. "Hayes collected the eavesdropping device from your house earlier and drove it to the crime lab in Austin."

She didn't miss the cool way he'd said his fellow Ranger's name. Obviously, Egan was still riled that Hayes hadn't been forthright about the secret affair with Kimberly.

"The lab just examined it…" Egan continued "…and were able to determine that it hadn't been left there the night of your break-in. The level of fine dust particles that had collected on it indicated it'd probably been there at least a week."

Caroline wanted to curse. For at least a week or more, she'd had no privacy whatsoever. "I guess there were no fingerprints to tell us who put it there?" And whoever it was, she wanted to throttle them.

"No fingerprints."

Of course not. It couldn't be that easy.

"Was the crime lab able to tell who was on the receiving end of the eavesdropping?" she asked.

Egan shook his head. "It wasn't a cheap device. Top of the line, actually. It had a quarter of a mile range for reception."

That both alarmed her and gave her some hope. "I have only five or six neighbors who live within a quarter of a mile of me."

That obviously wasn't new information to him. "Your parents, Taylor, Kenneth and Tammy Sutton, and your parents' best friends, the Jenkins."

Caroline nodded. "So, we're back to Kenneth and Tammy Sutton?"

"Not necessarily. The eavesdropping device could have been transmitting to a remote receiver, one that'd been planted somewhere near your house. That transmitter could have in turn fed the info to a receiver farther than a quarter of a mile away. Much farther."

Now she cursed under her breath. They hadn't narrowed down anything. The killer could be anywhere in Cantara Hills, or merely have access to it.

Which brought her to something she needed to tell Egan. "A little while ago, Taylor called. Her security guru is over at my house now, changing all the locks and updating my security system. I hope that won't interfere with your investigation."

"No. Actually, I think it's a good idea. The CSI guys are checking the grounds, of course, but there isn't any reason for them to go back in your house just yet because they've already processed it."

Egan paused the surveillance frames and whirled his chair around so they were facing. But he was a good twenty feet away, and he'd kept his distance since the "incident" the night before.

"So, think back to the past two weeks. Who's visited your house?" he asked. "And who would have had access to the kitchen?"

So they were back to more questions. Official ones. Where Egan was all Ranger.

She sipped her coffee while she gave that official question some thought. "My parents visited, of course. So did Kenneth and Tammy. Taylor, too. She comes over nearly every day. But I don't suspect her," Caroline quickly added.

"Neither do I. But what about her brother, Miles, and Carlson? Have they visited recently?"

"Unfortunately, yes." Why she hadn't thought of it sooner, she didn't know. Caroline stood and walked closer. "About a week and a half ago, maybe, Miles came by to ask if I knew where Taylor was, and Carlson was with him."

Egan groaned softly. "Let me guess—they came into your kitchen?"

She nodded. "Miles wanted to take some meds for a headache, or so he said, and he followed me into the kitchen for a glass of water."

"How about Carlson? Was he in the kitchen, too?" Egan asked.

It took her a moment to replay the events of that night. "Yes. He came in with Miles. And either of them could have planted the device because my back was to them for several seconds while I was at the fridge getting the water."

"It wouldn't have taken much effort. The device comes

with adhesive. And we already know Carlson's capable of doing something like this."

Oh, yes. He was capable of anything petty and nasty. But murder? She wasn't sure about that.

"Do you know if Carlson called your parents yet?" Egan wanted to know.

"He did." She drank more coffee. Avoided eye contact with him. "I'm sure they'll want to talk to me when they get back from their trip. But that's four days away." She'd have plenty of time to rehearse what she was going to say to assure them that she knew what she was doing.

Maybe during that time she could assure herself, too.

"Carlson's right about one thing," Egan continued. "Your parents will be upset. To them, I'm the equivalent of that vintage chopper you have hidden away in your garage. Fast and dangerous."

Caroline shrugged, tried to look flippant and walked even closer. "They don't want me to get hurt."

He caught her gaze. "Then you should keep your distance because with me, you will get hurt."

That was the first and only personal thing he'd said to her all night and morning. Too bad it had some merit. Merit that seemed way too serious for her already serious mood.

Trying to keep things light, Caroline gave his arm a gentle pinch. "You're like a truffle, Egan Caldwell. All solid on the outside, but I'm betting inside, there's a creamy soft filling."

She would have preferred a counter comment about his lack of richness, or something. Instead, he looked at her as if she'd missed a dose of meds and turned his attention back to the surveillance images. "Don't bet on that."

"Right. You're the guy who's never said I love you." Caroline chuckled. Not from humor. This conversation was too close to what they'd both been tiptoeing around for hours. Still, she didn't hush. The wound was there, and she had to examine it, even if she knew it was better off left alone. "My ex-fiancé used to say I love you all the time, and look how that turned out."

Egan turned back around and Caroline could almost read his mind. He was silently saying that it would turn out equally bad with him.

Or worse.

Again, he was right. But why did she want to be wrong? And then it hit her. With her mouth filled with coffee, it occurred to her that she was falling for Egan.

Really falling.

Well, damn. This couldn't happen. It just couldn't. When this investigation was over, she'd have to kiss Egan goodbye, and he'd go back to his office in Austin. That would be the end of it.

Wouldn't it?

She was still debating that when she realized something other than her had caught Egan's attention. He was leaning closer to the computer screen, where he was studying a still image on the surveillance disk.

It was Carlson Woodward.

"This footage was filmed about an hour before you arrived home and realized you had an intruder," Egan explained.

Caroline walked closer to get a better look. Yes, it was Carlson all right. He wore his usual tennis clothes and was coming out of the locker room. He had a gym bag clutched in his left hand.

"What do you see?" she asked Egan.

He tapped the gym bag. It was unzipped, and she could just make out a pair of shoes tucked inside.

Almost frantically, Egan used the keyboard to adjust the image. He zoomed in. And they got a much better look at the shoes.

"Those are Razors," he insisted. "The same type of shoes your intruder was wearing."

Oh, mercy. Was this the smoking gun? But then she looked closer. "There's a name or something on the tennis bag."

More key strokes, and Egan zoomed in on the monogram at the center, near the top zipper. The initials were MAL.

"Miles Andrew Landis," Caroline provided. "That's not even Carlson's bag."

He grunted in frustration. "So, why would Carlson have Miles Landis's bag?"

Caroline could think of a reason. "Miles plays tennis at the country club. Well, he does when he's sober. Maybe he left it in the locker room. Of course, if you question Carlson, he'll probably say he found it and was just returning it to Miles. He certainly wouldn't admit he'd planned to wear those shoes and break into my house to steal a dream journal."

"No. And Miles will likely claim he doesn't remember." Egan paused a moment. "I need answers about Miles because he seems to be the key to information we need."

She couldn't disagree with that. "What do you have in mind?"

"How about we ask Taylor to come down to the country club for a visit?" he asked, reaching for the phone.

"Any chance we can drive up to see her? Then, I can

stop by my house and get some things." Like a different set of clothes and a pair of more practical shoes.

He eased the phone back into its cradle. "I don't want you out in the open."

He had a point. She hopefully had a solution because she had major cabin fever and wanted to get out of there. "We could call ahead and park in Taylor's garage. We could do the same at my place. That way, we could walk directly into the houses. No being out in the open."

Again, he gave that some thought before he finally nodded. "Okay. Let's go talk to Taylor and ask her if she thinks her brother is capable of murder."

Chapter Twelve

Egan made Caroline's trek to the vehicle as fast as he could manage. He had his Jeep parked directly in front of the country club, and with his arm around Caroline, they practically ran to the vehicle so they could make the short drive to Taylor's.

He hoped to hell this wasn't a mistake.

All things considered, he would have preferred to keep Caroline locked away so the killer couldn't get to her. But the truth was, she might not even be safe at the country club. After all, the suite had windows, and there were no guarantees that the killer couldn't break in. The only thing he could do was continue to put himself between her and whoever this monster was who wanted her dead.

"Taylor moved her car out of the garage," Caroline relayed to Egan after a brief call to her friend. "When we get there, just pull into the empty space."

He nodded and started the drive up the winding hill. Taylor's house wasn't far, less than two miles, but each passing second only escalated his concern—and raised it even higher when a car burst out of a side street.

Egan slammed on the brakes, gave the steering wheel

a sharp turn to avoid a collision and reached for his gun. But he realized a gun wasn't necessary. The driver was a teenage boy with short, spiky black hair, and he gave them an indignant wave before he sped off.

"Wait a minute," Caroline insisted when Egan started to move again.

He glanced at her and saw that the color had drained from her face. "What's the matter?"

"I remember something about the hit-and-run. I remember Vincent Montoya."

All right. The timing was bad with them out in the open, but the shrink had said her memories might return. "What about him?" He volleyed glances between her and their surroundings. Even though this memory could be critical, he couldn't risk their being ambushed.

"Because of a streetlight, I saw his face. Right before he rammed into my car. I saw him. God, Egan." She started to tremble, and he slid his arm around her. "That wasn't the face of an angry man. But a determined one. Cold, unfeeling. Like a shark sitting there waiting to attack."

So Kimberly's death had likely been just a job to Montoya. That confirmed what Egan had already suspected. Now, the question was—who had hired Montoya to do that?

Egan glanced around them again and saw the car approaching from behind. The road was too curvy for the vehicle to pass, which meant he needed to get moving. Besides, he didn't like sitting there where anything could happen.

Even though Caroline was clearly upset, he eased his arm from her and continued the drive. "Do you remember anything else?" It was better to get her to focus on the details rather than the emotion, but Egan wasn't sure he could accomplish that just by getting her to talk about it.

She shook her head. "It was a flash, a quick glimpse of his face."

"But this is a good sign. You've remembered most of the accident now. And the parts you can't remember, that's because you were unconscious."

"Yes." She paused. "And those memories still haven't gotten us closer to the killer."

"You're wrong. Because of you, we know about Kimberly's argument with Kenneth, and we know Kenneth either lied or was mistaken about Montoya's motives. Montoya didn't kill Kimberly because she rejected his advances. He killed her because someone hired him to do that."

Caroline's breath shuddered. "And the person who hired him could be…anyone," she concluded with a heavy sigh.

No. Not just anyone. The list of suspects was pretty solid. Kenneth, Tammy, Carlson and Miles. Now, he needed to look for the link between these four and Montoya and Kimberly. Once he had the motive for Kimberly's death, then he would know the identity of the killer.

Egan turned into the stone-and-brick driveway. Taylor's car was parked on the side of her sprawling southwestern-style house, right next to the open garage. There was indeed a space waiting for them. So was Taylor. The slender blonde was in the doorway that led into the house, and as soon as Egan turned off the engine, she pressed the button to close the garage doors.

"Are you okay?" he asked Caroline as they got out of his Jeep.

She nodded, but he could tell that her nod was a lie.

The memory of Montoya had shaken her and this on the heels of the attempt to shoot her.

Taylor and Caroline hugged each other, and Taylor's gaze met his. It was a question—how's Caroline holding up? Egan only shrugged.

"Come in," Taylor invited, ushering them into a garden room just off the kitchen. She wore a perfectly tailored royal-blue business suit and heels.

"Thanks for delaying your business meeting," Caroline said.

"Don't worry about it. I told the bank trustees that I'd be about a half hour late. I hope that'll be enough time for our chat."

"It will be," Caroline assured her. "We only have a few questions."

True. But they were potentially volatile.

A gleaming silver tray of coffee was waiting for them on a granite-and-glass table, and both Caroline and he sat in the white wicker chairs and helped themselves to cups of the brew.

"This is about your brother," Egan started.

"I figured as much. I heard about the search warrant and the shoes taken from his condo. Please tell me those shoes didn't match the prints left by the intruder on Caroline's bedroom floor."

"They didn't. But that doesn't rule him out."

Taylor nodded. "Because he could have gotten rid of them." She reached out and gently touched Caroline's hand. "I'm so sorry if Miles is responsible for any of what's happened to you."

"I know. But you're not his keeper. You don't have to apologize for him."

Egan was relieved. Judging from Taylor's comment and attitude, she might not get defensive about his next question. "Do you think Miles might have had something to do with Kimberly McQuade's death?"

Taylor's only reaction was that she blew out a long breath. "I wish I could say no, but I've been thinking about this. No proof, just a theory. Miles and Montoya weren't friends, exactly, but I know that Montoya loaned some money to my brother. And I'm sure it was a sizeable amount. Maybe the hit-and-run had something to do with that?"

Egan couldn't see an immediate connection, but he'd dig deeper. "But what about what's happened recently? Have you seen or heard anything to indicate that Miles wants Caroline dead?"

"Nothing." Her answer was fast, which meant Taylor had likely given it some thought as well. "I know he asks her for loans all the time, but he's never had anything bad to say about her."

"What about anyone else?" Caroline asked. "Have you noticed anything about Kenneth, for instance, that would make you think he's involved?"

"No."

"I remembered seeing Kimberly and Kenneth argue the night of your Christmas party," Caroline volunteered.

"Oh, yes. That," Taylor agreed. "I remember it, too. They were in the corridor of the guest wing. I walked by there, heard voices and opened the doors. There they were."

This was the first Egan had heard of this. "Why didn't you tell us sooner?"

Taylor dismissed it with a head shake. "Because I didn't remember it until you asked. You think it's important?"

"Could be." And it brought them back to Kenneth, again.

"I didn't actually hear anything they said," Taylor continued. "In fact, I can't even be sure it was an argument. They looked intense. But it could have been they were just discussing business."

Egan doubted that.

"I didn't hear the argument, either," Caroline added a moment later. "But I remember that Kimberly was upset with Kenneth and she wouldn't say why."

"That's not usual. Kenneth can rub people the wrong way. Sometimes ambition doesn't leave a lot of room for tact." Taylor poured herself some coffee. "I take it he's a suspect?"

Egan avoided the question. He glanced at both of them. "I want you both to think back to the night of the party. Was there anything unusual going on at the City Board or here in Cantara Hills?"

After several moments, Caroline spoke up. "I think it was just normal business at the City Board. There was a big contract bid that was about to be revealed. But that was it."

"And as for here in the neighborhood..." Taylor answered "...there was the party here at my house, of course. It wasn't just a Christmas party. It was to celebrate the recent success of the City Board."

Yes. Egan had looked into that success. Funds, a huge amount, had recently been approved to build a new west-side library and extend the tourist area of the Riverwalk, the main artery of the thriving downtown area. But Egan hadn't found anything about that to tie to the murders.

Maybe it was time to take another look.

"I'll go over all the City Board records for that time period," Egan explained. He stood. "Maybe something will turn up."

Caroline stood as well. The two women shared another hug. "I'm worried about you," Taylor whispered.

"You don't have to be. I'm in good hands."

That sent Taylor's gaze sliding his way. But not just a gaze. A friend's scrutinizing one. Egan silently cursed. What, were Caroline and he wearing god-awful big signs on their foreheads so that anyone near them could read that they were attracted to each other?

Egan vowed then and there to focus just on the investigation. But one look at Caroline, at her sleep-starved eyes and her too-pale skin, and he knew he was kidding himself. He couldn't keep his mind off her for even a minute.

Somehow, he'd have to deal with that.

"If I remember anything else, I'll give you a call," Taylor assured them. She followed them out of the garden room and back to the garage. When she got to the exit, she pressed the button again to open the doors.

"Do your parents know?" Taylor asked Caroline.

Caroline didn't say "about what?" She merely sent a warm glance his way. "Probably."

"So you haven't talked to them about Egan," Taylor clarified.

Caroline shook her head.

"My advice—you'd better. Tammy called this morning with the latest gossip. You two are the hot topic of Cantara Hills. The chauffeur's son and the socialite. Everyone thinks you're having an affair."

"Do they now?" Caroline mumbled. There was no weary breath or heavy sigh. Nor did she look uncomfortable.

Probably because there was nothing she could do about it. Carlson had already spilled everything to her parents.

"Be careful," Taylor added, and she gave Caroline another hug before closing the door.

"Gossip," Egan repeated under his breath. "That, and your parents' reaction to an involvement with me are two Texas-size reasons for me to keep my hands off you."

He sounded like he was trying to convince himself.

He was.

"Your *hands?*" Caroline questioned. The slight smile she sent his way let him know that it wasn't his "hands" they had to worry about.

Egan scowled, knowing it was true, and he headed for the Jeep. He made it only one step when the explosion ripped through the garage.

IT WAS HAPPENING ALL OVER again.

At the sound of the explosion, Caroline instinctively tried to drop to the ground. Thanks to Egan and the impact of the blast itself, that wasn't a problem. Both of them ended up on the garage floor, and both of them were pelted with flying debris.

Caroline caught just a glimpse of the source. Or rather what remained of the source.

It was Taylor's car. The car she'd parked outside the garage so that Egan could park inside.

So they'd be safe.

There wasn't much left of Taylor's vehicle. It had literally been blown apart and was now on fire. Black coils of smoke rose from it, smearing into the air. Stench from the burning leather seats and rubber tires boiled into the garage, and Caroline couldn't breathe.

The door between the house and garage flew open, and Taylor gasped when she looked out. "My God, are you hurt?" She proceeded to drag them aside.

Caroline and Egan went willingly. She wanted to put as much distance as possible between them and that fireball in Taylor's side yard.

"We need to move away from the garage," Egan ordered. He grabbed on to both Taylor and her, and they raced to the other end of the house.

Once he had them shoved into the library, he drew his gun and his cell phone. "Hayes," Caroline heard him say after he pressed in some numbers. "I need backup at Taylor Landis's house. There's been another explosion. Caroline and I have only been here fifteen minutes, so the perp might still be around. Come, and bring Brody."

Caroline's stomach twisted into a knot. *Not again. Please, don't let this be happening again.* She grabbed Taylor and moved her away from the window.

Egan stayed at the door, looking out. He had a firm grip on his gun. "Taylor, is your security system armed?"

"Just for the windows. I disengaged the doors when I let you in."

Oh, mercy. That meant someone could be walking right into the house. Or could already be inside.

Egan obviously realized the same thing because he glanced around the room. "Get under the desk," he insisted.

They didn't argue. Caroline and Taylor hurried to the massive oak desk and climbed under it. Egan locked the library door and went to the window to stand guard.

"Do you see anyone?" Caroline asked.

"No."

But that didn't mean *someone* wasn't there.

Had the killer planted that bomb while Egan and she were inside talking? If they'd stayed just another minute, Egan would have been backing out when the explosive device detonated.

They would have probably been killed.

"Caroline, check and make sure you aren't hurt," Egan called back to her.

She hadn't even thought of that, and she was probably too numb and in shock to feel actual pain. She held out her hands. No injuries. And she looked at Taylor, who reached out and wiped something from Caroline's cheek.

Blood.

"It's just a scratch," Taylor whispered.

Caroline quickly tried to clean it all off. She wanted no trace of blood because she knew that would only incense Egan. She didn't want him going after this vile creature. Without backup, it could be suicide.

And then it hit her.

"Egan, are you hurt?" she asked.

"No."

But he wasn't telling the truth. She saw the trickle of blood making its way from his forehead down his cheek. Caroline started to go to him, but Taylor stopped her. "Not now," Taylor said.

Her friend was right, but it took every ounce of Caroline's willpower to stay put and not try to make sure that cut wasn't the only injury he had.

"Taylor, any chance you have surveillance cameras around the garage area?" Egan asked.

"Sorry, no."

So there'd be no footage of someone setting the bomb. Their only chance would be to find some kind of evidence he'd left behind. But if this bomber was also her intruder, then he had already left so much with those tracks on her floor, and they hadn't caught him yet.

Furious at not being able to do anything, Caroline reached up and grabbed the phone from Taylor's desk so she could make a call. To Kenneth. To his personal cell phone. She pressed in the numbers. Waited.

But there was no answer.

Of course, that didn't prove anything, but it certainly made her consider if he could be out there running away from an explosion he'd set.

"Call Miles," Caroline said, thrusting the phone at Taylor. "See if he answers."

Almost frantically, Taylor punched in the numbers, and a moment later, she shook her head. "It went straight to voice mail."

"How about Carlson?" Caroline asked. "Do you have his number?"

Taylor scanned through the index function on her phone and nodded. She pressed the key to automatically dial it and then put in on speaker so they'd all be able to hear what he said.

"Taylor," Carlson answered, obviously seeing her number on his caller ID. "To what do I owe this call?"

He seemed distracted and out of breath, and Caroline didn't think it was her imagination. Apparently, Egan felt the same way because he cursed under his breath.

"I dialed the wrong number," Taylor told him, probably because she didn't know what else to say.

"You're sure? You're not having any problems there, are you? Because I don't mind coming over to check on you."

Carlson not only sounded out of breath and distracted,

he somehow managed to sound a little smug. Caroline wished she could reach through the phone and smack him.

God, had he been the one to set that bomb?

Had his pettiness gone this far?

Caroline remembered what Egan had told her about the man. Carlson had tormented a pet, all because he didn't like Egan. Cruelty to animals was a sign of deviant and even dangerous behavior. Was he capable of doing something even more sinister now that he was an adult?

"No problems here," Taylor lied to Carlson, and she hung up.

"Carlson needs to be questioned," Caroline relayed to Egan.

"Yeah. I heard."

Outside, she could hear the sirens, indicating the Rangers were getting closer. Inside, Egan's phone rang. Caroline listened, hoping that it was someone calling to say they'd captured the person responsible. But judging from Egan's body language, that hadn't happened.

"Brody, Hayes and the guards are outside," he relayed. "They don't see anyone."

"So, what do we do?" Taylor asked.

"Come on. We're getting out of here. It's not safe because there might be another bomb."

Chapter Thirteen

From the driveway of Caroline's house, Egan sat in the bulletproof CSI vehicle and watched the activity. Something he'd been doing all afternoon and something that he would continue to do deep into the night.

And Caroline was in his arms.

With her head on his shoulder.

Egan hadn't even tried to put some distance between them, either physical or otherwise. This was the third attempt in just as many days to kill her, and Caroline was rightfully upset. If being in his arms seemed to soothe her, then that's where she would stay.

To hell with regulations and protocol.

The bomb squad had finished with Taylor's house and hadn't found a second explosive device. Now, they had gone over to Caroline's, just in case the killer had decided to hit her property for a second round. For over an hour, the squad had been in her house to search every inch of it with dogs and equipment, but they were now trickling out and heading for their respective vehicles.

"It doesn't look as if they found anything," Caroline commented.

Even though her head was on his shoulder, her attention was glued to her house. Like Egan, for the past hour she'd no doubt been holding her breath, waiting to see if it, too, would explode.

So far, so good.

The remainder of the bomb squad came out, leaving only Hayes inside to do the final wrap-up.

The medics had already tended to the cuts on his forehead and Caroline's cheek. She had a small white bandage angled just beneath her right eye. Egan could barely stand to look at it because it was a reminder of how close she'd come to being seriously hurt. Or worse.

"You think Taylor's okay?" Caroline asked, glancing over at her friend's house. The place had been marked off with yellow Do Not Cross tape that was fluttering in the summer breeze.

"Brody will see to her," Egan assured her.

But Egan doubted Taylor would be "okay" for a while. She was no doubt shaken to the core. Right now, Taylor was probably being interviewed, but once that was done, she'd be staying the night in Brody's own suite.

Just a precaution.

Egan and Caroline had almost certainly been the targets, but Taylor had been there, right along with them in the line of danger. Besides, Taylor probably wouldn't feel comfortable spending the night in her own home.

Hayes finally came out of the front door of Caroline's house, and she lifted her head and moved slightly away from Egan. For propriety's sake, no doubt.

"All clear. No additional bombs," Hayes announced, volleying his attention between Caroline and Egan. "We checked the security system—it's working. And like you

requested, your security company put some motion acti-
vators around the exterior. If anyone comes near the place
tonight, we'll know about it because it'll set off the
alarms. If they're tripped, you'll be able to hear a series
of beeps from inside the house."

Egan nodded. "Good. Thanks." At least they wouldn't
be ambushed again.

"There's more," Hayes continued. "I had the security
guards question the residents in the immediate area, and
the Roberts just up the street said they saw Kenneth out
for a jog. It was about two hours before the bomb went
off. Ms. Roberts was in her rose garden, and she thinks
Kenneth turned into Taylor's driveway."

Egan didn't like the sound of that. It put a prime
suspect in the vicinity.

"Ms. Roberts was quick to say that she didn't think
Kenneth would do anything wrong," Hayes added.

"Of course not," Egan mumbled. The residents would
protect one of their own, even if that person was the one
trying to kill Caroline.

Egan turned to Caroline. "Here's the plan. While
Hayes transports some of this bomb evidence to the lab
in Austin, you and I will wait in your house. With all the
security updates, your place would be easier to keep safe
than the suite at the country club." There were too many
nooks and crannies there to set bombs, and the surveillance system seemed to be constantly malfunctioning. Or
being tampered with.

"Then what?" she asked.

Egan took a deep breath, not knowing how she would
react to what he was about to say. "Once he's back from
Austin, which shouldn't take more than two to three

hours, Hayes will stay here at the house with you tonight. You're in his protective custody now."

"I see." Which seemed to be another way of saying, *Egan, you're avoiding me.*

He was. Still, Egan wasn't under any illusions that avoiding her would make him want her less. But this way, he might be able to keep his focus and solve this case.

She glanced uneasily at Hayes and him. "Did you two mend fences with each other?"

"No," Hayes and Egan said quickly and in unison.

"But you will." She sighed.

The irritation was still too strong for Egan to admit that she was right. But, by God, Hayes had screwed up. Egan had wasted valuable time investigating Kimberly McQuade's so-called secret lover, a man he thought might be a killer. He could have used that time to find the real killer and therefore make Caroline safe.

Yeah. That was worth another day or two of irritation.

Egan and Hayes exchanged a rather frosty "See you later," and Egan pulled the car up close to the porch. As close as he could get to the steps.

"Go in your house as fast as you can," he instructed. She nodded, and they barreled out of the vehicle, both hurrying inside. Egan immediately double-locked the door and engaged the security system.

"Don't go near the windows," he added. He figured there'd be a lot of such warnings while he was with her. And confusion. Since the only place without windows was where they were standing.

Caroline didn't protest his orders. In fact, she didn't say anything. Neither did he. They just looked at each other.

That look. It needed no interpretation, and it was effective in making him more mindless than he already was.

Egan hooked his arm around her waist and pulled her to him.

And he kissed her.

He didn't even bother to try to stop himself. Egan needed to feel her against him if only for a couple of seconds. He made those seconds worth the risk. He took her mouth, letting the taste of her slide through him. But then, he let go and eased away from her.

She didn't hold on, but she did look at him as if he'd lost his mind. "This protective custody arrangement with Hayes is a matter of semantics," she accused.

Egan had anticipated this conversation. It had the potential to turn into an argument. Not necessarily a bad thing. Because anger might keep them apart.

Then he shook his head.

Nothing, perhaps not even paralysis or near death would keep them apart. He wanted her that much. And then there was the torturous ache. His body wanting hers.

Wait.

Not wanting her body. Wanting *her*. The subtle difference was massive, and Egan didn't even want to explore the implications of that.

"Maybe it's semantics to you," he said. He felt himself halving the already narrow space between them. "But there's paperwork that makes a protective custody arrangement legal."

She halved the half. Until her body was so close to his that he could feel the heat. And they were generating a hell of a lot of heat.

"So?" she challenged. "You think if you legally assign

me to someone else, then you can pretend that nothing happened in your suite last night?"

The question was solid, argumentative. But her tone was all silk, sex and fire. Then she made it worse by moistening her bottom lip with her tongue.

"Look," he started. But he had to stop. Because he'd lost his train of thought. Instead, he did something totally stupid. He reached out and slid his thumb through that moisture on her bottom lip. "Assigning you to Hayes is a way of relieving my guilt over wanting you. A way of keeping this badge on my chest."

She caught his hand to stop him from pulling it back. So his thumb stayed brushing against her lip. "That badge. My parents. Your crummy childhood. Our socio-economic backgrounds. Yes, we have more than enough reasons to forget what happened last night. And there's absolutely no logical reason to remember it, is there?"

And she waited. Staring at him.

Hell.

No logical reason. Plenty of the other variety, though. The illogical, emotionally career-suicidal reasons. But it was useless to try to think about them when his body and mind wanted only one thing.

Caroline.

He reached for her so fast that Egan saw the split-second of shock in her eyes. But it wasn't shock he heard in the throaty sound she made when he kissed her. That sound was approval, maybe even relief, and then moments later, absolute pleasure.

Without taking his mouth from hers, he pulled them against the door. His back hit hard, so hard that he'd have bruises. He didn't care. Nothing else mattered right then.

Her mouth was as hungry as his, and while he had his hands occupied with holding her, Caroline put her own fingers to good use. She went after his shirt.

Egan went after hers.

He wanted to take his time with her. To savor every bit of Caroline. But that was a pipe dream. There was only one way this could happen between them. Explosive and fast. They'd have to burn off some of this white-hot energy and need before they could get to the foreplay.

She jerked back the sides of his shirt. The badge, pinned to the shirt, clanged when it hit against the door. Egan knew that should have been a reminder of exactly what was at stake there, but a reminder wasn't going to stop him.

With her hands playing havoc on his bare chest, Egan shoved up her top. Her bra was all lace, barely there, and he unclipped the front hook and created some havoc of his own by taking her right nipple into his mouth.

She made another sound—a deep, rich moan—and melted against him. Egan savored her while Caroline obviously savored what he was doing.

But only for a few moments.

That nipple kiss only made the heat more impossible, and she began a war with his belt buckle and zipper.

Her eyes were wild, and even though her touches and kisses were blurring his vision, he savored the sight of her, too. She was amazing. Beautiful. With her face flushed with arousal.

Then she slid her hands into his jeans and sent the battle to the next level.

Egan had to take a deep breath just to try to clear his head. But her touch made a clear head impossible. She ran her hand down the length of him. By the time she finished, Egan had no self-control.

She smiled as if she knew exactly what she was doing to him. So Egan turned the tables on her. Pinning her against the door, he shoved up her loose white skirt. Found a pair of white lace panties that matched her bra. But he didn't take the time to appreciate her taste in underwear.

He put his fingers inside those panties, inside her.

No more smiling. She moaned. Gasped. Her eyelids fluttered. She let the door support the back of her head. And she angled her hips so that his fingers would go deeper into her. That seemed to satisfy her for a moment or two, but soon it obviously wasn't enough.

"Do something about this," she said.

Oh, he intended to do something. He wanted her so much that waiting was agony.

"Here?" Egan asked, already stripping off her panties.

"Here," Caroline insisted.

Good. Because they wouldn't have made it to the bed anyway. Egan wrapped her legs around him and freed himself from his boxers. Because they were practically eye-to-eye, he watched her as she took him inside her. Inch by inch. She was tight and wet, and the sensations of that intimate caress robbed him of what was left of his breath. He didn't care.

Compared to this, breathing was overrated.

He moved inside her. Caroline moved, too. Matching him thrust for thrust. She buried her fingers in his hair. Rocked against him. Man, she was a picture all right. The wild child. No inhibitions. No doubts about what she wanted from him.

Egan watched her get closer to the edge. Her eyes

shimmered and were on him, but with each now-frantic thrust, her vision became pinpointed, not on him, exactly, but on the release that was a necessity.

She said his name. *Egan*. Using that classy silk voice. First, just a whisper. She repeated it, and her voice drove him harder. Deeper. Faster.

Until she shattered.

Egan felt her close around him like a fist. He smelled her sex. And kissed her so he could taste her release. He hung on to each of those sensations as long as he could—which wasn't very long.

Caroline's climax brought on his. Egan could only do one thing: hold on tight and ride over that edge with her. It was a damn good ride, too.

She laughed. Part enjoyment. Part exhaustion. Part relief. He knew exactly how she felt.

"Did we survive?" she asked.

"I'm not sure." Either way, it'd been worth it.

Egan had to close his eyes a moment when the little after-shock of her climax gave him an aftershock of his own. She slid against him. Teasing him and herself in the process.

"That wasn't because you felt sorry for me," she insisted. Her breath was rough and jolted against his sweat-dampened face. She kissed him. And moved against him.

Hell. He was getting hard again.

"No." With her still pinned to the door, Egan slid them to the floor and disengaged. What he didn't do was let go of her. He kept here there in his arms. At the rate they were going, they'd have sex again in a few minutes anyway.

She latched on to his face and forced eye contact. "And it wasn't ordinary."

Egan didn't even consider lying. "No. It wasn't."

Caroline cocked her head to the side. And laughed again. That laughter probably would have initiated a conversation they should have—because he knew she wasn't the type to have casual sex. But his cell phone rang, the sound echoing through the foyer.

Egan let go of Caroline so that he could retrieve the phone from his pocket and answer it. The caller ID indicated it was Brody. *Great.* It wouldn't be an easy call to take just then. In other words, Egan had to sound as if he hadn't just had sex against the door with Caroline.

"Brody?" he answered. Caroline, obviously out of breath, rolled away from him and landed on a nearby area rug. No panties. Her skirt up around the tops of her thighs. And her breasts exposed for the taking.

He wanted her all over again.

"Anything wrong?" he asked Brody.

Brody didn't say anything for several seconds. "Are you all right? You sound funny."

Egan silently groaned. Sometimes, like now, he swore Brody had ESP. "I'm fine. Why'd you call?"

"The bomb squad just gave me a prelim report on that device that took out Taylor's car. Like the other one, it'd been set on a timer."

"That doesn't surprise me. The killer probably timed it when he thought Caroline and I would be in the garage. Or backing out of it."

"Not quite. The timer went off exactly when it was set to go off." Brody paused. "I don't think this bomb was meant for Caroline and you."

Egan quickly went through the details of that meeting with Taylor and came to the same conclusion. "Taylor delayed an appointment to see us. If she hadn't, she would have been in her car driving at the time the device detonated."

"That's what I think, too."

Oh, man. This was not a complication they needed. "So Taylor's a target now."

That brought Caroline off the floor, and the alarm was immediate in her eyes. "What happened to Taylor?"

"Nothing. She's all right." Egan relayed what Brody had just told him. Caroline's eyes registered the fear and concern as well.

"Once Hayes is back from Austin," Brody continued, "I'll bring Taylor to Caroline's. I think it's a good idea if both women are in protective custody."

It was a logical plan. Besides, it would free up Brody to keep a closer eye on his fiancée, Victoria, who perhaps was also still in danger from the Cantara Hills killer. Of course, with Taylor in the house, there'd be far less chance that he'd have sex with Caroline again.

Egan tried hard to see that as a plus.

It sure didn't feel like a plus.

Caroline got to her feet, put her panties back on and fixed her clothes. "I'll call Taylor and see how she's handling all of this."

He stood, too, zipping his jeans.

Just as the beeping sound began to pulse through the house.

It took Egan a moment to realize what was making that sound. It was the security system. Specifically, one of the motion-activated devices that had just been installed around the perimeter of the house.

Someone had set it off.

And that meant the killer could be out there, maybe trying to plant another bomb.

Egan checked the security keypad next to the front door. None of the indicator lights were on. So at least the killer wasn't inside, and he intended to keep it that way.

He took out his phone. "I need to call Brody and tell him what's going on."

But before he could press in a single number, the doorbell rang. Egan drew his weapon and stepped back, putting himself in front of Caroline.

"Who is it?" he called out.

No one answered right away, and that caused his heart rate to spike. It spiked even more when he heard the man's voice.

"This is Caroline's father. Let me in. I want to speak to my daughter *now*."

Chapter Fourteen

Caroline thought there were few things worse than hiding out from a killer. However, facing her father definitely wasn't something she wanted to do mere minutes after having sex with Egan.

But she had no choice.

She'd have to let him in.

There was no way she could talk her father into coming back later after she'd composed herself. He'd heard of the attempts on her life from Kenneth. And of course, Carlson had made that call to tell them all about Egan and her.

"Let us in," her father insisted.

Us. So her mother was with him as well. Not surprising. They were joined at the hip when it came to matters pertaining to her.

"If you don't let us in, I'll use my key," her father threatened.

And he would, too—even though with the changed locks, the key she'd given him for emergencies would no longer work. That probably wouldn't stop him. Not because he delighted in invading her privacy, but in his frame of mind, he might think she was being held hostage or something else unsavory. He wouldn't be content until he could see her face-to-face.

"I'll be right there," Caroline answered in the calmest voice she could manage. She finished straightening her clothes and looked at Egan. "You might want to go in the bedroom and give me some alone time with my parents."

"Right," he said in a tone to indicate that wasn't going to happen.

"It won't be pleasant," she added. She only hoped the inevitable argument didn't turn physical. It wouldn't on Egan's or her part. He wouldn't lose his cool enough to take a swing at her father.

Caroline quickly finger-combed her hair and disengaged the security system. She gave Egan another look while her hand was poised on the door lock. "Last chance to escape."

Egan just shook his head. "I'm not leaving you alone to face this."

She hadn't expected that he would. Egan was a rescuer, with all those bad-boy traits. An odd combination. And an appealing one. He wouldn't hide behind her, and he wouldn't steal her parents' money.

But a broken heart was probably just on the horizon for her.

That didn't stop Caroline from brushing a kiss on his hot, surly mouth before she opened the door.

There they were. Her parents. And Egan's father, Walt. *Oh, great.*

"We figured it was a good idea for Walt Caldwell to be in on this," her father announced. "So we called Link and told him we wanted Walt to meet us here."

Caroline knew for a fact that idea wasn't good. Her

own parents were enough of a challenge without adding in Egan's dad.

"Well?" her father said. James Edward Stallings III was wearing khaki Bermuda shorts, brown leather sandals and an absurdly perky tropical shirt littered with exotic flowers. The perkiness didn't extend to his expression. He was scowling.

Her mother, Elaina, just looked concerned. Her normally perfect brunette bob was mussed, her makeup slightly smeared and her white linen dress wrinkled. Probably because they'd left their Cancun hotel room in a rush and hadn't stopped until they'd arrived on her doorstep.

In contrast, Walt looked as he always did. Dressed in his perfectly pressed chauffeur's uniform, he stood almost subserviently behind her parents and dodged her gaze completely.

"Are you all right?" her mother asked. "Kenneth said you weren't hurt in the explosion, but I had to see for myself."

"I'm okay. *Really,*" Caroline added when her mother frowned and gave her a questioning stare.

"If you're okay," her father pointed out, "then why the bandage on your cheek?"

Amazingly, she'd nearly forgotten about that. "Just a scratch. Truly, I'm fine. And while I'm sure you're concerned about my safety, I doubt that's the sole reason you're here, especially since Mr. Caldwell is with you."

"They say you're playing around with some big trouble, boy," Walt grumbled after no one else said anything.

Her father gave a stiff nod and glared at Egan.

Caroline's mom stepped in ahead of her husband as if to put herself between James and them. It wasn't necessary. Her father wouldn't hit her or anything, not even close. He wouldn't even raise his voice, to her, but her mom no doubt knew there was going to be an ugly argument.

There wasn't much chance of stopping that.

Caroline decided the best defense was a good offense, and the offense she had going for her was the truth. But where to start?

She took a deep breath. "Carlson called you because he wanted to cause trouble for Egan."

"Are you sleeping with Sgt. Caldwell?" Her father obviously bypassed her comment and went right to the heart of the matter.

"James!" her mother scolded.

Caroline put a hand on Egan's chest when he stepped forward. "Don't worry. I'm not going to answer that question because it's none of his business." She looked at her father. "I'm sorry, Dad, but you're not entitled to the details of my sex life." Then, she looked at Walt. "And for the record, neither are you."

"It's my business when your parents brought me in on this," Walt countered.

"And it's my business if you're going to get hurt," her father added.

Because there were beads of sweat rapidly popping out on her father's forehead and because he looked ready to implode, Caroline caught him by the arm and urged him inside. Walt followed, barely stepping inside, and Caroline shut the door. No sense airing their argument for the neighbors to hear, and at least this way the A/C would keep them physically cooler.

"I want you to calm down, James," her mother insisted.

Caroline nodded. "That's good advice. This isn't worth having another heart attack. Heck, it's not even worth this brouhaha you're causing." She felt Egan stiffen and looked at him. "I didn't mean it like that."

Crud. Now, she was upsetting everyone, including herself. "What I'm trying to say, and not saying it very well, is that Egan isn't a thief. He's a highly respected Texas Ranger with an incredible commitment to his badge."

"He had no right to get involved with you," Walt interjected.

Egan stepped closer to him. He stabbed his index finger at his father. "And you have no say in any part of my life."

"I do when you're screwing up. What you do with the likes of Caroline Stallings washes back on to me."

"Why? Because Link Hathaway and his cronies won't like it? And because you'd do anything to please your boss? What you and your boss think are not my problem."

Caroline was about to intercede. She wanted to defend Egan. To tell his father what a wonderful man he'd become despite the lack of attention from his parent. But after one glance at Egan, she knew he had to handle this by himself.

"Caroline Stallings is in the Rangers' protective custody," Egan calmly explained to his father. "That means I decide who comes in and who leaves. You're leaving."

Walt shook his head. "Not until you agree to keep your hands off her."

Egan latched on to his father's arm. Not roughly. And other than the iron set of his jaw, he showed no emotion. "I owe you no promises. Nor any agreements. But here's a promise—if you don't leave now, I'll have you arrested for hindering my investigation." With that, he opened the door and muscled his father onto the porch. Without so much as a glance, he shut the door.

The silence came. With all of them staring at each other.

"I'm sorry," Caroline said to Egan.

Egan shrugged. She didn't think it was an under-reaction, either. More like an acceptance that some relationships just couldn't be fixed.

"So you really are involved with Sergeant Caldwell?" her mother asked.

Silence met her question.

Not that Caroline expected Egan to supply some magic answer that would please everyone. But as the person who responded, it left her having to bare her soul. "I care for him, Mom."

There. She'd said it. A handful of words that would likely send Egan running because they smacked of commitment and other things he'd spent a lifetime avoiding.

More silence followed.

She didn't dare look at Egan. Instead, she kept her attention on her mother, who was the most likely ally Caroline had right now.

"I'm thirty years old," Caroline reminded her parents. Then, she told them something they probably didn't know. "I've been celibate for three years since that slime bucket, Julian, crushed my heart and robbed us blind. I gave up dating the kind of guys I like. I gave up sports cars. I work a sixty-hour week and don't take vacations. And I'm a little tired of playing it safe because safe isn't what I want."

She certainly knew how to shut down a conversation. She glanced at them, and at least they all appeared to be thinking about what she'd said.

"I'm worried you'll get hurt again," her father said.

Caroline turned her attention back to him. "I know. But

I'm not going to stop seeing Egan unless he wants to. He and I will be the ones who'll continue or end things between us. Not you, Mom and Dad, and not Walt Caldwell."

Glances were exchanged all around. Her father stared at Egan. "Did you sleep with her?"

"Yes," Egan admitted. "Not that it's any of your business, but I did. And now I suppose you're going to ask what my intentions are?"

Her father gave a too-stiff nod. "I am."

Could this get any more embarrassing? She felt like a schoolgirl who'd been caught stuffing her bra with toilet paper. "Don't answer that," she told Egan.

Egan didn't listen. "My intentions first and foremost are to protect her. I'm not interested in her money. Nor yours. I only want to catch a killer and put him behind bars so that Caroline will be safe."

Her father looked a little shocked with Egan's sincere explanation of his intentions. And perhaps because those intentions obviously didn't include anything personal. He made a sound that could have meant anything and reached for the doorknob.

"Call if you need us," her father instructed.

She released the breath she didn't even know she'd been holding. Then Caroline nodded, brushed kisses on both their cheeks. "I love you."

"We love you, too," her mom answered. A moment later, her dad echoed the same.

When they walked out, Caroline quickly closed the door, locked it and reset the security system. "I'm so sorry you had to go through that."

Egan stayed quiet a moment. "Even after the argument, you still told them you love them."

She blinked, surprised that after all she'd said that was the first thing he wanted to address. "Because I do love them. They're not bad people, Egan. They're just my parents, and they think if they can protect me from being hurt, then they've done their job."

He shook his head as if he didn't get that, maybe because he'd never been on the receiving end of any real parental affection.

"You've really been celibate for three years?" he asked.

Now *that* was one of the questions she had anticipated. "*Been* is the operative word. Obviously, my celibacy ended when I met you."

He shrugged uncomfortably, followed by another shake of his head. "Why?"

"Why what?" Best to clarify because it was a question that could get her in trouble.

"Why end your celibacy with me?"

She thought about it before she answered. "Because I was telling the truth when I said I really like you." To ease the tenseness in his face, she smiled and brushed a kiss on his mouth. "Don't worry, I'm not going to get all clingy."

Even if clingy suddenly didn't sound so bad.

Oh, mercy. She really was speeding her way to that broken heart.

The phone rang, and she automatically turned to answer it, but Egan caught her arm. "I don't want you near the windows," he reminded her. He went into the kitchen and came back with the cordless phone.

She glanced at the caller ID on the small screen. "It's Michael DeCalley, the manager of the Cantara Hills Country Club," she relayed to Egan.

"Caroline," Michael greeted her after she answered

the phone. Egan's phone rang as well, and he stepped a few yards away to take the call. "I just wanted you to know that I went ahead and talked with Carlson Woodward about that issue your father and I discussed. I terminated his employment, effective immediately."

Caroline hadn't thought she would feel guilty. But she did. Still, it would make Egan's job and her life easier without Carlson around. "Thank you," she told the manager.

"Don't thank me yet. Carlson was outraged. I think he'll probably try to sue you and your father."

"I can handle Carlson Woodward," she insisted.

Caroline thanked him again, clicked off the phone and waited until Egan finished his call. Judging from his responses, he was talking to Brody or Hayes because he mentioned the crime lab.

"What did the manager of the country club want?" Egan asked.

"He wanted to tell me that he fired Carlson."

A muscle went to work in Egan's jaw. "Did Carlson make threats about you?"

"Probably. But I doubt he said it to the manager's face. He'll need a reference to get another job so he likely held his tongue."

Egan shook his head. "References won't stop him from doing something petty to get back at you."

She remembered the story of Carlson's kidnapping the puppy. That sounded a few steps beyond petty.

"I'm more concerned about the killer right now." Caroline tipped her head to his cell phone, which he slipped back into his pocket. "Did you get news from the crime lab?"

"The crime scene analyst tested the lock they took

from your exterior bedroom door. It wasn't picked or tampered with. Whoever broke into your house and stole your dream journal used a key. It was a new key, one not used very often, if at all, because it left tiny shavings inside the lock."

That sent a chill through her. "And you want to know who has a copy of my key?"

He nodded. "Your father obviously has one because he threatened to use it. Who else?"

"Taylor." Someone she trusted with her life. But Caroline really hated to give the whereabouts of the final key she'd given out in case of an emergency. "Kenneth and Tammy Sutton have one."

Egan groaned. "Was it a new key?"

"Yes, a copy. And to the best of my knowledge, it's never been used."

"Hell," Egan cursed under his breath. He pulled out his phone and pressed in some numbers. "Brody," he said a moment later. "We need a search warrant. Kenneth Sutton has a copy of Caroline's house key. We need to have it checked for trace shavings. I want it compared to those that the crime lab found in the lock they removed from Caroline's bedroom door."

Caroline waited, her breath caught in her chest. "And then what?" she asked when Egan had finished the call. But she already knew the answer.

If the shavings were a match, then it likely meant that the person who wanted her dead was a man she'd known and trusted her entire life.

Kenneth Sutton.

Chapter Fifteen

Sitting on Caroline's pantry floor, Egan rubbed his hands over his face and checked his watch. Barely 8:00 p.m. This had already been one of the longest, and most eventful days he'd ever lived through. He hoped the eventfulness was over, but he wasn't holding out hope that the long day wouldn't turn into an equally long night.

Brody had just called to say he'd gotten the search warrant for Kenneth's house, and Hayes and he were on the way over to look for the copy of the key Caroline had given her neighbors in case of an emergency. Once they found it, the key would have to be taken to the lab, and those trace shavings would be compared to the ones found in the lock.

If it was a match, Kenneth and/or Tammy would be arrested. If they got lucky, one of them might even confess. And that meant this soon might be over.

"You should eat," Caroline insisted. She was sitting across from him, her legs stretched out in front of her, while she munched on Oreo cookies and bottled water.

It wasn't exactly great cuisine, and the pantry was stuffy, but it beat being in the kitchen with all those windows. As an extra precaution, Egan and Caroline had crawled from the foyer, and that would have to be her mode of travel throughout the house. Then tomorrow, if Kenneth or Tammy weren't in custody, he'd have to decide what to do about their living arrangements.

That included having Hayes swap places with Egan.

Egan wanted to stay with Caroline. And that was the problem. She was a major distraction to him. Especially now, with her bare feet, bare legs, rumpled clothes and his scent still all over her.

"Uh-oh," she mumbled. "I recognize that look. You're thinking about sex."

He lifted his eyebrow.

"About the sex between us that by now you believe shouldn't have happened," she clarified. Smiling, she leaned over and gave him a mouth-to-mouth kiss. "Don't worry. I have no expectations."

Well, she should. She deserved something better. And she sure as hell didn't deserve being stuck with a Texas Ranger bodyguard who couldn't stop thinking about her in a carnal sort of way. That kiss went through him like warmed whiskey, and he wanted her all over again.

Something that'd been happening all night.

"I'd like a hot bath," she said, putting her stash of snacks back on the shelf. She also put on her flip-flops. "How about you? Would you like to join me?"

Oh, man. That was some offer, and it was tempting. But if he got in that tub with a soapy, naked Caroline, they'd be all over each other again. Slick soap against slick body. Her breasts, and the rest of her, ready for the taking. That couldn't happen because he wanted to be alert and unaroused in case something went wrong.

"The security system will go off if someone breaks in," she reminded him.

True. He looked at her again, and the rationalizations started. Bad rationalization, about how he could have her one more time and that would somehow lessen his desire for her.

Yeah, right.

"Well?" she prompted.

Egan was on the verge of crawling down the hall with her to the bath, but his phone rang. Saved by the bell. But it wouldn't save him for long.

"Go ahead," he told her. "Keep the lights off, and stay away from the windows. I'll join you in a few minutes."

That earned him a chuckle and another kiss before she crawled away.

Egan motioned for her to go, cursed himself under his breath and answered the phone. "It's me, Taylor. Brody came by and got Caroline's house key, which she gave me months ago. He wouldn't say what was going on. Is everything okay with Caroline?"

"Caroline is…fine." It took him a moment to settle on that description, and Egan hated that it sounded sexual. Of course, he was thinking about sex so it probably came out in his tone. "We just need all the keys for some comparisons."

Egan left it at that. Best not to announce too many details of the investigation. But he did think of something else he wanted to question Taylor about. "Does your brother, Miles, have a gym bag with his initials on it?"

"Yes. I gave it to him for his last birthday. Why?"

Well, that was one mystery solved. "Have you seen it recently?"

"Funny you should mention it, I saw it just this morning. Miles had it with him when he dropped by on his way to the country club to play tennis."

Interesting. "Did he say anything about misplacing it a couple of days ago?"

"No. But that wouldn't surprise me if he had. Miles is always losing his things."

And in this case, Carlson simply could have been returning it. Nothing nefarious. No killer plans. "What about his shoes? Do you know if Miles owns a pair of tennis shoes called Razors? He would have bought them recently, in the past month probably, because they just came out."

"Let me check his credit card account. I pay his bills," Taylor added after a heavy sigh. He heard her make some key strokes on the computer. "I don't see any purchases at shoe stores or athletic stores. No online purchases, either."

"Could he have paid cash?" Egan asked.

"Miles doesn't have cash. If he bought them, he used the credit card, and it has a limit on how much he can spend."

Egan went in a different direction. "How about his friends—could one of them have purchased the shoes for him or given them to him as a gift?"

"Not likely. Let's just say my brother has tapped out all his friends when it comes to getting them to buy things for him. And despite Miles's penchant for spending money he doesn't have, he's never shoplifted."

So that left Egan with some big holes in the theory of Miles's possibly being the intruder. Of course, Miles could still be guilty, but right now Egan's money was on Kenneth.

If Kenneth had ordered his goon, Vincent Montoya, to kill Kimberly, then Kenneth could have killed Montoya and now simply be covering his tracks by trying to set up someone else, including Miles. And he could be trying to eliminate Caroline because he was afraid she'd remember something incriminating about that night.

Egan heard the slight click that indicated he had another call. "Thanks, Taylor. I'll talk to you soon." And he switched over to the other call.

"It's, uh, your father," the caller said.

Egan wasn't just surprised—he was shocked. He certainly hadn't expected to hear from him. "Look, if you're calling to put me in my social and economic place, forget it. I'm busy."

"I'm calling to save you some grief." He paused. "Egan, our kind doesn't mix with their kind."

That set his teeth on edge, even if it probably had some truth to it. "Is that fatherly advice?"

"No. I don't have a right to give you anything that's fatherly. I'm not apologizing for it, either. I did the best I could do."

"Did you?" Egan fired back.

His father cursed, but for once, it didn't seem to be aimed at Egan. "I was twenty years old when you were born. Just a kid myself. And then your mother…"

Egan waited. Holding his breath. "What about her?"

"She died, Egan." His father's voice cracked. "Her name was Mary, and she died right there in the hospital because the lowlife doctor at the charity hospital messed up something when he did the C-section to deliver you."

"Mary," Egan repeated. Yes, that was the name on his birth certificate, but until that moment it was the only thing he had known about her. That, and that she'd been barely nineteen. "I checked for a death certificate and didn't find one."

"Probably because her name wasn't Caldwell. It was Mary Buchanan. We never got around to getting married." His father paused. "I blamed you for her death."

Yes. Egan had always known he'd been blamed for something. Still, it hurt like hell to hear it confirmed. "Why didn't you just give me up for adoption?"

"Couldn't. Mary used her dying breath to tell me to take care of you. I told her I would. But I failed."

"Yeah. You did." Egan didn't intend to cut him any slack.

His father cleared his throat. "But you still turned out all right. You stood up to me tonight. You stood up to the Stallings, too."

No thanks to you, Egan wanted to say. But he couldn't. Because in an ironic sort of way, he could thank his father for his backbone. His father's neglect had taught Egan to stand up for himself because no one else ever had.

No one but Caroline.

"Do you love her?" his father asked.

Since the question seemed to come out of the blue, it took a moment to sink in. It took Egan another moment to realize he wasn't going to answer. And he wasn't going to think about it, either.

Hell, he wasn't even sure he knew what love was.

There was another clicking sound on his phone. Another call. He was obviously in big demand. Egan wasn't upset because it was a good time to end this chat with his father so he could have some time to process what the heck had just happened between them.

"I have to go," he told Walt. "Another call." He didn't wait for his father's response. Later, though, he might call him back and finish this conversation.

"It's Hayes," the caller said. "I'm at the Sutton house,

and Kenneth isn't here. He's supposedly downtown at a City Board meeting, but he's not answering his cell phone. Convenient, huh?"

Too convenient. But not being there wouldn't stop them from trying to learn the truth. "What about his wife?"

"Oh, she's here all right, shadowing my every move." And Egan could hear Tammy in the background. It sounded as if she was more than upset with Hayes's search. "When we got here, Tammy went to the kitchen drawer, where she says she kept Caroline's key. Guess what?"

Egan groaned. "It wasn't there."

"Bingo. Tammy says it's missing."

"Maybe because her husband has it," Egan quickly suggested.

"My thoughts exactly. Brody just left to try to find Kenneth at that meeting. I'll be here, probably all night, helping Ms. Sutton look for the key."

"Let me talk to him," Egan heard Tammy insist. A moment later, the woman came on the line. "Your Ranger friend here doesn't believe me. He thinks I know where the key is."

"And you don't?" Egan hoped his question conveyed his skepticism.

"I have no idea where it is. I think someone stole it," Tammy concluded.

"Who would do that?" Egan asked.

"Miles Landis." There wasn't a shred of hesitation in her voice. "He was here last week, asking for another loan. And I left him alone in the kitchen while I answered the phone. When I came back, he was rifling through the drawers."

Egan took a moment to process that. If she was telling the truth, and that was a big *if,* then it would explain how

Miles had gotten access to Caroline's. But if Miles had wanted a key, why hadn't he just taken it from his sister's place? That would have been far less risky than stealing from Tammy and Kenneth.

"Put Hayes back on the phone," Egan instructed.

"Yeah?" Hayes answered a moment later.

"Dust the kitchen drawers for prints."

"Will do."

Although they both knew it was a long shot. If Miles had indeed stolen the key, he'd probably wiped away his prints. Of course, sometimes criminals didn't do smart things, and Miles didn't appear to be that smart.

"I'll call Brody," Egan added. "Once he's located Kenneth and questioned him, the next person we should be interrogating is Miles."

"I agree. It might be a good idea if we got him off the street for a while. Or at least out of the neighborhood."

Yes. Miles Landis's name was popping up in all the wrong places, and Egan wanted to ask the man face-to-face if he was the one trying to kill Caroline.

WHILE EGAN WAS ON THE PHONE, Caroline crawled her way out of the kitchen, through her bedroom and onto the tiled bathroom floor. Just as Egan had instructed, she didn't turn on the lights. The room was definitely dark, the only illumination was the moonlight filtering through the crackled-texture thick glass blocks in the lone window at the far end of the room.

Fumbling around, she located the faucets and began to fill the tub. She considered adding bath oil, but she doubted Egan would want to smell like gardenias, and it was the only scent she had.

She caught a glimpse of herself in the mirror. Her face was there among the shadows. A troubled face, she noted. Despite her cavalier comment about having no expectations when it came to a relationship with Egan, she did have concerns. Not about him. But her.

Somewhere along the way, her feelings for him had crossed the line.

Her body wanted Egan. But her heart wanted him, too. And Caroline could see them having a relationship until the lust burned out. Which might take decades. Or it might end tomorrow. She wasn't sure how she would recover from that.

"Don't you dare fall this hard for him," she mumbled.

But realized it was already too late for that.

She closed her eyes and tried to deal with that in a logical sort of way. Unfortunately, no logic was going to change her mind.

Caroline turned to check the tub. She didn't hear footsteps exactly, because of the running water, but she sensed the sound and that she wasn't alone. She turned off the water and whirled around, expecting to see a crawling Egan making his way to her.

But it wasn't Egan.

Before she could even react, someone stepped out from the shadows, and a hand clamped hard over her mouth. He shoved the barrel of a pistol against her right temple.

"Oh, God," she mumbled beneath the intruder's hand. And she just kept repeating that because she didn't know what else to do.

The killer had obviously gotten in and had come for her. If she tried to call out, if she tried to scream, he'd put a bullet in her and would no doubt do the same to Egan when he came into the room.

"What do you want?" she asked, but her words were muffled.

He didn't answer. Instead, he dropped something on the floor. Something small that made a slight pinging sound when it landed on the tile.

Caroline could almost make out his reflection in the mirror. The man with the gun to her head.

But it wasn't till she heard his voice that she knew the truth.

"Ready to play a little kidnapping game, Caroline?" he whispered.

Chapter Sixteen

Egan cursed when he ended his call with Brody. Things just weren't going their way. Brody had located Kenneth at the meeting all right, but Kenneth was giving the same song and dance as his wife: that the key had obviously been stolen. If the pair stuck to that story, there wasn't much Egan could do, but he wasn't giving up.

He slipped his phone back into his pocket and got into a crouching position so he could make his way to Caroline's bathroom. Egan didn't even try to talk himself out of what he was going to do. Even if it was probably a mistake.

Too bad it didn't feel like a mistake.

But Caroline would be the one to pay for this so-called relationship. He'd seen the look in her father's eyes. The man thought Egan was scum.

Of course, Egan had seen the look in Caroline's eyes, too. And he'd heard her defend him. Still, in the back of his mind, he had to wonder if she knew what she was truly getting into with him.

He stood upright when he made it to her bathroom, and he picked through the darkness so he could find her.

Naked, hopefully. But he didn't see her there in the shadow-filled room.

"Caroline?" he called out softly.

Nothing.

Was this some kind of game? That's what Egan wanted to believe, but as a Ranger, he'd been trained to expect the worst. Besides, this wasn't a game Caroline would play.

He drew his weapon.

"Caroline?" His voice was louder now. His heart began to beat faster. Lots of really bad scenarios started to slam through his head.

Egan walked toward the tub to see if she was in the water, and his right boot landed on something small and hard. Maybe a shell casing. Keeping a vigilant watch around him, he reached down to retrieve what he'd stepped on.

It was something hard, but not a shell casing. More like a bit of molded plastic. A cracked button, maybe.

He held onto it and hurried to the tub. Caroline wasn't there. Thank God. She hadn't hit her head or drowned. That was the good news.

But the bad news was that she wasn't in the bathroom.

"Caroline?" he practically yelled.

Still no answer.

His instincts were to go racing through the house looking for her, but Egan held himself back. He had to think—not like her lover but like a Texas Ranger. If someone had broken in and was holding her at gunpoint, he had to figure out how to find her and get her free.

But was that what had happened?

Had someone broken in? Egan certainly hadn't heard anyone, and the security alarm hadn't gone off. Still, he knew that no security system was foolproof.

Keeping his gun drawn, he eased out of the bathroom and checked her bedroom. He tried to hurry. And he tried not to panic. That wouldn't do Caroline any good. But with each place he searched—under her bed, in the closet, in the sitting room—he had the sickening feeling that she was in grave danger.

Egan turned on the lamp in the sitting room to get a better look. She wasn't there. In case it was a clue of some kind, he checked the object he'd picked up from the bathroom floor.

He stared at it, a little blob of plastic painted gold. It took a moment to figure out exactly what it was.

"A golden Lab," he whispered. And he shook his head, not believing what he was seeing.

It'd been over twenty years since his pet had been stolen. Kidnapped. Locked in a storage shed.

By Carlson Woodward.

The impact of that slammed into Egan like a heavy-weight's fist.

Hell.

Carlson had somehow broken in. He had Caroline. And he'd left the toy as a sick clue so that Egan would know his childhood nemesis was responsible. But responsible for what? Did Carlson intend to hurt Caroline?

Or worse—was Carlson the killer?

Egan whipped out his phone and called Hayes. "I need Brody and you here, *now*. I think Carlson kidnapped Caroline." He didn't wait for Hayes to respond. He shoved his phone back into his pocket and checked the closet of the sitting room in her bedroom suite. She wasn't there, either.

"Caroline!" he shouted.

Still nothing.

She had to be alive. She just had to be. Carlson wouldn't just kill her. No. He enjoyed the game too much for that. Was that what this was? A sick game?

Some movement caught his eye, and he spun in that direction. But it wasn't Caroline. It was the curtains on the window at the rear of the house. He bracketed his right wrist with his left hand and inched toward it.

The breeze didn't help. It stirred the white curtains, making them look like ghosts reaching out for him. Egan held his breath, and with each step, he listened and prayed.

He caught hold of the curtains. Snapped them back. And looked out into the backyard. The window screen had been removed and was lying on the ground.

Carlson had no doubt taken her out this way.

Egan heard the sound then. Well, *sounds* actually. Someone opened the garage door and started a car engine. He turned and raced toward the sound. Toward the garage.

But it was already too late.

Egan threw open the door, smelled the gas fumes and caught just a glimpse of Caroline's red Mustang as it sped away.

Cursing, and with his heart in his throat, Egan ran toward his Jeep, which he'd parked just off the side of the garage, extracting his keys as he ran. He rammed the key into the ignition. Turned it.

And nothing.

Damn! Carlson had obviously tampered with the engine. Egan didn't have time to figure out what was wrong. He had to go after Caroline. But how? He'd be useless on foot, and he couldn't wait for Hayes to arrive. That would mean precious moments lost.

He glanced around the garage, and he remembered the vintage Harley that Caroline had hidden away in the storage room. Egan raced toward it as if his life depended on it.

Because it did.

If he didn't get to Caroline in time, Carlson would kill her. And Egan would be dead inside if he wasn't able to save her.

"WHERE ARE YOU TAKING ME?" Caroline asked. She tried to make it sound like a demand, but even she could hear the fear in her voice.

Carlson had gone insane.

Thanks to the Cantara Hills streetlights, she could see his face. The muscles were tight. He was covered in oily sweat. His breathing was way too fast. And his eyes were wild and unfocused. Caroline didn't know if his present state was drug-induced or if this was a side of him that he'd kept hidden away, only allowing it to break free so he could kidnap her at gunpoint.

Driving too fast and steering with one shaky hand, Carlson made a sharp turn, not out of the neighborhood but toward the part of it that had yet to be developed. Caroline hiked there sometimes, and it was rugged, with dense trees and shrubs littered with limestone bluffs. Some low. And some, like the one they were approaching, high. This one was at least thirty feet up and rimmed the narrow two-lane road for several miles.

Carlson kept the gun gripped in his right hand, and it was pointed right at her heart. She could try to knock the gun away, but it would be a huge risk, especially at the speed he was going. If he didn't shoot her, there would certainly be an accident, and neither of them would survive if the car plunged off the limestone bluff.

Since he hadn't answered any of her questions so far, Caroline took a different approach. She had to get him talking so that she could maybe distract him. "How did you get past the security system at my house?"

"I followed your parents." His voice was soft, which was more unsettling than a shout would have been. That voice was also an alarming contrast to the rest of his appearance and body language. "Put on your seat belt," he insisted. "I don't want you trying to jump from the car."

Of course not. Caroline stretched the belt across her lap and shoulder, but she didn't fasten it.

"I need to hear the click, Caroline," he demanded. "Do it. Because I don't want to have to shoot you in the car."

But he would.

His tone made that very clear.

Caroline fastened the seat belt and prayed she'd get an opportunity to escape.

"When you turned off your security system to let your parents in your house, that's when I broke the latch on your sitting room window," he calmly explained. "All of you were talking so loud, you didn't even hear me. Then I climbed in and hid. I figured you'd eventually come back there to that part of the house."

Oh, mercy. That meant Carlson had been inside for an hour or more. Lurking. Waiting. It made her skin crawl.

And unfortunately, his plan had worked.

He'd waited, and now he had her. But why? Did he really intend to kill her?

"Where are you taking me?" she repeated.

"We're going to play a game." His voice was even softer now. Practically a whisper. "With Egan."

That chilled her to the bone, and Caroline glanced behind them to see if Egan was there. He wasn't.

But he soon would be.

Somehow, someway, Egan would find her. Carlson knew that as well, and he was probably going to set some kind of a trap so he could kill them both or make Egan watch while he killed her.

"This doesn't have anything to do with the murders?" She wanted to know.

"Why would it? Caroline, this is between me and you. Oh, and of course, Egan."

Of course. She'd known that Carlson disliked both Egan and her, but she'd obviously underestimated just how far he'd go. "If you want revenge for getting fired, then leave Egan out of this."

He smiled. "What, and have him miss all the fun? He's missed too much fun in his life."

Anger began to replace her fear. This sick SOB actually planned to use her and his being fired from his job to get back at Egan. "This isn't fun, and it wasn't fun when you kidnapped Egan's golden Lab puppy twenty years ago. It's sick, Carlson. *You're* sick. You need help."

He took his eyes off the road and glared at her. Not an ordinary glare. She saw nothing but savageness in those feral eyes.

With his jaw muscles working as if they'd declared war on each other, he stomped on the accelerator, right before he made the final turn that would lead them to the peak of the bluff. Because she was watching him so closely, she saw the surprised look. For just a split second.

Before he grabbed the steering wheel with both hands.

Caroline knew this was her chance. Maybe her only chance. She had to escape.

She reached for the handle of the door, but reaching for it was as far as she got. The car went into a sharp skid. Carlson grappled with the steering wheel and slammed on the brakes. It didn't help.

The Mustang plowed right into a tree.

Air bags burst out from the dash, and hers slammed into her face. Her father had insisted that she add the bags after she had bought the vintage vehicle. Good thing, too. Because it only took Caroline a few seconds to realize the air bag had probably saved her life.

It'd saved Carlson's life, too.

He cursed, and she followed his gaze to the rearview mirror. Caroline heard the sound, too. A motorcycle. Her Harley. She glanced back and spotted Egan riding straight up the hill toward them.

"Let's go," Carlson ordered.

He got her out of the seat belt, and with a death grip on her arm, he practically dragged her from the car. If he had even minor injuries, he didn't show it. Carlson maneuvered her into the thick trees that lipped the bluff, and he started running with her in tow.

Caroline stumbled. Partly from the flip-flops she was wearing and partly because she wanted to slow him down. It didn't work. Carlson simply wrenched her arm until she was back in a standing position, and they ran again.

Behind them, she heard Egan kill the engine on the Harley. She also heard his running footsteps. He was coming after her.

Carlson obviously realized that, too.

Because he stopped and dragged her in front of him, putting her between Egan and him.

Caroline got just a glimpse of Egan.

As Carlson fired a shot at him.

Chapter Seventeen

Egan dove behind a scraggly mesquite oak.

Barely in time.

The bullet from Carlson's gun flew past him and slammed into a limestone outcropping to his right. Too close. The mesquite wouldn't be much protection if Carlson continued to fire at him. Besides, he couldn't stay put and try to keep himself out of harm's way.

He had to get to Caroline.

With a firm grip on his service pistol, Egan glanced out to assess the situation. He didn't like what he saw. Carlson had his arm curved around Caroline's throat, and he had the gun pointed at her head. There was no way he could get off a safe shot to take Carlson out because the man was literally using Caroline as a human shield.

That in itself was enough to make Egan's pulse pound out of control, but the gun and Carlson weren't the only danger. Nature wasn't on their side, either. Carlson was standing in the moonlight just a few feet from the edge of a jagged limestone bluff. Egan knew from experience that the limestone was often unstable and could give way. If that happened…

Well, he refused to think beyond that.

His only goal was to save Caroline.

Egan peered out and met her gaze. For only a second. It was all he could handle, or it would distract him at a time when he needed no more distractions. But he couldn't completely dismiss that look he saw on Caroline's face. Not fear. Not even a hint of it. And that cut him to the bone. Because he knew it cost more to hide the fear than to show it.

"You aren't doing yourself any favors," Egan told Carlson. "Surrender your weapon, and you won't be hurt. You've got my word on that." He kept his voice calm, void of any emotion. Like the look on Caroline's face, it was a well-concealed lie. Beneath the badge and the gun, there was a storm of emotions. He didn't intend to let Caroline die.

"Surrender my weapon?" Carlson repeated. He gave a hollow laugh and backed up a step, moving himself closer to that lethal edge of the bluff.

"Carlson, you're going to fall. Look behind you. The fall will kill you. You really want to die at the bottom at that bluff?"

Carlson didn't take the bait. He didn't look away and divert his attention from Caroline. "Death is death," he concluded. "We all have to go sometime."

Egan cursed. "What the hell happened to you to make you do this?"

He expected Carlson to launch into a tirade about how getting fired had humiliated him, about how all that garbage during their childhoods had affected him. But Carlson only shook his head and looked at the gun he held as if seeing it for the first time.

"Are you wasted on something?" Egan asked. If so, that made this situation even more dangerous. It was hard to bargain with someone whose mind was in a drug-hazed cloud. Strange, though, Egan had heard no rumors or reports that Carlson was a user.

Carlson didn't respond to Egan's question, but his expression changed. The cockiness evaporated, and he kept shaking his head as if trying to clear it. What he didn't do was let go of Caroline.

And he kept the gun pointed right at her.

Egan eased out several inches from the tree so he'd be in a better position to get off a shot. If the opportunity arose. If it didn't, then he'd have to create one.

"Don't come any closer," Carlson warned.

He moved.

Not backward, thank God. But to the side. Toward a dense cluster of cedars and underbrush. Beyond that was a wooded area and perhaps even an escape route. Egan wasn't familiar with the area, but he knew there were old ranching trails and dirt roads that snaked around the property.

Hopefully, Carlson didn't have another vehicle stashed out there somewhere.

Caroline's expression didn't change, but she no doubt knew what this scum was capable of doing. Her life wouldn't be worth a dime if he somehow managed to get away from Egan. Carlson would just take her to a secondary crime scene.

"Tell me what it'll take to get you to release her," Egan bargained. "You've got to give me something to bargain with here." He hoped it would stop Carlson from moving.

It didn't.

Carlson just kept inching toward those cedars that would conceal him. "Nothing will make me release her."

"He's playing the kidnapping game," Caroline said. "He didn't hurt the puppy twenty years ago. I don't think he'll hurt me, either."

Carlson stopped and made direct eye contact with Egan. "I made a mistake that day. I should have hurt that damn dog and set you up to take the blame. They would have sent you somewhere. Maybe juvenile hall so I wouldn't have to live on the same street with you."

It sickened Egan to hear Carlson speak so casually about doing harm to an animal. And it made him think of something he should have already asked. He wanted a confession. "Did you hire Montoya to kill Kimberly McQuade and the others?"

The corner of Carlson's mouth lifted into an uneasy smile. "No."

Egan didn't believe him, even if Carlson seemed adamant about it. "Then if you're not a killer, why start now?"

"Because Caroline deserves to die. And you deserve to watch her die." Carlson tightened his arm around her throat, and he shoved the gun even harder against her temple.

Caroline dug in her heels when he tried to drag her closer to those cedars. "Okay. I'm not saying this because I think I'm going to die. I won't. But just in case, I want you to know this isn't your fault. And I have no regrets about what happened between us."

It was pure bravado. Egan could hear the fear in her voice. She was trying to say goodbye.

And Egan wasn't going to let her.

"Carlson, I'll trade places with Caroline," Egan insisted. "It's me you really want to kill anyway."

He blinked away the sweat that was sliding down his face. "Oh, I want both of you dead. I just want her to be first so you have to watch."

Carlson stood there. Staring at Egan. His hands were shaking now. And he dragged his tongue over his bottom lip. For just a moment, Egan thought Carlson might change his mind. He prayed that whatever drug was clouding his mind the effects were dissipating and Carlson was coming to his senses.

Egan inched out from the tree. He kept his gun aimed. Just in case he could get a clean shot. But that wasn't his first course of action. He wanted to talk Carlson into surrendering his weapon. And Caroline.

"Let's talk," Egan calmly suggested. He got to his feet. Stood. And stared Carlson down.

Carlson's mouth opened slightly. As if he were about to say something. But he didn't utter a word. Neither did Egan. Before he could say a thing, Carlson shifted his gun. Away from Caroline.

Carlson fired.

And the pain exploded through Egan as the bullet hit him.

CAROLINE HEARD HERSELF scream.

But the sound was muffled by the deafening blast of the shot.

Everything slowed to a crawl and felt thick and syrupy. Maybe because her mind couldn't absorb the sheer horror of what she was witnessing.

Egan had been shot.

Caroline's breath vanished. Her heart kicked against

her chest. In front of her, Egan dove back to the cover of the tree. But it was too late.

The blood. God, the blood. She'd seen it spattered across the front of his shirt.

"Egan!" she called out.

Caroline fought to get loose from Carlson so she could go to him. Egan needed help. But Carlson held on to her, even tightening his grip, and he growled some kind of warning in her ear. She didn't care about warnings or what this SOB might do to her.

She had to get to Egan.

"Keep fighting me, and I'll finish him off right now," Carlson added.

Caroline clearly heard that. The words made it into her adrenaline-spiked, fight-mode brain. And because Carlson would carry through on that threat, she stopped struggling. For a moment, anyway, so that she could figure out what to do.

Begging was the easiest option. "Please, Carlson, let me help him."

Carlson didn't react to her plea. He started to move again, dragging her in the direction of the dense cedars.

Caroline tried to hold her ground, but her shoes didn't cooperate. The jeweled flip-flops obviously weren't meant to navigate rugged terrain, and she couldn't keep her footing. She practically fell face-first into the cover of those trees and shrubs.

She looked back, trying to get a glimpse of Egan. He was still there, behind the mesquite. And he was moving. Well, he was glancing at them. But she couldn't tell if he was alert or if he was losing consciousness. He was certainly losing blood, and he needed an ambulance.

And Carlson was responsible for this.

Along with the adrenaline, Caroline felt the anger ripple through her. The enraged emotion took over, and she ignored Carlson's warnings, drew back her elbow and jammed him hard in his belly.

Carlson staggered back. Just a step. Not enough to get him to release the grip he had on her, though.

"Try that again, and you die." He called her a name. Not a flattering one, either, and gave her another shove.

Caroline didn't give up. She couldn't. Egan's life was at stake. This time, she went for the gun. She turned, using her body to ram into him, and in the same motion, she tried to grab the gun. She wasn't quite successful, but she did manage to latch on to his right wrist. She dug her nails into his skin, drawing blood.

"Caroline, don't!" Egan shouted.

From the corner of her eye, she saw Egan come out from the cover of the tree. Carlson obviously saw him, too, because even though she still had a grip on his wrist, he managed to turn the gun in Egan's direction.

Carlson's sheer strength stunned her. He threw off her grip as if she were a gnat, and he fired another shot.

At Egan.

Egan dropped to the ground again, and the bullet kicked up some dirt and rocks just behind him. He took aim at Carlson, but he didn't shoot. Because of her. Carlson moved behind her again, preventing Egan from returning fire.

"How badly are you hurt?" she called out to Egan.

"I'll live," was his answer. But he sounded weak, and in that brief glimpse of him, she'd seen the blood that now covered the right shoulder and sleeve of his shirt.

It felt as if someone had clamped a fist around her heart.

She'd known Egan was important to her. She'd known she cared about him. But she hadn't known how much.

Until that moment.

Caroline blinked back the tears that tried to form in her eyes. It wasn't exactly an ideal moment to realize that she was in love with him.

Carlson hooked his forearm around her neck and got her moving again—toward those cedars. She couldn't go there. It would give Carlson the perfect cover to dodge any gunfire from Egan. And it would give Carlson the perfect place to kill her. Then he would lie in wait so he could ambush Egan when he came after her.

Caroline had no doubts whatsoever about that. Which meant she had nothing to lose. She had to get away now if she stood any chance of getting Egan help in time.

She dropped down, using her weight to propel herself toward the ground. Egan reacted. He came out from the tree and took aim.

Carlson's grip slipped from her neck.

That was her opportunity. And she took it. Caroline started to run.

She'd made it only a few steps before Carlson fired his gun.

EGAN IGNORED THE PAIN that speared through his arm and shoulder, and he got to his feet. He didn't have time to take aim at Carlson before the man tackled Caroline. He could only watch as the two plummeted to the ground, and Carlson scrambled into the cedars with her.

Carlson had her—again.

Caroline hadn't been able to escape.

Hell. It'd taken ten years off his life when he'd seen

Carlson fire that shot at her. But she hadn't been hit. Thank God. Egan was sure of that. The bullet had landed against a limestone boulder. He'd seen the spray of pellets and dust. Close. But not close enough.

They'd gotten lucky.

That luck might not continue.

"Caroline?" Egan yelled.

"Stay back, Egan," Carlson warned. His voice was frantic now, and he sounded out of breath from the exertion of the struggle with Caroline.

"Is Caroline all right?" Egan had to know. It was a battle just to stand there, but if he went charging into the cedars, Carlson would likely shoot her first.

"For now," Carlson answered.

Good. That was a start. "Carlson, this has to end. You have to let her go."

"So you've said. But we haven't played the game yet."

Egan groaned and clamped his left hand over his shoulder when he felt the flow of blood increase. "There's no game to play," Egan shouted. "Just release her."

Carlson didn't say anything for several seconds. "You won't win this time, Egan. I swear. You won't win."

The words chilled him to the bone.

Egan stood there. Listening. Praying. It was hard to hear anything with his heartbeat drumming in his ears, but he was sure he didn't hear the sirens or Hayes. With his attention and his weapon aimed on those cedars, he took out his phone.

Hayes answered on the first ring. "Where the hell are you, Egan?"

"Cantara Hills. Top of the bluff. You'll see Caroline's wrecked Mustang." Egan had to force himself to steady his breathing. And hell, he was getting dizzy. "Carlson took her hostage, and he shot me."

Hayes cursed. "How bad?"

"It hurts worse than it is." Egan hoped.

"I'm on the way, and I'll call an ambulance."

Good. Because he would need one. He hoped he'd be the only one who did. Egan ended the call and put away his phone so he'd have both hands to continue this battle.

"Caroline?" Egan shouted.

She didn't answer.

But he did hear something.

Something that put Egan's stomach in a hard knot. The sound of footsteps. Hurried ones.

Carlson was on the move with her. That was good news. In a way. It meant he hadn't tried to kill her. Instead, he'd likely continued what he considered to be a game. Some game. Caroline and he were fighting for their lives.

Egan couldn't stay put, and he couldn't wait for help from Hayes. It might be too late. He left the meager cover of the tree and raced in the direction of those footsteps. With his hand still pressed over his wound, he made his way through the cedars.

They weren't there.

But there were signs of a struggle. Snapped tree branches and swirls of shoe prints on the moonlit ground. A red fake gem from Caroline's shoes sparkled amid the crushed limestone.

There was a small clearing ahead of him, and just beyond that, more trees. He paused to get his bearings and to figure out the best way to approach the area.

Then a shot tore through the hill country.

A single bullet. Followed by no sounds. No screams. No shouts for help. *Hell.* Caroline might be hurt. Or worse.

Egan didn't stop, although he knew in the back of his mind that Carlson could be waiting in those trees to ambush him. He tore through the clearing, ignoring the pain and the dizziness. He had to get to her.

He raced into the trees, bashing aside the low-hanging branches. Egan had to hurdle over a large fallen oak, and he cursed when the landing caused pain to stab through him. Still, he didn't slow down. He headed straight for the moonlight that was threading its way through the trees.

And he came out the other side.

Still no sign of Caroline. No sign of blood, either.

Egan barreled over a six-foot-high uneven limestone outcropping.

And practically skidded to a stop.

Dead center in front of him was Caroline and Carlson. He still had her in a death grip. Arm around her throat. A gun to her head.

She was alive.

And other than some scrapes to her knees, she appeared to be unharmed.

Egan was more than thankful for that but not for what else he saw. There was another limestone bluff. Higher than the first one he'd encounter.

That was where Carlson had Caroline.

On the edge of it.

The heels of Carlson's shoes weren't even on the ground. With the grip he had on Caroline, if Carlson fell, then she would, too.

"Carlson, you don't want to do this," Egan bargained. But he apparently did want to do this. Carlson's expression was flat now, and his skin had turned pale. Whatever drug he was on, it was playing havoc with his body and his mind. The man was obviously insane.

"I'm tired of this game," Carlson mumbled. He shook his head and took aim at Egan. "It's time for it to end."

Egan walked a step closer. "It doesn't have to be this way." Maybe he could keep Carlson talking until Hayes arrived.

Caroline's gaze met Egan's. Carlson might be ready to end this, but she wasn't. There was resolve in her eyes. And concern. She kept glancing at his blood-soaked shirt.

"I'm okay," he lied to her.

"No, you're not." She angled her eyes back at Carlson. "Please let me call for an ambulance. For both of you. You need help, too."

"She's right," Egan added. "Whatever drug you took has messed with your mind."

"I didn't take a drug." And Carlson was resolute about it. For a second or two, anyway. Then he shook his head again. "Did I? I don't remember taking anything."

"That's why you need to put down the gun and come away from the bluff. The drug will wear off, and you'll know then that you made the right decision."

Carlson seemed to think about that. He stared at Egan. Glanced at Caroline. Before looking at his gun. It finally seemed to be registering that what he was doing was stupid and reckless.

His attention landed on Egan again. Specifically, at the fast-spreading blood pool on his shirt. Hopefully, Carlson wouldn't notice that Egan was having trouble seeing. The dizziness was making everything flash in and out of focus.

"If I put down my gun," Carlson said, "I'll go to jail

for attempted murder of a Texas Ranger. If you don't kill me first, that is."

Carlson put the gun back to Caroline's head. And the corner of his mouth lifted into a smile. "I might as well win part of this game. I can take her away from you, Egan. I can make you have to live with seeing her die."

The anger went bone-deep inside Egan, and he went a step closer.

Carlson leaned back. Nearly tipping himself off-balance. And he laughed. It was as sick as that stupid grin on his face.

"Say goodbye to him, Caroline," Carlson insisted.

Her bottom lip quivered a little before she hiked up her chin. "I love you."

Egan couldn't have possibly been more stunned if she'd shot him. He didn't question it, nor did he take the time to consider if it was the adrenaline talking. He made his decision about what to do and then said a quick prayer that Caroline would do what was necessary to survive.

Egan lifted his gun. Aimed it.

At Carlson.

Maybe the dizziness would wait until he finished this.

"No!" Caroline yelled. Her voice echoed through the canyon below. It echoed in his head.

"Move!" Egan shouted to her.

Carlson reacted. He whipped the gun from her so he could aim it at Egan. Caroline did exactly what Egan wanted her to do. In the chaos of the moment and the re-shifting, she slung both arms at Carlson's body. Her elbows battered him. Then, she dropped to the ground.

Carlson fired.

Egan didn't even take the time to feel if he'd been hit again. He did what he was trained to do. He took aim.

And fired.

Two shots. A double tap of gunfire. Shots meant to kill. The gun blasts ripped through the air, drowning out everything else.

The bullets went where Egan had intended them to go. Straight into Carlson's heart.

Carlson went stiff, his hands dropping to his sides. His gun clattered to the ground. There was almost no life left him, but he met Egan eye-to-eye. For just a split-second, Egan saw the shock. The realization of what had just happened.

Maybe even the regret.

Egan watched as Carlson's eyelids closed, and he dropped backward over the ledge. Seconds later, he heard the thud. Saw Caroline scrambling to get to him. But the dizziness took over. And Egan felt himself fall to the ground.

The last thing he heard was Caroline screaming his name.

Chapter Eighteen

Egan struggled to open his eyes. The fight was still with him, and the images of Carlson ripped through his head. He automatically reached for his gun.

Which wasn't there.

But the pain was.

Cursing, he forced himself to focus and realized he wasn't in the woods near Cantara Hills. He was in the hospital with an IV in the back of his right hand and with his left shoulder and arm bandaged. Machines beeped around him.

"Carlson shot me," he mumbled. "I shot him."

"Yes," he heard someone say. He knew that voice. It was Caroline. "But you're alive, and you're going to make a full recovery. The bullet went clean through and didn't do nearly as much damage as it could have."

Wincing as he moved his shoulder, Egan turned slightly and spotted her. Not that he had to look far. Caroline was there, right next to his bed. Behind her, looming over her, stood Brody and Hayes. Both were staring down at him and had plenty of concern on their somber faces.

Caroline looked concerned, too.

And she had blood on her top.

Adrenaline shot through him. *Hell*. She'd been hurt. Carlson had hurt her. Egan tried to get up so he could make sure she was okay.

Caroline stopped him. She gently but firmly put her hand on his uninjured shoulder and eased him back onto the bed. She followed his gaze and shook her head. "No. I wasn't injured. This is your blood."

His blood. Egan had to give that some thought, but yes, that made sense. "Right," he mumbled.

"You left a lot of your blood in the woods, in the ambulance and on Caroline," Hayes informed him. "It could have been more if Caroline hadn't put pressure on the gunshot wound. I don't guess it occurred to you to wait until I got there before you went after Carlson?"

Egan ignored the mandatory scolding, and his gaze connected with Brody's. He got no such scolding from him, because Brody likely understood why Egan had done what he did. If Brody's fiancé, Victoria, had been Carlson's hostage, Brody wouldn't have waited for backup, either.

"Carlson is dead," Brody explained.

Yeah. Egan knew that. No one could have survived that fall from the bluff. "Make sure the coroner does a tox screen. Carlson was high on something."

Brody nodded. "Caroline told us." He paused. "She also told us that Carlson said he was playing some kidnapping game."

Egan remembered that as well, and it made him sick to his stomach. "We'll have to connect Carlson to Vincent Montoya," Egan said, thinking out loud. "Carlson probably paid him, or blackmailed him, to go after Kimberly the night of the hit-and-run."

Which meant Carlson had tried to kill Caroline that night, too. But why? Maybe because Carlson thought when Caroline's memory fully returned that she would be able to link him to Montoya and the hit-and-run? Maybe this was Carlson's way of tying up potential loose ends that could send him to prison and even get him the death penalty.

Was that it?

But Carlson had also tried to kill Egan. Of course, there was bad blood between them. Carlson hated him, and he probably didn't mind adding Egan to his kill-list so that he could stop him from learning the truth and get some revenge for all the petty things that'd happened between them as kids. Carlson had probably spent a long time stewing over that bad blood, and along with the help of some kind of drug, he'd finally got the *courage* to do something.

Thank God he hadn't succeeded.

"*We'll* connect Carlson to Montoya," Hayes insisted. He was adamant about it, too. "As in Brody and I will do that. You're looking at a minimum of two days here in San Antonio General and at least two weeks of time off after that. Those are orders from the captain."

Egan was already shaking his head before Hayes finished. "The case—"

"Will be taken care of," Brody finished. "Hayes and I will finish off things."

Egan looked at Caroline to back him up, but she only folded her arms over her chest and gave him a flat stare. "I watched you nearly die, and I'm wearing a pint of your blood. If you think I'm going to give you my blessing to go straight back to work, then you're wrong."

And then she did something else that surprised him.

Caroline leaned over and kissed him.

Not a peck, either. A real kiss. Slow. Deep. Long. Under different circumstances, he would have thought it was foreplay, but when she pulled back, he saw the tears in her eyes.

She quickly blinked them away. "Seeing you shot scared me." Simply explained, but he could see the intensity of her feelings. This had shaken her to the core.

Egan understood that. Seeing Carlson's gun at her head had shaken him, too.

"You owe me," Caroline added.

He wasn't in so much pain that he couldn't feel a little outraged, and confused, by that. "Excuse me?"

"Because you scared me so much, you owe me your cooperation. You're going to take that time off, and you're going to get well."

He didn't argue, mainly because her tears started to return. And with Carlson out of the picture, time off didn't sound so bad.

Brody cleared his throat. "We'll be going. Caroline's right—heal. Get better. And don't worry about the case. There are just a few loose ends that need to be tied up. That's all."

Yes. A killer was dead. And Caroline was no longer in danger. All in all, that was worth the bullet hole he had in his shoulder.

Brody nodded a goodbye. Hayes punched him on his good shoulder. "I'm leaving Caroline some rope in case she has to tie you up," Hayes joked.

Caroline waited until they'd left before she winked at Egan. "You think you'd like being tied up?" She smiled, and it was dazzling despite the fatigue and worry he could see in her eyes.

"Tied up by you?" Egan caught her arm and eased her down beside him. "How could I say no to a woman with a Harley, a rope and some apparently really raunchy ideas?"

He pulled her closer and kissed her this time. The taste of her went right through him, and he could have sworn that it lessened the pain.

She pulled back, licked the taste of him from her lips. "Your father called a couple of minutes before you woke up."

Egan had to repeat it to himself to make sure he'd heard her correctly. "My father?"

"Yes, he sounded worried."

Egan was about to dismiss it. But he didn't. Maybe that phone call in the pantry had really been the start of some fence mending. Egan wasn't sure that was possible, but after being given a second chance at life, he wasn't about to close any doors just yet.

"I asked Hayes, and he said you have a great little house in Austin. Maybe I could stay there with you while you're recovering?" Caroline asked.

He thought of his house and suddenly didn't feel so warm and fuzzy. And he rethought that door closing part. "It's a fixer-upper."

"Sounds perfect."

He shook his head. "It's not exactly your style."

"Sounds perfect," she repeated. The smile returned. "You've got to revise this notion you have of me, Egan, that I have to live in luxury. I own a Harley, remember? It's my prize possession, not that Victorian house my parents bought me."

Yes. He was beginning to see that. Cool and expensive on the outside. But inside, Caroline Stallings was, well, hot. And she was his kind of woman.

Now, the question was—what was he going to do about it?

He could keep things status quo. Give them time to build a relationship and be absolutely certain that they were right for each other. It was what he would usually do when faced with a complex decision.

Approach with caution.

Stay guarded.

Then walk away before things could develop into something deeper.

But the idea of walking away from Caroline actually made his heart ache.

And what he felt for her was already something deeper.

"Uh-oh," she mumbled. "You're thinking about breaking up with me."

"No." He said it quickly to get it out of the way. Breaking up was the last thing he wanted to do with her.

Smiling, she moved closer, until her mouth was hovering over his. "Well, you can't do *that* with me right now. But after you've recovered…" She let her words linger between them, and it fueled a fantasy or two.

He whispered one of those fantasies to her. It involved her naked and on her Harley. Actually, on his lap while on the Harley.

She moved her mouth against his ear. "You're a wild child, Egan Caldwell." She kissed his earlobe. Laughed. "I love that about you."

Then she stiffened and got that deer-caught-in-the-headlights look. Probably because she thought that would be his sign to start building a wall between them. The leave 'em time.

But Egan had something else in mind.

It was a risk. A Texas-sized one. Still, it was time he took a risk like that.

He held her chin and forced eye contact, something she was suddenly avoiding. "What would your parents say if I were to ask you to marry me?"

She blinked. Then, stared at him. "W-hat?"

His heart started to pound, and he wondered if that Texas-sized risk was about to be a Texas-sized mistake. "What if I asked you to marry me?" he paraphrased. "What would your parents say?"

And he held his breath.

Caroline seemed to have a little trouble breathing as well. "They wouldn't like it. Well, not at first, but I think after they got to know you, they would warm up to the idea. Why?" She swallowed hard. "Was that a proposal?"

He skimmed his thumb over her bottom lip. "You're my type, you know that?"

"Really? You're my type, too," she said quickly. "Now, back to the other thing. Was that an honest-to-goodness marriage proposal?"

Egan tried to look self-assured and was certain he failed. "What if it was, hypothetically speaking?"

She eyed him with skepticism. "Hypothetically speaking—then I'd have to say that I'd marry you in a heartbeat."

"A heartbeat?" *Okay.* That sounded good. To him. But he had to wonder. "You could have anyone you want."

"Good." Her voice was hardly more than a whisper, but she cleared her throat to give it some sound. "Because I want you." She paused and fondled her locket. "Does that mean I can have you?"

Did it? Egan thought he'd better clarify things first. "Life with me wouldn't be easy. I'm the surly one, remember?"

She didn't disagree. "Okay."

"And I work long hours."

Caroline pressed her fingers over his mouth. Frowned. "Are you trying to talk me out of my hypothetical yes that I'd marry you in a heartbeat?"

He eased her fingers away after he kissed them. "I'm just trying to make you understand that I'm no prize."

A sigh left her mouth, and before he could guess what was coming, she kissed him, Caroline-style. "I." She kissed him again. "Love." Another kiss. "You."

That was the answer he was looking for, but it still took him several moments to let it sink in. It sank in very well. "So, the question is no longer hypothetical. Caroline Stallings, will you marry me?"

"In less than a heartbeat." She smiled against his mouth. He could almost taste that smile, and he could feel her happiness.

Well, for a couple of seconds, anyway.

She pulled back slightly so they were eye-to-eye. "Why do you want to marry me?"

Oh, man. There it was. The question he'd tiptoed around for the past five minutes. And his entire life.

"I know it's not for my money," she said when he didn't answer. "Or my house." She lifted her shoulder and gave him a teasing look that he was becoming familiar with.

She was going to give him an out.

She wasn't going to make him say it.

"But it could be because we have great sex," she continued. She snapped her fingers. "I got it. You want to marry me because of my 1951 Panhead Harley Chopper."

"No." He could do this. He wasn't a wimp. But facing down bad guys seemed easy compared to this.

He took a dose of courage by sliding his hand around the back of her neck and hauling her to him so he could kiss her. He didn't stop until they both had to gasp for air.

"I'm not marrying you for the money, the house or the Harley," he let her know. Clarifying that was important.

And it was something he'd waited his life to say.

"Caroline, I'm marrying you for one reason. Well, two, actually. I want to marry you because I want to spend the rest of my life with you."

Those beautiful eyes shimmered with tears, and they were definitely of the happy variety. "And the other reason?" Her voice was all breath and hope.

Egan was filled the same hope. "Because I love you."

He pulled her into arms and showed her just how much.

* * * * *

THE SILVER STAR OF TEXAS:
CANTARA HILLS INVESTIGATION
*comes to an explosive conclusion next month when
award-winning author Rita Herron presents*
Beneath the Badge
only from Mills & Boon® Intrigue.

DAREDEVIL'S RUN

BY
KATHLEEN CREIGHTON

Kathleen Creighton has roots deep in the California soil but has relocated to South Carolina. As a child, she enjoyed listening to old timers' tales, and her fascination with the past only deepened as she grew older. Today she says she is interested in everything – art, music, gardening, zoology, anthropology and history, but people are at the top of her list. She also has a lifelong passion for writing, and now combines her two loves in romance novels.

This book is for DAVE and TIM…
the two sweet, wonderful guys who have dedicated
themselves to making my daughters' lives happy
(a task requiring more than a small measure
of patience, empathy, and of course, love).
How on earth did my girls get so lucky?

A SPECIAL THANK YOU…
To Dawn, my firstborn (who calls to my mind
words from *The Sound of Music*: "Somewhere…
I must have done something good…") and to the
other wonderful people at Kern River Outfitters in
Wofford Heights, California – Dwight Pascoe, his
wife, Trudy, and whitewater photographer Bob Walker
– for making it possible for me to ride the river
without once getting my feet wet.

Prologue

Part 1

It started the way it always did, with the dream of waking up in the darkness, of being afraid, terrified. Heart racing, pounding, sweating and shaking, wanting to cry but knowing he was too big to cry. He didn't want to be a baby, did he?

He didn't cry, he *didn't*. But his chest and throat hurt as if he did.

Then the noise. Terrible noises—things crashing, breaking, thumps and bangs, voices yelling…screaming. A man's voice yelling. A woman's voice screaming.

There were other voices, too, small frightened voices—*not his!*—whimpering, "Mommy…"

And finally…finally the *other* voice, the one he'd

been waiting for, praying for, soft as a breath blowing warm past his ear. "Shh... It's okay...it's gonna be okay. I won't let him hurt you. Nobody's gonna hurt you. You're safe now. It's okay."

He felt safe then, and warm, and when the loudest noises came, he crouched down in the warm darkness and waited for the crashing and banging and screaming and yelling to stop and the lights to turn on, so bright they hurt his eyes. So bright he woke up.

"Wade—Wade—"

Mattie's voice. Mattie was standing beside his bed, poking him, shaking his arm.

"Wake up, Wade. Wake...up!"

"I am awake. Stop poking me." He glared up at his brother's face, just a dark blob in the darkness of their room, and scrubbed furiously at his eyes. "What's the matter? What did you wake me up for?"

"You were crying."

"Was not."

"Yes, you were. I heard you. Did you have a bad dream, Wade?"

"Maybe. So what?" He was the older brother, after all. "Big deal. It was only a dream. Go back to sleep, Mattie."

Mattie's shadow didn't move, just went on standing there beside Wade's bed. A small voice said, "I can't. I'm all awake now, too. Can I get in bed with you, Wade?"

Wade let out an exaggerated breath, but the truth was, he didn't mind. "Okay...but you better not kick me this time, or I'm pushin' you on the floor."

He scooted over and Matt lifted the edge of the

blankets and crawled in beside him. For a few minutes Wade lay still, listening to his brother's uneven breathing, feeling the warmth of his body drive away the last lingering chill of nightmare.

After a while, he heard a whisper.

"Was it the pounding dream, Wade?"

Wade's voice felt gravelly as he answered, "Yeah."

"And…did he come?"

"Did *who* come?"

"You know who. *The angel.* The boy angel."

After a pause, Wade said on a long breath, "Yeah…"

"I *knew* it," Mattie said, wriggling down into the pillow with a yawn. "He always comes when you need him…."

A moment later his breathing became a soft snore, and a moment after that, Wade, too, was asleep.

Part 2

Wade dialed the phone from his hospital bed. He closed his eyes as he counted the rings, but it didn't help to shut out the image of his brother the way he'd last seen him, making his way slowly and awkwardly through his apartment in his wheelchair.

The rings stopped after only two, surprising him. Always before when he'd called, it had taken at least six rings for Matt to get to the phone.

"Man," he said, "that was fast."

"Cell phone," his brother said. "Who's this?"

"It's me—Wade. How are you, buddy?"

"Hey…Wade. Wow—been a while."

"Yeah." He gritted his teeth against a double

whammy of pain waves, one from his leg, suspended in a sling and swathed in surgical dressings, the other in his heart. Pure guilt, that one. "Listen, about that—"

"Forget it, bro. It's cool. I understand. So…how you been? Bad guys keepin' you busy?"

Wade laughed—tried to do it without moving anything that might hurt. "Yeah, well…I guess I've been better. But hey—that's not why I called. I've got somebody here who wants to talk to you." He paused. "You sitting down?"

"Oh, yeah, funny. Very funny. So who is it? Hey, don't tell me. You got married?"

Wade looked at the woman standing beside his bed, reached for her hand and squeezed it tightly. "Not quite," he said in a voice gone raspy with emotions he knew better than to try and hide. "Not yet. Soon though. We want you to be there. And I promise you, man, you're gonna love her. No—this is…" He paused, looked up at the other faces bending over him, and muttered half to himself, "Jeez, I didn't think this was going to be so hard. Uh…Mattie? Remember those nightmares I used to have? I told you about 'em, remember? There was this voice—you said it was—"

"An angel. Sure, I remember. I was a kid—what can I say. So? What about it?"

Wade took a deep breath and grinned up at the man standing poised, his face a mask of suspense that didn't come close to hiding his emotions, either.

"Well, little brother…guess what? He's real. And here he is. In person." His voice broke, and he barely got the rest of it out as he handed the phone over to Cory. "Mattie, say hello to our Angel. The brother you didn't know you had."

Chapter 1

Alex Penny gave a start when the front door to the offices of Penny Tours, located in the tiny town of Wofford Heights, California, opened to admit a stranger. Almost nobody used the front door, since most people wanting to make reservations did so by telephone or online, and when they showed up in person, they would have been directed to the Rafting Center farther along and on the other side of the highway. Guides and drivers coming in from the equipment yard and warehouse used the back door.

Once in a great while, though, someone did wander in looking for information on available tours, or maybe directions to the Rafting Center, so she gave the visitor an automatic smile and was well into her customary speech. "Hi. If you're looking for the Rafting Center, it's about a block down on…" Then the man's face came into full focus.

Behind rimless glasses, the stranger's eyes were a dark and penetrating blue, but it was his smile that made her heart give a kick she wasn't prepared for.

"I think I'm in the right place. I'm looking for Alex. Are you…?"

"That would be me." She could hear her own voice, hear that it was even more hoarse than her normally froggy croak, and she cleared her throat as she clicked the save button and pushed back from the computer.

"We spoke on the phone. I'm—"

"Yeah, you'd be Matt's brother. Cory, right?" She was on her feet, hand extended, the expected words— she hoped—on her lips. But her mouth was on autopilot and her heart in overdrive, because her brain had temporarily disengaged, having gotten hung up, for the moment, on that smile.

Mattie's smile.

"Cory Pearson. I hope I haven't come at a bad time. You did say afternoons were usually best."

"No…no, this is, uh…fine. Can I get you anything? Water? Coke?"

"Water's fine. Thanks…"

Ridiculously glad to have a specific job to do, Alex darted into the kitchen alcove, opened the refrigerator and took out two bottles of water. She turned to find that the stranger—who was no stranger at all, it seemed— had followed her.

"Nice Lab," he remarked, gazing at the large slumbering form sprawled on the floor, taking up most of the space between the fridge and the small sink and counter.

"That's Annie." Alex stepped over the dog to hand one of the bottles to her visitor. The other she cracked open for herself. "She was Matt's, actually. She's pretty old, now. Mostly just sleeps. So—" she took a gulp and waved the bottle at the empty office "—you said you wanted to—"

Before she could finish it, the back door opened a crack and a voice called through it. "Hey, Alex, Booker T just called. The Las Colinas group's on its way in. I'm heading over to the center, unless you want—"

"I'm kinda busy right now, Eve."

The door opened wider, and Eve Francis, one of the river guides who sometimes doubled as office staff, stuck her head through the opening. Her blond hair was caught up in its usual style—messy ponytail with wisps flying around—and sticking to her face, which, since she'd been working all morning in the warehouse, was red-flushed and sweaty. And she still managed to look disgustingly gorgeous. Partly, Alex was sure, because of the smile that lit up her face when she saw they had a visitor.

"Oh—hey!" She turned the smile, full wattage, on Cory Pearson. "I didn't see you come in. Welcome to Penny Tours." The smile didn't dim as she switched it to Alex. "I'll take care of him, if you want to go. Those guys were kind of your babes, I know."

Cory looked a question at Alex and had his mouth open to spit it out, but she waved it aside before he could say the words. "No—no, it's okay. You can take it. This is something I need to, uh…" She paused to take a breath. "Eve, this is Matt's brother. Matt Callahan, my, uh…"

Eve's smile went out like a light. "Oh *yeah!* Matt—your old partner—right. So…well. Okay, I guess you…" She cocked her head to give Cory a long look, eyes glittering with curiosity and something Alex couldn't define, then shrugged. "Hey, I'm gone. See you later." Her head vanished and the door thunked closed.

"Look," Cory said, "if you need to go take care of something, I can wait."

Alex waved a hand at the chair she'd vacated and settled her own backside onto the edge of her desk. "No, it's just that…well, the kids from Las Colinas Academy are kind of a special bunch, is all. Teenagers. They're all mentally disabled."

As he took the relinquished chair, the visitor's eyes lit up with a new kind of interest, and Alex remembered what Matt's brother Wade had told her—that their long-lost and recently found older brother was a journalist. A reporter, and a fairly famous one at that. "You take disabled people down the river rapids?"

"Oh yeah, sure. We take all kinds—physical and mental disabilities both. These people come every year. Have a ball, too—you should see 'em. But hey, Eve can take care of things. She's a guide—also a friend. She won't mind."

She drank the last of the water in the bottle, then looked around for a place to put it. Finally she set it on the desk with great care, as if she'd never done such a thing before. After that there was no place else to put her eyes that wasn't Matt's brother Cory. And since he looked way too much like Matt, she went on staring at the bottle. The silence stretched.

Which they both broke at the same time.

"You said you wanted to—"

"I guess Wade told you I—"

Cory's face broke into Mattie's smile as he gestured for Alex to go first.

So she did, in a voice gone gruff and edgy again. "Yeah, so…Wade said you got separated from him and Matt when you were little, or something?"

"I did." Cory still smiled, though there was a deep sadness in his eyes now, and Alex remembered the way Matt used to smile like that, sometimes, in a way that made her heart ache. That last day… "How much did Matt tell you about his childhood?"

She shrugged and shifted the empty water bottle from one spot to another on her desktop. "Just that he was adopted—he and Wade—when they were little. He told me he had a happy childhood, though. Said his adoptive parents were great—older, but nice. Good people. I don't think he even remembers anything before that."

Cory nodded. "Wade didn't, either. Actually, I was hoping you could tell me—"

"So, what happened?" She broke in on the question, hoping to stall it. "How did you guys get separated?"

He smiled again, wryly, and his eyes told Alex he was onto her tactic and okay with it—for now. "Wasn't just us 'guys,' actually. We have two sisters, too. Twins. They were toddlers at the time." He hitched a shoulder apologetically. "Haven't had any luck finding them, yet."

Alex glared fiercely down at her hand and the empty bottle, daring the burn in her eyes and the ache in her throat to produce tears. She won that battle but didn't trust her voice, and finally just shook her head.

"Our father was a good man, before Vietnam changed him," Cory said softly into the silence. "I was born before he left, old enough to remember how he was then. I remember his gentleness, and the way he liked to tell me stories. Then he was gone. And he never came back. Some stranger came in his place. Wade and Matt were born after that, and then the twins. But Dad never told them stories. He'd drink instead. And he'd have flashbacks. At those times, Mom would lock us kids in the bedroom and tell me to look out for them—keep them safe. Then she'd try to talk Dad back from whatever hell he'd gone to. She took…a lot from him, to keep him from hurting us, or himself."

He drew a hand across his face, and the movement caught Alex's gaze like a magnet and held it fast so she couldn't look away even though she wanted to.

"Then…one night I guess she couldn't bring him back. He tried to break down the door to the bedroom where us kids were hiding. I don't know exactly what happened, but…anyway, that night he shot her, and then himself."

"God…" The whispered word slipped from her before she could stop it.

"We were taken away to some sort of shelter—a group home. I don't remember much about it. Then we were divided up among several foster homes. I kept running away from mine, trying to keep in touch with the others. I was considered a disruptive influence, I guess, because nobody would let me see them. Eventually, I landed in juvenile detention. While I was there, Wade and Matt and the twins got adopted by two different sets of parents. I got out when I was eighteen, of course, but nobody would tell me where they were. Nobody would tell me anything. Which was probably a good thing, I suppose, in retrospect. I was angry enough, I don't know what I'd have done if I'd been able to find the little ones. Kidnapped 'em maybe. Something stupid, I'm sure."

"So…how *did* you find them? I mean, after so long—that had to be, what, twenty-five years ago?"

"Well, it hasn't been easy. I have my own resources, but we didn't make any real headway until we hired a P.I. who specializes in this kind of thing—reuniting adoptees with biological parents. A man named Holt Kincaid. He's the one that made this happen. He found Wade first. Up in Portland. And Wade put us in touch—"

"With Matt." She folded her arms across her middle and frowned at him, concentrating on keeping all traces of emotion out of her voice. "So…have you seen him?" *How is he? How does he look? Does he still have the smile, now that he can't walk? Can't climb, can't do any of the things we both loved to do.*

"Matt, you mean? I've talked to him," Cory said. "On the phone, a couple of times. I'm on my way to meet him now. But I wanted to…" He shifted abruptly, leaned forward and propped his forearms on his knees, hands clasped between them, head bowed in what seemed almost an attitude of prayer. After a moment he cleared his throat and looked up at her. "I wanted to talk to you first," he said carefully. "I need to know what I'm in for."

Alex pushed away from the desk, scooped up the water bottle and went to drop it into the recycling bin that stood beside the door to the warehouse. "What can I tell you?" she said without turning. "I haven't seen him since he left rehab."

"I mean, about the accident. You were with him when it happened."

She shrugged. "We were rock climbing, he fell, broke his back, now he's paralyzed. That's about it."

"Come on." The smile in his voice made it a gentle rebuke. "That much I got from Wade."

She spun back to him, firing questions in a breathless rush, again hoping maybe with the sheer volume of them she might hold him off a little longer. "How is Wade, by the way? I didn't even ask you—he told me he got *shot?* What's up with that? And he said he's getting *married?* Man, that's just… I didn't think Wade would ever settle down. I don't think cops do too well with relationships. So I'm really surprised. What's she like? Have you met her?"

"I have," Cory said, while his eyes regarded her steadily from behind the rimless lenses in a way that made her feel he could see inside her head. And knew how desperately she was trying to avoid this—talking about Matt. *Thinking about Matt.* "Tierney's…something special." He paused, then added with a secret little smile, "I think she and Wade will do well together."

"What about you?" She tilted her head back, still

smiling at him, though his steady eyes told her it wasn't fooling him one bit. "Are you married?"

And she watched his face light up in a way that altered his whole being. It reminded her of watching a film of a land blooming from winter into spring in fast-forward. "Yes, I am. My wife's name is Sam—Samantha. She's the reason for all this, you know. The reason I decided to start looking for the little ones."

"Wow," Alex said, her own smile hanging in there, resolute and meaningless. "Sounds like there's a story there."

"Several, actually."

Cory studied the young woman facing him with arms folded and smile firmly in place, barricades she struggled valiantly to maintain. She wasn't tall, he'd noted, but looked wiry and fit, with long, thick dark hair worn in a single braid. Not beautiful, but definitely attractive. Her skin was a warm golden brown, with a sprinkle of freckles across her nose and the tops of her cheeks that gave her face a poignancy she probably wasn't aware of and would have hated if she'd known. Beyond any doubt, her eyes were her best feature, hazel fringed with thick black lashes. They had a brave and haunted look now, and he felt a deep sympathy for her, along with an aching sense of familiarity.

I know what you're doing, Alex Penny. I know because it's what I used to do. Ask the questions to keep from having to answer any. Concentrate on someone else's story to avoid having to tell your own.

He said gently, "I'd gotten very good at burying everything that had happened to me...the loss of my family. That, along with the anger. Fortunately, I'd learned to channel that anger into writing, and I think I took to writing about—and reporting on—wars because on some level I was trying to understand what had happened to my dad. But I never let myself think about my brothers and sisters. That was an emotional mine-field I didn't cross—didn't even want to try. Sam changed all that. But not before I almost lost her, trying to keep my secrets."

There was a silence, one that seemed longer than it was. Then she let out a breath and unfolded her arms, and although she remained distant from him, she relaxed enough to lean against the wall. "Okay, so what do you want to know?"

"How did it happen? How did my brother fall?"

"I don't *know*." She slapped that back at him, defensive again, chin thrust out. "The rigging failed. That's all I know. Believe me, if I—"

"I'm not blaming you for what happened," Cory said quietly.

"Well, swell, that makes one of us!" Her eyes seemed to shimmer, but with anger, not tears. Then she lowered her lashes to hide them, and after a moment went on in a wooden voice, as if reciting something she'd committed to memory long ago.

"We were going to expand the business—offer combination adventures, rafting *and* rock climbing. We'd already checked out several climbs—this one wasn't any more difficult than some of the others we'd done. We were almost to the top. I was ahead of Matt. I heard him shout—not a scream, like he was scared, just…a shout. There was some scraping, the sound of rocks falling. I looked back, and Matt was lying on a ledge about halfway down. I knew he was hurt. I thought, you know… I was afraid he was dead.

"When I got to him, he was conscious, and I was just so glad he was alive. I didn't even think about anything else. But he had this scared look on his face. Like…he *knew*. He told me he couldn't move, and I kept telling him not to move. I made sure he wasn't bleeding anywhere—well, except for some cuts and scrapes— and I went for help. They got him out with a helicopter. They were good, those guys—they handled him like he was made of glass. They did everything they could—"

"I'm sure they—and you—did everything you could."

Her freckles stood out almost in relief against her golden skin, and he wished he knew her well enough to go to her and offer more comfort than the words she'd probably already heard too many times before.

"So…" And he hesitated, the journalist in him struggling against the compassionate man he was and the brother he was only just learning to be, trying to put the question he had to ask in the least hurtful way he could. "After my brother got out of the hospital, and had been through rehab, whose decision was it for him to stay in Los Angeles?"

"*His,* of course." Again, she swatted the words back at him, as the hurt she'd so far been able to hide spasmed across her face like summer lightning. "He…broke things off with me. Told me it was—quote—better for both of us. I wanted him to come back, stay and run the business with me. I tried to convince him. I told him it didn't matter—" She broke off, looking appalled, probably because she'd said so much, and to a total stranger.

"I wonder why," Cory said, keeping his voice dispassionate—the reporter's voice. "You told me you take physically disabled people on the river. It doesn't seem as though being in a wheelchair should have kept him from continuing on with you in the business, if he'd wanted to."

"Yeah, well…that's the point, isn't it?" Her voice was quiet, and rigid with controlled anger. "Evidently, he didn't."

Cory studied her thoughtfully and didn't reply. There were so many things he could have said…asked about. Things like his brother's pride, and hers, and whether she'd ever told Matt how she felt about him. Whether she'd ever asked him to stay—actually said the words. It was obvious to Cory, who'd spent a good part of his life ferreting out the feelings behind the words people employed to hide them, that Alex Penny's feelings for his brother ran deep. The kind of anger and pain he'd seen in those golden eyes of hers didn't come from nothing. There'd been something more between those two than a business partnership—a lot more. In Alex's case, at least, the feelings were still there.

And he'd be willing to bet she'd deny it with her last breath.

He looked at his watch and rose, smiling apologetically. "Wow, look at the time. I've taken up more of yours than I intended to. I'd figured on being halfway to L.A. by now."

"You'd have hit rush hour traffic," Alex said stiffly. "Probably better this way."

"Yeah, maybe. Well—" He held out his hand. "I really appreciate you taking the time to talk to me."

"No problem," she said as she took his hand and shook it—a quick, hard grip.

"It's been a big help. I think I understand a little better what I'm dealing with now."

"Glad one of us does." She said it with a smile, but her voice had the funny little rasp to it that told him she was keeping a tight grip on emotions she didn't intend to share.

They exchanged the usual goodbyes and thank-yous and Cory left the offices of Penny Tours feeling lighter of heart and of mind than when he'd arrived, for reasons he couldn't quite explain.

After Matt's brother had gone, Alex made her way to her desk and lowered herself carefully into the chair he'd just vacated. She felt shaky and weak in the knees—a fact that both frustrated and infuriated her.

"*Damn* you, Matt," she said aloud.

As if she'd heard the name, or—which was more likely, since she was practically deaf—sensed something, the dog Annie came padding across the room to thrust her white muzzle under Alex's hand. After receiving her expected ear fondle and neck hug, the old Lab collapsed with a groan at Alex's feet and went instantly back to sleep.

That was where they both were some time later when Eve returned from the Rafting Center.

She opened the back door a crack and peeked through it, then, seeing Alex was alone, came to claim the chair at the empty desk next to hers. She slouched into it and spun it around with a noisy creak to face Alex.

"Hey," she said, with a poorly suppressed grin. "Your visitor take off?"

"Yeah," Alex said, rousing herself. "So, how'd it go with the Las Colinas kids?"

"Great. Everybody had a ball, as usual." The grin blossomed. "Bobby got dunked."

"No way."

"Oh yeah, way. Twice, actually—he'd just managed to climb back in the boat when he went over again. The kids loved it. Randy got some great footage."

"Nice." Alex produced a grin in return, though her heart wasn't in it.

In the silence that followed, Eve rotated her chair back and forth with that annoying creaking sound, and finally said, "So, the dude with the glasses. You said he's Matt's brother? Sure didn't look like a cop."

"Cop? Oh, no, no, different brother." Alex waved a hand dismissively, hoping Eve would take the hint from that and leave it alone. The last thing she felt like doing was explaining Matt Callahan's family to Eve. The last person she wanted to talk about in *any* way was Matt Callahan.

He was the last person she wanted to *think* about, too, and she knew she was going to do that whether she wanted to or not, as well.

"So, what did he want with you? I thought you and that guy were finished."

Alex scrubbed her burning eyes with the hand she'd

used to try to fend off the question. "We were—we are. It's not—it's nothing to do with me, actually. He just…had some questions about Matt. About the accident, and…stuff like that."

"That's kind of weird, isn't it? Why ask you? Why not just ask his brother?"

"It's not that simple. He doesn't really know Matt. He hasn't seen him since they were little kids. Look, it's a long story, okay? And I don't really feel like talking about it right now."

And instantly she thought, *Damn, why did you do that? You know Eve's going to have her feelings hurt.*

And yes, now she was looking like a kicked puppy. Which she really didn't deserve.

"Sorry," Alex said gruffly. "Hey, you know me. I just…really don't want to talk about it. Okay? I'll tell you all about it later, I promise."

"Well, you better," Eve said sternly, then grinned as she levered herself out of the chair. "Hey, the guides are getting together at The Corral to toast Bobby's double dunking. You coming?"

"I…dunno. I have a killer headache and a bunch of paperwork to do here before I can call it a day. You go on. Maybe I'll catch up with you later."

"Okay." Eve paused at the door to look back at her, head tilted. "Hey, Alex."

"Yeah?"

"He's not thinking about coming back, is he? Your ex? I mean, you're not thinking about taking him back?"

Alex gave a short hard bark of a laugh. "Oh, *hell* no."

"Well, good. Because the guy ran out on you, right?

I mean, I remember how it was. It was pretty rough around here for a while."

"Hey, don't worry about it," Alex said with a flip of her hand, as if she were swatting at a fly. "Matt Callahan and I are ancient history."

Eve hesitated, then nodded. She gave the door frame a slap. "Okay. See you later. I'll save you a cold one."

For a few minutes after she'd gone, Alex sat without moving. Then, slowly, she swiveled to the desk and reached for the phone. Picked it up. Held it for a long time, then put it back in its cradle without dialing the number she still remembered, even after five years.

Just as she remembered the words they'd spoken to each other then. Words she didn't want to remember. Words that made her cringe to remember.

"Ah, jeez, Matt. Don't do this."

"Do what? It's not like I'm asking you to run off and get married tomorrow. Just talk about it. Why's that so hard? We've been doing this—whatever it is we're doing—for five years. Don't you think it's about time?"

"Doing what? What've we been doing? Seems to me we've been fighting for five years! So now you want to get married?"

"Yeah, and what is it we fight about? I'll tell you what we fight about—we start to get close, and you get scared, so you do something to screw it up."

"I don't! That's bull—"

"Sure you do. Every damn time things start to get really good for us. Just because your mother messed up your head—"

"Don't you dare blame my mother for this!"

"Why not? She's managed to convince you every man's a jerk like your father, leaving her cold when he found out she was pregnant. Well, I'm not your father, okay? I'm not a jerk. We've been working together, sleeping together—hell, we've been best friends—for five years, you should know that by now. We've got a good thing going. Or it could be good, if you'd quit trying to ruin it. It's no big secret how I feel about you, I tell you often enough. So, now I'm asking you." He paused to give her a hard, burning look. "Do you love me?"

Do I love you? The question was a white-hot fire burning inside her head. Somewhere inside the fire was the answer she feared even more than she feared losing Matt. The answer she couldn't bring herself to grab hold of or even look at, as if, like some mythical curse it would sear her eyes blind, or turn her to stone.

"It's…complicated," she mumbled, her face stiff with pain.

"I don't see what's so complicated about it. You either do, or you don't."

She'd turned away, then. But she remembered Matt's face…tight-lipped, stubborn as only he could be. And his hands…their movements jerky and hurried as he packed his climbing gear.

Cory heard the ruckus before he saw it, as soon as he entered the foyer of the rec center. He was able to follow the sounds of mayhem to their source, the indoor basketball arena, where, from an open doorway, the noise pulsed and billowed like a heavy curtain in a high wind. He braced himself and paused there to assess the likelihood that carnage either had already ensued within or was about to. He'd been in battle zones, live ammo firefights less noisy and less violent.

What he saw inside that huge room confirmed it: people here were trying to kill each other.

What it reminded him of was an epic movie battle scene set in medieval times. War cries and shrieks of pain and rage echoing above the thunder of horses' hooves and the clash of steel swords on armor plating and chain mail. Except these battle chargers were made of titanium, not flesh and bone, and carried their riders on wheels instead of hooves.

Out on the gleaming honey-gold hardwood floor, four wheelchairs were engaged in a no-holds-barred duel for possession of what appeared to be a regulation-size volleyball. Now the ball rose above the fray in a tall arc, to be plucked from the air by a long brown arm and tucked between drawn-up knees and leaning chest. The four chairs swiveled, drew apart amid cries of "Here here *here!*" and "Get 'im, get the—" and "No you ain't, mother—" then smashed together again more violently than before.

Cory's fascination carried him into the room, where he found a spot in the shadow of a bank of bleacher seats from which to watch the mayhem. Now that he could see it more clearly, the contest on the court seemed less like a battle between medieval knights and more like a grudge match being settled via amusement park bumper cars—though the canted wheels on the low-slung chairs did resemble warriors' shields, even down to the dents

and dings. The occupants of the wheelchairs—four
young males of assorted ethnicities—all wore expressions of murderous intent, but the chairs moved clum-
sily, slowly, and their clashes produced more noise than
effect.

Again the white ball arced into the air, to be retrieved
by a lanky black kid wearing a Dodgers baseball cap—
backward, of course. After tucking the ball into his lap,
the kid hunched protectively over it and slapped at the
wheels of his chair with hands wearing gloves with the
fingers cut off, pumping as hard as he could for the far
end of the court. The other three chairs massed in frantic
pursuit. One, manned by a stocky boy of an indetermi-
nate racial mix, seemed to be angling to cut off the pos-
sessor of the ball, before it was smashed viciously from
the side by another pursuer. Over they went, toppling
forward almost in slow motion, chair and occupant together, spilling the latter facedown onto the court.
Above him, the chair's wheels spun ineffectively, like
the futilely waving appendages of a half-squashed
beetle.

Cory lunged forward and was about to dash onto the
court to render assistance when his arm was caught and
held in a grip of incredible strength.

"Leave him be. They got him down there, they'll
get him up."

The reflexive jerk of his head toward the speaker was
off target by a couple of feet. Adjusting his gaze downward, he felt a jolt of recognition that made his breath
catch, though the face was one he'd seen only as a very
small child's. It only reminded him of one he'd last

seen nearly thirty years before, and since then only in his dreams.

You have our mother's eyes.

He didn't say that aloud but smiled wryly at the broad-shouldered young man beside him and nodded toward the knot of wheelchairs now gathering around the fallen one out on the court. "You sure they won't just kill him? They sure seemed to be trying to a minute ago."

"Nah—he's safe. He's not who they're mad at." The young man reached across his body and the wire-rimmed wheel of his chair to offer his cropped-gloved hand. "Hi, I'm Matt."

Cory put his hand in the warm, hard grip and felt emotions expand and shiver inside his chest. He fought to keep them out of his voice as he replied, "I'm Cory. We spoke on the phone. I'm your—" He had to grab for a breath anyway.

So Matt finished it for him. "My Guardian Angel. My bro. Yeah, I know."

Chapter 2

He'd seen him come in, of course he had.

He'd thought he was prepared for this. Should have been. Hell, he'd talked to the guy on the phone two or three times since the day Wade had called him from the hospital to tell him the Angel he'd always thought was a figment of his childhood imagination was real.

"You look like Wade," he said, feeling like he needed to unclog his throat. "A little bit—around the eyes."

"Well, we both got the blue ones, I guess."

This brother's eyes were darker than Wade's, Matt noticed. And looked like they'd seen a whole lot more of what was bad in the world. Which was saying something, considering Wade was a homicide cop.

"Yeah? Whose did I get?"

"Mom's. You got Mom's eyes."

About then, Matt realized he was still holding his brother's hand, and evidently it occurred to Cory about the same time. There was a mutual rush of breath, and he got his arms up about the same time Cory's arms came around him.

Matt had gotten over being shy about showing emotions five years ago, so he shouldn't be ashamed to be tearing up now. And he wasn't.

He could hear some hoots and whistles coming from the court, though, so after some throat-clearings and coughs and a backslap or two, he and Cory let go of each other. Dee-Jon, Frankie and Ray had gotten Vincent picked up off the floor, and all four were churning across the floor toward them, along with Dog and Wayans in their regular chairs, moving in from the far sidelines.

"Woo hoo, look at Teach, I think he got him a girl-friend!"

"Hey, Teach, I didn't know you was—"

"Yo, Teach, who the ugly bi—"

At which point Matt held up his hand and put on his fierce-coach look and hollered, "Whoa, guys—I won't have any of that trash talk about my *brother*."

By this time he and Cory were surrounded, and the exclamations came at him from all sides.

"Brother!"

"He yo *brothah?*"

"Hey, you told us your bro was a cop. *He* don't look like no cop."

"Yeah, he look like a *wuss*."

Matt glanced up at Cory to see how he was taking

this, but Cory was grinning, so he did, too. "Nah, this is my *other* brother. He's a reporter."

"You got a *othah* brothah? How come you never—"

"Reporter—like on CNN?"

"How come I never seen you on TV?"

"Yeah, Dee-Jon, like *you* watch the news."

Cory waited for the chorus to die down, then said, "I'm the other kind of reporter. A journalist—you know, a writer."

The kids didn't have too much to say about that. The chairs rocked and swiveled a little bit, and some heads nodded. Shoulders shrugged.

"Huh. A writer…"

"A writer—okay, that's cool."

"He's been in more war zones than you guys have," Matt said, which got the kids going again.

Dee-Jon shot his chin up. "Yeah? You ever been shot?"

"I have, actually," Cory said.

Obviously thrown a little bit by that, Dee-Jon hesitated, then said, "Yeah, well, I have, too. That's what put me in this chair. I was just walkin' down the street, doin' ma' thing, not botherin' nobody, know what I'm sayin'? And this car comes cruisin', and this dude starts in shootin'—like, eh-eh-eh-eh—an' next thing I know I'm down on the sidewalk lookin' up at the sky, and I don't feel *nothin'*. Still don't. But, hey, I can still satisfy my woman, don't think I can't."

That brought a whole barrage of hoots and comments, most of them in the kind of language Matt had pretty much gotten used to and given up trying to ban entirely. He wasn't sure about how his big brother was taking it, though.

But Cory hadn't batted an eye, just started asking questions, asking the kids how they'd gotten hurt, what had happened to them that put them in the chairs. In about ten seconds he had them all pulled in close around him, and was listening while each one told his story, sometimes yelling over the other eager voices, sometimes almost whispering in a respectful silence.

Ray, describing how his dad liked to beat up on him and throw him up against a wall when he was crazy drunk, and one day missed the wall and threw him through a third-floor apartment window instead.

And Dog, admitting how he'd been living up to his nickname hotdogging it on his dirt bike out on the Mojave Desert, showing off for his friends the day he'd flipped over and broken his neck. "I was stupid," Dog said with a shrug. "Now I gots to pay."

Wayans wasn't stupid, just unlucky, having been born with spina bifida. And Vincent hadn't had much to do with the automobile accident that had injured him, either, just happened to be in the wrong intersection at the exact time when a corporate lawyer on his way home from entertaining a client at a Beverly Hills nightclub failed to notice the light was red.

Frankie tried to get away with his favorite story about getting attacked by a shark, but the others shouted him down, so he had to admit he'd gotten his injury skateboarding illegally in the Los Angeles River's concrete bed.

Matt hung back and watched his brother, the way the kids responded to him, the way he listened, not with sugary sympathy, but with his complete attention, interest that was focused and genuine, and that made people want to open up and spill things they wouldn't normally think about telling a stranger. He could see what had made his brother a Pulitzer Prize–winning journalist, although the whole war-correspondent thing was still hard for him to grasp. He'd been prepared to like this newfound long-lost brother—particularly since he'd had those dreamlike memories of him protecting him from the bad scary stuff of his nightmares. What he hadn't expected to feel was respect. Maybe even awe.

"Hey, guys," he said, breaking into the chorus of questions now being fired at Cory from all sides, "you want to know about my brother, go home and do an Internet search on Cory Pearson. That's P-E-A-R-S-O-N for you semiliterates. Now get out of here so he and I can spend some time together. We've got a lot to catch up on. Go on, hit the showers."

The response was predictable.

"Ah, *man.*"

"Hey, it's early—how come we gotta quit now?"

"Yeah, I wanna *hit* something."

"You can't hit nothin'—you a wussy."

"I'm 'a show *you* wussy—you hit like a little girl."

The noise drifted off across the court as the six kids headed for the locker room. Matt and Cory followed, slowly.

"I see what you meant when you said it's not each

other they're mad at. That game they were playing—
it's what they call Murderball, right?"

"Officially," Matt said, pausing to scoop up the forgotten volleyball, "it's called quad rugby. It's been an
official sport of the Paralympics since…I think, Atlanta."

Cory nodded. "I've done some reading up on it. The
rules allow them to do just about anything they can to
the chairs, right? But they can't go after the occupant.
Whoever thought up that game was a genius. Gives
them a chance to beat up on the thing they hate most
and can't live without. One thing, though. Doesn't the
'quad' stand for—"

"Quadriplegic—yeah, it does. And most people
think the same thing, which is that quads can't move
their arms, but that's not true. There's a whole range of
motion, depending on where the SCI occurred."

Cory glanced at him. "But you're not—"

"No—I'm a para-T-11, to be exact." He grinned lop-
sidedly up at his brother. "That's how we refer to our-
selves. These kids are mostly paras, too. Dee-Jon is the
only one who's a quad, and he'd like to try out for the
U.S. Paralympic team someday. No, when I started this
program, it was supposed to be wheelchair basketball.
But the kids had other ideas. They were so rough on the
chairs, I finally quit fighting it and went looking for
some sponsorship so we could get some rugby chairs.
You might have noticed, they're built a little differently
than regular chairs, even the sports models." He slapped
the canted wheel of his own chair.

Cory grinned. "I noticed. Also noticed you're short
a couple."

"We're working on it. Those suckers cost a couple thousand apiece. We got lucky right off the bat, because the guy that hit Vincent got his law firm to cough up the cost of the first two. The U.S. Quad Rugby Team gave us one. And…you know, it's taken us a couple of years to get the other three, but we'll get there. Eventually."

"I might be able to help with that," Cory said, so offhandedly Matt wasn't sure he'd heard him for a moment.

Then, when he was sure, he didn't know what to say. He bounced the volleyball once and coughed and finally said, "That'd be cool, man. Really. Thanks." He looked over at his brother, but Cory wasn't looking at him. *Carefully* not looking at him. His profile gave nothing away.

"No problem."

They'd reached the gymnasium door. Matt swiveled his chair about halfway to facing his brother and said, "I've got to supervise these guys, but I'll be free in an hour or so, if you want to…uh, I don't know. Like… hang out?"

Okay, he'd been hanging out with teenagers too long.

Cory grinned as if he'd had the same thought, and in the spirit of the moment, said, "Okay, cool. I'll be here."

Matt nodded and went wheeling into the hallway, leaving his brother standing in the doorway. Halfway to the locker rooms, from which he could hear the usual racket and hair-curling language as his team got themselves and each other into the showers, he paused and looked back. The doorway was empty.

So. He was alone. Nobody to see him when he let his head fall back and exhaled at the ceiling, not sure whether he felt like laughing or crying. What he wanted to do, he supposed, was both. So instead he smiled to himself, like a little kid with a new bike. Shook his head, whooshed out more air, scrubbed his hands over his face, smiled again. Sniffed, wiped his eyes and muttered some swear words he'd never let the kids hear him use.

After a few minutes, when he had himself under control again, he swiveled and wheeled himself on down to the locker room.

Matt slid a dripping medium-rare hamburger patty onto Cory's plate and said, "Don't be shy, bro. Dig in."

"Looks great," his brother said, helping himself to slices of tomato and onion.

But behind the rimless glasses, his eyes held shadows. He hadn't said much, either, the whole time Matt had been fixing the burgers, just watched everything he did with that quiet focus that seemed to be his natural way. Now, with food on the table, and nobody with any particular reason to say anything, silence fell. It didn't seem like a comfortable silence.

Matt doctored up his burger the way he liked it, took a bite, chewed and swallowed, then said, super-casually, "Hey, man. I hope you're not blaming yourself, or anything like that."

Cory put down his burger, and one corner of his mouth went up as he glanced over at Matt. "For what part?"

"What part? For losing track of us—Wade and me and…the little girls. Waiting so long to try to find us. What the hell did you think I meant? This?" He hit the rim of the wheel and threw him a look. "Why would you be blaming yourself for this?"

Cory shrugged and picked up his burger. Put it down again and stared at it as if it had turned bad on him all of a sudden. "Why wouldn't I?"

"Okay, wait." Matt couldn't believe this guy. He huffed out a laugh. "You're not thinking you could have changed what happened to me. If you'd been here. That's crap. That's just… Look here, okay? I probably would have found some other way to screw up my life. It's just the way I am. You've got no way of knowing this, but I've always been a daredevil, taking chances I shouldn't, even when I knew better. You being around wouldn't have changed that."

Cory gave him an appraising look, and the light was back in his eyes, as if he'd put the guilt away, for now. "A chance-taker, huh? That why you chose to teach in an inner-city school?"

Matt snorted. "Hadn't thought about it quite like that, but…yeah, maybe. Probably."

"Wade told me he was surprised—that's an understatement, by the way—when you decided to become a teacher. He said you weren't ever much for school…being indoors. Said you reminded him of Tom Sawyer. You'd always rather be outdoors, mixed up in some sort of adventure. And by the way, he blames you for any and all trouble you two got into when you were kids."

Matt laughed silently, nodding while he chewed. "He would."

"You did get through college, though. That's something."

"Yeah, well, I guess it's a good thing I did…as it turns out. Gave me something to fall back on, career wise. Not that I'm any great shakes as an academic, you understand. I started out teaching phys ed, substitute teaching now and then. Now I teach ninth grade social studies in addition to the PE. Seems to be working out okay. It's a challenge, though, I grant you, going up against the gang influence—drugs, the whole culture of violence. I like it, though—and you're right, maybe because it's a challenge. Like…maybe I had something to prove to myself. Maybe."

Cory said mildly, "Seems like you could have done that just as well by going back to your old job."

"Hey," Matt said, letting himself back away from the table. "Forgot the beer. Can I get you one?"

"Sure."

He could feel those dark blue eyes boring into him as he made his way to the fridge, got out two cold ones and came back to the table. His brother didn't push, though. Just waited, as Matt was discovering was his natural way.

Matt slid one of the cans across to Cory and popped open the other. Took a drink, then figured there was no use avoiding the subject. He should have known it would come up, and was going to come up again, his brother being who he was.

"The mountains, you mean. The river." *There. That wasn't so bad, was it?*

"I had a talk with your former partner," his brother said quietly.

Matt took another swallow of beer. Not that it helped

wash down the knot in his throat. "Yeah? How's she doing? The rafting business going well?"

Cory's half smile and steady gaze told Matt he wasn't fooled. "Seems to be. Although Alex...maybe not so well."

The kick under his ribs caught him by surprise, made him check with his beer halfway to his lips. He coughed to cover it, set the beer down and said carefully, "What do you mean?"

"She's pretty angry with you, you know. And hurt. Doesn't understand why you broke things off with her."

Matt leaned back in his chair and steadied his hands on the wheels. Emotions he'd learned to control threatened to break loose, something he didn't want, not now, not with the brother he was trying so hard to impress watching him like a hawk. He huffed out a laugh he hoped didn't sound bitter. "That doesn't surprise me. I wouldn't expect her to understand." He added, as an afterthought, "Don't expect you to, either."

"I'm pretty good at understanding," Cory said.

There was a moment when Matt thought he wouldn't answer, when he swiveled away from the table. Then for some reason he came back.

"Okay," he said, then paused while he thought about how to start. "Look. All during rehab they tell you the hardest part of getting your life back is facing up to what you were before. Like, as long as you're in the hospital, in rehab, you're in this completely different world, and you're surrounded by others in the same boat you're in, or worse off than you. You look forward to going home, that's what you're working toward, the light at the end of the tunnel. And then when you finally get there, instead of being this great thing, it's like bam, everything hits you at once. Everywhere you look you see stuff that was part of your old life, stuff you can't do anymore. That's hard." *And how's that for understatement?*

Cory nodded. "I can see how it would be. So you tried to avoid that part altogether. By not going back to the life you had before."

"Yeah, I did," Matt said, quietly defiant. "Do you blame me?"

"I'm not into blaming anybody—" Cory's smile flashed "—except maybe myself."

"And I told you not to do that. I mean it. I'm okay with my life. I mean, hell no, I'm not okay with being in a wheelchair, but I've accepted it. What else can I do? Look, I went through all the stages—first, you're just numb, then you're in denial. You tell yourself you're going to get over this, you're going to get well, you're going to walk again. When you realize you're not, you hit bottom. There's rage, despair, bitterness—some people never make it past that. Some people choose to end it right there. I don't know why I managed to get through it, but I did, and I'm glad I did. I've got a job doing something important. At least, I think it is. I think maybe I can make a difference in some kids' lives, and that keeps me going, getting up every morning."

"I think so, too. I hate to sound like a big brother, but I'm proud of you." Cory coughed and took a swallow of beer—a ploy Matt was familiar with, had used himself a time or two—then frowned at the can in his hand. "But there's more to life than a career. Trust me—this I know from personal experience."

It was an opportunity, and Matt jumped on it with great relief. Leaned forward, grinning, and said, "Speaking of which, I haven't heard about yours, yet. You're married, I know that much. Your wife's name is Samantha, right? So, tell me about her."

This time his brother's smile was different, somehow, as if somebody had lit a whole bunch of candles behind it. "You'll meet her yourself, soon enough. She's flying out tomorrow."

"No kidding? Hey, that's great. No kids, though, I'm guessing?"

The candlepower went just a shade dimmer. "Not yet. Sam's been busy with her career—she's a pilot, did Wade tell you?—and then we've both been occupied with this search. Still two missing, you know. The twins—the little girls are out there, somewhere. We're not ready to give up just yet."

He took off his glasses, frowned at them, then shifted those deep, dark, see-everything eyes back to Matt. "What about you? You broke things off with Alex, so…what now? Do you have anybody special in your life? Do you plan to get married someday, have kids of your own? I'm assuming everything's…"

Matt jumped in with a cough and a hurried, "Oh, yeah. Everything's fine. Works just…fine. You know…." And after an awkward pause, "I'd like to find somebody, sure." From out of the past a pair of hazel eyes fringed with black swam into his mind and gazed at him accusingly. *You found her, you idiot. And you were too stupid to know it.*

His consciousness protested. *Hey, I wasn't the stupid one.*

You could have changed her mind if you'd tried hard enough.

I would have. I meant to. I thought I had time....

Cory's voice broke into his inner debate. "You and Alex..."

"Whatever we were," Matt said evenly, "it's history."

"That's...not the impression I got from her."

Matt jerked away from the table, needing a physical outlet for the anger that spasmed through him. "Look— you don't... You have to know her." He gave a short, hard laugh as he wheeled into the kitchen and lobbed his empty beer can into the sink, liking the clatter it made. "She's got some issues, believe me."

His brother's mild tone told him he wasn't impressed by the display. "So, tell me about her."

Sam's "Hey..." was mumbled and sleepy, and Cory closed his eyes in contrition.

"I woke you. I'm sorry. I didn't think about the time difference."

"No...no, 'sokay." He could hear rustlings, and for a moment, knowing she preferred to sleep nude, enjoyed the mental picture of his wife getting herself propped up on pillows and the sheet pulled up across her breasts. "Tell me. You've seen him? Talked to him?"

"Just came from having dinner with him. He fixed us hamburgers."

"Umm. Yum."

"Sam, I wish you could have seen him. He coaches

a bunch of teenagers with SCIs. Have you ever heard of 'Murderball'?"

"I have, actually. Well, gee, Pearse, what did you expect? He's your brother. So, how *is* he? I mean, you know, about…"

"Being paralyzed? He seems to have adjusted very well. Ask me how it was seeing him like that."

"Okay."

"In a word, awful. I kept thinking I could have changed things if I'd…you know. That he wouldn't be in that chair if I'd been there for him."

"Pearse—"

"I know, I know. He already told me what he thought of that notion. There is something I'd like to do for him though. This is something I think I *might* be able to fix." *And maybe it'll help with these guilt feelings…*

"Okay, tell me. Can I help?"

"I think so, yes. You're still coming tomorrow, right?"

"Right. Hitched a ride with the U.S. Navy. Leaving at O–six hundred. You're picking me up at Edwards, right?"

"You bet." Cory let out a breath. "I'm going to take Matt back to the mountains, Sam. He's adjusted okay in most ways, but…he'd never admit it, but I think he's lonely. He'd like someone—a wife, kids—but I don't think he's ever going to be able to find anyone as long as he's got this unresolved thing for Alex Penny. His ex-partner. I'm positive he's still got feelings for her, and it's a big hurting empty inside him."

He listened to some more rustlings, and then,

"Darlin', I know you want to help your brother, but meddlin' in his love life? I don't know about that... Do you think taking him back to the life he used to have is such a good idea? Seems like that could be pretty hard."

"Oh, yeah. He admitted that. He said it was the reason he chose not to go back. But I think there's more to him not going back than not wanting to face his old life. He's got more guts than that." He paused. "I think he'd have gone back if she'd asked him to."

"Well, why didn't she? Maybe she doesn't have the same feelings he does."

"That's just it—I think she does. Sam, she's still hurt and angry after five years. That doesn't come from nothing."

"True." He heard a swallowed yawn. "Then why? Is she just proud? Stubborn? What?"

"Mmm, I don't know. Some, maybe. But Matt told me some things about her that might help to explain why she didn't ask him to stay. Apparently she grew up in a trailer park in a little town on the Mojave Desert. Single mom, father deserted her mother as soon as he found out she was pregnant. Mom was bitter but tough, and raised her daughter to fend for herself, be self-sufficient, not depend on anybody but herself, and especially not a man. She died of cancer about the time Alex met Matt."

"Oh boy."

"Yeah. Add to that the fact that Matt's got his pride, too, and he's trying to prove to himself he can make it on his own, doesn't want pity, doesn't want charity, so the only way he's going to stay on the river is if his partner convinces him she really wants and needs him."

"Which goes against the whole mind-set she was raised with. So, how do we go about fixing this?"

"I told you. We're going to take him back to the river. I want to book us a rafting trip—you, me and Matt. They do trips with all sorts of disabled people, so I know it's doable. Then, once we get him there, we let nature take its course. I'll butt out, I promise."

"Okay," Sam said, softly laughing, obviously not believing that for a minute. "That's fine…but how do you intend to convince this little brother of yours to go along with your plan? From the sound of things, he's got a mind of his own."

"I'll put it to him in the one way he won't be able to refuse," Cory said, letting his smile into his voice. "He's a bit of a daredevil. So, I plan to dare him."

"No way," Alex said. "Not in a million years. Out of the question."

"You go, girl," Eve said, clinking beer bottles with her across the remains of their burgers and fries.

"That's what I'm gonna tell him, too. First thing tomorrow." Alex took a chug from the bottle, then lowered it and demanded of Booker T, who was gazing at her from under his beetling white eyebrows and shaking his head, "*What?* You don't think I won't? Eve's right. Why in the hell should I let my paraplegic ex-partner book a tour with me when he friggin' deserted me? Didn't even have the guts to come back here and help me run this damn outfit? Who needs that? Who needs *him?*"

This time Eve's "Hear! Hear!" was echoed enthusiastically by Bobby and Ken and a couple of the other river guides who were obviously a beer or two up on the rest of the crew. Randy, the photographer, who had his mouth full, gave a thumbs-up gesture. Linda, Booker T's wife, who also manned the Rafting Center's store and was too kind and sweet to say a bad word against anybody, just smiled and shook her head. Booker T scraped back his chair and stood up.

"We got boatin' to do tomorrow, people," he announced to a chorus of boos, which he ignored. "Time to be headin' on home. C'mon, sweet pea." He pulled out Linda's chair for her and offered her a hand with a gesture like an old-time gentleman, which he did sort of resemble with his sweeping handlebar mustache with its waxed and curled-up ends. Then he gestured at Alex. "You, too, baby doll. Morning comes early."

"Ah, hell, Booker T, we're just getting warmed up. The night is young!" And as far as Alex was concerned, home was the last place she wanted to be. Home was quiet, and empty. She wanted music and noise and a few more beers. Hopefully enough to block out the memories.

Evidently Booker T could read her mind, because he shook his head and said, "Come on—we'll drop you off home," as he took her by the shoulders and guided her up out of her chair. His touch was gentle, and although Alex could have resisted it, she didn't. It was a mystery to her *why,* but Booker T was the only human being on the planet she'd let boss her around like that.

So, she laughed and hollered her goodbyes and Booker T hooked one arm around her waist and the other around Linda's, and he danced them both out the door

of The Corral with a Texas Two-Step to the Billy Ray
Cyrus song that was playing on the jukebox. By the time
they got to the parking lot, they were all singing along
with Billy Ray at the top of their lungs, having a *good*
time. Alex thought it would be a fun idea to ride in the
back of Booker T's king cab Chevy truck and keep right
on singing all the way—the whole half mile—to her
house, but Booker T somehow managed to maneuver her
into the backseat instead, where she had to sit on some
coiled-up rope and leather gloves and a bunch of other
stuff she couldn't even begin to guess the nature of.

Booker T slammed the door on her complaining and
got into the driver's seat while Linda climbed in beside
him. He started up the truck and pulled out of the
parking lot, and Alex scooted forward and put her
folded arms on the back of his seat.

"Booker T?"

"Yeah, baby doll?"

"I'm tellin' him tomorrow. I mean it. No way am I
booking Matt Callahan for a tour. Huh-uh."

"And why's that?"

"Well…*hell,* isn't it obvious? I mean, he's a—"

"Cripple?"

The word stabbed into Alex like a thorn, and she
sucked in a shocked breath because she'd never thought
Booker T would say such a thing. Something so mean.
But it's what you were thinking.

I was not!

"No! You know it's not—shoot, we take disabled
people on the river all the time, you know we do."

"Well, then?"

"Jeez, Booker T, he wants to go on the Forks. That's a class V. He can't—"

"He's done it before, dozens of times."

"Not in five years, he hasn't!"

Booker T pulled up in front of Alex's little house, set among the granite boulders and bull pines with the privacy and isolation she normally loved. He cut off the motor, and in the silence said quietly, "That's what's bothering you, isn't it? The fact he's been gone five years. What are you afraid of, Alex? That he can't do it, or that he still can?"

Still can...make my heart hammer and my skin hot? Still can...make me want him?

She sucked in another breath—an angry one, this time—and whooshed it out along with, "No, that's not— Look, I'm not afraid, okay? That's just stupid." *I'm not afraid. I'm not.*

"Okay, you're not afraid. So, why not book his trip?" He opened his door and got out, then opened hers for her and held out his hand to help her down. "You're not chicken, are you, baby doll?"

She could see the snaggletoothed smile lurking underneath that mustache. Damn him.

"Damn you, Booker T." She let him walk her to her door and open it for her and turn on the lights, then paused in the doorway to give him a sideways look. "You know you're the only person on God's green earth that gets to call me 'baby doll.' You know that, don't you?"

"Maybe that's what's wrong with you," Booker T said as he started off down the pine needle–strewn walk, heading back to his pickup.

"What's that supposed to mean? Hey, Booker T—"
She stomped her foot and started after him, and he
paused with one hand on the truck's door handle to turn
back to her.

"You never got to be any lovin' daddy's little girl,"
he said, then yanked open the door, climbed in and
drove away.

He left Alex standing there with tears smarting her
eyes, cussing out loud and ashamed at herself because
she'd just remembered. Booker T and Linda's only
daughter, Sherry Ann, had died in a car accident when
she was just seventeen.

But she still wasn't booking Matt Callahan and his
brother on a trip down the Forks of the Kern. No way, José.

Chapter 3

Alex spent a restless night in the company of dreams that weren't quite awful enough to be called nightmares, but close.

First, she was back on the Mojave Desert where she'd spent her childhood. She, the grown-up Alex, was climbing the tree that stood beside their mobile home. It was an old tree shaped by decades of desert wind so that it seemed to hover with its limbs spread protectively over the trailer, sheltering it from the relentless desert sun. Down below, her mother was yelling at her to come down from there before she fell and broke her neck. Alex smiled and kept climbing. And then she fell.

Except, instead of the tree, it was a rocky cliff she was falling from, and as she was falling she looked up and saw a face peering down at her from a ledge up above. Matt's face. He was yelling at her, something she couldn't hear because of the wind rushing past her ears, and he was holding out his hand for her to grab hold of. But she wouldn't. She scowled at him and kept falling, and just before she hit the ground, she woke up.

She was drenched in sweat, so she threw aside all her covers and pulled off the oversized T-shirt she'd worn to bed, flipped the pillow to a dry side and went back to sleep.

And she was right back on that cliff, still falling. Only now she was naked, and Matt was still peering down at her, holding out his hand for her to grab on to, and instead of yelling at her, he was smiling. Smiling that beautiful Matt Callahan smile that could melt her heart like vanilla ice cream in the Mojave sun. She watched the smile get smaller and farther away as she fell, and fell, and fell, and again, just before she hit the ground, she woke up.

The ringing telephone woke Matt in the darkness. He groped for the handset, squinted at the time in the lighted window. Jeez, was that…4:00 a.m.? He thumbed it on, swearing under his breath. "Who the hell is this?"

"Are you insane?"

"Alex?" He jerked himself half upright, got himself propped on one elbow and his throat cleared, stalling for time, waiting for his heart rate to get back to normal. When it didn't appear it was going to anytime soon, he tried instead for the lazy Clint Eastwood drawl he sometimes adopted with the kids when he wanted to appear cool. "Nice of you to call. Haven't heard from you in a while. What's it been, five years?"

"You're the one who broke up with me, remember?" He heard some heavy nasal breathing, and then, "The *Forks,* Callahan? Have you lost your mind?"

His scalp prickled in a familiar way, and instead of confessing to her that the whole river trip had been his brother's idea and he'd only insisted on the Forks of the Kern run and its Class V rapids to scare Cory off the notion, he dropped the temperature of his tone a couple more degrees and said, "No, don't think I have."

"Okay, then, you can't be serious."

"Why's that?"

"Oh, for—" There was a long pause, filled with some more of that breathing. "You're going to make me say it? Okay, I'll say it. You can't do a Class V run. Not the Forks."

Another shower of prickles enveloped him, and it was like getting hit by a gust of wind-driven sleet. Five years he'd dreamed of hearing her voice again, talking to her, and he should have known it would be like this, picking up right where they'd left off. Shouting at each other. Just proved he'd been right to end it when he did.

He closed his eyes and fought to hang on to his temper. "I've made that run a dozen times. You've been with me on most of 'em. What's the problem?"

"Jeez, Matt. That was more than five years ago. Before—"

"Before I got hurt? Before I was paralyzed? Last time I checked, you didn't need legs to row a boat.

Somebody change that when I wasn't looking?" He felt
a childish urge to brag, to tell her how he played basketball and tennis and won medals in wheelchair races
all over the country and had a good chance of making
the U.S. Paralympic Team, if he put his mind to it. But
he managed to keep his mouth shut, and after listening
to the silence on the other end of the line, said in his
coolest drawl, "Alex? What's the matter? Scared I won't
be able to do it, or scared I will?"

"Okay, but I'm sending two Class V guides." She'd
cleared her throat, but her voice sounded raspy anyway.

He'd always loved that little froggy voice of hers.
Never failed to stoke his fires, not then. And evidently
not now, either.

"Why? You already got me. You only need one
more." *You, Alex? You're a Class V guide, too.*

"Two. Besides you. And that's not negotiable."

He sat for a minute, smiling to himself, savoring the
moment. Making sure to keep the smile out of his voice,
making it sound grudging, he said, "Who've you got?"

There was an exhaled breath. "Tahoe, for sure."

"Tahoe—he's that big dude with the beard, the one
that does trips in the Andes in the off-season, right? Surprised he's still around."

"He isn't, always. But he's here right now. He's the
most experienced Class V guide we've got. Him, definitely."

"Okay. Who else?" *Come with us, Alex. Come on—
I dare you.*

Another whoosh of breath. "I don't know. I'll have
to think about it. I'll find somebody, okay? I just need

to— Jeez, it's four in the morning, Callahan, you really expect me to *think?*"

"Hey, you called me, Alex." He tightened his fingers on the handset, half expecting her to hang up. When she didn't, he eased himself back onto the pillows and said softly, "So. How are you? Doin' okay?"

"I am. I'm good." A caught breath…a pause. "How are you?"

"I'm doing just fine. I guess you heard…my brother—"

"Yeah, he stopped by here. That's so amazing. How's it been? The two of you…"

"Oh, it's been—" he gave a short laugh "—a little unreal, actually. I find out I not only have a brother, but a couple of little sisters, too. I'm still trying to get my head around it. But, yeah, it's amazing." *Lots to tell you, Alex. I'd like to tell you all about it, the way we used to tell each other everything. We used to be friends—best friends, remember? When we weren't being lovers…or mad at each other and yelling—or not speaking.*

God, I miss you, Alex.

Had he said that out loud? He didn't think he had. But he could have. The nearness of that disaster made his scalp crawl.

"So…I guess I'll see you in a couple of days, then." Was it his imagination, or did her voice still sound strange? Sort of muffled.

The handset had grown slippery in his grasp. He put his free hand over his eyes and pressed on his closed lids, and was surprised to discover there was moisture there, too. "Okay—yeah. Guess you will."

"Well…bye, then."

"Yeah. Take care now."

"You, too."

The phone went dead in his hand, and for a while he sat with his eyes closed and held it. His chest had a hard lump of emotion in it he didn't know what to do with, a little like that moment right after he'd met Cory for the first time, in the hallway outside the locker room. Like he'd done then, he tried laughing and swearing and whooshing out a breath, but none of those things helped. Not this time.

It hurt too much. And he was too damn big and strong to cry.

"Dieter's gone? He's the only other Class V guide we've got, besides Tahoe. What do you mean, he's *gone?* Since *when?* Ah, jeez, Booker T—"

"Hey, don't kill the messenger." Booker T held up his hands and tried—unsuccessfully—to look innocent. "You know how these guides are—come and go as they please, especially those Class V guys. Bunch of adrenaline junkies. I guess the season's about getting started up there in Idaho, on the Salmon, and Dieter told me he wanted to get there for the spring runoff—said that's the best water. Who am I to tell him he can't?"

"You told him he could go? You *told* him? You *knew* I needed two fives for this Forks run. I don't have anybody else available."

"Sure you do. Tahoe and you. That makes your two."

"Yeah, but I'm not going. How can I? Somebody's got to stay here and run this place."

Booker T was in the process of shouldering a pair of oars. He paused to snort. "You know good and well if you don't go you're not gonna be worth a nickel around here anyway. All you're gonna do is sit here and worry the whole time they're gone."

"Dammit, Booker T, who's the boss of this outfit, anyhow?"

"Well, you are, sweet pea." He got the oars balanced and started for the bus, but not before he threw her a wink.

"Yeah, well, I don't know very many employees get to call their boss 'sweet pea,'" she yelled after him. "Tell me why I don't fire your ass!"

Booker T's cackle drifted back to her. "Because if you fire my ass, the rest of me'd have to go along with it. Then you wouldn't have anybody to tell you when you're full of—"

"Booker T—"

A shadow blotted out her sun. She whirled to face the man-mountain who had cast it—her one remaining Class V river guide, whom she knew only by the unlikely name he'd given her when she'd first hired him five years before: Tahoe Jones. His wild auburn hair, backlit by the sun, formed a fiery halo around his deeply tanned face, and his full, dark brown beard failed to hide his grin.

"Looks like it's you and me, boss." Tahoe jerked his head toward the blue SUV with handicapped plates that was just then pulling through the open gate. "Can't very well cancel now."

Alex opened her mouth to offer a retort, but found it

had gone dust dry. *Keep it together, Alex. Don't give him the satisfaction. Don't you dare.* She stood stock-still and watched the SUV roll across the yard and into a parking place beside the half-loaded bus. Like it belonged there.

The hell it does! Anger blew through her. Blessed anger. Cold fury.

She started across the yard toward the SUV, all set to inform the person driving the damn thing that he was going to have to park down at the Rafting Center, like any other client. But Booker T and Tahoe were already converging on the driver's side of the vehicle with grins and gestures of joyous welcome. The tinted window rolled slowly down, but from where she stood, Alex couldn't see who was inside. A wave of dizziness washed over her, a reminder that it had been some time since she'd taken a breath. She hissed one in, whooshed it out, put her hands on her hips and elected—wisely— to stay where she was.

As she watched, the world around her seemed to shrink; her focus narrowed down until it was like watching the scene through a telescope turned the wrong way around. From far, far away Alex saw the SUV's side door slide back, saw the wheelchair lift emerge, then slowly descend.

Oh God, this hurts.

A hard, painful knot formed beneath her breastbone. Once again she reminded herself to breathe as her mind flashed back to those awful days and weeks and months of visiting Matt at the rehab hospital.

Oh God, he looks just the same.

Same brown hair, maybe a little longer, maybe a little more wavy. Same finely honed features that were in no way effeminate, and he'd shaved off the beard he'd worn the last time she'd seen him. Same poet's mouth curved in a Huck Finn grin. Mattie's grin. Mattie's smile.

How dare he look just the same!

From a vast unbridgeable distance she watched the wheelchair disengage from the lift, and Booker T move in for some macho hand-gripping, backslapping, and yeah, some male-bonding-type hugging. Then Tahoe and Matt did the cool hand thing all guys seem to understand and know how to do. Nobody appeared the slightest bit constrained by the fact that one of them was in a wheelchair. To them, obviously, he was just…Matt.

Why can't I feel like that?

I wish I could, but I can't!

Because he's not the same, dammit. Matt—my Matt—is strong and graceful and full of life and mischief and laughter. His body is beautiful. He moves like a thoroughbred racehorse. It's a pleasure just to watch him. And his hands…he has the hands of a sculptor. And when he touches me—

"Alex?"

She jerked around to face Cory, letting go of another forgotten breath that told her one thing: plainly, the pain in her chest had nothing to do with breathing. Thrusting the pain ruthlessly aside, she pasted on a brilliant smile and said, "Well, I see you guys made it."

"Alex, this is my wife, Samantha."

The woman standing beside Cory was tall, athletic-looking and blond, her hair cut short and worn casually tousled, styled by natural influences rather than expensive hairdressers. She wore light tan cargo pants, a khaki T-shirt, aviator shades, and judging from the part of her face Alex could see, a pleasant though neutral expression. Which didn't change as she thrust out her hand and said, "Hi, Alex. And it's Sam."

Her grip was strong, Alex noted. Firm, no-nonsense. She'd do okay with the paddles. "Sam," she repeated, still automatically smiling. "Nice to meet you. And welcome to Penny Tours."

She tried not to, but from the corner of her eye she could see Matt wheeling himself across the yard flanked by Tahoe and Booker T. The three were making their way toward the warehouse, making slow progress as other members of the crew, loaded down with supplies for the trip, paused to extend greetings or be introduced, depending on how long they'd been with the company.

The pain under her ribs twisted sharply. *What, he's not even going to say hello? He can't even face me? What the hell is that?*

"As you can see," she went on, with an arm sweep that took in all the activity around them, "we're in the process of packing for your trip." She glanced at Cory and dryly added, "Most of our clients don't get to see this part. Guess Matt's having some trouble remembering he's the customer on this run."

Cory gave her a smile and one of his piercing looks but didn't comment.

As the three of them began walking toward the open warehouse, Sam moved closer to Alex's side. "I know it's not easy," she said in a low voice, and with a Southern accent that was unmistakable but not strong enough to be annoying. "Believe me, you're talkin' to one who's been there." She paused, then took off her sunglasses and gave Alex her eyes—unexpectedly dark, and even more unexpectedly, filled with compassion. "Pearse tells me it's been about five years since you two saw each other. That's about what it was for us, too— maybe not quite as long, but close. It was hard. And trust me on this, too. Him bein' in a wheelchair's got nothin' to do with it."

Since she couldn't think of a thing to say to that, Alex replied with a short huff of breath—what Matt would have called a snort. She saw Sam and Cory trade smiles and long looks before Sam once again tucked hers behind her aviator shades.

He could at least have come over to say hello to me. He started this. He's the one that wanted this craziness. I'll be damned if I'm going to him.

She set her lips—Matt would have said stubbornly— as she separated herself from her clients and veered toward the office's back entrance. "Since you're here, you might want to watch the guys pack up the gear. It's kind of interesting to see what goes into a run. The big scary-looking guy with the beard is one of your guides. He can explain everything, answer any questions. I'm going to…uh, I've got some things…some paperwork to take care of, so if you'll—"

"*One* of our guides?" Cory had paused with one hand on his wife's shoulder. "Matt tells me we're required to have two for this run. May I ask—who's the other one?"

Alex flashed him a desperately brilliant smile. "Looks like that would be me." Before he could respond, she brushed past Eve, who was leaning against the wall near the office door, pushed it open and escaped into the air-conditioned office.

Since what she wanted at that moment more than anything was to be left alone, she wasn't thrilled when Eve followed her in.

"So, they made it." Alex didn't comment, so Eve went on. "He looks pretty good—considering."

"Yeah," Alex said, studiously avoiding looking at her, instead picking up a handful of mail and giving it her focused attention. She glanced up briefly to add, "Why don't you go say hello? You knew him, right?"

"Sure." Eve gave a one-shoulder shrug. "I will."

But she stayed there, fidgeting, getting on Alex's already frayed nerves. Being in no mood to deal with one of Eve's sulks, Alex smacked the stack of envelopes down on her desktop. "What, Eve?"

"Jeez, don't get mad."

"I'm not—"

"I just don't see why you have to be the one to go on the run. Okay? There's only three of them, it's not like Tahoe can't deal with it."

"Yeah, well…I'm going. Okay?" Alex paused, took a breath and made an effort to soften her tone when she saw Eve's lips compress in that hurt way she had. Was that what they called passive-aggressive? "Look. They're my responsibility, and I'm not handing them off to someone else. You can handle things around here while I'm gone, right?"

"Yeah." Eve exhaled grudgingly. "Sure." Still she made no move to go.

"It's three days, Eve. Then he's gone."

"You're sure about that?"

"Hell, yeah."

Eve lifted one shoulder and turned to go.

Alex did a double take. "Wait. What would make you think— Wait, dammit. Eve—"

The door closed quietly. Alex clamped a hand to the top of her head, then closed her eyes and swore.

What the hell are you doing, Alex, hiding in here? Making such a big deal about this? Get out there and face the man, you know you have to sooner or later. Did your mama raise you to be a coward?

She made a growling sound and strode with grim determination to the door. Her heart was pounding and her hands were cold as she pasted her smile back on her face and opened the door.

But the blue SUV and its passengers had already gone.

Matt paced the open space in his brother's motel room, as someone wheelchair-bound paces, rocking forward and back, angled first this way, then that way. Going nowhere, while his mind raced in circles.

Shouldn't have gone over to the yard, man. You don't have the right...and anyway, what were you thinking? Maybe she'd fall on her knees and beg you to come back? Yeah...right—after the way you brushed her off? When snowball fights break out in hell.

So you went over there. Then you don't even go and say hello to her? What's that say? That you care too

*damn much, or you're a gutless coward. A wuss, as my
kids would say. Either way, you're screwed.*

Either way, it hadn't been his finest hour.

And instead of having gotten it out of the way, he still
had it to look forward to—his first face-to-face with
Alex since that day at the rehab hospital. *Awful day.* He
closed his eyes, pressed his fist against the pain in his
chest and whooshed out air, but the memories came
anyway.

*Alex fidgeting, arms folded across her waist, looking
anywhere but at him…looking like she'd rather be anywhere but there, with him.*

*"They tell me I'm going to be ready to leave here in
a couple weeks."*

She nods, says, "Good. That's good. I'm glad."

"I'm getting a place…." He waits, she nods. *"Physical therapy…you know. I guess that goes on for a while
yet. So…I guess I'm gonna need to be close to this place
for now."*

*She nods again. He sees her swallow. His chest is full
of knots, and his mind is screaming,* What the hell's wrong
with you, Alex? This is me—Matt. Don't stand there like
you're a million miles away—say something, dammit!

*Then she does, and it's, "Okay, so I guess that's
what's best, then. I understand. That's cool." She
sounds like a stranger.*

And he wants to yell at her, No, it's not cool. It sucks.
It's my body that's all busted up—inside I'm the same
guy. The one who runs the big rapids with you, makes
you laugh. The one who loves you…makes love to you.
My God, Alex, can't you see that?

He knows it's not true, even while he thinks it. He'll never be the same man he was. And he can see she knows it, too.

Smart woman, Alex.

Hey—I made it easy for her, that's all. Clean break—that's always best. Right?

A knock at the door kept the rest of it at bay, for now. He knew from long experience the memories would be back. The memories from before…and after. He had a feeling they always would.

It was the *during* memories, the ones of the accident, he didn't have.

Sam came from the bathroom, having changed her khaki T-shirt and cargo pants for walking shorts and a sleeveless top that left a lot of smooth golden skin showing. Matt saw his brother give her an appreciative look as he went to open the door, and couldn't help feeling a sharp stab of envy. Woulda been nice, he thought.

Then the room was filling up with people and noise, and he put all thoughts and feelings aside for the moment. Put on his happy face. Or, if not happy, at least *cool.*

Alex came in first, naturally. Then Booker T and Linda, then a tall, good-looking blond girl Matt didn't know. Last came Tahoe, the Class V guide, which pretty much filled up the room. There was a lot of noise and friendly handshaking, since mostly everybody had met everybody else that afternoon at the yard. Matt hung back out of the way through most of it, rocking forward to extend a hand as he was introduced to Cheryl, the blonde, who turned out to be the guide assigned to food duty for their trip.

"A newbie, huh?" He noted, smiling at her in his most charming way, that her hand was warm and firm, and seemed to want to linger in his a little longer than was really necessary.

"Yeah… How'd you guess?" Her voice was breathless, husky and a little shy.

"Tradition. Newbie's get the food detail."

"Oh, that's right, you used to be—"

"Yeah. Guess some things don't change."

"You got that right." Now, *that* voice he knew. Edgy as a squeaking door, and it still made his skin shiver in predictable ways. "Better watch him, Cheryl. Still thinks he can charm the britches off a girl with that grin."

"Hey, Alex." He made it nice and cool…easygoing. Clint Eastwood would have been proud.

"Hey, Matthew."

Matthew. He couldn't remember the last time anybody'd called him that. Only two people in the world did, and one was his mother. He let his gaze find her eyes, and Cheryl the good-looking blonde and everybody else in the room disappeared.

Still has those lashes. Like soot rings around live coals.

She had some sun wrinkles he didn't remember, a couple around her mouth and at the corners of her eyes. Maybe a few more freckles, too. She never had been good at remembering sunscreen.

"'Bout time you got around to saying hello."

"Got things to do. Hey, you think you're the only customer I've got?"

Her tone was light, teasing. Her smile was in place,

just like his was. Twin smiles. No getting around it, people were going to be watching this. They'd put on a good show.

He felt as if the paralysis he'd grown accustomed to in his lower half had crept up his body all the way to his chin.

"So—" she turned away from him and raised her head and her voice to encompass Sam and Cory "—in case you didn't read your information packet yet, this is your 'pre-trip meeting.' We're supposed to go over the details of the trip with you all, but since you probably got that already this afternoon, or from Matt here, I think we can probably skip that. Unless you have any questions?"

She paused, waited, then gestured to Tahoe, who stepped forward to dump some waterproof gear bags on the nearest bed. "Okay, these are for your stuff. Matt can tell you what you need to take and what you should leave behind." She paused to dust her hands off and grin. "And that, boys and girls, concludes the business portion of our evening. Shall we all adjourn to The Corral for burgers and…whatever?"

There were general cries of approval and seconds to that motion, which got even more enthusiastic when Cory announced he was buying.

Everyone shuffled and jostled their way out of the room and into the soft summer twilight. Nobody was inclined to drive, since The Corral was just across the park and the main road through town. As the group strolled along the roadway, taking the long way around instead of cutting through the park for Matt's sake, Alex moved in alongside his chair. Making it seem a casual thing, as if it were only the natural ebb and flow of the crowd that had brought her there.

They strolled along in silence for a while. Then Alex said in a low voice, "You do know this is insane."

He gave a short dry laugh. "Wouldn't be the first time you and I did something wild and crazy."

"Yeah, and look where that got us."

Something in her voice—a slight catch, maybe— made him look up at her, wanting to see what was in her face…her eyes. But she was already moving away from him, into the dusk.

The crowd at The Corral was rowdy; at least some things hadn't changed—much. The place had gone smoke-free, along with the rest of California, but there was enough of the familiar smells of sweat, booze and charred meat to make up for it, still make it the place he remembered. That, and the noise—laughter and conversation and loud foot-stompin' country music playing on the jukebox. Matt wondered whether they still had live music on weekends. And whether Alex went there to hear it, and who she danced with these days.

There was a lot of calling out and waving back and forth as their group moved through the crowd to a table near the dance floor. Obviously, the river guides were still regulars here. Several people Matt knew came over to say hello, with varying degrees of awkwardness and constraint. Which he was used to, and had long ago stopped being bothered by. He figured he'd probably be the same way, if the situations had been reversed.

They put in their orders for beer and The Corral's

famous black angus hamburgers, then settled back to watch the raggedy line dance in progress. It ended, to hoots and cheers and some sporadic applause, and a Garth Brooks classic—"The River"—came on. Linda and Sam started to sing along, and then Booker T got up and with old-fashioned courtesy, asked his wife to dance. A respectful silence fell over the table as they all watched Booker T guide his wife around the small dance floor, kind of bent over at the hips like the rump-spring cowboy he'd been in his youth. Then Sam jumped up and grabbed Cory's arm and hauled him onto the dance floor.

Among the four remaining at the table—Cheryl and Tahoe, Alex and Matt—an awkward silence fell. Tahoe sat sprawled in his chair, nursing his longneck beer and watching the dancers with his usual unreadable gaze. Cheryl tapped her fingers on the table and rocked her body in time to the music. Alex picked up her beer and took a sip.

Matt said, "How 'bout you, Alex—you used to like to dance." He spoke in an easy drawl, but he could feel his heart thumping, out of sync with the music.

Above the rim of the beer bottle her eyes widened briefly, flared and then faded the way banked coals do when you blow on them. He could see she didn't know what to say, that he'd surprised her, probably. Hell, for sure, he had. What had he expected her to say? He hadn't even asked it out loud. *Dance with me, Alex. Won't be the way it used to be, but I'll make sure you enjoy it. Maybe not quite, but* almost *as much.*

While Alex was hesitating, swallowing her mouthful

of beer and evidently trying to think of a reply, Cheryl hopped up and stuck out her hand and said, "Hey, I'll dance with you."

So, what could he do? He reached out and took the hand she offered, looked up at her and smiled. "Well, let's go, then."

After that, he just concentrated on the music, Cheryl's warm hand in his, and her pretty baby-blue eyes.

Tried to, anyway. Trouble was, a different pair of eyes kept getting in the way. Hazel-gold eyes filled with fire and fringed with black, and a smart-alecky mouth that never lacked for something bossy to say. He kept remembering how that mouth felt, laughing up against his, how incredibly inventive it could be, exploring his body's most sensitive places—back when his body had had senses. Kept remembering how her body felt—small, but round where it needed to be, and as she liked to say, "freakishly strong." One little bitty package made up of muscle and fire—that was Alex. *My Alex.*

He rotated his chair in time to the music, one hand guiding Cheryl as she sashayed in a circle around him. She looked down at him, eyes lit up and smiling, and he looked back at her and winked. And his mind followed its own steps…its own dance:

Not your Alex anymore, you fool. What the hell do you think you're doing here? She's right—it's insane, going on this run. What is it you hope to accomplish? What are you trying to prove?

It came to him, finally, sometime out there on that dance floor as he was rocking and swaying to Garth

Brooks's anthem comparing life to the flow of a river. In a way, he'd staked everything on this run down the monster rapids known as the Forks of the Kern. This was it—his one chance to make it all right again. As far as his future happiness was concerned—and that meant his future with Alex Penny—to borrow a poker term (and he'd played a lot of poker during his months in rehab), he was All In.

Alex watched the dancers from a great unbridgeable distance, while thoughts and feelings rocketed through her mind like an oarless boat on a river full of rapids.

My God, he can *dance. And who would have thought a man in a wheelchair could look so graceful? So sexy.*

So...beautiful.

So virile? I wonder if he...

No. I don't want to wonder.

Damn, but this hurts. I don't want to watch him, but I can't help it.

How can he dance with someone else? To this song? Not that we were sentimental, either one of us, to have had "our song"—but if we had one this would have been it. We used to dance to it, me with my hands around his neck, and he'd have his hands on my butt, and we'd sing along while we danced. Sing about the river we both loved.

How could you, Mattie? How could you have messed everything up so badly?

"Hey, boss, leaving so soon?"

She realized only then that she was standing, looking down at Tahoe, who was looking back at her with heavy-lidded eyes. And she was proud of the brisk and businesslike way she replied. "Hey, I'm runnin' the Forks tomorrow. I don't know about you, but I'm planning on getting a good night's rest."

She walked out of the room without a backward glance, fully aware of the fact that she'd left before the hamburger she'd ordered had arrived. And that everyone there would know that. And probably guess why.

In the foyer she almost bumped into Eve, who'd been lurking in the doorway, evidently watching the dancers, too.

Oh, damn. Of all the people in the world she did *not* want to have to deal with just then, Eve topped the list. Not that Eve wasn't a good friend, but she was just so darn *needy.* And at the moment... *Dammit, right now I might be "needy" myself. Okay? When do I get to have somebody comfort me?*

The thought was so foreign to her nature, it shook her. Terrified it might show, she compensated by being overly jovial.

"Eve—hey, where you been, girl?"

Eve shrugged and looked away. Looked at the dancers, the empty coat rack, the beer signs on the wall. She mumbled something about having stuff to take care of. Paperwork to catch up on.

Okay, so she was still miffed about Alex taking the Forks run? Tough. Covering her own inner turmoil, Alex gave a shoo-fly wave. "Forget that—it's the weekend, right? You don't have a run scheduled. Why don't you go on in? Join the gang. They've got a regular party goin' on."

She'd started out, bent on making her escape, when it occurred to her. She said to Eve without turning back, "Oh, hey—you can have my burger, too, if you want it."

Chapter 4

It was the part he'd dreaded. He thought he'd gotten over feeling humiliated by the limitations of his physical body; falling on his face in public places and having to be lifted back into his chair by strangers had pretty well cured him of that. He was finding out it was much, much worse when it was friends doing the picking up. Especially friends who'd known him when he was able-bodied. Especially when one of those "friends" was Alex.

They made it as easy on him as they could, he'd give them that. Tahoe, who could probably bench-press a Volkswagen, picked him up as effortlessly as he did the coolers full of food and set him down on the back of the mule—an old-timer named Mabel he remembered well—before he really had time to think much about it.

Booker T strapped him into the saddle while Tahoe held him steady, and Alex supervised the whole operation with a frown of laserlike concentration and never once made eye contact with him.

It probably shouldn't have bothered him, but it did. He endured it with what he hoped was expressionless stoicism, but inside he was seething with humiliation and anger, flashing back to his early days in rehab.

Jeez, Alex, couldn't you have the tiniest shred of sensitivity? Did you really have to watch? *So how did it make you feel, seeing the man who used to share your bed picked up and plunked on the back of a mule like a baby in a stroller?*

The flare of anger passed and bleak realization came in its place.

Hell, who am I kidding? She probably doesn't feel anything at all. No more than she would for any other "physically challenged" customer, anyway. She's responsible for my safety, so naturally she's going to check everything out. It's her job.

He watched in grim silence while Tahoe strapped his chair onto the back of one of the other mules. Then Booker T mounted the lead horse and the train moved off onto the winding, switchbacking trail. Up ahead of Booker T, Matt caught a glimpse of Cory and Sam, top-heavy with their thirty-pound backpacks, and Alex trotting to catch up with them before they dropped out of sight into the canyon.

He looked up at the sky, checking out of habit for the haze of forest fire. But the weekend with its invasion of crazy or careless flatlanders from L.A. and the San

Joaquin Valley was still a day off, and all he saw was clear, cloudless blue, and a hawk circling lazily in it. He sniffed the air for the scent of smoke, then hauled in a chestful of air that smelled only of pine and dust and horse sweat. With it came a whole avalanche of memories. Good memories.

Almost against his will, the anger and hurt faded, and he felt instead a fierce kind of joy. And that prickling, tingling ache that made him not know whether to laugh out loud or cry. Seemed like he'd been having that feeling a lot lately.

He let go of the breath and settled in to enjoy the descent into the river gorge and the rocking gait of the mules beneath him, and the Sierra Nevada mountains spread out all around him like a great big welcome home.

Alex walked away blindly, leaving the rest of the mule-packing to Tahoe and Booker T.

Oh God, I shouldn't have done that. Why did I do that? Stay and watch? It hurts. It hurts me to see him like this. I can't even imagine what it must be like for him.

She caught a quick breath to ease the pain inside her, and was grateful for the anger that helped even more. *Why is he doing this? What is it, Mattie, the challenge of it? You always were a daredevil. Or are you trying to prove something? Who to? I wonder. Yourself, your big brother, or...me?*

Oh God, I hope it isn't me.

I wish I hadn't watched.

She closed her eyes for a moment...and saw her own hands checking over the saddle and the rigging. Then her mind flipped backward in time and she was seeing Matt's hands, instead. Matt's strong, sure hands, jerkily checking over his climbing gear. She heard his voice…

"It's no big secret how I feel about you, I tell you often enough. So, now I'm asking you. Do you love me?"

What might have been, she wondered, if only I'd answered?

If only I'd checked his rigging that day…

She exhaled with a shudder, jerked off her sunglasses and wiped her eyes with her sleeve. Then she put the glasses carefully back in place and broke into a downhill jog to catch up with Cory and Sam.

"Okay, quit beatin' yourself up, Pearse."

Cory gave his wife a rueful smile as she sank onto the granite boulder beside him. "Is it that obvious?"

"Probably only to me." She jerked her head toward the figure sitting alone a little way off, hunched in his chair and gazing intently at the river. "Right now you're asking yourself, 'Was I out of my mind, bringing him here? What was I thinking?'"

He snorted, shook his head, then after a moment looked up at the sky as if the answers to the questions in his mind might be found written up there. "What have I done to him, Sam? Do you know what it must have been like for him, to have her see him—"

"Pearse. You know I'd tell you if you were wrong. Okay, well, I'm not going to tell you you're wrong. I'm not quite sure if you're right, either, but I do know this. If anything is gonna happen between those two, they're gonna have to face this sooner or later. I mean, he's gonna have to let her see him bein' weak and helpless and vulnerable and get over bein' bothered by it. And she's gonna have to see him that way and not have it affect how she feels about him. That's the way it is with two people when they get to be a couple. You have to be okay with the other person bein' the strong one now and then."

"Oh, yeah," Cory said, "I've felt that way with you a time or two."

"A time or two?" Sam pretended to look shocked, then grinned and leaned over to give him an affectionate nudge.

"The thing is," he went on, after nudging her back, "I think there's got to be some sort of balance—you know, offsetting measures of strengths and weaknesses." He paused, and his gaze found his brother again before it moved on to where Alex was engaged in conference with Tahoe and Booker T down by the river's edge. "I don't think either of those two would be happy if it's too one-sided."

"True…" She turned her head to look at him along one shoulder. "You don't think Alex has any weaknesses? Vulnerabilities?"

He gave a dry laugh. "Except for having some ambiguous feelings for my brother, I sure haven't seen any so far."

Sam's gaze drifted back to the trio by the water's edge. "Everybody's vulnerable about something. Some people just hide it better than others."

"That's true." Cory shaded his eyes with his hand.

"What do you suppose is going on down there? Does that look right to you?"

She shook her head, shading her eyes, now, too. "Huh-uh. Appears to be a problem of some kind."

"Well," said Cory, getting to his feet, "I don't know about you, but I'm for finding out what." He offered his wife a hand up, grinning slyly.

Sam grinned back as she took it. "Hey—I'm not too proud to show my weaknesses."

"How could this happen?" Alex had one hand clamped to the top of her head, as if doing that might help keep a lid on her temper. So far it wasn't working. "The equipment was checked—thoroughly. I double-checked it myself. You *know* I did. How could the damn thing not be holding air?"

Down on one knee beside the slowly deflating oar boat, Tahoe tilted his head to give her an inscrutable look. "Looks to me like the valve's damaged, boss."

"What?" Alex added a second hand to the one already attempting to keep the top of her head from flying off. *"How?"*

Tahoe shrugged and rose to his feet, dusting off his hands. "Pretty much had to be deliberate. Must have happened last night, after the equipment check."

She opened her mouth, but all that emerged was a wordless squeak of incredulity. She couldn't believe what she was hearing. *Sabotage? Why? Who?*

As if she'd uttered the words out loud, Booker T said mildly, "At a guess, I'd say somebody doesn't want us to make this run."

Her mouth clamped shut as she realized both men were staring at her. She stared back at them in utter silence for a long moment. Then, "Good Lord, Booker T, you can't think I—"

Booker T shrugged. "Honey, you've been throwing a hissy fit over this trip ever since you booked it."

She uttered another outraged squeak and looked at Tahoe, who was carefully not looking at either one of them. She closed her eyes for a quick three-count to get a grip on her temper, then said slowly and carefully, "Look. I was against it to begin with and I'm still not happy about it, but I'd never sabotage my own equipment just to get out of a run. Hell, I'd just cancel it, if it came to that. Booker T, you know me better than that."

"Yeah," said Booker T, "I do know you." He jerked his head toward the three people approaching. "I'm just not so sure they do. You know how this is gonna look to them."

Oh Lord, Alex thought. *Matt. He's going to think I did this. He knows what I think about making this run.*

"The other boat seems okay," Tahoe offered. "And we've got the kayaks."

"Yeah…I guess. We'll have to leave some of the gear behind, though. You guys—"

"Is there a problem?" That was Cory. He'd reached them first, those inquisitive, see-everything eyes intent behind his glasses.

Alex glanced at Tahoe, then Booker T. Carefully avoided looking at Matt, who was just now rolling up behind his brother, the going being a bit slow for his chair on the riverbank sand. She looked at Cory and

Sam and offered them a bright gung ho smile. "Nothing we can't deal with. Seems one of the boats doesn't want to stay inflated."

"That can't be good," Sam muttered.

Alex gave a chortle of laughter and tried not to think about the intent and curious stare Matt was giving her as he joined them. "Definitely not. Which is why we always bring backup. We have a couple of kayaks, just in case something like this happens. Sam, you think you can handle riding along with Tahoe?"

"Sure. No problem."

No hesitation, no looking at her husband first. She had her chin up, fingers tucked in her back pockets, confident and ready for anything. Alex decided she liked this woman.

"Okay, then. Gather up your gear, folks. Meet back here in ten minutes for your final safety briefing. We'll be putting in in fifteen."

Cory and Sam nodded and headed back up to the campsite. Booker T gave a little salute and went off to see to the horse and mules. Tahoe was already unloading one of the two-man inflatable kayaks from the other oar boat. Which left Alex to face Matt, whose eyes were steady and full of questions, and who wasn't showing any inclination to leave without answers.

"You want to tell me what's going on?" He asked it softly, for her ears only.

She looked at him, then away, telling herself she didn't need to tell him anything more than she would any other client.

"Alex?"

Maybe she didn't need to tell him, but oh, how she wanted to. *In the old days I would.*

But how could she tell him about this? *Sabotage?* It was just too crazy. And Booker T was right. Matt would probably think she'd done it herself in some sort of desperate ploy to get out of making the run.

She let out an exasperated breath. "Look, it's just embarrassing, okay? How do you think I feel, having something happen on this, of all runs? I mean, *you,* of all people…and your brother… *Jeez.*"

"Hey, I know the feeling." He gave her his crooked smile and leaned into the job of turning his chair in the sand.

She watched him, words clogging up her throat. He'd made a few yards progress before one broke free. "Wait—"

He paused and looked at her over one shoulder. She took a step toward him, then another. He waited patiently, not saying anything.

"Matt—" *God, why is this so hard?* "—hey, look, I'm sorry about…" She made a helpless gesture, then tucked her fingertips in her pockets to keep from doing it again. "You know—back there. With the mule."

He tilted his head. "Why?"

"Why? Because—" There was a lump in her throat. She swallowed, but it wouldn't go down. "I shouldn't have stayed. I mean, I should have given you some privacy. I wasn't thinking. And I'm sorry." She let go the breath she'd been holding.

He lifted one shoulder. "Hey, you were there in rehab. It is what it is, Alex. It's been five years. I've learned to deal with it." His look lingered, and there was no accusation in his eyes at all.

So why did she feel so guilty? And why did the words he hadn't said echo so loudly in her mind?

Five years, Alex. And if you'd shared them with me, maybe you'd have learned to deal with it, too.

He'd tried to explain to the shrink they'd sent him to, those first months after the accident, what it was about running the river. He thought the doc was probably hoping to help him find some equally enjoyable hobby to occupy him, something more suitable for a man with his physical limitations. Matt had tried to make him understand—there *wasn't* anything else like it. Not even close. It wasn't all about the adrenaline rush, either. He still got that, in other ways, like at the start of a race, in those frozen seconds waiting for the starter's gun, when his focus narrowed down so he could hear his own heart-beat, feel the blood surging through his arteries. And then the shot...the explosion of energy through every cell in his body, even the ones he no longer felt. There was challenge there, too, him against the field, man against man.

But man against the river. That was something else.

Just him...him against a force so immense, so un-imaginably powerful, he knew if he gave it one chance, made one mistake, one error in judgment, it could easily kill him. It tested a person, going up against the river. Tested his mental and physical strength and stamina, and yes, his courage, in ways nothing else he'd tried ever could. To go up against the river and all its might and unpredictability and *win*—that was something nothing and nobody could take away from him.

The river had never bested him—not yet. He'd fallen off a mountain, most likely due to his own carelessness or stupidity, but he'd never lost a battle with the river.

Him versus the river. One on one. And the river didn't know or care whether his legs worked. There would be no special category for people like him, no different set of scoring rules, no allowances made for the fact that he was "disabled." The river didn't know mercy.

God, how I've missed this!

For the first time in five years, he felt whole.

As the first set of rapids churned and thundered around him, Matt lifted his paddle to the sky and let out a whoop of pure joy.

Matt's shout went through Alex like an electric current, a bolt of emotion that was both exhilaration and pain. It made her smile—she couldn't help it. And brought tears to her eyes—she couldn't help that, either.

They'd made it through the first rapids. The first test, and he'd passed it with flying colors. The laughter that bubbled through her as they drifted into the quiet water below the rapids was partly relief, partly something she couldn't even name. Gladness…joy…even a peculiar sort of pride?

Exasperation, she thought, would be more like it. She should have known he wouldn't stay put in the bottom of the boat. Of course he wouldn't. Obviously, some-body paralyzed from the waist down couldn't sit on the tube, the way passengers normally would. Passengers had to sit sideways to the bow and use their leg muscles to steady them while they turned to face forward and paddle, while the guide sat up on the back of the boat and steered with two oars and called commands. Physically challenged clients sat in the bottom of the boat. But not Matt. Oh, no. The minute they'd hit the first rapids, he'd pulled himself to the edge with his chest against the tube, braced himself with his elbows and begun paddling.

And, dammit, she had to admit she'd needed him. Normally there would be a lot more people manning the paddles. With only Cory to respond to her commands, the big oar boat would have been a lot harder to control.

Now they sat in the quiet water with oars gently backpaddling, waiting for the kayak to make its run. It was standard procedure for the boats to go through rapids one at a time, so they could watch each other and be ready to assist in case of emergency. In this case the oar boat, carrying the emergency equipment, had been the first to go. Now they waited...and watched.

Alex glanced at Cory, who was tense as wire. Of course he'd be worried about his wife. She gave him a reassuring smile. That Sam was a tough one. She'd do just fine.

This is wild, thought Sam. *Crazy wild. Pure insanity. But, oh Lord, it's fun!*

Sam hadn't time for much more thought than that; she was much too busy trying to stay alive. At some point it occurred to her that she was in a real life-and-death fight—not the first time she'd found herself in that situation, but this was different, somehow. Here, she was up against an adversary not driven by human intelligence. One that would kill without discrimination, mercy or remorse.

Terrifying.

Here were forces so powerful they could only be ridden, never mastered or controlled—something like riding a bucking bull, she imagined, only here getting bucked off was not an option!

It was oddly tempting to surrender to the forces, just give in and let them take her where they would. But she couldn't give in, she knew that.

Have to keep my head…stay on top of it…

She had no time to marvel at the skill of the guide, Tahoe. No time to worry or think about Cory…or Matt. Just focus on hanging on to the paddle, following Tahoe's lead, and staying upright.

Then, in an instant, they weren't upright.

She was in the water, icy-cold water. She was in the monster's grip. In its mouth. Being chewed up, eaten alive. Every limb was being pulled in a different direction. Twisted and turned, like a rag doll in a washing machine. She had no idea which way was up. She swallowed water and her chest screamed. Her brain exploded in panic.

Then—her head was free! She gasped in air, choked on it. She was bobbing like a bit of flotsam in the frothing, seething turbulence, and from somewhere a pinprick of reason broke through the chaotic darkness in her mind. Something Alex had told them during the safety briefings: *If you fall in, get into tuck position!*

Like lying in a recliner—sit with feet up and pointed downstream! So you don't get a foot caught in the rocks!

There. She was still alive. Reason was returning. She was alive, floating down the river in the wake of the kayak, which she could see from time to time as it was flung skyward like a broken branch in a flash flood.

But she didn't see Tahoe. *Oh God. Where is Tahoe?*

They all saw it happen, Alex and Cory maybe a split second before Matt did, since they were sitting up higher than he was on the sides of the boat. And Alex didn't waste her time blowing the emergency alarm whistle, since they were the only boat there. She did yell, "Paddle!" Which they were already doing anyway.

It was a drill he'd been through so many times before, sometimes in practice, often enough for the real thing—capsized boat, bodies in the river. It was gratifying, at least, how fast it all came back to him. Alex working like a demon to get the bag line ready, he and Cory digging at the water with all their strength. Trying not to think about or look for the people now at the mercy of the river's hydraulics…just pulling, pulling to get the boat into position to snatch them out of the maelstrom before it carried them on by, out of reach.

Hang in there, Sam!

He couldn't imagine what Cory must be going through. Couldn't let himself think about that.

Then he heard Alex yell, "There she is!" And felt the boat rock as she heaved the bag line across the current.

He gripped his paddle, held steady against the current and watched Sam shoot toward them, riding the water feet first, just as she'd been taught. Good girl, he thought, and his chest was bursting with adrenaline, exhilaration and relief.

"Grab the rope!" Cory had abandoned his paddle and was leaning over the side, calling instructions and encouragement to his wife.

Matt saw Sam nod and begin to paddle toward the line. Her head was wet and sleek as a seal's, but her face was calm…intent. No panic there.

"Grab hold—hang on, Sammi June, darlin'—we've got you, babe!"

Then she got hold of the line, and Alex and Cory were hauling her in…pulling her into the boat.

Matt had seen a lot of people pulled out of the river, both customers and guides. The guides usually came in whooping and laughing—a little bit embarrassed, maybe. The customers—well, they'd be gasping, choking and on the verge of tears, if not outright hysterics. Not this lady.

Sam toppled into the boat like a landed marlin and instantly sat up, shook her hair out of her face and grinned at her husband. Matt figured his brother's heart had to be about jumping out of his chest right now, and what he'd be wanting to do more than anything in this world was grab his woman and hold on to her and thank the Lord for giving her back to him. But all he did was grin back at her and murmur, "Show-off."

All that took only a moment. Then Sam raked more water out of her eyes and gasped for breath, and managed some words. "Tahoe—I couldn't see—is he—"

Alex didn't answer. She was staring intently up-river, watching the foaming, swirling current. Watching the kayak come shooting out of the white water and sail toward them—empty. She threw Matt a look as she let the kayak drift past them. A look full of anger...helplessness...desperation...futility.

He knew how she felt. Because he knew what could happen when a boat overturned, how many different ways there were for a man to die. Even someone as experienced and strong as a Class V river guide. He gave Alex the same look and their eyes held for what seemed a long time. Held on until someone's hoarse cry—Sam's or Cory's; it was hard to tell in that moment—galvanized them both.

Alex spun back to the rapids and a moment later echoed the cry. Matt heaved himself up and braced himself with the strength of his arms so he could see what everyone else had seen already. It took him seconds to find it—the spot of dark in the sea of white. Tahoe's head, barely keeping above the water, sometimes dipping under.

Matt yelled, "He's lost his vest!" at the same moment Alex started shouting commands—commands mixed with some passionate swearing.

"He's not buoyant, may not be conscious, might not be able to grab the rope! Get those paddles in the water, dammit! *Now!*"

Matt knew what had happened, and he was sure Alex did, too. Tahoe's life vest had evidently gotten caught on something underwater. Anybody with less experience, less presence of mind than the guide, would have been dead, but somehow the man had managed to keep his head, extricate himself from the vest and get his head above water. Problem was, without the buoyancy of the life vest, he was at the mercy of the river's hydraulics—the action of the water. No way to keep himself from being bashed and battered against the rocks.

Alex was right. He might be barely conscious, unable to grab hold of the line.

Matt knew what needed to be done and didn't stop to ask permission. He knew he was the only one who could do it. Grabbing hold of the boat's fat slippery tube, he hauled himself up and over the side, and slid headfirst into the river.

Chapter 5

Matt heard the shouts as he went over the side, and ignored them.

Surfacing, he yelled, "Throw me the line!" He shut out of his mind the vision of his brother's face peering down at him, pale with shock and fear, and focused on Alex's furious one instead. "Dammit, Alex, give it to me—*now!*"

Then the bag was arcing through the air above him, and he reached up and snagged the line and got it around his chest and snugged up tight. He got a bead on the head he could just see drifting toward him, riding the current at what seemed an impossible speed, and struck out swimming crosscurrent to intercept. Swimming harder than he'd ever done in his life, knowing if he missed the rendezvous…

Missing the rendezvous wasn't an option.

Then he had the man in his arms.

"Hold on, buddy—I've got you." Did he say it out loud, or only in his mind?

He felt Tahoe's broad body, slippery and cold in its wet suit, turned him and hugged him tight to his own chest. He felt the pull of the rope fighting hard against the pull of the river, and let others fight that battle while he concentrated on keeping the river guide's head above water. He could hear yells of encouragement above the rush and roar of the river, coming closer and closer, and then hands were reaching for him, reaching down to grab hold of Tahoe's arms.

Matt lifted from below with all his strength, and with everyone pulling from above, they managed to pull the big man into the boat without capsizing it. For a moment, then, Matt clung to the side of the boat and rested his forehead against the giving rubber fabric and hauled air into his lungs in great hungry gulps. Then he let himself lie back in the cradle of his life vest and give in to the rocking of the current, while a wave of euphoria washed over him.

You did it, man. You're not done yet. Not by a long shot.

"Hey, buddy, were you planning on getting back in the boat?"

It was Cory, grinning, reaching down to him. He reached up with his gloved hand and took his brother's hand and felt a leap in his chest because that felt so good. Then Sam was there, too, grabbing hold of his life vest, and with the help of the two of them, Matt got himself hauled up and over the side. Sprawled in the bottom of the boat and breathing hard, he threw off the safety line, raked back his wet hair and said, "How is he?"

Alex didn't answer. She had the first-aid kit open and was trying to stem the flow of blood from a gash in the big man's scalp with a wad of gauze bandage. Trying to keep her hands from shaking.

She'd never lost a client. Or a guide. But today—

Today you would have. She tried the mental equivalent of clamping her hands over her ears, which didn't keep her from hearing any better than it did in the actual physical world. *If it hadn't been for Matt.*

Tahoe lifted a hand to his head and growled feebly, "Cut it out. I'm okay—just a scratch."

"Like hell," Alex growled back, batting his hand away. "This is gonna need stitches—at least. Probably a concussion. And look at your arm. No—jeez, don't move it! Looks like it could be broken." She threw a furious look over her shoulder at the rest of them. "Get those paddles in the water. We're taking out. There's a spot just downriver. I'll need to call for a chopper. No way he's gonna be able to finish the run."

"What? Hey, wait—I'm okay, Alex—"

She jerked back to Tahoe. "Shut up—I mean it. I'm your boss, remember? One more word and you're fired. I swear to God."

You almost lost him, Alex. You couldn't have reached him with the boat in time, not with only three other paddles in the water. If Matt hadn't gone in...

If Matt hadn't been here...

We wouldn't be on this damn run!

Furious, she snatched up the oars. "Forward—*right!* Left—*back!*"

She'd let the roar of the river and the splash of the oars and the rush of her blood through her veins drown the voice in her head. The one that kept saying his name.

Mattie...Mattie...

Matt knew the spot where they took out for the emergency pickup. He wondered if Alex remembered.

They'd scouted it, the two of them, back when they were first talking about adding the Class V run. They'd decided it was too small and too close to the start of the run for a camping spot, but would do for an emergency take-out. Like this one.

They'd also discovered a cozy little nook behind the boulders that lined the river's edge. A protected spot, with a thick carpet of sun-warmed pine straw over which they'd spread every article of clothing they had, and it had still been prickly as hell. Matt had done the chivalrous thing, of course, which Alex gave him no credit for since she liked being on top anyway. But afterward, she'd made him roll over and she'd kissed the places where the pine needles had left their marks on his skin. Kissed and licked them...every single one.

He wondered if Alex remembered. He sure as hell did.

He'd elected to stay in the boat with Tahoe while Alex hiked up to higher ground to find a signal for the satellite phone. Cory and Sam had gone off in opposite directions to find some privacy, after having been reminded of the two basic rules of wilderness comfort stops: One, watch for rattlesnakes, and two, leave no trace. Matt and Tahoe had made desultory conversation for a while, until it became obvious the guide was in some serious pain and not really up to the effort.

So he'd had plenty of time to think about it. To remember.

To remember making love in the warm pine needles and then swimming naked in the icy-cold river, whooping and shrieking like kids. Lying on the rocks in the sun afterward to warm up, and forgetting to put sunscreen on the exposed places. Singing Bruce Springsteen songs and Alex teasing him about being old enough to remember when "Born to Run" first came out...

To remember the day the memories always returned to, sooner or later. Their last day, as it turned out.

It was a good day. We were so excited, driving up to the meadow. Talking about how great it was going to be, adding rock climbing to Penny Tours's schedule, and how the meadow would make a great base camp. We spent the night there in the shadow of the Devil's Fortress, made love under the stars. I can still remember the way her skin smelled...the way her mouth tasted. We were good together, when we weren't arguing.

It had been so good that day. Which was probably why he'd gotten to thinking about making it official.

Thinking about it, he could probably have gotten away with. Talking about it—that was his big mistake.

He could see Alex coming back down the hill in a hurry, slipping and sliding around the boulders and bull pines. She joined him, only a little out of breath, with her long dark braid over one shoulder and wisps of damp curls sticking to her flushed face. Her skin was all warm colors…autumn colors: golden tan, cinnamon brown and the deep blush pink of old roses.

And it hit him then, with the sharp sense of loss he'd thought he was long past: he was never going to make love with her in that secluded spot among the boulders again. Never go there, with her or anyone else, or even see it…ever again. He'd have to be able to walk to do that.

"Okay, the chopper's on its way." Alex tipped her head toward Tahoe, who was leaning back against the side of the boat with his injured arm cradled across his waist, and lowered her voice. "How's he doing?"

"Hangin' in," Tahoe replied, without opening his eyes.

"Hey, Alex." Matt felt restless, antsy all of a sudden. He nodded toward his chair. "Think you can help me with that?"

She looked startled, opened her mouth, then closed it again and shrugged. "Sure." Carefully not looking at him. "What do I do? Just… You want it—"

"Just lift it out of the boat. Unfold it. Set it down as close to the boat as you can."

His insides cringed, and if he'd been able, he'd have done what his body's defense system yearned to do— get the hell away. But he'd learned a long time ago he couldn't run away from what was. *It is what it is, Alex.*

He clamped his teeth together and focused on what had to be done.

Alex picked up the chair and lifted it out of the boat. It was surprisingly light. She unfolded and placed it carefully on the hard-packed decomposed granite, mentally steeling herself for whatever came next.

It is what it is, Alex. He's obviously okay with this, why can't you be?

Because it hurts, *dammit.*

And if you let him see how much it hurts, you'll never forgive yourself.

"Okay," she said, straightening up and planting her hands on her hips, all business now. As if this were any other client. *As if.*

Looking at him was like looking straight into the sun. She wanted to close her eyes. Look away. "What now?"

He smiled at her, crookedly, as if he knew. "Just steady it. And stand by in case I need you."

Oh God, please don't make me watch this.

But she did watch. Watched him push his body up with the sheer strength of his arms and shoulders until he was sitting on the tube. Watched him swivel and reach for the chair, brace and maneuver himself into it. And somehow, it wasn't awful at all. It was…amazing.

She'd expected to feel pity. Instead, she felt awe. She'd expected—no, *feared*—she'd feel revulsion, but instead she felt stirrings deep inside…an awakening of emotions she hadn't allowed herself to feel in a very long time.

She was used to being around athletic, physically fit people, but even so, Matt's arms and shoulders, chest, back and torso were…amazing. Rock-solid, sculpted muscle. His body was…*beautiful.*

"*What?*" The belligerence was reflexive, because she realized she'd been staring, and Matt was sitting there watching her with that crooked grin on his face. And a gleam in his eyes that made her insides quiver.

"What's the matter, Alex? Didn't you ever see a paralyzed man get into a wheelchair before?"

She shrugged and turned as he did, falling in beside him as naturally as if he'd been walking. "Not from a boat, anyway."

He gave a snort. "It is—"

"If you say 'It is what it is' again, I'm gonna smack you."

He laughed.

They moved slowly, away from the boat, as far as the terrain would allow. When they reached the place where piled boulders blocked the wheelchair's path, Alex leaned her backside against the sun-warmed rock and scanned the rugged hillside. "So, where are the others?"

"Went looking for privacy."

"What about you?" She didn't look at him. "You don't need—"

"Nah, I'm fine." Alex tilted her head, cut her eyes at him. He grinned, then shrugged. "I'm okay for now."

She laughed, and it felt good. Almost as good as she remembered it being with Matt. When they weren't arguing. She drew a deep breath, knowing they were about to do it again.

"I'm canceling the run," she said, at the same exact moment he said, "You're not canceling the run."

She let out the breath, and again they spoke together.

"Matt—"

"Alex—"

Alex raked her hand over the top of her head and muttered, "God, you're just the same. Stubborn…"

"Hell, yeah, I'm stubborn." There was an angry

edge to his voice. "I didn't get to this point with this thing—" he pounded the gloved heels of his hands on the wheels of his chair "—by quitting when things got tough."

And yet, you did. You quit on me, *dammit.*

But she didn't say that out loud, and silence fell like a wall between them.

Ah, hell. Matt closed his eyes and counted. *Why does it always have to be like this between us, Alex? As close as we were—once—were we ever* honest *with each other?*

He took a deep breath and said softly, "Alex, be honest—do you really want to quit? Don't you want to keep going, too?"

She gave a short laugh. Looked at the ground, then at him. And did he imagine it, or had her eyes kindled for just a moment, the way they did sometimes, like live coals when a soft breath touches them?

She looked away again, nodding. "You did good out there," she said stiffly, not looking at him. "Really good. You saved him—you know that, don't you?"

"*We* did. We were good together, weren't we?" *Like old times.* He waited for her to say it: I've missed you. I need you here. I want you to come back.

But she didn't say it. Instead, Alex shaded her eyes and looked skyward, and they both listened to the staccato beat of the fire department chopper, making its way steadily toward them up the river canyon.

"I thought sure she was going to cancel the rest of the run," Sam said. "Didn't you?"

Cory didn't reply.

They were standing on a huge boulder overlooking the river, arms around each other's waists, watching the helicopter bank sharply and begin its long gradual climb out of the canyon. Down below them they could see Alex and Matt at the river's edge, getting the boat ready to put in.

"Wonder why she didn't?" She craned to look up at her husband. "Think maybe that's a good sign?"

She felt him exhale. Looking out across the river, he said, "Lord, I sure do hope so."

"You're worried, aren't you? Why—because of the accident? Seemed like Matt handled that real well."

"You're forgetting the reason you were in that kayak to begin with. I don't know, Sam. Seems like too many things going wrong."

Because she didn't want to think too much about how it had felt, being at the mercy of the river, she poked him teasingly in the ribs. "Are you being paranoid, Pearse? Or just superstitious?"

He didn't tease her back. The gravity of his voice sent a chill down her spine. "Not paranoid or superstitious, but maybe a wee bit…suspicious."

She pulled away from him a little. "Pearse? What are you thinking?"

He glanced down at her, then quickly away. "I don't know. I mean, you'd tell me if—"

The doubt in his voice jolted her. "Jeez, Pearse, you can't think—no!"

"Tell me the truth, Sam." His body felt rigid next to hers. "This isn't the Philippines all over again, is it?"

"Listen to me," she said, and her voice was low and

even. "That was before you were my husband. I'd tell you if I had anything goin' on. Especially if there was any chance it might put your brother in danger. I don't know how you could think I wouldn't."

He exhaled, and she felt him relax as he kissed the top of her head. "I don't. Not really."

Her own heartbeat slowed to its normal rhythms and the prickles faded from her skin. But she wasn't quite ready to let him off the hook. "Why would you mention it, then?"

"Because it sure does seem like somebody doesn't want us to make this run," Cory said quietly. "And I can't for the life of me think why—or *who*."

There were no more incidents, no more mishaps that day.

Because of the wait for the chopper, it was later than normal when they put in for the night, so everybody volunteered to help Alex with the food prep. She'd warned them it would have to be a wilderness camp, since a lot of their gear had had to be left behind with the malfunctioning oar boat. They'd have to make do without the folding table and chairs and tents. Nobody seemed to mind.

Cory and Sam unloaded supplies from the boat while Alex got the fire going and set up the camp stove and oven. She had baked brie, toasted sourdough bread and fresh raspberries ready by the time the unloading was done. Meanwhile, Matt made margaritas for everybody. Alex thought it was probably a toss-up, which was appreciated more.

It may have been partly the fault of the margaritas,

but Alex realized she was actually enjoying herself. It was weird, but it felt almost like being part of a warm family gathering—at least, the way she'd always imagined that experience would be. Cory and Sam were telling stories about each other, affectionate or hilarious, embarrassing, maybe, but never mean, cracking each other up and making it impossible for anyone listening not to laugh along with them. Matt and Alex listened and laughed, and it felt so good to her, watching Matt laugh. Seeing that smile she remembered. *So good.*

Meanwhile, potatoes roasted in the coals and an apple pie baked in the Dutch oven, and Matt tended the grill, waiting for the right moment to put on the thick, lean beef tenderloin steaks. Fresh green salad stayed cold and crisp in the cooler, along with plenty of tequila and margarita mix and whipped cream for the pie. A few yards away, the river chuckled peacefully to itself on its way down the canyon, and an owl hooted in the gathering dusk.

I'm happy, Alex thought in surprise. *Here, tonight, with these three people, I...am...happy.*

And it came to her, because she knew at this moment how it felt to be happy, that she had not been for a very long time.

After dinner, Alex adamantly refused Cory and Sam's offer to help with the cleanup.

"Okay if we go for a walk?" Cory then asked with studied innocence.

"Sure," said Alex, wondering why they felt they had to ask.

He and his wife exchanged a secret look and went off, holding hands. Alex called after them, "Watch out for rattlesnakes. And don't get lost…" Their laughter drifted back on the twilight breeze, and Alex felt a sharp pang of envy.

Then it hit her. *That secret look. Could it be, that the reason for this whole crazy run… Could it be?*

No.

But she hadn't imagined it.

Her chest prickled. Her heartbeat quickened and heat flooded into her cheeks. She glanced sideways at Matt, wondering if he'd caught the look. Wondering if he had any idea what his brother and sister-in-law were up to.

"What?" he said, and she looked away quickly.

"Nothing…" She hitched in a breath. "They're sure being good sports."

"What'd you expect?" Matt's smile was crooked. "None of this was your fault."

"Yeah, but not everybody would have been so understanding." She paused. "They even seem to be enjoying themselves."

He bent down to open the cooler…dropped in a foil-wrapped package of leftovers and closed it again. He gave a short laugh as he straightened. "I imagine they've been in worse situations. A helluva lot worse. I mean, steak, margaritas and apple pie? Jeez, Alex."

She felt the warmth leave her and a chilly disappointment take its place. She looked away and said distantly, "I just meant…Sam getting dunked…Tahoe almost—"

"I know what you meant. Sorry." Matt's voice was

gentle. Then, in a different, almost conversational tone, "My brother's seen some stuff. Did you know he spent several months in an Iraqi prison?"

"No!" Her braid snaked over one shoulder as she jerked her eyes back to him. "Really? Good Lord."

"Yeah. And Sam's kind of closemouthed about what it is she does, exactly, but I wouldn't be surprised if she's been in a hairy situation or two herself. You know she's a pilot, right?"

Alex shook her head. She was remembering Cory's words, that day in the office, when he'd come to ask about Matt. *"...I almost lost her, trying to keep my secrets."*

"Cory told me there were stories there—about her, the way they got together." But she hadn't asked. She hadn't been able to think about anything except the fact that Matt was back in her life. After five years…

"Probably more than one," Matt said dryly, and Alex smiled, remembering his brother had said almost the same thing. "What?" he demanded, seeing her smile.

Again, she shook her head and said, "Nothing." Because there was so much she wanted to say and knew she never would.

She finished packing away the remains of dinner, silently handing things to Matt to put in the cooler. Securing the camp, setting up for breakfast. Doing things she'd done hundreds of times before. Things they'd done together, she and Matt, so many times before.

The ache inside her came from nowhere and quickly became intolerable.

Just before it turned, in self-defense, to anger, she

heard the crunch of wheels on the hard-packed earth and felt the nearness of Matt's body in the growing darkness.

"Alex." His voice came barely above the whisper of the breeze in the pines. "What's wrong?"

"What's *wrong?*" She said it more loudly than she meant to, turning to lean her backside against solid rock and fold her arms across her middle. "Jeez, Matt, I wouldn't know where to start. You, this crazy run, Tahoe almost getting—"

"Yeah, look, why don't you forget about the stuff I already know, and just tell me what it is you're *not* telling me?"

"What's *that* supposed to mean?"

"You're worried, and it's not just about me, or making a Class V run you've made dozens of times before." He listened to her silence. Finally, sheer frustration made him add, "Come on. You used to tell me everything, Alex."

"Yeah," she shot back, breathless and angry, "*used* to." She shifted restlessly, and in silhouette he saw her look up at the deepening sky, at the stars just winking on up there.

"Back there at the put-in," he gently prompted, careful not to push too hard, "you were upset, and it wasn't—" he held up a hand to forestall her retort "—*just* because the boat failed. Booker T and Tahoe weren't happy, either. What happened, Alex?"

She hissed out a breath, unable to stop herself. "Somebody—" Her voice caught, and she cleared her throat and went on, tense and edgy. "Somebody filed the valve fitting."

"What?"

"Just enough so it had a slow leak. Couldn't have happened before we packed up the bus yesterday, because we'd have noticed it during the safety check. So it had to have been later. Last night sometime."

"Wait." He held up a hand now because he couldn't seem to get a grip on the words he was hearing. "You're telling me you think somebody deliberately…"

"Sabotaged the boat. Yeah, that's what I'm telling you."

"Come on, Alex. Who'd do such a thing? *Why?*"

"You think I haven't asked myself that at least a hundred times?" She lifted her arms and let them drop. "*God.* It's just not possible."

"Okay, you know what they say. If you eliminate the impossible, the alternative, no matter how improbable… So, what's the alternative? You missed the damage when you checked it—you all did."

She didn't reply. He couldn't see her face, but he could hear misery and self-blame in her silence.

"Don't beat yourself up," he said softly. "It happens."

"Yeah." And she muttered something under her breath as she turned her head away.

He could feel her tension, almost hear it, like a humming in the air. Knowing she was an instant away from walking off and leaving him there, he reached out and caught her hand. "Talk to me, dammit."

Her silence was impenetrable, her wrist like steel in his grasp. But the feel of it…the warmth, the wiry strength of it…the softness of her skin, touching his for the first time in so damn long. He gentled his grip, stroked his thumb over the tendons at the base of her palm, and wondered what would happen if he were to bring her hand to his mouth and put his lips there instead. Juices pooled at the back of his throat, and he felt like a starving man, starving for the taste of her… the smell of her.

"Matt…"

She was pulling against his grip, and reluctantly he let her go. But not before he felt her tremble. She took one step away from him, jerked back, lifted one hand toward him, then wrapped it with the other across her body. When she spoke it sounded as if the words were choking her. "That's what happened, isn't it? That day. I didn't check it. And I should have. I didn't—"

"Didn't—*what?*" He shook his head, trying to understand. She was talking nonsense. "Check what? What day?"

She took a step back toward him, then retreated, so upset he could see her shaking. "The day you fell. Your gear. I should have double-checked it. If I had—"

"What?" Sudden anger sent his voice off the scale. "What in the holy hell are you talking about? You think you were supposed to check *my* gear? What are you, my *mother?* Now I need *you* to check up on *me?*"

"It sure looks like you did!" She spat the words at him like an angry cat.

Matt shook his head, gave an incredulous bark of laughter. "Do you even *know* how insulting that is? You think you should have double-checked my gear…why? Because you think I was careless? Why—oh, wait, because we were arguing? Because I suggested maybe we should get married? Because I asked you if you loved me?" He paused, not really expecting an answer. In the silence he could hear her breathing. In a voice heavy with irony, he went on. "Maybe it was a question I shouldn't have had to ask after five years, and sure, I know it was lousy timing. But do you really think I'd be so upset over it, I'd forget to check out my gear?" Again, he tested her stubbornness. Finally, softly, he said, "I've been over it a thousand times in my mind, Alex. I swear to you, the gear was okay. I checked it thoroughly."

She answered him, a whisper of misery. "Then why did it fail?"

She waited, but he had no answer for that. He hadn't had one for five long years.

Chapter 6

Alex slept badly that night. She woke up several times, once in time to watch the almost full moon rise above the rim of the canyon and flood the river gorge with silvery light, and the stars go into hiding. She watched the river carry the moon's broken reflection along on its rippling current without ever taking it away. She saw the pines in black silhouette, and the smooth granite boulders huddled along the riverbanks like herds of great slumbering beasts.

Except for the chuckle of the river and the whisper of the breeze in the pines, the world was silent.

Across the camp she could see Cory and Sam, their sleeping bags close together, touching. And Matt's, on the other side, some distance from her own.

I can't hear him breathe. He always used to snore. I wonder if he's awake, too.

She fought the urge to call to him, whisper to him in the darkness. If she did, would he answer? What would she do if he did? Would she go to him? And if she did...then what?

Images...feelings... Before she knew it, they came tumbling in. She didn't want them but couldn't stop them, couldn't make them go away. So she closed her eyes and surrendered, let herself drown in the sweet, aching memory of how it had been...with Mattie, making love.

He was so sensual, for a man. He loved to be touched, not just there, *but everywhere. And I loved touching him, with my lips and tongue and fingers and breasts. I loved the way his skin felt...smelled...tasted. I could spend hours just...touching him.*

And he loved to touch me, too. He never seemed to be in a hurry to get inside me, as if that were the only thing that mattered. No...he would kiss me and kiss me...everywhere. Not as if that was something he had to do to get where he wanted to be, but as if this...the kissing...was all that mattered.

Oh, Mattie. I wonder...would it still be like that now?

What would it be like now? Even if you can't move, can you still feel?

We used to laugh a lot when we made love. I wonder, Mattie...would we...could we...still laugh?

The smell of coffee woke her up. She sat bolt upright in the morning chill and saw that it was early, just breaking day, and the pale ghost of the moon was slipping below the mountains on the far side of the river. And that Matt was already up and in his chair, with the stove going and coffee made.

Her sudden movement must have alerted him. He turned and saw her sitting up in her sleeping bag and made a little beckoning head-jerk, as if to say, *Hey, get up and get your lazy self over here.* A tremor ran through her, and she saw herself rising, going over to him and putting her arms around his neck and breathing in the warm, sleepy-man smell of him.

And so, contrarily, she took her time disentangling herself from her sleeping bag, stretched...shivered in the shorts and tank she'd slept in as she slipped on her shoes, and finger-combed her hair that had come loose from its braid. Then, and only then, did she get up and make her way across to the fire and the warmth where Matt waited to pass her a mug of coffee.

She smiled at him as she took it and murmured, "Thank you." Then, watching him reach to take a package of bacon out of the cooler, "You don't have to do that."

The smile he gave her back was crooked. "Figured you could use a little extra sleep, after the day you had yesterday."

She feigned outrage in a squeaky whisper. "Me! You're the one that went for a swim."

He handed her a stainless steel bowl, a whisk and a carton of eggs. "Okay, then, make yourself useful. First morning out—omelets, right?"

"Surprised you remember that." She set her coffee on the grill's prep shelf, and as she leaned past him to take the milk from the cooler, inadvertently brushed against his arm.

Her heart jolted and her skin shivered at the touch.

Had she done it on purpose? *Surely not.* But she hadn't tried very hard to avoid touching him, either.

"Some things you don't forget." His voice was a husky drawl, so close she could feel his breath on her temple. She turned her head to look at him, and her braid tumbled over her shoulder to dangle between them. He didn't have to move his hand much in order to grasp it.

An involuntary breath escaped her, not quite a gasp. She glanced down at his hand in its fingerless glove, holding her braid, his thumb stroking across the bumps and crevices, then lifted her eyes to his. They were so close, gazing back into hers. *So close.* If he tugged on her braid, even a little, and if she obeyed that summons... It would take no more than that.

Their eyes held. Time stopped.

A twig snapped in the quiet. Voices murmured across the camp. Alex straightened up, breathing again, as her braid slithered through Matt's loosened grasp.

"Our guests are awake," she said in a croaking voice, and only realized she'd said *our* when it was too late to take it back.

It was a picture-perfect day. As if, Alex thought, the river were trying to make up to them for its surliness the day before. The rapids were hair-raising enough to get everybody's adrenaline pumping, but they all came through them without mishap. And in the quiet water between, there was time for picture-taking and story-telling, to surprise a doe and her fawn drinking in the shallows, and to catch an even more rare glimpse of a bobcat bounding away across the rocky hillside.

As the guides usually did during the quiet times on the river, Alex gave talks on the river's history, geology, flora and fauna, although she felt self-conscious doing so now, with Matt there. He'd always been the better storyteller.

She said as much at one point, after forgetting a key point in the lecture she'd been giving on the role the Kern River Valley had played in the gold rush. Cory had smiled and said, "It runs in the family."

"Really? How's that?" Matt had seemed surprised.

"Dad loved to tell stories," Cory had explained. "Used to make them up himself. That was before you were born, though. Before Vietnam."

And it had hit Alex then, with a chilly sense of shock and shame, that this river run wasn't even about her and Matt and whatever may or may not have been between them. She'd been so caught up in her own issues and emotions—how could she have forgotten what it must be like for *him?* Not just coming back to the river, and the life he'd once loved so much, but trying to get to know a brother he hadn't known existed, a whole family history he didn't know anything about.

Yeah, you're one selfish bitch, Alex. The least you could do is quit thinking of your own issues and try not to make things any harder for him.

They took out for the noon break—a sumptuous spread of cold cuts, fruit and veggie plates, breads and cold drinks—nonalcoholic, since they still had more rapids to run that afternoon. Another of the cardinal rules of river rafting, right up there with "Watch for Rattlers" and "Leave No Trace," was "Don't Drink and Boat!"

After lunch, Sam volunteered to help Alex with the cleanup, while Matt and Cory went up the river—presumably to take care of personal and private needs. Alex was glad to have the help, and the company, since she wasn't all that comfortable with the course her own thoughts had been taking lately. Not after her lightbulb moment on the river.

And besides, she genuinely liked Sam. Not being one who got close to very many people, and being an only child besides, Alex didn't exactly know what having a sister would be like. But if she *did* have a sister, it would be okay with her if she was something like Samantha Pearson.

Which—combined with her chastened mood—was probably why, when Sam asked her how it felt, being around Matt again, she didn't try as she normally would to evade the question. But she couldn't answer it, either, thanks to the unexpected knot of emotion that came from nowhere to clog up her throat and make it impossible to do more than shake her head and give a meaningless little ripple of laughter.

"I do know how it is," Sam said gently. "From personal experience."

Alex cleared her throat, buying herself the time she needed to tuck her emotions safely away. "Yeah, you said that before. What…I mean, how do you know? From…what…"

Sam laughed. "What personal experiences, you mean? Okay, well, in a nutshell, Cory and I met when I was really young. He was a friend of my dad's, and thought he was too old for me. Or, maybe that I was too young for him—because I *was*. Too young to settle down, anyway. Too young to know what I wanted. He was patient for a long time, willing to wait for me to do all the stuff I wanted to do, that I thought I wouldn't be able to do once we—well, long story. Anyway, the upshot of it is, he got tired of waiting and we broke up. And then Cory got married to somebody else."

Alex made a shocked sound. "You're kidding."

"Nope. The marriage didn't last, but I was devastated."

"I can imagine!"

Sam's smile was wry. "Stupid me. I always thought he'd be there for me, forever. And then one day he wasn't."

Yeah, thought Alex, *I know how that is.*

"I didn't think I could ever forgive him for that. But then…a few years later, we met again under…let's just say, difficult circumstances. Again—long story, but we came close enough to losing each other forever that it kind of put things into perspective for both of us. In the end, it wasn't easy, but we just…had to forgive each other."

She paused, then added, "And for Cory there was the other thing—this issue about his family."

"Yeah," said Alex, "he told me about that."

"Well, he'd been keeping all that inside, and it was really hard for him to open up to me. Once he did—" She shrugged and Alex saw the sheen of tears in her eyes. "But what made it possible for us to get through all that was…" she brushed at her eyes and gave a small, self-conscious laugh, the kind of thing Alex could see herself doing if she got caught with her emotions showing "…we really *really* wanted to make it work. You have to have that. Otherwise, I think…it's just too darn hard."

Alex murmured, "Yeah…" Those emotions she preferred to hide were percolating dangerously.

Sam turned to give her a piercing look, weighing a plastic bag full of cut-up veggies in her hand. "So I guess my question would be…do you? Want to make it work with Matt?"

Oh Lord. Do I? Now Alex resorted to that painful little laugh as she muttered, "It's complicated."

"Always is, hon."

Oh yeah. Especially right now. "He's got a lot going on," she said carefully.

"About his family, you mean." Sam snorted—something else Alex wasn't above doing herself now and then. "There's always gonna be family issues. Now me—my dad disappeared from my life when I was ten."

"Hah," said Alex, "mine split before I was born."

"Yeah, well, *mine* turned up alive and well when I was eighteen."

"Okay, you win," Alex said, laughing. "You definitely take the blue ribbon for father issues." But she was remembering Booker T's words: *You never got to be any lovin' daddy's little girl.*

Sam was smiling. "Not really. My dad and I get along great, now. Turns out it wasn't his fault he was gone so long. He'd been shot down in the Middle East and was in an Iraqi prison all that time. Nobody knew he was there until Cory got himself kidnapped. He was this famous journalist, see, so they sent Special Forces to rescue him. And, whoops, they found my dad with him. That's how I met Cory."

"Wow." It was the only thing Alex could think of to say. What *did* you say to someone with a story like that? Filled with a vast, inexplicable sadness, she became very busy arranging plastic bags full of food in the cooler.

"So," Sam said casually as she passed the bags to her, "your mom never remarried? After your dad left?"

"Never *married*. Period. Nope, I think she'd about had her fill of getting her heart broken. She raised me all by herself, which couldn't have been easy. I wasn't exactly an easy kid. But...my mom was a tough cookie."

"Was? So...she's gone now?"

Alex nodded, staring down at her hands, guarding that private pain carefully. "She died—cancer. The same year I met Matt."

The silence that fell was only in the small space between them. Beyond it, the river sang its usual song, scrub jays screeched in the manzanita and a hawk whistled high in a cloudless sky. And from somewhere out of sight came the rich harmonies of two brothers' laughter.

Listening to it, Sam said softly and with a catch in her voice, "It's meant so much to him—finding Matt. Both of his brothers. I can't even—"

"Yeah," said Alex, and cleared her throat. "I can imagine. Too bad he didn't find him before—" She stopped, appalled, but Sam finished it for her and didn't seem to find it terrible.

"Before his accident, you mean. Yeah. You know, I

think Pearse believes if he'd been around it wouldn't have happened."

Alex smiled crookedly. "He's not the only one who's played the 'what if' game." She shrugged. "It happened. Can't be undone." *It is what it is, Alex.*

There was a pause. Then Sam said, "You and Matt were close, though, right? Before he got hurt?"

"Close?" The question surprised her, not the asking of it, but because she realized she didn't know the answer. *Close. Were we close, Mattie? We were together a lot...worked together...played together...slept together...talked...quarreled...laughed...made love. But were we close? I don't even know what that means.* She gave a one-shoulder shrug. "Yeah, I guess. If you mean, were we sleeping together." Then, as realization collided with guilt, she threw Sam a look and added defensively, "Look, it's not like I abandoned him, okay? I visited him as often as I could while he was in rehab. He's the one who abandoned *me*."

Sam said quickly, "I didn't mean it like that," but Alex held up a hand as if to stop a flood of accusing words.

She said in a choking voice, "You don't know what it was like, okay? I was there. I saw him fall. I thought he'd died, I really did." She paced a few steps, then back, arms wrapped around the pain inside her, pain she'd thought she'd put behind her. *Hoped I had.*

"But he didn't."

"No. No—but in a way, he did. Or...*something* did."

"Your feelings for him?"

"No. *No.*" She stared at the other woman as shock lanced through her, then sank back onto a boulder and brushed a furious hand across her nose. "No, but…the life I'd always thought we'd have together," she said thickly. "I never thought that would end."

Sam leaned against the rock beside her and looked at her along one shoulder. "Did it have to?"

Because her eyes were filling with tears, Alex did the only thing she could: looked away, looked at the sky, the mountains, the river. "I don't know." Her voice ripped raggedly through her throat. "I know I was so mad at him I could have killed him myself." She gave a sharp, bitter laugh. "Does that make sense? I mean, it's not like he wanted to get hurt, right? So then, I was mad at myself for thinking that. Oh hell, I was just…so angry. I wanted to scream at someone. Hit somebody." She shook her head and her voice betrayed her by becoming an airless squeak. "I missed him so much I thought I'd die. And when he told me he wasn't coming back, that he'd decided to stay down there in L.A. and it would be better if we—" She clamped a hand over her mouth and drew a shuddering breath.

Bluntly, without the gentleness and sympathy Alex was sure would have been her undoing, Sam said, "Did you tell him how you felt?"

Alex shook her head, not yet willing to risk actual speech.

"Why not?"

Alex shot her a hot, angry look. "I don't know— pride, maybe?"

"How about fear?"

"Fear!" Alex opened her mouth to deny it, then hesitated. "I don't know. I know I really hate needing anyone. It makes me feel…"

"Vulnerable?" Sam was smiling.

"Weak," Alex countered firmly.

"How about…human?"

Alex gave a bark of laughter—pure self-defense. After a moment she cut her eyes at the other woman over one shoulder. "Okay, don't think I don't know what you guys are up to."

Unrepentant, Sam grinned. "Is it working?"

For a moment longer Alex tried to keep up the banter, smile back. Keep it light. But her emotions were too close to the surface. Before she could stop it a wave of frightening longing swept over her. Horrified, she felt her face crumple, its expressions no longer hers to control. Appalled at her own vulnerability, she looked down at her shoes and whispered, "Do you really think it could?"

"Why not? If the feelings are still there…"

"Yeah, well, I guess that's the big question, isn't it?"

"Is it?" Sam seemed surprised. "For you, or for him?"

Alex couldn't answer. Safety doors came clanging down inside her head, shutting out the question, cutting off the voice she could still hear echoing faintly in her memory. *Do you love me, Alex?*

But Sam was waiting, and so after a moment she shrugged and said testily, "How would I know how he feels?"

Unperturbed, Sam said in pushy Southern, "Well, sweetie pie, don't you think you should find out?"

"Yeah, how?" Alex demanded, pushing back. "Seduce him?"

"Well, why not?"

Alex glared at her for a long moment while the self-sufficient loner inside her arm-wrestled with the pathetic weakling that secretly longed to confide in this woman. Giving up the battle, she drew a shaky breath. "Yeah, and what happens then? I mean, how do I know…" She halted and glared at the distant trees.

"Ah," said Sam, nodding. "You mean…"

"Yeah. I mean, how embarrassing would it be if…" She stopped again. Coughed. Made some sort of vague gesture. Then laughed and put a hand up to cover her eyes. "I looked it up—would you believe it? On the Internet. At first." She jerked her hand away and threw Sam a defiant look. "Well, hell, neither one of us seemed to be able to bring up the subject during rehab, and I was curious. Wouldn't you be?"

"Oh, yeah," said Sam. "And?"

Alex hitched a shoulder and watched the toe of her shoe dig at the hard-packed dirt. "It seems to pretty much depend on the person—the location of the injury, stuff like that," she said with studied diffidence. "Basically, it's mostly doable, with patience and—and I quote—'an understanding partner.'"

"So…?"

"That's just it," Alex said carefully, hoping the anguish she felt inside wouldn't come through in her voice. Confiding was one thing; stripping naked was another. "I don't know if I'm the understanding type."

And Sam said—gently, this time, "Oh, hon'. If you care enough, you will be."

"I just wanted to hug her," Sam told her husband. "I wanted to, so bad."

"I'm surprised you didn't."

"Yeah, well, in case you haven't noticed, Alex Penny isn't exactly the hugging type."

It was evening, past sundown but not yet dusk, and Sam was feeling a wee bit grumpy. Dinner had been another amazing feast—she didn't know how they managed it under such primitive conditions, she really didn't. At the moment, she felt entirely too full and too tired out from the day's adventures to move, much less go rambling through the rocks in yet another ploy designed by Cory to leave his brother alone with Alex. A ploy she was beginning to think might be a lost cause.

She'd said as much to Cory, who'd then asked why she felt that way. So she'd related most of her conversation with Alex, which, she admitted, had left her feeling sad.

"I think she loves him, I truly do, Pearse. But she's got some serious abandonment issues. I don't know if—"

"'Abandonment issues'?" Cory smiled and slipped his arm around her waist and pulled her snug against him. "That's something we know a thing or two about. And we managed to get together in spite of them."

For a moment Sam allowed her head to nestle in the comfortable hollow of her husband's shoulder. Just for a moment. Straightening, she said, "Yeah, but we didn't have the disability thing to deal with, either. I mean, think about it. They have to figure everything out all over again. Like, back to square one, really."

"Figure 'everything' out? You mean, the sex thing, don't you?" She heard the smile in his voice even before she felt the warmth of his lips against her hair. "I wouldn't worry too much about that. Those things have a way of working themselves out. Where there's a will…"

"Assuming there *is* a will."

"Hmm," Cory murmured. And after a moment, "I guess you didn't notice the way she was looking at him."

She craned to look at him. "Yeah? How?"

He grinned. "Like a hungry wolf."

"When? Today?"

"This afternoon. When we were going through the rapids."

"Oh, *well.* I might have been a *little* busy right then. You know…trying to keep from getting pitched into the river? *Again*…"

He laughed and pulled her back against him. "Well, let's just say she couldn't take her eyes off him. Watching him wield that paddle…"

"Hmm…well, I have to admit, Pearse, your brother does have an amazin' body. Those shoulders…" Her voice dwindled to nothing as her husband's fingers worked their magic over *her* shoulders. She chuckled low in her throat and slipped her arms around his waist. "Darn it, I really do wish we hadn't had to leave those tents behind."

"Hmm…why's that?"

"Because, honey-bunch…Alex and Matt aren't the only ones who could do with a little privacy."

He laughed softly and let her go. Then he bent down and gathered up his bedroll and tucked it under his arm, smiled at her and held out his hand. Her heart skittered like a teenager's as she took it. Smiling back at him, she walked beside him into the deepening dusk.

* * *

Matt watched his brother go off hand in hand with his wife, and only realized he was smiling when Alex looked over at him and said bluntly, "You know what they're trying to do, right?"

His grin slipped away. "They're not exactly being subtle."

He worked in silence for a moment, once again occupying himself by clearing away the remains of dinner and setting up for breakfast, while questions chased themselves in circles in his mind. He paused, then threw them at her all at once, so he wouldn't lose his nerve. "Is it so terrible an idea, Alex? Being with me? Do you find me that repulsive?"

Oddly, she didn't seem surprised he'd asked. She went sort of still for a moment, then shook her head, not looking at him. "What scares me is that I don't."

His heart began a slow, heavy thumping he could almost hear. "I'm not sure I know what to say to that." He paused, and the smile found its way back. "Fact is, you always were a puzzle to me."

"I'm not that complicated," she muttered, keeping her face turned away from him.

He gave a wheel a shove, edging closer to her. "Yeah, you are. Plus, you don't let on how you feel. And I've never been much good at reading minds." He rubbed the back of his neck as he added wryly, "The only time I ever knew how you felt is when I was touching you."

She threw him an arrogant look he remembered well. "Ha—you only *thought* you knew."

"Maybe." But then she shivered. He saw it…*felt* it.

And entered a zone of certainty and confidence he hadn't felt in a long time. "You cold?" he asked softly, knowing she wasn't.

Hugging herself, she glared at him in annoyance and shook her head. He touched the wheels again and brought himself closer, close enough to reach out and take her hand. It felt so familiar to him, and yet...not. It seemed smaller than he remembered. More vulnerable. Maybe because she wasn't resisting?

He turned her hand over, and with his other hand gently uncurled her fingers to expose her palm. Ran a fingertip over the bumps and ridges of calluses...then the softer, smoother hollow in its center. Her fingers curled involuntarily, and he looked up at her. Her cheeks looked moist and flushed, though her chin still had that defiant tilt.

"Okay," she demanded in a raspy voice that made a shiver crawl over his own skin, "what am I thinking now, smart-ass?"

"Oh, too easy." He laughed, and lifted her hand slowly to his mouth. He brushed the warm damp palm with his lips, smiling at her with his eyes as he murmured, "You're thinking, 'What is this guy doing? Promising something he can't deliver?'" He saw and felt her flinch. Laughing, he tightened his hold on her hand to keep her from pulling it away. "Oops, right on the money, huh?" She didn't reply, and he swiveled his chair just enough and tugged her toward him.

"Wait—what are you doing?" The fear in her voice as he guided her into his lap made his chest clench.

"Relax, darlin', I just want to show you something."

He moved her hand to his shoulder…watched her eyes while he took her other hand and placed it against his chest. He held his breath and felt his heart thumping against her hand. After a moment he let the breath out and said softly, "There…you see? Muscle and bone. I haven't changed that much. I still—" He paused, and the pressure in his chest reminded him he'd forgotten to take another breath. He hitched about half of one in and finished it. "I still like to be touched."

Chapter 7

Her hands were small and strong, the way he remembered. Just as he remembered. They began to move on his shoulders…his chest, stroking him, dipping under the fabric of his T-shirt to touch his skin. And it felt so good he wanted to cry or laugh out loud with sheer joy, because it had been so long since he'd been touched that way.

He felt a compulsion to close his eyes, the better to savor the sensation of her wicked little fingers working magic on his skin, but he didn't; having lost a good part of one sense, he wanted to make the most of the ones he did have. With all his senses at full alert, he listened to her quickened breathing, inhaled the scent of her hair and breath, touched her hair and then her face, and watched her intently even though he couldn't really see her eyes in the growing dusk. He watched them anyway, and imagined he saw them darken, first with confusion, then with desire she couldn't stop or deny.

Her hands slid to his neck and then upward to his head, cradling it between them as her fingers threaded through his hair and rasped against his scalp. Shivers enveloped him. He cupped the side of her face in his hand…then abruptly ripped off his glove and gently stroked her hair back and filled his hand with the silken thickness of her braid. As she dipped her head closer to him, just for a moment the firelight splashed across her face and he saw her eyes were closed, and droplets of moisture in her lashes caught the light like tiny jewels. His heart ached with tenderness, and he murmured her name, but only in his mind.

He didn't kiss her then. He wasn't sure why—he wanted to, more than he wanted his next breath. Maybe he wanted it too much, and knew it was something not to be rushed. Whatever the reason, something inside him held back. *Not yet…not yet.* The words whispered warnings in his mind.

He slipped his hands down her back but didn't use them to compel her closer. Instead, he moved them onto her waist, ignoring her initial gasp of protest as he lifted and turned her, rocked his chair into better alignment, then resettled her astride his lap. *Now?* his body and heart pleaded. But again his mind whispered, *Not yet.*

Between his hands her torso felt supple…vibrant. The muscles in her back were as firm as he remembered, and when he let his hands slide downward over her bottom, that was as he remembered, too. On they went, his roving hands, over her hips to her thighs, sleek and bare in the jogging shorts she'd worn that day beneath her wet suit. And her back bowed and her head dipped lower, closer to his, while her breath flowed warm over his lips. And still he didn't claim her mouth, although he could have with no more than a deepened breath. *Not yet...*

Down the length of her thighs, then back up again, his hands stroked slowly, savoring the matte textures of her skin. And now, on their return journey it seemed only natural for his hands to follow the path of least resistance and slip under fabric and elastic to maintain contact with that sweet warmth. He felt her belly quiver and contract at his first touch there, and then she gave a little whimpering cry of surrender and *she* was the one to bring her mouth to his. And in his mind the voice whispered, *Yes.*

After that, for Matt, for a time all thought ceased. He knew only *feeling,* the way a starving man feels such intense relief when given food, he spares no thought at all for manners or customs, flavor or substance, but simply devours all he can. He'd been hungry for her for so long. Now he could not get enough.

He didn't even notice—not then—that she was as hungry and heedless as he. It was only unknown minutes later when they broke apart, panting, that he realized his lips were swollen and tingling and tasted of blood, and that her body was arched in a way that brought it into intimate contact with his. That his fingers were nested in her warm, moist places, and that she was rocking in sync with his gentle probing, demanding more.

With silent urgency, she twined her fingers in his hair and pressed her forehead to his while her body writhed against his hand. He turned his head and buried his face in the hollow of her neck, seeking and finding the leaping pulse there, at the same time his fingers were locating its counterpoint deep inside her body.

It came to him that she was making sounds—gasps and whimpers—sounds he'd never heard her make before, even in all the times they'd made love. He wrapped one arm around her and his hand came to cradle her head, and when her body went rigid in his arms and her breath came screaming in a high, thin cry, he held her close against him and rocked her with his own body. He felt her throb around his fingers, and gentled the runaway pulse in her neck with soothing strokes of his tongue, while something inside him leaped and surged in primitive masculine triumph. He laughed softly and deep in his throat with the sheer joy of that feeling.

A moment later, he realized, too late, that what Alex was feeling wasn't joy, or anything close to it. She'd sagged against him, at first, breathing in irregular gulps and gasps, the way she'd always done postclimax. But now she pulled jerkily away from him, shaking, her hands fisted in the fabric of his shirt.

"How…could…you…do…that…to…me?"   She sobbed the words, punctuating each one with blows from her knotted fists, rained against his chest and shoulders. Then she slithered backward, out of his grasp and off his lap, to stand facing him, hugging herself, hunched and shivering with fury. "How could you think…that was what I *wanted?*" She gave a hiccupping sob and amended it. "That it was…*all* I wanted?"

"Alex—"

"*No.*" She held out her hand like someone bent on stopping a train. "No—don't you say anything. Don't…say…anything." Then she jerked around and stumbled off toward the river, heedless of the gathering dark.

Matt watched her go in a state of bemusement and shock. The woman had obviously lost her mind. Her words made no sense. All *I wanted…*? What more could he have given her? The first time they'd made love in five years—hell, the first time they'd touched each other since the accident—and all he'd done was give her a mind-blowing—

All *I wanted…* He played the words she'd spoken again in his mind, and this time heard them overlaid with sounds from other times, past times they'd made love. The little feminine pleasure sounds she'd made as she touched him…aroused him…blown *his* mind. And it came to him then, a glimmer of understanding, a tiny inkling of why she might be upset.

Clearly, he was an idiot. A thick-headed jerk.

Chastened, he put a hand down to check himself and found wetness, and swore out loud, then laughed silently at the irony. He wondered if Alex would be happier if she knew he'd climaxed, too.

Alex awoke at the first hint of light and smelled wood smoke. She lay with her arm over her eyes, envisioning Matt in his chair, starting the fire, putting on the

coffee, setting up for breakfast. Envisioning him in his
T-shirt, with his broad shoulders and bulging muscles
and sculpted chest and the strong, sturdy column of his
neck…reliving the cool feathery feel of his hair on her
fingers, the smell of his skin, the taste of his mouth…

The sensation of sexual climax rocketing through
every nerve and cell in her body. The agonizing, sickening, chilling sense of humiliation that came after.
And she almost groaned aloud with misery.

Oh God, how will I face him? Look at him? Talk to
him? How did I let that happen? How could it have
happened? He barely had to touch me and I—

Oh, get over it, Alex.

Mom?

*I thought I taught you to stand on your own feet and
not depend on anybody. So why are you making a big
deal out of this? You were long overdue for some sex,
and he gave it to you. Enjoy. And get over it.*

She shook with silent, rueful laughter.

And in the silence, heard a familiar sound. Unmis-
takably a snore. Coming from somewhere on her left,
which was where, the last time she'd checked, Matt
had his sleeping bag. So…Matt wasn't up yet, and could
not have started the fire. Who, then? Sam, or Cory?

She took her arm away from her eyes and sat up. The
camp was silent, the campfire dark and cold. On her
right she could see the elongated bundle that was Sam
and Cory's combined sleeping bags. On her left, the
bundle that was Matt's. Across the river the slightly
flattened circle of the moon was preparing to dip below
the canyon's rim. Somewhere a bird woke up and joined

its song to that of the river. The air was cool and dry and smelled of burning wood and brush.

Swearing under her breath, Alex rapidly unzipped and scrambled out of her sleeping bag. She was fumbling in her backpack for the satellite phone when Matt's sleeping bag stirred, and his voice came, raspy with awakening.

"Alex? You up? I smell—"

"Yeah, yeah, I know." She was jabbing buttons with her thumb. "Smells like there's a fire somewhere. What else is new? It's the weekend." She put the phone to her ear and listened to clicks and then a ring. Covering the mouthpiece with her hand, she nodded toward the double sleeping bags. "Better wake up your brother." She couldn't have said why, but she had a bad feeling about this.

And was shamelessly grateful for a crisis that made it possible to pretend last night had never happened.

Across the river, the moon glowed orange behind an ominous veil of smoke. Alex kept her eyes on it as she replied to the crisp voice of the fire department dispatcher, a friend as well as the husband of one of her guides.

"Hey, Dave, it's Alex. I'm with a group up on the Forks. What's happenin', man? You got a fire up here, or what?"

"You're up on the Forks?" The dispatcher uttered some profanity, and then, "Not a good time to be up there, Alex."

"Well, shoot. Tell me when's a good time—we got tourists every damn weekend."

"I don't think this was tourists."

"Are you kidding me? You're saying this was—"

"I'm saying it looks suspicious from the get-go. Right now it's heading right toward you. We got aircraft warming up as we speak—they'll be in the air come daylight, but if I were you guys, I'd get my butt in gear and get on down the river—*now*. If the wind stays steady, you're fixin' to get cut off."

Alex disconnected and stood for a moment with the phone in her hand, the back of her hand pressed against her forehead. *Focus, Alex. This is no time for an emotional…whatever. You…Matt Callahan…whatever that was last night—that's history. Right now—*

"Problems?" Cory joined them, shivering in T-shirt, shorts and flip-flops and rubbing vigorously at his arms. Right behind him, Sam was doing the same.

"Yeah…maybe a little one." Alex caught Matt's eye as he heaved himself into his chair. She jerked her eyes back to Cory and Sam and forced a smile for their benefit. "There's a fire farther on down the mountain—no big deal, but they might need to shut down the road. So we need to get to the take-out point before they do. Looks like the eggs Benedict I was planning on serving you guys for breakfast is gonna have to wait."

"I'd settle for some coffee," Sam muttered through a yawn.

"Sorry, folks, no time for a fire," Alex said in her brisk tour-guide voice, cheery as all get-out. "Grab some cold cuts and make yourselves a sandwich while I get the boat ready to go. For you caffeine junkies, there's Coke in the cooler." She tucked the phone in the waistband of her shorts as she started toward the river.

"Alex."

She turned back, heart galloping, smile fixed in place. *Matt, if you say anything…one word about last night, I swear I will push your ass in the river.*

He rolled closer to her, eyes dark shadows in the gray dawn light. "Need any help?"

She let out a breath, and with it a small shaky laugh. "Yeah—you can hurry those two along. And get yourself fed and ready to shove off, ASAP."

"Is it that bad?" He asked it in a low voice, for her ears only, and she answered the same way, but with a bite in it.

"Look, don't worry about it, okay? I've got it under control. You're not… You just…look after your brother and his wife." She walked away from him, chilled and shaky with poorly timed adrenaline and emotions she didn't need and didn't know what to do with.

She didn't need this. She really didn't. She hadn't wanted to make this damned run to begin with, and being able to say "I told you so" wasn't going to make up for what was turning out to be a total disaster. In so many ways.

First thing she was going to do when she got back was kill Booker T. But before she could do that she had to get three people through a forest fire and some dangerous water. And she had to do it all alone.

Then, for some reason that thought—the *alone* part—made her angry. Furious. Resentful as hell. Which was odd, since if there was anything Alex Penny had always prided herself on, it was how gosh-darned self-reliant and independent she was.

Since when do I need anybody? Alone is the way I like it.

But, banging around inside her head the thought had a curious echo. And it came to her as she methodically checked over the boat and gear—an activity that brought a measure of reason and calm to her mind— that those were the same words she'd repeated over and over to herself during the first days and weeks after Matt's accident.

Now, as then, she tried very hard not to hear the little voice way in the back of her mind whispering, *Liar...*

When they hit the first set of rapids Sam forgot all about the fact that she was a quart low on coffee. She felt like she was finally getting the hang of this rafting thing, and about time, too. She'd played loop the loop with clouds and raced the wind and won, but she'd never run up against anything quite like the Kern River. Flying was still her first love—okay, her second, after Pearse— but white-water rafting was rapidly moving up on third place for sheer heart-pumping, mind-blowing exhilaration.

They all did a lot of whooping and hollering like a bunch of kids on a roller coaster, and by the time they'd come through the rapids everyone was laughing and drenched, and had pretty much forgotten, at least for the moment, that there was a forest fire burning somewhere between them and home. Well, not quite forgotten; that would have been hard to do with the sun glaring redly down on them through a haze of smoke like an angry god.

They drifted in the quiet water below the rapids, resting, making jokes and doing some bragging and back-patting.

"I'm glad you're all feeling invincible," Alex warned them, as the current picked up and the unmistakable roar of more hydraulics came from up ahead. "You ain't seen nothin' yet. Grab those paddles, people."

Then, from one breath to the next, the boat became a bucking bull. Sam gave a whoop as the bow lifted into the air, and almost at the same moment, Matt threw himself chest first onto the bow's tube to give it more weight.

The boat went into a spin, and Alex yelled, "Right— *pull!* Left—*back!*"

Sam was pulling on her paddle with all her might, and from the corner of her eye she could see Cory dig in with his and twist his body to hold steady against the force of the current.

Then suddenly he wasn't there.

A scream she couldn't hear ripped through Sam's throat. She didn't remember dropping her paddle, but in the next instant she was lunging across the boat with only one goal in mind—to rescue her husband. She would have hurled herself into that maelstrom, too, but for the hand that gripped her arm and sent her flying.

Struggling like a netted trout in the bottom of the boat, above her she saw motion…heard Alex scream, "Matt— *No!*"

She got herself upright just in time to watch Matt snatch up the safety line and slip headfirst over the side.

Alex didn't know whether she was too angry to be

scared, or too scared to be angry. The turbulence inside her head and heart would have made the river look like a lily pond.

"Matt—I swear I will *kill* you!" She probably screamed that aloud, but inside she was sobbing, *Damn you, Mattie, don't you dare die!*

It was the nightmare she'd thought she was finished with. Or the most horrible déjà vu she'd ever experienced. Here she was again, seeing him fall, and fall, and fall, and helpless to do anything—not one thing—to stop it.

Who was she, anyway, a little bitty woman, no more than a hundred and ten pounds soaking wet? What could she do against a force like the river? Who did she think she was, to challenge Class V rapids with only another woman to help her? Sam was a tall woman, and strong, but hell, the two of them put together didn't have enough weight to keep the damn boat from flying around in the turbulence like a cork in a typhoon.

She'd never felt so scared. So angry. So helpless.

All she could do was hang on to the oars and struggle to keep the two men in sight. At some point she realized Sam was doing the same thing, and that they'd both reached out unconsciously and were clinging to each other's hands as they watched the two dark heads disappear again and again beneath the white foam.

Matt had only one thought in his head when he went over the side of the boat for the second time: *I am not going to lose this brother before I get a chance to know him. I just found him. I'm not gonna lose him now.*

He'd grabbed the safety line before going in, but that

could be a liability, if it got hung up in the rocks, or if he let himself get tangled in it. But he knew if he could just get to Cory and get the line to him, he'd have a chance. He told himself Cory had a good chance—he had his life vest; at least he wouldn't be like Tahoe, with no buoyancy and only his own strength to keep him afloat.

He beamed silent messages across the waves, like prayers. *Hold on, man, I'm coming. Keep your head up, bro, and get those legs up, like we practiced during the safety drill. You don't want to end up like me....*

Then he saw Cory. And Cory saw him. Matt focused on his brother's eyes, dark as coals in all that white, kept watching them as he pulled himself through the swirling, racing current with all the strength he had in his body, watched them until he was close enough to reach out and grab hold of his brother's vest.

"Hold on, bro, I got you. You're okay now—I've got you."

Did he yell that aloud, or was it only another silent prayer? He didn't know, couldn't have heard anyway in the rush and roar around him.

He went under, swallowed water, but didn't lose his grip on his brother's vest. Came up choking and gagging, but managed to get the safety line looped around them both. He couldn't see what was happening in the boat, which was bounding and leaping like a wild mustang, so he just started hauling himself one-handed along the line, and kept his other arm snugged across his brother's chest. The line stretching between him and the boat grew shorter, and then he was able to throw his arm over the tube, and he felt hands reaching for him, grabbing him, pulling on him.

"No—take him!" he was able to choke out, and only when he felt Cory's weight pulled from his arms did he allow himself to relax. He held on to the side, then, panting and coughing up river while the boat galloped over the last of the rapids and loped into quiet water.

He was hauling himself up the side of the boat, grateful for his gloves and wondering if he had enough strength left to make it when he felt Alex grab hold of his shoulders.

"This part I got," he told her, laughing…panting. "Could use a lift on the hind end, though."

"I should let you stay in there," she said, in a voice as gritty as it ever got. But she leaned over and got a grip on the back of his vest and heaved, and before he had time to grab another breath, he was on his back in the bottom of the boat with his legs still up on the side.

He'd forgotten how strong she was for such a little woman. Plus, there was the fact she was mad enough at him to spit nails. Was he a crazy fool to think that was a good thing?

He caught a breath to stifle a threatening grin, then twisted around, looking for Cory. "How is he?"

Sam was kneeling beside him, and Cory's eyes were closed, his face contorted with pain. "Broken collar-bone, I think. Maybe some broken ribs." She threw Matt a look over her shoulder, then gasped and swore. "Lord, Matt, what about you?"

"What about me? I'm fine."

"You're bleeding, you idiot," Alex said tersely.

That was when Matt noticed the barber-pole spiral of blood running down the calf of his elevated leg. Well, hell. He figured it probably wasn't a good time for a flippant remark about the perks of being paralyzed, with Alex already of half a mind to kill him—which he *still* couldn't convince himself was not a *good* thing.

Alex mad at him he could take—gladly. Time was, she'd been mad at him half the time anyway. Alex not giving a damn—that was what he couldn't accept. And had decided he wasn't going to, not anymore.

He watched her pick up his foot—not gently or gingerly, either, so it appeared she wasn't squeamish about touching him—and bit down on his lower lip to keep from grinning as she scowled critically at his injury.

"You'll live," she announced, bending his knee and placing his foot on the same level he was, handling it as deftly as if she'd been doing it forever. "Probably won't be bleeding to death anytime soon, either. Must've scraped it on a rock. Next time keep your feet up." Muttering about rookie mistakes, she offered him a hand, and didn't flinch from meeting his eyes when he took it and let her anchor him as he pulled himself to a sitting position.

Her eyes. Greenish, now, and dark as quiet water, fringed with black and filled with accusation and anger, confusion and pain. Looking into them, he felt the elation leave him. He wanted to take her in his arms and hold her and tell her everything was going to be okay.

Or, he ruefully amended, it would be, if only she could get over her issues, whatever they were—pride, independence, mom, commitment—and realize she needed him as badly as he needed her.

There—he'd said it. Not aloud, but to himself, which was halfway there, right? *I need you, Alex Penny. I thought I had everything figured out, things were going okay, my life was on track. But Cory's right, there's more to life than a career. And the truth is, I really need you in mine.*

"Think you can handle a paddle, Matthew? If you're not too beat up, you can help me get this boat to shore." Alex's voice, rough and cranky as nine miles of bad road, and music to his ears.

"Hand me a paddle," he said, grinning because he knew how much it must have cost her to ask for his help, even for something like this.

But it *was* something. Baby steps, he told himself.

Alex hated to admit defeat, but she'd had enough. Enough of this damn run, enough of Matt, and enough of this damn river. Should've listened to her instincts in the first place. Why had she agreed to it, when every ounce of common sense had told her it was crazy?

Yes, why did you, Alex? Because...admit it, you wanted to see him again. Yes, you did.

With Sam and Matt helping, she managed to beach the boat at a spot they sometimes used for emergency take-outs because it was a fairly easy hike up to the road—for someone with working legs. The first thing she did, once her feet were on dry land, was call the Rafting Center. She was a little surprised when Linda handed the phone right over to Booker T. He gave her his usual, "Hey, sweet pea," but Alex could tell he was worried.

"Don't you 'sweet pea' me. Right now I'd just as soon kill you as look at you. How's Tahoe?"

"Pretty much out for the season, so he's not a happy man, but other than that, he's fine. How're you doin'?"

"'Bout as well as you'd expect, considering this was insane to start with. We've got another injured man. Need you to come pick us up."

"Aw, shoot. Who—"

"Cory went in at Vortex—broke some ribs, I think. Look, there's no way we're taking those last rapids— the Falls—with only three able bodies."

"Three? And…one of those would be Matt, I take it?"

"Don't push it, Booker T. I mean it." She scowled at Matt, who was listening to every word and grinning, damn him. And sitting there with the paddle across his knees, his looked as able as any body she'd seen lately. "We're at that take-out point below Vortex—you know where I mean. You know Matt can't get up to the road, so you're gonna have to come get us. How fast can you get here?"

"Uh…got a problem with that, honey. We just got word they've closed the road above the Johnsondale Bridge because of that fire."

Alex felt as if the bottom had fallen out of her stomach. The world went cold and quiet for a moment. Then, realizing three pairs of eyes were watching her like hawks, she hauled in a breath and said brightly, "Bloody hell."

"Sorry, baby doll. I'll get the bus up to the take-out at the bridge, but you'll have to get down that far on your own."

"Yeah. Okay."

She disconnected, swearing under her breath, and

punched in the number for the fire department. It rang several times before Dave picked up. He listened to her request, then broke the news: all available choppers were out on the fire.

"Unless you've got a dire emergency, I can't pull one off the fire right now. Obviously, lives come first, so if you tell me you've got lives at stake, we'll come and get you."

Alex hesitated, biting her lip, looking at the three people sitting in the boat, watching her intently. Cory, pale and tight-lipped with pain. Sam, calmly holding his hand. Matt.

"Alex? Say the word."

"No. No, that's okay. We'll make it," she said. And thumbed the disconnect button.

Chapter 8

Alex tucked the phone back in her waterproof duffel bag and zipped it shut. One way or the other, she wouldn't be needing it again this trip. It was all up to her now.

She straightened and turned to face the others. But it was Matt's eyes she held on to as she spoke. "Okay, troops, here's the situation. The road's closed because of the fire, so the bus can't get up here to us. Choppers are tied up fighting the fire, so they can't pick us up either. So…looks like we're pretty much on our own."

"No problem," Sam said. She gave her husband's hand a squeeze and let it go. "We've come this far, we can finish it. How much farther is it?"

"Not that far…but the problem is, the last rapids we run before the take-out below the bridge—"

"Carson Falls," Matt said, nodding.

Alex glanced at him, then back at Sam, who said, "Yikes. *Falls?* That sounds like fun."

Alex hauled in a breath and tried a smile. "It can be, actually. They're not that high, but it'll seem like a mile, going over. And it can be tricky. But normally, see, there'd be a few more people to help navigate. I don't know if I can—"

"*We* can," Matt said quietly. "We've done it before, Alex. You and me. We can do it again."

It had been a while since he'd given in to frustration over his lack of mobility, but right then he desperately craved privacy. Privacy with Alex. To be alone with her and do…well, whatever it took to make her see she didn't have to go it alone. That she was *not* alone.

But he couldn't do that, not with his chair strapped on the back of the boat, and nothing but a narrow strip of riverbank among the rocks even if he'd had access to it. And he couldn't very well ask his brother and Sam to give them a few minutes, not with Cory in pain and barely mobile himself. So he just looked at her as hard as he could and hoped she'd see the confidence and conviction in his eyes.

Dance with me, Alex.

It came back to him suddenly, that evening at The Corral, when he'd had his epiphany about what this river run was all about, what it meant to him and his future. And it seemed to him he must have known somehow that it was all going to come down to this. This moment. This question. *Are you gonna dance with me, Alex?*

A gust of wind chose that moment to come skirling up the canyon, bringing enough smoke with it to make his eyes water.

Alex held on to her braid with one hand as she looked up at the sky. "Yeah, but the river's not the only thing we've got to worry about."

Cory cleared his throat and tried to straighten up, grimaced and had to brace his ribs with his good arm in order to speak. "Hey—for what it's worth, I've had my life saved on more than one occasion, and it happens two of the people who've done that for me are right here in this boat." He coughed, grinned and looked first at his wife, then at Matt, and finally at Alex. "If I get a vote, I can't think of any three people I'd rather trust to get me home safely than the two of them…and you, Alex."

Sam laughed the way people do when they're moved and trying not to let on and said, "Well, shoot, Pearse."

"What about it, Alex?" Again, Matt put everything he had into his smile, his voice, his eyes. "Are we gonna do this?"

What about it, Alex?

And for some reason she was remembering that moment at The Corral, when he'd almost asked her to dance. Except he hadn't said the words, not really. Had he? And even if he had, she wouldn't have known what to say. Anyway, she'd hesitated and let the moment go by. And regretted it—she could admit that, now. She'd underestimated him then. What if—

It's not the same! That was a stupid dance, dammit— this is life and death. If you make the wrong choice this time it'll cost you a helluva lot more than a Corral burger.

Then…without even realizing she'd made her decision, she was bending over, giving the boat a shove, stepping over the side. "All right, then, let's do it," she said tersely.

With Sam and Matt helping, they pushed off from the riverbank and the boat caught the current.

Not much was said. Alex didn't give her usual speech, reminding everyone of the commands, going over the safety rules. Sam and Matt had already taken up their positions in the bow, one on each side. It was Cory who was in the bottom of the boat, now, wedged in among the backpacks and sleeping bags to cushion him as much as possible. Alex climbed carefully around him to her seat up high on the back and took hold of the oars.

It was deceptively peaceful, at first, drifting on the river past stands of bull pine and sycamore, manzanita and chaparral and cottonwoods, and the great gray boulders scoured smooth and carved into fantastical shapes by rushing waters over uncounted millennia. But above them the sky roiled with billows of windblown smoke, and the sun seemed far away and inconsequential, only a glaring, brassy disk, like an old tarnished coin.

The wind blew stronger and hotter, a thermal wind now, fed by the fire as much as driving it. Ash rained down on the river and the boat and the people in it, and no one spoke of it. No one spoke at all.

I wonder, Alex thought, *if they're all as scared as I am. Are you afraid, Mattie? Or is this just another adventure for you? You used to love to dare the Devil.*

At that moment, as if he felt her gaze, he turned his head and smiled at her. His beautiful smile, like the old Mattie. And in a gravelly voice that wouldn't have been out of place in a biker's bar, he began to bellow "The River," the Garth Brooks song that had been running through her own head. She felt a kick under her ribs and a tightness in her throat that kept her from joining Sam and Cory when they chimed in on the chorus, but then the last lines of the second verse flashed into her mind and she had to laugh out loud. *Dare to dance...* How had he known what she was thinking?

The singers repeated the chorus with lusty enthusiasm, then let it die away. And in the quiet, they heard it—the rushing roaring sound that wasn't wind.

Sam threw Alex a look that wasn't quite alarm. "Good Lord—is that the falls I'm hearing?"

"I don't think so," said Matt. "Look..."

They all looked where he'd pointed with a tilt of his head, toward the timbered ridge that rose on the right bank of the river, no more than a quarter of a mile away. Sam spoke for all of them when she murmured, "Oh my God."

Flames were shooting upward along the top of the ridge, tornadoes of fire, twisting, twirling, leaping and roaring like something alive. Like a monster, hungry, voracious...*alive.* As they watched, a bull pine on the downslope of the ridge exploded in flames. The monster gave a great roar as if in triumph as it devoured that tree and instantly bounded on to the next...and the next. Heading straight for them.

Alex was already down in the boat, tearing through the packed gear. "Here," she yelled, "grab a sleeping bag. Dip it in the river." She was putting her words into action, tossing a sleeping bag at Matt, who caught it and unrolled it over the side of the boat. "Get yourself covered. Everybody get down in the boat and cover up. Cover as much of the boat as you can!" She didn't want to think about what would happen if one burning cinder hit the boat. Going over the falls in an oar boat was one thing; going over in wet suits and life jackets, especially with an injured man…that wasn't an option she wanted to contemplate.

As she struggled to drag the sodden sleeping bags into the boat and get them wrung out enough to work with, Alex heard a new note above the demonic roaring of the fire—the metallic hum of aircraft engines. And now she could see the helicopter zooming toward them up the valley, its water bag swaying out behind as it banked into the path of the inferno. It dropped its load and swooped away into the distance, where she could see another chopper angling into position. They seemed so tiny, she thought, like sparrows circling the head of a dragon.

The image had barely formed in her mind when the beast let go a blast of fiery breath-searing heat, choking smoke and stinging ash—straight into their path. Fear, blacker and more suffocating than the smoke, enveloped her. Her mind stopped. The oars slipped from her hands as she lunged blindly for the side of the boat.

Then, from somewhere outside the terror, came a sound. A voice. Matt's voice, yelling.

"Get *down!* Cover up! And paddle like hell if you can!"

And somehow she was gripping the oars once again, leaning into them with all her might and at the same time trying not to breathe. The boat galloped beneath her, gathering speed. The wet sleeping bag was heavy on her head and shoulders, and peering from under it like a terrified creature hiding beneath a rock, she saw the world disappear in a roiling billowing holocaust of smoke and flame.

"Don't look!" Matt's voice, like a raucous note of a blackbird's call in the midst of a storm. "Keep your eyes on the water! Pull...*pull!"*

Alex focused on his voice, shut out everything else, listened only to that voice.

Her lungs screamed in agony, desperate for air. Her eyes streamed tears and her throat made whimpering sounds without breath. *Oh God oh God don't let me die like this not like this!*

Then...just when she thought she could not make her arms and shoulders go one more pull on the oars, when her muscles seemed on the brink of total rebellion...the noise and heat and smoke were behind her. She could hear sounds again—the clatter of choppers, the rush of the river, grunts of effort, coughs and ragged breathing from the others in the boat. She threw back her head, shook off the wet sleeping bag as she gulped in air, as much as her lungs would hold. The oars went slack, and she slumped over, trembling.

Incredibly, someone—was it Matt? Sam?—began to laugh. Alex tried it, and discovered it felt good. Laughing and sobbing with the sheer joy of being alive, she looked up and found Matt's eyes, found them gazing back at her, red-rimmed and burning, as if they still held pieces of the fire they'd come through. He wore a black mustache from the smoke and she knew she probably did, too. Yes, they all had them—Sam, holding the paddle with one hand and a death grip on her husband's life vest with the other; Cory hunched over with one arm braced across his ribs and a grin on his face; and Matt, holding his paddle across his knees like a victorious gladiator.

Gazing at them, Alex felt chastened…humbled. And overwhelmed by a tremendous wave of…something— *my God, was it* love?—for each of them. Amazing, in- credible, wonderful people, these three—they'd come through with flying colors, while *she,* on the other hand, had come within a breath of losing it. If it hadn't been for Matt calling her back from the edge of panic…

"Don't get too comfortable, guys," Matt yelled in a voice reduced to a frog's croak by the smoke and fire. "Hear that? That's the falls. Comin' up fast. Now listen up—when we get close, you want to make sure to keep the boat pointed straight ahead. Got it? Don't let her slip sideways, or we're all goin' for a swim."

He half expected Alex to say something, take back the lead, but she didn't. In fact, she seemed awfully subdued, for Alex. Knowing her the way he did, he was pretty sure she was feeling bad about being scared when they were going through the fire. He knew she'd hate that she had been, because she liked to think of herself as up for anything. But brave as she was, she wasn't a daredevil, not like he was.

Daredevil. He'd been called that, by Alex, and prob- ably some others, too. So he supposed he must be. He knew he'd never felt so alive—well, not in a long time, anyway. Maybe he did need to skirt the edge of danger, walk the tightrope, meet the challenge in order to feel fully alive.

And if that was so, how had he managed all these years, being only half-alive? More important, how could he go back to being half-alive after this? The river's roar was music to him. It sang through all his muscles and nerves and bones, and he felt he could dance its dance forever and never get tired.

He looked over his shoulder at Alex, and thought he'd never seen her look more beautiful, with her hair coming loose from its braid and her cheeks streaked with soot and tears. He wanted her to know how happy he was, being here on the river again, with her. He wanted her to be happy, too, having him with her again. But she looked haunted, not happy, and he saw ghosts of the terror that had been in her eyes as they were heading into the fire.

Remembering that, he realized it wasn't the first time he'd seen that look in her eyes. He'd seen the same fear and panic staring down at him as he lay on his back on a rocky ledge, feeling nothing at all, no pain...nothing, and she, hovering over him, begging him not to die.

He had a sudden bright flash of empathy, or insight, and it struck him that of all things Alex hated most, to be afraid must top the list. Was that why she hadn't fought for him, argued with him when he'd told her he didn't want her in his life? Was that why she couldn't let herself love him? Because to love someone is to know the worst kind of fear?

He looked at her and smiled, his heart sore with

wanting to take her hand and tell her it was okay, and not to be afraid. Or, not to be afraid of *being* afraid, because that was part of being alive, after all. *Take my hand, Alex, dance the river with me, like the song says.*

He wanted to tell her that, and maybe he'd have a chance to, someday. But right now, there were the last of the rapids yet to run. Carson Falls.

So he nodded at her to tell her he was ready, and picked up his paddle. She nodded back but didn't smile, and he saw her fingers flex on the handles of her oars. "Okay, let's do this!" he yelled.

As he twisted to face front again, he felt the river surge under him, felt it in his chest and in his arms, and even in the part of him that no longer had feeling. The river's music swelled louder, louder, and the banks rushed by in a blur. High on her seat in the back of the boat, he knew Alex was focused on the water ahead, working her oars, calling orders to him and to Sam. He wished he could just stop for a moment and watch her. In his mind's eye he could see her—cheeks flushed and braid flying, her eyes fierce as a warrior's, riding headlong into battle, her hard-muscled little body taut as a bow. *God,* how he loved her.

He wanted to shout it.

Yeah, I love her! Always have…always will. How did I think I could turn my back on that? I love her. Why didn't I have the guts to fight for it? For us?

As the boat plunged over the falls, he gave a whoop that was part joy, part adrenaline, and maybe there was some sort of promise in there, too. *I'm not giving up on us. Hell no. I'm comin' for you, Alex Penny!*

Then they were chest-deep in snowmelt surf and the hydraulics of the river took over, tossed them back toward the sky as if they were no more than leaves, twigs, bits of flotsam. Matt hung on to the tube with one elbow and thrust his paddle high in the air, riding the water like a rodeo cowboy on a bucking bull. He heard yells and whoops from the others in the boat and his heart soared as he recognized one of the voices as Alex's.

Helluva ride, huh, Alex? One helluva dance…

And just like that, it was over. The river flowed along as if the turbulence had never happened, chuckling to itself as if enjoying a secret joke at their expense. Everyone in the boat was drenched and laughing, slapping high fives—even Cory, with his good arm. And Alex tumbled headlong off her perch and dove straight into Matt's arms.

It was feeling that drove her. Sheer overabundance of feeling she didn't know what else to do with. If she'd thought about it, she probably wouldn't have done it, but at the time it seemed the only possible thing to do. And then his arms came around her—hard around her—and his hands framed her face and wiped the water away, and she did the same to him, both of them laughing and shaking the way they used to after mind-blowing sex. The laughter grew faint and fitful, and she felt his hand grip the back of her head, his fingers push into the loose wet mass of her hair. He looked into her eyes for an instant, then brought her face to his and kissed her.

She gasped a breath and found he'd become a part

of it. Her fingers curled in the shoulders of his life vest as she opened her mouth and drank him in. She forgot her anger and humiliation as completely as the river forgets its rapids once past them. His mouth meshed with hers, his body solid beneath her hands—they felt so familiar to her, had been so achingly missed for so long. She felt like an exile finally allowed to come home.

And it was over too quickly. He released her mouth so suddenly her eyes smarted with tears and her lips felt bruised, cold and bereft.

"We're here, babe—we made it." His voice was a hoarse and ragged whisper. He gave her head an intense little shake, then let go of her hair and picked up his paddle.

She heard it then: yelling and cheering coming from far off. She lifted her head and through a haze of tears saw the bridge up above, and a line of fire crew vehicles parked all along the road, and the Penny Tours bus was there, too. And up ahead, at the take-out spot, Booker T and half a dozen of her guides and crew—even Tahoe, sporting an arm sling—were waving and cheering, waiting to bring them in.

Sam had her paddle in the air and kept yelling, "My God, we made it, Pearse. I can't believe we made it." And Cory was grinning, too, not seeming to mind, now, being injured and in pain.

Aware that Matt was watching her, Alex encompassed them all with the best congratulatory smile she could muster, and concentrated on breathing through the dull ache that had crept in to fill her throat, her chest, her stomach, her whole inside. "Hey, guys, you did it—you ran the Forks of the Kern! Great job!"

And inside her mind was wailing, *It's over. It's over. It's over.*

The bus was winding cautiously down the mountain road—slower going than usual because of the stream of firefighting vehicles clogging up the road in both directions—when Alex left her customary seat up in front and made her way to the back of the bus, where Matt sat in his chair, locked in place on the lift.

He grinned when he saw her. "Hey—I was wondering when somebody was gonna come back and keep me company." And his tone was the husky, low-in-the-throat one he used for seduction, the one that once had made pulses start up in all the feminine response outposts in her body.

She gave him a look that warned him she was onto him and in no mood to be wooed. She took the seat nearest the chairlift and said bluntly, "Matthew, we need to talk."

His eyes darkened and his smile slipped sideways. "Yeah, we do."

She made an impatient motion with her hand. "Not…that. Not about us." Then she closed her eyes. "Okay, we do, but not now. That's not what I meant." She opened her eyes and let out a breath. "Doesn't it strike you as strange that so many bad things happened on this run? I mean, we've had accidents before, but jeez—it seems like everything that could happen did. So, I'm wondering…why right now?"

"I'm not sure what you're asking." But he was

looking at her intently, not smiling at all now. "What are you thinking? Thought we agreed the notion that somebody sabotaged—that's just crazy, Alex."

She looked away, waited a moment, then brought her eyes back to him. "I didn't tell you before, but Dave told me the fire was set."

"What—you mean, on *purpose?*"

"They're pretty sure. Think about it—why on earth would anybody set a fire up here? In just the right place for it to spread up the river canyon, where we just happen to be?" She shook her head and looked away again. "I don't know what to think. But what can I think?" She paused and lowered her voice to a murmur. "How much do you know about your brother? Or Sam? Maybe somebody has something—"

Matt was making frantic gestures to shut up, so she wasn't all that surprised when Sam spoke from close behind her.

"It's okay, Matt," she said as she took the seat across from Alex. "Cory and I have been talking about it, too, actually. Too many things going wrong, it stops being coincidence and becomes…"

"Enemy action," Cory finished in a croaking voice as he eased carefully into the next seat down. He grinned wryly. "That's James Bond—from a book, not a movie. So," he said after a pause, "the question is, which one of us has an enemy who might have taken action?"

They all looked at each other, then shrugged, one by one, and shook their heads. Matt rubbed the back of his neck and muttered, "Hell, I'm just a schoolteacher, man."

Sam looked at Cory and said softly, "I told you, Pearse. It's not me, I swear."

He let out a breath that sounded oddly relieved. "Right."

"Alex?" Matt was looking at her—they all were.

She reared back, holding up her hands. "Come on, guys."

"If it *was* sabotage," he said quietly, "it would almost have to be somebody with access to the equipment. Wouldn't it?"

"One of my—" She broke off to stare at him, cold in the pit of her stomach. Then shook her head. "*No*. No way. We're like a family. Nobody would do such a thing. Not to me, not to the company."

Matt shrugged.

Cory nodded.

"So," Sam said in her down-to-earth way, "coincidence it must be."

Matt was sitting in his van in the Penny Tours equipment yard. He had the motor running and the air-conditioning on, and he was waiting for Alex to finish up inside so he could catch her on the way to her car. His brother and Sam were in Booker T's king cab pickup truck on their way to the hospital on the other side of the lake. Matt was supposed to go back to the motel and wait for them, but he had no intention of doing so, not without talking to Alex first.

He watched people come and go through the yard, some with finished tours coming in and unloading, others prepping and loading up for future runs. Sometimes they waved at him, and he'd smile and wave back, but his mind was chewing over the problem of how he was going to convince Alex to come away with him for a while. He couldn't very well invite her to lunch or dinner, since it was the middle of the afternoon and they were both still stuffed to the gills with the burgers they'd stopped for on the way through town. He didn't know if she'd be willing to come with him, just to talk, but he felt in his gut that if he could just get her to someplace where they could talk in private…maybe do more than talk…everything would be all right.

He didn't know how, but…since the alternative wasn't acceptable, it had to be all right.

He'd waited long enough. He was beginning to consider getting back in his chair and going into the building to look for her, when he saw her coming through the open warehouse door. The blond guide was with her—Eve, that was her name—and watching the two women walk out into the sunshine, Matt had the weirdest feeling. It was a jolt of gut-level animosity that, if it had been a guy walking beside Alex, he'd have had to say it was jealousy.

He dismissed it with a wry snort and a shake of his head, reminding himself he and Eve never had gotten along, even back before his accident. He'd pretty much tolerated the woman because she was a friend of Alex's, but he never had understood what Alex saw in her. As far as he was concerned, the woman was a real pain in the ass, always getting her feelings hurt about something or other—usually nothing important. Matter of fact, he was kind of surprised to see she was still around. In his experience, people like her were always moving on, figuring all their problems would be solved if they were somewhere else.

But who gave a damn, anyway? All he cared about was Alex. Watching her emerge from the warehouse into the bright sunlight, he felt hungry juices pool at the back of his throat. She may have been a full head shorter than the lanky blond "California girl" beside her, but she'd command any man's eye first. She was... The word that came to his mind wasn't *beautiful,* although to his mind she was. What she was, was...*vivid.* She'd changed into jeans and a yellow tank top that lit fires in her golden-tan, dark-freckled skin, and with the sun striking red highlights into her dark hair, freshly braided and snaking over one shoulder as she turned to call to someone across the yard, she put him in mind of a painting by that Frenchman whose name he couldn't recall, the one that painted scenes from the South Pacific. She was warmth and light and life. And so damn hot she sizzled.

He rolled down his window and called to her, and she changed course and headed toward the van. After a little hesitation, Eve did, too, throwing a look his way that told him she wasn't pleased.

And in that moment, Matt caught a glimpse of something in her face... A flash of something came and went in his memory, like a lightbulb's little mini-explosion before burning out. *Something...about Eve. Something... That look. I've seen it before. Something...*

But it was gone.

And anyway, who cared? The only woman he gave a damn about was Alex.

"Hey," he said when she came to his window. She had a wary look, a half smile, as if she hadn't decided whether she really wanted to be there and might leave in a heartbeat if he said the wrong thing. So he kept it light, and the dimmer half-down on his own smile. "Where are you off to? Were you gonna leave without sayin' goodbye?"

She gave a defensive half shrug. "I thought you'd already left. Gone back to the motel."

"Figured I'd wait, see if you wanted to grab a cup of coffee…or something." He waited, watched her eyes slide away from his, then drop, a flush wash over her cheeks. And he took a chance…let some of what was inside him leak into his voice when he softly added, "It's been five years, Alex." *You owe me this much.* The last part silently, of course, and what he'd really meant was, *Us—you owe us, Alex.*

He could hear his own heart hammering as he waited, not breathing, for her reply.

She looked at Eve, who promptly looked away into the distance. Pouting, probably. Well, screw her, he thought. *Alex?*

"Okay," she said, "I guess we could do that." And he started to breathe again. "Eve, I'll catch you later, okay?"

Eve shrugged and said sullenly, "Yeah. Sure. No problem."

Alex gave the woman a distracted glance as she made her way back across the yard with arms folded, like someone in a sulk, and when she looked back at Matt he saw doubt in her eyes, and all sorts of other things he wished he hadn't.

"I have my car," she said. "I'll see you at the motel, okay?"

"Sure," he said, and she nodded and walked away.

He told himself, as he drove out of the yard and onto the highway, that it was okay, because at least she'd agreed to come to him. It would all be okay, he told himself, if they could just…talk. In private.

Yeah, and what will you say to her, dumb-ass? That you were a stupid fool to let her go out of your life? That you love her? Can't live without her? Want to stay here and make a life with her? Marry her and raise a bunch of little river rats with her?

Yeah, right—you know how she is. You'd scare her so bad you wouldn't see her for the dust.

What, then? Remind her how good you were the past couple of days, together again on the river? Ask her to take you back, maybe pick up where you left off before the accident? Partners…battling lovers?

Except, even if she was willing, you know that's not what you want. It wouldn't be enough for you. Not anymore.

And if that's all she's got to give you? What then?

He knew the answer to that, even though it made his belly sore thinking about it.

Pray, man. Pray you've got the strength to walk away.

Chapter 9

Alex parked her SUV next to Matt's van, turned off the motor, then sat still, staring at the motel room door in front of her and listening to her heart hammer.

Why am I doing this? What do we have to talk about?

We were great today, on the river. Admit it, Alex. It seemed almost like before the accident.

But it's not like it was. It won't ever be again.

Yet a voice whispered…and it was the voice of a temptress, *It could be. It could even be…better.*

Tears threatened, and she fought them off with anger. *He broke my heart when he told me he didn't want to be with me and wasn't coming back. Didn't want to come back.*

I was stupid enough to let myself depend on him. Let myself need him.

I won't ever do that again. Ever.

With her resolve thus recharged, she got out of the car and knocked on Matt's motel room door. He opened it almost immediately, and her heart slammed up against her throat. She wondered if he'd been sitting by the window, watching her, wondering when she was going to get up the courage to get out of the car and face him.

"Hey," he said, in a voice that was warm and rich and deep…the voice of seduction. "You want to come in?"

She tucked her fingertips into the hip pockets of her jeans and tried not to look at him. Did anyway, and couldn't help but notice he'd changed into a clean T-shirt and that under it his pecs and biceps and shoulder muscles stood out in smooth, rounded mounds. And that his hair was mussed and his jaws were shadowed with a weekend's growth of beard, and that his eyes burned bright as embers in his dark tanned face, giving him the fiercely jubilant look of a victorious warrior fresh from the battlefield.

She said, "Why don't we walk, instead?"

"Sure—okay." He rolled one-handed across the threshold, tucking his room key in a hip pocket with the other. "Where do you want to go?"

"I don't know. Like…maybe the park?"

"Fine with me."

So, they walked without talking, across the street to the riverfront park and onto one of the paved pathways that followed the riverbank. They paused to watch children playing with inner tubes in the quiet water near the bank, and kayakers training farther out in the shallow rapids. The sky was clear; there was no smell of smoke—the fire was north of town and heading away from it. Alex tried not to think about it, probably into the high-country timber by now, destroying God only knew how many acres of forest. Tried not to think about the fact that it had been deliberately set. Except for cold-blooded murder, she couldn't think of a more despicable act than arson.

Softly, and without taking his eyes off of the kayakers, Matt said, "That was one helluva run."

Alex gave a little whimper of a laugh. "Yeah, it was."

"Thanks," he said, and she looked at him in surprise. "What for?"

He glanced at her and gave his wheels a turn, moving on. "You didn't want to do this."

"No," she said, with another short laugh. "I sure didn't."

He paused to give her a long look. "You want to tell me why?"

"Are you kidding? You know why. I thought it was nuts. I still do. And I was right, wasn't I? Two people injured, and your brother and Sam, they both could have been killed."

"But they weren't."

Because you saved them. But she didn't say that, not out loud. She walked slowly, watching cottonwood fluff drift by on a warm breeze, smelling the river smell, and feeling an ache deep inside.

After a moment, Matt said in a gravelly voice, "We were good together up there, Alex. Admit it. We were."

But of course, even though the same thought had been in her mind, she wasn't about to admit it, and since she couldn't deny it, either, she turned her face away so he couldn't see the tears in her eyes.

"Alex—"

She threw up a hand to stop him. "Don't. Don't. Just…don't." So they walked on in silence.

Some children ran by, heading for the sandy beach farther down, yelling to each other, flip-flops flapping, beach towels draped across their shoulders flying back in the breeze. Alex watched them through a blur, then blinked her vision clear and halted. She turned to him, furious but controlled. "What do you want from me, Mattie?"

He said nothing for a moment, then slowly turned his face to her. "Nothing more than I've ever wanted, Alex." His voice was low and even, almost without expression.

Frustrated, she threw up her hands and let them drop. "Which is something I can't give you—I thought you understood that."

Anguished, she could only look at him while her mind wailed the rest. *Isn't that why you left me? Because what I did have to give you wasn't enough?*

He might have seen what was in her eyes, the pain she couldn't tell him about, if he'd been looking at her. But he'd pivoted slightly and was gazing at the river now, and she wanted to scream at him, pound his shoulders with her fists. Cry. All those emotional woman things Alex Penny would never do. Couldn't do.

She stood there, clenching and unclenching her fists, breathing through her nose and fighting for control for what seemed like forever, and just when she thought she would have to walk away and leave him there, he began to speak. Slowly, at first, in a low and rough voice that sounded nothing like his earlier seductive murmur.

"You told me once…about when you were a little kid. You'd climbed up in a tree that was growing beside the trailer you and your mother were living in then." He looked up at her and she nodded, surprised because she didn't remember telling him about her dream.

But then he went on, and she realized it wasn't her dream, but a memory she'd half forgotten.

"Anyway, you were up in the tree, hollering for help because you couldn't get down. And your mother came out, and told you you'd gotten yourself up there, you could get yourself down. So, you told me…you managed to climb down as far as the roof of the trailer, but then there was no way down except to jump." He stopped there and looked at her.

She wrapped her arms across her waist and lifted her chin as she gazed defiantly back at him. "Yeah, so I jumped. Sprained my ankle, but I made it down. All by myself, too."

"You told me," he said, still speaking slowly…painfully. "You said your mother wrapped your ankle in Ace bandages, and you wore that bandage like a badge of honor. Like battle ribbons."

Now it was her throat that felt wrapped in bandages; she couldn't say anything, couldn't do anything but stare at him. And he gazed back at her, his eyes dark amber, and sadder than she'd ever seen them.

"The proudest moment of your childhood. Proving you could take care of yourself. You didn't need anybody."

How could she deny it? She swallowed…looked up at the sky. Swallowed again; it seemed like the only part of herself that was capable of movement.

"I can't compete with that, Alex. I knew that five years ago. I thought maybe I could fight it, but I can't. It's who you are. Who you were taught to be, maybe, but still…it *is who…you…are.* You don't need anybody. And for sure you don't need me."

She shook her head, then clamped a hand over her mouth. Tears sprang to her eyes. But he saw none of that. Because he had already turned and was slapping at the wheels of his chair with his gloved hands, wheeling himself slowly along the path, back toward the street, back to his motel. Back to his life.

He didn't hurry. She could have stopped him…called out to him. Run after him. But she didn't. Of course she didn't. What would she say? She couldn't deny the things he'd said, because they were true. Even if right now she felt like wild animals were gnawing on her insides, and at this moment somewhere inside her there was a little girl, the one Booker T called baby doll, sobbing and crying and longing to be held and comforted, she knew it wouldn't last, not in the long run. She was Alex Penny, daughter of Carla, who'd taught her to be independent and self-reliant and to never depend on anyone but herself. And right now she was hurt and sad and bereft, but she was angry, too.

Okay, dammit, I missed you, Mattie. I did. Right now, I guess…I want you. Oh, I do. But…you want me to need *you. You need to be needed, and I can't do*

*that. I can't…let…myself need you. I'm sorry…damn
you. Matthew!*

Alex stood there by the river, alone, hugging herself
and watching him roll away, with her hand clamped
over her mouth to keep from calling out his name.

Booker T had dropped Sam and Cory off at the door
to their motel room, and they were in the process of
saying their thank-yous and goodbyes when Sam happened to look across the hood of the pickup and see
Matt coming along the river path alone. And Alex
standing by herself farther back, watching him go.

"Oh hell," she said under her breath, "that can't be
good."

"What?" her husband said, and she tilted her head to
draw his attention to the silent drama evidently unfold-
ing across the street. "Oh…damn."

Linda looked out the passenger-side window and
Booker T ducked his head and peered across her to see
what they were all looking at, then turned back to them
with a half smile showing under his swooping mustache. "So, looks like you had some plans for those
two."

"We did," Sam said with a sigh. "Hopes, anyway."

"Yeah," Booker T said after a glance at his wife, "we
did, too. Tell you what, though—I'm not ready to give
up on 'em just yet." He winked as he put his pickup
truck in gear and drove out of the parking lot.

"You know what?" Sam said as she watched them
go. "Neither am I."

"Samantha…dearest," her husband said gently,

"what do you think you're going to do? You can't make two people fall in love."

"Oh, horsefeathers, Pearse, they're already in love—anybody can see that. They're just bein'...*bullheaded.*" She said the last word with emphasis, and a meaningful glare for Matt, who was just joining them.

"Referring to me, I suppose," he said as he rolled past them and inserted his room key card in its slot. He opened the door and gave it a shove, then looked up at Cory and Sam and added evenly, "But you're talking to the wrong person. Trust me." He pushed his way into the room, closing the door on Sam, who would have followed him in if her husband hadn't grabbed her in time to prevent her.

"Pearse, you're not going to let—"

"Shh...not now. Can't you see he's hurting? Give him some time."

"Time? How much time? What are we supposed to do now?"

At that moment Matt's door opened up again, framing him and his chair in an attitude Sam thought wouldn't have been out of place on a Murderball court.

"How soon can you guys be ready to leave?" he inquired without preamble. "Because I'm thinkin' it's time to go home."

"Ah..." Cory glanced at Sam. "Give us twenty minutes?"

"Right—twenty minutes." The door closed.

Cory's lopsided smile told her he was blaming himself for the pain his brother was in. She wanted to tell him something to make him feel better, at least let him know she understood how he felt, probably wishing he hadn't tried to meddle in his brother's love affairs. But what could she say? In the end she simply snuggled against his side when he hooked his good arm around her and kissed the top of her head.

"Right now," he said with a sigh, "I guess we'll do what we have to do—take him home."

Alex pulled up in front of her house to find Booker T's truck parked there and him sitting on her front steps, waiting for her.

She got out of the SUV and slammed the door, and held up her hand as she stormed up the walk. "Don't you start with me."

"I'm not doin' a thing." He slowly and creakily got to his feet. "Looks to me like you've about done enough already, all by yourself."

"I mean it, Booker T." She halted in front of him, hauling in quick deep breaths, which was way more air than she really needed and had the effect of making her feel all swelled up, like a toad.

Booker T paused, gave her a long, hard look, then took her by the arms and turned her around and sat her down on the step. He eased himself carefully down beside her and planted a hand on each knee, then let out breath in a gust. "Baby girl, what'm I gonna do with you?"

Alex stared down at his hands, all gnarled and beat-up from his days roping calves and breaking horses. Then all of a sudden the hands were swimming, and her nose was running a stream, and dammit all, she couldn't help it, she had to *sniff*.

Booker T reached in his back pocket and took out a blue bandanna handkerchief and handed it to her. "You know Linda and I love you like you was our own, but—and I know this sort of thing ain't done much anymore, but right now what I feel like I oughta do is turn you over my knee."

Alex blew her nose and stared at him over the handkerchief. "What'd I do? I didn't do a damn thing. I was getting along just fine. And *he* has to come along, and…and… Why'd he have to come back, dammit?"

"You know why he came back," Booker T said, giving her a look, as if she'd said something incomprehensible. "He came back for you."

"Yeah, well, he can just go on back to L.A., then," Alex said angrily, "because I sure as hell don't want him."

"Now that is just a big old lie." His face was as stern as she'd ever seen it.

Chastened, she blew her nose again, then leaned her head on his shoulder and sighed. "What am I gonna do, Booker T?"

He didn't say anything for a minute or two, just sort of rocked her. Then she felt him nudge her head with his chin. "Tell me something, baby girl. Do you love him?"

She straightened up as if he'd stuck her with a pin and clapped a hand to her forehead. "I don't *know,*" she wailed. "How the hell would I know?"

Booker T chuckled. "Oh, I think you know."

"Okay, if I do, then how come it's so complicated and hard? How come I'm not all gooey and dopey and nothing else in the whole world matters?"

"Because," Booker T said, "that's not you."

"Yeah…" Suddenly she felt wrapped in misery, weighed down by it. Every part of her seemed to *hurt*. "Okay," she said in a low, uneven voice, "even if…say I *do* love him. It doesn't really matter—"

"Oh, it matters."

"No—because what he wants is for me to *need* him. Think about it, Booker T. He's not the kind of man who's gonna be happy with a woman who's bossy, and opinionated, and independent and used to running the whole show." She glared at him, waiting for him to deny it. But all he did was smile. She hitched in a breath and looked at her feet, watched one of them scrape at the stones in the walk. "He wasn't before—that's probably why we used to fight all the time—and he sure as hell isn't now. Even more now that he's…" She couldn't bring herself to say it. Caught another breath, shook her head and went on. "Anyway, he needs to feel he's carrying his own weight, and probably half of mine besides."

Booker T cleared his throat noisily. "Well, you do seem to understand the man pretty well." He paused, evidently intent on studying the two cars parked out at the road. "Too bad you don't understand yourself as well."

"Okay, what's that supposed to mean?"

He glanced at her, smoothed his mustache with a thumb and forefinger, then shook his head. "Not just you, honey, don't get mad. It's just the way people are made. Human beings are not meant to be alone. They're hardwired to need each other." He held up a hand when she started to interrupt. "No, now, hear me out. Of *course* you don't need a man to defend your cave and go out and whomp a yak and bring it home to feed you and the kiddies. These days, women are pretty much capable of defending their own caves and whomping their own yaks. But see, the thing is, human beings with their great big brains have got to be born small and helpless or they can't be born at all, and that means they've got to be protected and cared for and taught for years and years, and like it or not, sweet pea, that's a job best done with two people."

Alex snorted, ignoring a new little spike of pain, one she didn't even know the cause of. "Yeah, well, that's assuming you mean to have kids."

Booker T kind of reared back and looked at her, and she remembered, again too late, about the child he and Linda had lost. Then he shook his head. "Doesn't matter. We're all still hardwired the same way. Tell me this. Do you *want* him? Do you want this man?" And then he held up a hand to stop her before she could answer. "No. Don't think on it—don't try and parse this, like it was a problem in logic to work out with your brain. This is a gut thing. What does your gut tell you? You want him, or don't you?"

Do I want him? Memories swamped her. Memories of the way his hands felt, sliding up along her ribs, under her T-shirt. Memories of the way his mouth tasted, the way his laugh sounded, and the happy shiver that ran through her whenever he smiled.

"Yeah," she said gruffly, then cleared her throat and said it again. "Yeah, I do."

Booker T threw up his hands, the way a rodeo cowboy does when he's finished throwing and tying a calf. "There you are, then. If you love him, and you want him, you *need* him. It's as simple as that."

A bubble of laughter fought its way up through the pain inside her and she caught it in the handkerchief. She sniffled, sighed, then muttered, "How'd you get so wise?"

He laughed out loud. "Me? I'm nothin' but an old cowboy that had the good sense to get down off a horse and marry a smart and beautiful woman. Everything I know about love and relationships I learned from Linda, I'm not ashamed to say it."

Alex sat still, suddenly feeling empty…tired. Bewildered. Lost. "So," she said carefully, "what should I do, Booker T? Do you really think Matt and I could…" She hitched one shoulder and let it trail off.

"I think," said Booker T, evidently addressing the stones in the walk, "you can if you want to bad enough." Then he angled a look at her. "From what Samantha and Cory were telling me about what happened up there on the Forks, seems like the two of you can work together just fine when you need to."

"Yeah…" She tried to smile. Tried to feel better about things. But she was remembering the way Matt had looked at her, with his eyes full of such terrible sadness, and his words: *You didn't need anybody.*

Booker T gave her a nudge. "Hey—what's wrong now?"

"I think—" she tried to laugh, though she'd never felt less like laughing in her life "—it might be too late."

"Nah," said Booker T, "it's never too late. 'Course,

you might have to swallow some of that pride of yours first."

She began in automatic defense. "*Me?* What about—"

"For Pete's sake, girl, *love, want, need*—the words don't matter. Get your butt in gear and get over there to that motel and say whatever it takes to keep one of the best men I've ever had the pleasure of knowing from driving out of your life for good. Tell him you need him, if that's what he needs to hear. You think you can do that?"

Alex drew a breath, nodded and was finally able to laugh, although it felt a little weak and shaky, like something newly born. She wiped her cheeks, leaned over and kissed Booker T's cheek, then got up and started down the walk to her car. Halfway there she began to run.

Her sense of purposeful euphoria lasted until she pulled into the motel parking lot and saw that Matt's van was gone. Something—*panic*—clutched at her stomach. She sat with her hands gripping the steering wheel while her heart raced and her thoughts raced faster, going nowhere. *Now what? What do I do? Where did he go? Did they leave? Oh God, what now?*

Shaking, she parked, got out of the car and went into the office. The girl behind the counter—someone Alex didn't know, roughly college age—looked up at her and smiled.

"Hi, can I help you?"

"Uh…yeah, the couple with the guy in the wheelchair—I'm not sure of the room numbers—"

"Oh yeah, you just missed them. They checked out about…um…ten minutes ago."

"Checked out?" She could hear it, it was her voice, but it seemed to come from far, far away.

"Yeah…sorry." The desk clerk was relentlessly cheery. "They had the rooms reserved until tomorrow, but I guess they decided to leave early. They said something about…um…wanting to avoid the weekend homecoming traffic into L.A. on I-5?"

"Yeah…okay…thanks." In a daze, Alex walked out of the motel office.

Her heart sank as she saw Eve's Jeep pull up beside her SUV. *Not now,* she silently pleaded. *I really do not need this right now.*

She fought for calm, searched deep inside herself for some shreds of patience. Remembered the sunglasses she'd pushed up onto the top of her head and flipped them down to cover her eyes. Fixed a smile on her face and angled across to the driver's side of the Jeep as Eve rolled the window down.

"Hey, what are you doing here?"

Eve planted her arm on the windowsill and shrugged that same shoulder in a way that seemed almost defensive. "Thought maybe if you were done with your meeting with Matt…" She nodded toward the row of empty parking spaces beyond their two cars. "Anyway, I see his van's gone. So…did they leave? Want to go get a beer, maybe a bite to eat?"

Alex felt waves of guilt, tempered with annoyance. She really did like Eve, and also felt sorry for her, since although she got along okay with the other guides, and the customers seemed to like her fine, she didn't appear to have any close friends. Which was her own fault, Alex thought, for being so damned high maintenance.

"Oh, darn, Eve—I wish I could, but right now I've got to…" And she was opening the door of her SUV, clearly in a hurry to be off.

Which was lost on Eve. She got out of her Jeep and came over to Alex's car, shading her eyes with one hand. "Where are you going? Do you need any help? I can—"

"No, it's just…I've got to catch Matt. They just left." As she spoke she was climbing behind the wheel, starting the car. And looked up to find Eve's hands pressed against her window. Her eyes were wide and her lips were moving. Inwardly chafing, Alex rolled the window down. "Eve, what is it? I really need to go."

"Why? Alex, what are you doing?" Eve was obviously upset, even more so than usual. Her fingers were gripping the windowsill so hard her knuckles were white, as if, Alex thought, she was trying to physically prevent the SUV from moving. What was wrong with the woman? *I can't deal with this now.*

"What I should have done a long time ago," Alex said impatiently, turning to back out of the parking place. "I'm going to tell him I don't want him to leave. Now—"

Eve's fingers caught her arm and dug in hard. "You're not going to take him back! You said—"

"I know what I said, Eve, and I was stupid. Now, please—I'll explain later. But I really have to go. If I leave right now I might be able to catch up with them before they hit the canyon." She put the SUV in reverse and began to back up, and Eve's hand slid away from her arm. Alex put her arm out the window and waved as she called back, "I'll call you later, Eve—promise!"

As she accelerated out of the parking lot, she glanced in her rearview mirror and saw that Eve was standing where she'd left her, hands down at her sides, curled into fists. Well, hell. Eve was pissed—what else was new? Couldn't be helped. Right now she had only one thought in mind, and that was to catch Matt before he vanished into the Los Angeles–bound Sunday afternoon traffic.

Matt had one thought in mind as he drove his van west on the divided freeway-type highway that was the first leg of the route down the Kern River Canyon to the San Joaquin Valley: Put as much distance between himself and the Kern River Valley and Alex Penny as he could, and hopefully get home to Los Angeles ahead of the Sunday incoming traffic. He was finding it a little hard to concentrate on his driving, however, due to the fact that his sister-in-law had been giving him an earful since they'd pulled out of the motel parking lot.

"Matthew, do not try and argue this logically," Sam said for the second or third time. "If you do, you're an idiot. And why are you smiling? This is not funny."

A glance in his rearview mirror told Matt he could expect no help from his brother, who'd evidently succumbed to the painkillers the doctors at the hospital had given him, and was asleep in the backseat. Either that or he was playing possum just to keep clear of the fray.

"You calling me Matthew—that's what I was smiling at," he said. "You're the third person to do that—my mom and Alex do, too. Funny, though—only when they're mad a me."

"Why do you think Southern women always give their kids two names? One syllable just won't do it when you need to chew somebody out. You need at least three— what's your middle name, by the way?"

"None of your business," said Matt.

"James," said Cory from the backseat. "It's Matthew James Callahan."

"Rat," Matt muttered.

"Okay," Sam crowed. "Matthew James, you are an idiot. What's with this *need* business? Don't you know, there's all kinds of ways to need somebody? 'Course Alex doesn't need you to support her or take care of her—what woman does? I sure don't need Pearse to support me—doesn't mean I don't need him about like I need my next breath. I need him because I like having him around, and without him I'm not a happy woman. I need him because he knows just where to rub my neck when it's stiff, and how to make me laugh, and a million other things besides. And I bet you Alex needs you in all kinds of ways she hasn't even thought of yet."

"So, go yell at her, then. She's the one who thinks she's an island, not me."

Sam lifted her hands and let them drop into her lap. "Well, I *would* have, if you hadn't been in such a hurry to hightail it outa Dodge."

"Look," Matt said, using the kind of patient tone he might have employed to explain something to one of his less-than-brilliant students, "I am not the one with the problem here. I know perfectly well how much I need *her,* but it kind of has to be a two-way street, you know what I mean? When one person does all the needing, then…hell, he's just *needy.* And that's not me. You understand? I can't be that guy. Not for Alex, not for anyone."

When she didn't reply, he glanced over at her and saw she was looking thoughtful. Confident he'd won the argument, finally, he turned his full attention to driving, as the freeway section of the highway ended and the winding Kern River Canyon road began.

A few minutes later, Samantha, peering out the side window at the deep drop into the canyon below, uttered an extremely colorful blasphemy, followed by, "Would you look at this *road?*"

"Yeah, helluva pretty river, isn't it?" Matt said, and smiled, even though his heart was aching. "I hope you guys don't get carsick."

Alex was frustrated. She hadn't been able to make good time going around the lake, due to the usual crush of boating and camping traffic and the abundance of idiots who seemed to enjoy those recreational pursuits. Her only comfort came in knowing Matt wouldn't have been able to go any faster than she did. Now, though, past the town of Isabella and on the freeway section of the canyon road where she'd planned to put the pedal to the metal and make up for lost time, she was being dogged by a car that, from a distance in her rearview mirror, looked suspiciously like a CHP SUV. She watched it, keeping within seven or eight miles of the speed limit and tapping her fingers impatiently on the steering wheel, until it edged up beside her. Damn—just the friggin' Forest Service. She stepped on the gas and in a few moments had left the SUV far behind.

But now…here was another vehicle looming in her mirror, and this one was coming fast. Jeez! Coming like a bat outa hell.

Instinctively, Alex eased up on the gas as she watched the other car zoom up behind her, then pull out to pass. She didn't have much time to look as the car streaked by, but what she saw made her gasp. It was Eve's Jeep. No mistaking that bright Day-Glo yellow. And Eve at the wheel, so intent on the road ahead she didn't even glance over as she accelerated around Alex's SUV.

Alex felt herself go cold clear through. Her heart began to pound as she watched the familiar yellow Jeep disappear around a wide sweeping curve ahead. Gripped by a fear for which there was no concrete explanation, only a notion that something bad was about to happen, she flexed her fingers on the wheel, pressed down on the gas and followed.

Chapter 10

"**W**e've got some pretty hairy roads in the Smokies," Sam said, "but I mean to tell you, I have not *ever* seen anything like this." She tore her fascinated gaze away from the rocky gorge flashing by only a couple of yards from the side of the van and turned to address her husband in the backseat. "Pearse, you don't know what you're missing. I swear, you need to—" She broke off as she caught a glimpse of the yellow Jeep careening around the bend in the road behind them, practically on their bumper. "Oh my Lord, now *what* is this guy doing? Matt—"

"I see him," Matt said, flicking a calm glance at the rearview mirror. "It's a her, actually. In fact, I know her. She works for Alex. You've met her. Eve…the tall blonde?"

"You're right—what on earth do you suppose—oh *jeez!*" She gave a squawk and instinctively threw up her arm as the Jeep accelerated suddenly, coming straight at them. There was a loud bang and a jolt that made her head snap back, and her heart dropped into her stomach. "Matt, what— Did she just *ram* us? Is she *crazy?*"

"I think she might be." Matt was busy controlling the van, which was careening dangerously close to the edge of the drop-off. He glanced up at the mirror. "Here she comes again—hang on." And he hit the gas.

Too scared now to swear, Sam jerked around in her seat to face front and settled her seat belt more securely across her chest. "Pearse," she yelled, "wake up! Are you buckled in?"

"Of course," came his reply, sounding groggy. "What the hell's going on?"

"A crazy woman's trying to force us off the road," Matt said. His lips were stretched in a grim smile.

It was odd, how calm he felt. Somewhere in his body, he knew, adrenaline had shifted everything into high gear, but he felt none of it. In fact, everything—heartbeat, breathing, all movement—seemed to be happening in slow motion.

Oh so slowly, he lifted his eyes to the mirror…saw the Jeep coming, closing the distance…slowly, slowly. Saw it veer—but *slowly*—out into the oncoming lane. He had all the time in the world to deduce what the woman's intent was, to know that this time, rather than ram him from the rear, she meant to swerve at him from the side and force him over the bank. And he was ready for her, knew just what he had to do. His hands were steady on the controls, ready to apply the brakes the instant she swerved toward him.

He saw the car coming toward them from the other direction, and that was in slow motion, too.

There was a screeching of brakes and his body strained forward against a seat belt gone rigid across his chest. As he stared through the windshield, dazed, the slow-motion spell broke. In a blink, almost too fast for the eye to follow, the Jeep swerved out of the path of the oncoming car and continued on, out of control, across the lane in front of his van to plunge, with a terrible screeching of tires and metal, over the side and into the river gorge.

Alex had managed to keep the yellow Jeep in sight, at some risk to life and limb. She saw it closing on the blue van traveling at a much saner pace, and the cold feeling of dread in the pit of her stomach spread through her entire body when she recognized the van as Matt's. What was Eve thinking? What was she *doing?*

Dear God, Alex thought, she's going to cause an accident.

Around a few more curves…and she realized that was exactly what Eve was trying to do. Her heart was racing so fast it hurt; she drove hunched over the wheel, eyes burning as she stared at the drama playing out on the road ahead, little whimpering sounds coming from her throat. And once again there was nothing she could do. Nothing.

She could only watch and utter an unconscious shriek of horror as the Jeep suddenly accelerated and rammed into the back of the van. She sobbed with relief when the van swerved and wobbled back and forth, then regained control, and realized only then that she was muttering aloud, over and over, "Hold on, Mattie, hold on, Mattie, hold on…."

The Jeep seemed to gather itself…and lunged forward once more, but into the oncoming lane, this time, moving up alongside the van.

And what came next happened so fast, Alex couldn't even process it until it was done. The flash of a car coming around a bend from the other direction. The Jeep swerving hard to the left. The van screeching to a halt, tires sending up puffs of smoke from burned rubber. The Jeep becoming a yellow streak that crossed in front of the van and disappeared.

Then the sounds. The whoosh of a car zooming by and continuing on down the winding road, its driver probably cussing the idiot in the yellow Jeep and oblivious to what was happening now behind him. The indescribable screeching and banging of tortured metal. Her own frantic sobbing breaths.

Somehow, probably on autopilot, she managed to stop the SUV behind Matt's van, and even remembered to hit the button for the emergency flashers. She flung open the door and half fell from the driver's seat, at the same time she saw the van's side door slide open, and heard the whine of the chairlift. From somewhere—the other side of the van—came the thump of a slamming door.

"Matt—oh God, Matt—" She ran to him on shaking legs.

"I'm fine," he said, with a little jolt in his voice as his chair touched down. "It's Eve—she went over the side."

"I saw. Oh God, Matt, she was trying—"

"Yeah. Go see if there's anything you can do for her." He turned to call back to his brother inside the van. "If you can get a signal, call—"

"Already on it." From the depths of the van, Cory's voice sounded eerily calm.

"I see her!" Sam shouted, turning as Alex ran to join her on the edge of the drop-off. "She's alive—out of the car—" She peered over the side and clamped a hand to her forehead. "Oh God—she's in the river. Alex—"

Down below, Alex could see the yellow Jeep lying upside down in the boulder-clogged river, its wheels still turning sluggishly, like the futilely waving legs of an overturned turtle. She could see Eve, too, now, a few yards downstream from the wreckage of the Jeep, caught in the white-water current. As Alex watched, she saw an arm reach out...and then another, as Eve struggled to swim, to keep her head above water...and then, miraculously, grab hold of a boulder. She was holding on...somehow, but how long she'd be able to was impossible to guess. And how badly was she injured? Alex had no way of knowing that, either.

"There should be a rope in the back of the SUV," she yelled back to Sam as she went over the side and began to slip-slide her way down the steep embankment. "When you get it, throw me a line. I'll try to hold her...."

"Got it, Alex—coming to you. Heads up!"

She looked up and saw Matt grinning down at her, his chair perilously close to the edge of the drop as he swung the end of the rope around his head like a cowboy preparing to lasso a steer. For the first time since the yellow Jeep had gone flying past her on the highway, Alex felt her heart climb out of her stomach. She even managed to grin back at him as she reached up to snag the snaking end of the rope out of the air and loop it around her waist. She knotted it firmly, then looked up and yelled, "Okay—you got me?"

"You bet," he yelled back. "Always!"

She felt giddy, absurdly happy—crazy, given the circumstances—but there was no other way to describe the feelings that swamped her then. She felt like a superhero—she could do anything! With the rope around her waist and Matt holding on to the other end, she felt safe and strong and able to swim rivers and climb mountains—or move them, if need be.

She all but flew down that bank, and in moments was waist-deep in rapids, scrambling over slippery rocks to reach the boulder where Eve was barely hanging on against the powerful current.

Eve could see her coming now, and she was staring up at Alex, staring with desperate eyes that seemed to cling to her as tenaciously as her arms and hands and fingers clung to the granite boulder. Blood poured down her face and was instantly carried away by the turbulent water that surged and splashed into her face. Her lips were stretched wide in a desperate parody of a smile as she screamed words Alex couldn't hear.

"Hang on, Eve, I'm coming," Alex yelled. And then

she was there, and Eve was sobbing, clutching at her, and dangerously near to losing her hold on the rock in the process. "Wait— Don't try to grab me, just let me— I've got you, okay? I've got you!"

Too panic-stricken to listen, Eve relinquished her hold on the boulder and wrapped her arms in a stranglehold around Alex's neck. And now Alex could hear what the other woman was saying, in panting words all mixed up with sobs. What she heard made every muscle in her body go slack with shock.

"Why did you do it? Why did you take him back? You lied—you said you wouldn't. You said— Oh, why didn't he die? He was supposed to *die*. But he didn't— but I thought it would be okay, because he was hurt, and couldn't be on the river anymore. But he came back. *He came back!*"

"Wait, Eve—" Alex couldn't breathe. She wrenched the other woman's arms from around her neck and held her away from her, stared at her, the roaring in her ears louder than the river. "Eve—" she gasped the words, shrieked them without sound "—what are you telling me?"

Eve's eyes stared back at her, swimming with anguished tears…tears of impotent rage, mixed with water and blood. "He wasn't supposed to come back. Alex— why did you let him come back? We don't need him— you and me—we don't need him, Alex. He's not what you need—don't you see that? I had to make him go…for good, this time. Don't you see?"

Alex's hands had lost all sensation. If she could have moved them, she might have flung the woman from her, flung her back into the rapids—she wanted to. Revulsion and horror filled her head—she couldn't think, couldn't feel. "It was you?" She said the words, not caring whether anyone heard. "Matt's accident—it was *you?*"

"He was supposed to die," Eve wailed. *"Oh God— why didn't he die?"*

"She's got her, I think," Sam said.

"Yeah," said Matt, "but what's she waiting for? What's she doing?"

He had the rope looped around his shoulders and had taken a good firm grip on it, ready to begin pulling when Alex gave the word. But now she seemed to be holding Eve off, and saying something to her—yelling at her. It almost looked like…some kind of struggle?

Behind him he could hear cars pulling up alongside the road and stopping, people getting out of their cars, calling 9-1-1 on their cell phones, coming with offers to help. Offering to take the rope.

"I've got this, but you can hold on to my chair," he told them all when they asked. No way he was giving up that rope. That was Alex down there, depending on him to bring her back. They'd have to cut his arms off before he'd let go.

What the hell is she waiting for?

Then at last, he saw Alex lift her head and look up at him. She'd shifted Eve, got her on her back, piggy-back style, and the rope looped around them both. And now she raised her arm to signal him she was ready. Matt waved back, then flexed his hands in the leather gloves all people in wheelchairs wore to protect their hands from blisters and calluses, thinking what a good thing they were to have at a time like this. And was aware even then of the irony in that.

He turned his head to address the two hefty guys standing behind his chair. "You guys got me?" They both affirmed they were ready, took hold of his wheels and braced themselves. "Okay, here we go."

He began to pull on the rope, not taking his eyes off Alex as he eased up the slack, then began to pull the weight of the two women slowly up the bank. Watching, gauging the obstacles Alex had to navigate over and around, careful not to hurry, careful not to jolt her, letting her find the best way up through the brush and boulders, wrapping the rope around his bent arm to take up the slack. His muscles burned and sweat poured down his face and soaked into his T-shirt. Not since his early days in rehab, when he was first learning to bear the full weight of his body with just his arms, had he worked so hard. Or felt such triumph in it.

All the while he was pulling on that rope, pulling the woman he loved more than his own life up that hill, all he could think about was that she was *here.*

She was here, where she'd no earthly reason to be, except for one: she'd followed him. She'd come after him. For Alex, that pretty much constituted a miracle.

And it told him all he needed to know. For Alex Penny to let go of her pride and come chasing after him, she had to have some powerful feelings. He wasn't foolish enough to think they didn't still have things to work out between them, but he wasn't ever going to ask her the question he'd asked her once before. He'd never ask her again if she loved him. She didn't have to say the words.

He knew.

He could hear sirens far down the canyon, coming fast. Moments later the rope went slack in his hands as people rushed to help Alex with her burden. He bowed his head, breathing in hungry gulps, and didn't see them bring her up the last few feet, over the edge and onto the hard-packed earth.

When he looked up again, Eve was sobbing and struggling against the restraints of the Good Samaritans trying to give her aid, while Alex sat motionless a few feet away. He tossed away the rope, gave his wheels a shove and rolled over to her. When he said her name, she turned her head slowly to look at him, and the look on her face scared him. She was pale, deathly so, and her eyes looked blank, like windows in a deserted house.

Shock, he thought, and reached out with a shaking hand to touch her cheek. Where in the hell were the paramedics?

So naturally, at just that moment, a paramedic came and dropped his kit on the ground beside her, then bent over to ask if she was all right.

She seemed to jerk herself back from whatever hell she'd been in and waved him away impatiently. "Go away—I'm fine."

The EMT glanced at Matt, then turned his attention back to Alex. "Ma'am, you need to let me look at you. Unless your ancestors came from another planet and blue-green is your natural color, I don't think you're fine. Okay?"

"Alex," Matt said gently, "let the man do his job."

"I am not injured," she said, speaking slowly and carefully, as if to a mentally deficient child. "I wasn't involved in the…accident. I just hauled that woman's sorry ass out of the river, and I'm a little *tired*. Okay? So…please—" she finished in a desperate whisper "—leave me alone."

The EMT gave Matt another look, shrugged, then straightened up and picked up his gear. Matt turned with him and touched his sleeve. "Uh, look," he said in an undertone, even though he was sure Alex could still hear him, "she's upset, but I think she'll be okay. But you should know, the reason she's upset—that woman, the driver of the Jeep, tried to run my van off the road. Rammed me from the rear, first, and when that didn't work, she tried to come at me from the side. She was in the oncoming lane when a car came from the opposite direction. I hit the brakes, and she swerved to avoid a head-on, lost control and went over the side. You need to tell the CHP—make sure she's taken into custody."

The EMT nodded gravely. "I sure will. But your friend, here, she could be in shock. You might want to keep an eye on her."

"I'll do that," Matt said. "You can count on it."

He waited until the EMT had gone to join his partner over by the wagon, then swiveled back to Alex. She was still sitting on the hard ground, with her forearms resting on her drawn-up knees. He said her name and she raised her head and looked at him. Just looked at him. Then slowly shook her head. Obscurely frightened, he reached out a hand to touch her arm. And found that she was shaking. Not great, huge shudders that would be visible to someone looking at her, but fine, vicious tremors that seemed to come from the very ground she sat on.

Truly alarmed, now, he tightened his hold on her arm and lifted her up, pulled her to him. She came without a sound, crawled into his lap and looped her arms around his neck and hid her face against him like a bereft child. He didn't know what to do, he'd never seen her like this before. Not Alex, his Alex, who never showed grief or pain or fear, and who, if she'd ever cried at all, had only in his experience cried tears of anger. And wasn't crying now, though it was clear even to him that she needed to.

Overwhelmed, he held her and stroked her hair and murmured comforting things to her, all the while wondering what in the world was wrong. Was it just some kind of shock, as the EMT had warned, or had she been so afraid for him...or so afraid of losing him... A shudder of emotion rippled through him and he almost laughed. *I wish.* But even if she'd been both those things, this wasn't like Alex.

And gentleness clearly wasn't working.

"Hey," he said sternly, "talk to me, Alex. Now. Come on…" He bumped her head with his chin and tried to push her away from him—or pretended to. And it worked.

She gave a settling-down sort of shiver, then spoke at last from the depths of the nest she'd made for her face in the hollow of his neck and shoulder, in a low, husky voice. "She tried to kill you."

"Yeah, she did," he said with a snort. "And damn near

killed herself in the process. She's gonna pay for it, don't worry."

Alex shook her head, and brought up one hand to cover her eyes, even though they were already well hidden. "Not this—*before*. She tried— Oh God, Mattie. I can't… I can't tell you. I can't—"

"Shh…sure you can. You can tell me anything, you know that. So, come on. She tried to kill me…before? When? How could—" He stopped. The words, his breath, even his heartbeat seemed to have frozen inside him.

He gripped her arms and did push her away now, forcing her far enough away from him so he could see her face. And it was a mask of tragedy, lips bruised and trembling, eyes shut tight. As he watched, tears oozed from under her lashes and ran in rivers down her cheeks. He gave her a quick, hard shake and said in a terrible voice, "Tell me, Alex."

Again, she shook her head. And moaned, as if the anguish inside her was simply too much to bear. Then…abruptly, she drew herself up. Pulled in a shuddering breath, and another…held it and finally the words came, all at once, in a rush.

"The day you fell—your accident—it wasn't an accident. She did it, Mattie. Eve did something to your gear. She wanted—tried—to kill you. Because of me. All this—it was *because of me*…" Her face, her whole body seemed to crumple, and she collapsed against him, crying as he'd never known her to cry before, in great wrenching sobs.

She didn't stop even when Sam came over a little

while later to see what was wrong, and to report that Eve had been arrested and taken to Bakersfield, where there was a county hospital that had a prison ward.

Matt just nodded and muttered, "Good…that's good."

Sam bent over to look at him with uncertain and worried eyes. "Matt, is she all right? Are you?"

He blinked her into focus, still in a state of shock himself, probably, the pain not quite reaching him yet. He gave a shaky laugh. "I think so. Yeah. I think we're gonna be okay, now. We will be…."

Sam made her way back to the van in a state of bemusement, letting autopilot steer her through the crowd of EMTs, CHPs and assorted helpful bystanders and looky-loos, now beginning to disperse. She found Cory sitting on the floor in the open doorway of the van with his head resting against the frame, looking exhausted.

He lifted his head to ask the question with his eyes, and she went to him and kissed him. "She's okay. He's okay. They're both…I think…more than okay." She sat beside him, being careful not to jostle his injured shoulder and ribs.

They sat in silence for a few minutes. Then Cory began to laugh, silently and with very little movement. Sam looked at him and said, "What's funny?"

"Oh God, no, not funny—but ironic, maybe." He looked at her, then put his good arm around her shoulders and drew her close. "I was just thinking…about when I went after you, after the Philippines, remember? Chased you down at your mom's place in Georgia."

"How could I forget?" Sam said softly. "And afterward…that's when it all came out—about you and your family. You were finally able to remember, and tell me what happened." She closed her eyes and drew in a shaky breath. Remembering the emotional roller coaster of that day…the terrible pain, and the indescribable joy. "You should see them, Pearse. I can't…" A tear rolled down her cheek and she brushed it away. Laughed a little. "It's like watching us, the way we were that day. It was so hard. But afterward…"

He kissed the top of her head. "Afterward, we weren't two separate people anymore. It was like we'd been through a crucible that melted us down and remade us into one."

"Trust you to use a word like 'crucible,'" Sam said huskily. "But yeah, that's what it was. I think this might be theirs. Pearse, I wonder…is it always so hard? Does everyone have to go through this kind of stuff before they can be happy together?"

"I don't know." He paused. "But this business of finding my family is turning out to be a bit more dangerous than I thought. Sam, I never meant for all of this to happen—you know that."

She laughed and leaned gently into him. "Yeah…but you'd do it again in a heartbeat, you know you would. And don't forget—we still have two to go. The little girls."

"Oh, I'm not forgetting. I don't know, though—maybe I should let Holt handle it next time. When I do it, people keep getting hurt. What do you think?"

"I think," Sam said tenderly, "that when he does find

them—and he will—you'll want to be there, even if it kills you."

Cory laughed—then winced. "Ow—don't say that...."

It was late when Alex and Matt drove up in front of Alex's house. They were both in Matt's van, Sam having volunteered to drive Alex's SUV back to town. Naturally, Cory had elected to ride with her. The two of them were tucked in at their motel down at the riverfront park.

"Maybe we should have gone to the motel, too," Alex said as she sat looking out the window at her pine needle–strewn walk, and the wooden steps leading up to her front porch. "I don't have a ramp."

"Not on your life," Matt said. "We'll manage."

A shiver of strange pleasure ran through her as she opened the door and climbed out of the van. *We'll manage.* She was going to have to get used to those words.

She waited while Matt descended in the chairlift, then walked beside him as far as the steps. There they stopped. Matt studied the steps for a moment, then said, "Here, hold my chair steady."

She watched, swallowing the protests and suggestions that leaped instantly into her mind, while he pushed himself out of the chair and lowered himself onto the nearest step. Then pushed himself up to the next step. He looked at Alex, grinned and barked, "What are you waiting for? Bring me my chair, woman!"

Her chest grew tight with the emotions that seemed to be running amok inside her at the moment, and she couldn't even trust herself to give that the answer it deserved. She hauled his chair up the steps and onto the porch without saying a word. She was maneuvering it into position so he could reach it, when there came a frantic scratching and whining from behind the front door.

"Oh gosh," she said, "that's Annie. What in the world? Here—" She thrust the chair aside and dug in her pocket for her keys.

"Annie?" Matt swiveled to look at her. "*My* Annie?"

The commotion behind the door escalated into frenzied barking. Alex got the key in the lock and had barely managed to open the door a crack when the dog pushed her way through it. She barreled across the porch, toenails scrabbling on the wood planks, and leaped into Matt's arms, wriggling like a puppy and trying to lick him everywhere at once.

In the middle of it all, Matt was saying, "Annie? My God, she's still alive? I thought— Jeez, it's been five years. Hey, girl, you still know me? You remember me, girl?"

Alex, being pretty much out of tears by this time, said in a husky croak, "Dogs don't have any sense of time, don't you know that? She probably thinks you just took a really long lunch break." She watched the dog, still wriggling in Matt's embrace, nuzzling and licking every place she could reach, and folded her arms across her chest where there seemed to be a permanent ache, now. Shaking her head, she murmured, "All this time I thought she was getting old, 'bout ready to die. Maybe she was just depressed. Like she was sleeping away the time until you decided to come back for her."

Matt grinned at her over the Lab's graying head. "What about you, Alex? You been depressed, waiting for me to come back?"

"Don't push it, Matthew." But she went to sit on the step beside him.

Annie gave a sigh and settled herself with her head in Matt's lap, and they sat there together in silence, the three of them. Annie drifted off to sleep, and Matt and Alex watched the moon come up.

Alex said softly, "You really hurt me, Mattie."

"I know. I'm sorry."

"I was there for you, all during rehab. How could you not know I…wanted you?" And how was it that even now it was so hard for her to say the words? *Want…love. Yes, both of those. Why can't I just say it?*

Matt reached for her hand. "I did know. I did." He looked up at the moon. "The truth? I was…angry, back then. At everyone, but especially at you." He waited, but she didn't say anything, so he took a breath and went on, and his voice was soft and hoarse with pain. "I was mad at you because you could still walk, still climb mountains, do all the things we'd always done together. I don't know if you can understand, but…I couldn't bear to be with you then."

Alex cleared her throat, struggling to understand. The tears she thought she'd run out of were falling again, silently. She brushed them away, but they were still there in her voice when she whispered, "I lost something, too, Matt. I did."

"I know…" His arm came around her, and she felt his body quiver.

She turned into him and held on to him, and felt his face press against her hair. After a while she drew a shuddering breath and said, "I don't think I ever cried for it, either—for you. Not 'til today."

He laughed, blowing warm puffs into her hair. "You sure made up for it."

She straightened up, brushing tears and stray hair back from her face with both hands. "I guess we've got a lot of things to make up for. And a lot of things to work out—you know that, right?" *It's not like a fairy tale, where it says "Happily Ever After" and that's it...no more problems.*

Matt was looking around him. "Yeah, like a ramp for this place. And I seem to remember some narrow doorways..."

She tried to smile, but a new heaviness was creeping over her. "What about your job? Down in L.A.? Don't you coach some kids? You can't just...abandon them."

He shook his head and murmured, "No."

The heaviness inside her became misery. For a moment she was angry. *This is why I didn't want to love him. This—the sadness, the pain. The not knowing how to live without him. I didn't want this! I hate this!*

"How about this?" Matt said, gazing up at the moon. "Rafting season's only half the year, right? The other half we'll spend in L.A. Or...I'll commute, if you can't stand to live in the city. It's only what—two and a half hours?"

And just like that, the heaviness lifted and happiness filled her again—but it felt so fragile, that happiness. So terribly, terribly fragile.

Chapter 11

Matt said, "Whatever it takes, we'll work it out."

She laughed, and it sounded more like a whimper. "Easy for you to say. You always were the brave one."

"What are you talking about? You're the bravest person I know."

But she was afraid. Terrified. He could feel it. Even though he couldn't see her eyes, he knew the fear was there, the way it had been up on the Forks when they'd been about to go through the fire.

If we'd known then what we were about to go through together…we didn't know it then, but that fire was the easy part.

He ran his hand down her back and felt her shiver. "What's wrong, Alex? Tell me."

"There's so much, Mattie. So much we haven't talked about. Things…we haven't…"

"Ah." He felt ripples of a new excitement vibrating deep inside his chest. Carefully, he said, "Things…like sex?"

She hitched in a breath. "Yeah, like that. I don't know…how it is with you. I mean…" and now she sounded testy "…well, obviously, you can still turn *me* on, but that's not really…it's not enough." She turned her face to him. "Is it?"

Tenderly, he traced the side of her face with his fingertips, then leaned to brush her lips with his. "This…is definitely something we need to talk about—a lot. But…showing you is probably easier. How about, if you'll get this dog off me and hand me my chair, we take this inside?"

"Matt—"

"Trust me, Alex."

She nodded, but he could feel the resistance in her still. She maneuvered his chair closer, then braced it for him while he hoisted himself into it, then stood hugging herself and looking scared. He held out his hand to her, and she hesitated, opened her mouth but didn't say anything. And he remembered.

"That night at The Corral. When I wanted you to dance with me," he said quietly, "and you didn't. Why?"

She rubbed her arms, shrugged, but didn't look away. "I guess…I didn't think you could."

"And you were wrong, weren't you? You didn't want to do the Forks with me. Why?"

More firmly, now, maybe getting where he was going with this, she replied, "I didn't think you could."

"And…you were wrong. So now I'm asking you."

Again he held out his hand, and said softly, "Come… make love with me, Alex."

He held his breath, and after a brief and suspenseful moment, she reached out and took his hand.

It was so much easier than she'd imagined, and at the same time, so much scarier. Maybe the scariest thing she'd ever done, because it was all so new. So different. And at the same time, in the most thrilling of ways, the same.

Matt used the bathroom first, after explaining to her why he needed to, and what he was doing. Then, when she told him she wanted—needed, after three days on the river, and all they'd been through since—to take a shower, he maneuvered his chair close to the bathtub and bathed her himself. Soaped her body with long, loving, sensual strokes, laughing when the spray made him and everything else in the bathroom as wet as she was. And when she told him she wouldn't be able to stand up if he kept doing what he was doing, he pulled her naked and soaking wet into his lap and took his time caressing her dry with a towel. Then…slowly, began to stroke her wet again, with his mouth, this time.

When she was shivering uncontrollably, he wheeled them both to her bedside. Holding her waist in his hands, he eased her off his lap and when her knees threatened to buckle, helped her to stand while he looked at her. Feasted on her with his eyes.

Then… "Touch me," he whispered hoarsely.

He'd always loved to be touched. Everywhere…she remembered that so well. The sheer pleasure of touching him. The way he'd close his eyes and seem to lose himself in her touch. It was the same now, except he didn't close his eyes. And that made it even more intense for her. More scary. The same, and yet different.

She let her open palms rest lightly on his chest, at first, on those sculpted pecs that were—again—the same Matt, only different. She let her hands glide, oh so slowly, over his chest, his torso, his hard-muscled belly…then up to his shoulders…down his arms and over his hands, guiding them down to her hips and then to her thighs…while she leaned forward and brushed his mouth with hers, barely breathing.

"I'd like to get into bed now…" His words blew gently against her lips.

She whispered, "Yes," and pulled shakily away from him to draw aside the covers.

And again, he didn't hide anything from her, neither the awkwardness nor the unexpected grace, as he shifted himself from chair to bed. She hovered, and helped him when he asked her to, with pillows piled up for his back, and to dispose of the rest of his clothes. Then, when he lay naked and completely exposed to her, he raised himself on one elbow, glanced down at himself and smiled—not his warm, beautiful Mattie smile, but one so wry and vulnerable it made her heart turn over.

"See?" And his voice had a rasp in it she'd never heard before. "I told you…it's still me."

And suddenly, she wasn't nervous or scared or uncertain anymore. She felt almost overwhelmed with strength and tenderness, and… *Yes, love. Booker T's right. I've always loved him. How could I not have known?*

Smiling, with all the confidence in the world in her eyes, she leaned down to kiss him, kissed him long and deeply while she straddled his body. He pulled away to whisper, with a small laugh, "You always did like to be on top."

"Hush up, Matthew," she growled against his mouth as she lowered herself over him, touching his body from chest to thighs with her own. "I don't care who's on top, or what goes where. As long as we go together. You hear me?" She kissed him again, for a long, long time…and finally drew back enough to gasp. "And we do…go together. Don't we? Can you feel that?"

"I don't feel *that*. I feel *you*." He closed his eyes and his arms came around her, vital and strong.

And as he held her, she felt him, too, felt him with every nerve and cell in her body, in a way she never had before. She felt him as though he were a part of her, as if they'd somehow become two parts of the same whole, and in that moment she knew that Booker T was right, that human beings weren't meant to be alone. Holding the man she loved in her arms, melding her body with his, she felt herself fill with the most intense joy she'd ever known, or could ever have imagined. Because half of herself that had been missing for so long had finally come home.

"Oh, Mattie," she whispered brokenly, "I love you. And I do need you."

With tenderness and a smile in his voice, he replied, "I know."

Epilogue

Several months later, in a motel room somewhere in west Texas...

Holt Kincaid sat on the edge of the unmade bed and punched a number on his cell phone speed dial. He listened to it ring, imagined it ringing in a room far away in South Carolina, on the shores of a small lake. It rang three times before a machine picked up.

"Hello, you've reached Sam and Cory's place. We're both away from home right now. Leave us a message and we'll get back to you."

He disconnected and sat for a moment with the phone in his hand, thinking. Then he pulled the laptop that lay open on the bed closer to him, found the page he was looking for, scrolled down the list of phone numbers on it until he came to the one he wanted. Dialed it.

Several minutes and several different numbers later, he'd learned several things. One: his employer was on assignment in Sudan, and there was no way in hell to reach him. Two: his employer's wife was also on assignment, God—and the CIA—only knew where. Three: he was on his own.

Holt Kincaid didn't often feel frustrated, but he did now. Here he'd finally managed to get a line on one of his client's missing twin sisters, and there wasn't anybody he could break the news to.

News that wasn't good.

And he was very much afraid that if he waited, it might be too late.

What the hell was he going to do now?

* * * * *

™ INTRIGUE

Coming next month

2-IN-1 ANTHOLOGY

BABY'S WATCH by Justine Davis

Bad boy Ryder is shocked by the connection he feels to the baby he helped deliver, as well as her mysterious mother Ana. But can he put his life on the line for them?

A HERO OF HER OWN by Carla Cassidy

From the moment she arrived in town, Jewel caught Quinn's attention. They're both overcoming tragic pasts, but does Jewel trust Quinn enough to let passion in?

2-IN-1 ANTHOLOGY

BENEATH THE BADGE by Rita Herron

Nothing matters more to Hayes than the police badge he wears. Protecting heiress Taylor is his sworn duty, but could she become the object of his desire too?

MATCH PLAY by Merline Lovelace

Special Agent Dayna jumped at an undercover assignment overseas. However she didn't expect to find former lover air force pilot Luke awaiting her arrival…

SINGLE TITLE

VEILED TRUTH by Vivi Anna
Nocturne

Lyra's skills as a witch can't help her solve a series of gruesome murders. She distrusts brooding Theron, but he could have the answers she seeks. And with the gateway to hell opening, it's imperative the two find common ground…

On sale 18th September 2009

Available at WHSmith, Tesco, ASDA, Eason and all good bookshops.
For full Mills & Boon range including eBooks visit
www.millsandboon.co.uk

⦿ INTRIGUE

Coming next month

2-IN-1 ANTHOLOGY

CHRISTMAS SPIRIT by Rebecca York

Michael doesn't believe in the ghosts said to haunt Jenkins Cove. Can Chelsea change his mind – or will they be forced to confront the spirits of Christmas past?

BEAST OF DESIRE by Lisa Renee Jones

Only in the throes of lust and battle does Des embrace his dark side. But in protecting Jessica from the Darkland Beasts, it is the animal in him that must rule!

SINGLE TITLE

THE HEIRESS'S 2-WEEK AFFAIR by Marie Ferrarella

Detective Natalie never got over former love Matt, and now he could be the key to helping her find her sister's killer. But can she keep a professional distance?

SINGLE TITLE

TALL, DARK AND LETHAL by Dana Marton

With dangerous men hot on his trail, the last thing Cade needs is Bailey seeking his help to escape her own attackers. Now it's up to him to tame the feisty free spirit...

On sale 2nd October 2009

Available at WHSmith, Tesco, ASDA, Eason and all good bookshops.
For full Mills & Boon range including eBooks visit
www.millsandboon.co.uk

From No. 1 *New York Times* bestselling author Nora Roberts

Nightshade available 2nd January 2010
When a teenager gets caught up in making sadistic violent films, Colt Nightshade and Lieutenant Althea Grayson must find her before she winds up dead…

Night Smoke available 5th February 2010
When Natalie Fletcher's office is set ablaze, she must find out who wants her ruined – before someone is killed…

Night Shield available 5th March 2010
When a revengeful robber leaves blood-stained words on Detective Allison Fletcher's walls, she knows her cop's shield won't be enough to protect her…

Passion. Power. Suspense.
It's time to fall under the spell of Nora Roberts.

The special gift of love at Christmas

CHRISTMAS WISHES – CHRISTMAS WEDDINGS!

BETTY NEELS
DEBBIE MACOMBER
JESSICA HART

Sleigh Bells and Wedding Rings

Three classic Christmas romances!

The Silver Thaw by Betty Neels

The Christmas Basket by Debbie Macomber

Mistletoe Marriage by Jessica Hart

Available 2nd October 2009

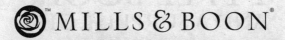

2 FREE BOOKS
AND A SURPRISE GIFT

We would like to take this opportunity to thank you for reading this Mills & Boon® book by offering you the chance to take TWO more specially selected books from the Intrigue series absolutely FREE! We're also making this offer to introduce you to the benefits of the Mills & Boon® Book Club™—

- **FREE home delivery**
- **FREE gifts and competitions**
- **FREE monthly Newsletter**
- **Exclusive Mills & Boon Book Club offers**
- **Books available before they're in the shops**

Accepting these FREE books and gift places you under no obligation to buy, you may cancel at any time, even after receiving your free books. Simply complete your details below and return the entire page to the address below. You don't even need a stamp!

YES Please send me 2 free Intrigue books and a surprise gift. I understand that unless you hear from me, I will receive 5 superb new stories every month, including two 2-in-1 books priced at £4.99 each and a single book priced at £3.19, postage and packing free. I am under no obligation to purchase any books and may cancel my subscription at any time. The free books and gift will be mine to keep in any case.

Ms/Mrs/Miss/Mr _____ Initials _____

_____

Surname _____

Address _____

_____

_____ Postcode _____

Send this whole page to: Mills & Boon Book Club, Free Book Offer, FREEPOST NAT 10298, Richmond, TW9 1BR